WHEN CRICKETS CRY

**Center Point
Large Print**

**This Large Print Book carries the
Seal of Approval of N.A.V.H.**

WHEN CRICKETS CRY

CHARLES MARTIN

CENTER POINT PUBLISHING
THORNDIKE, MAINE

This Center Point Large Print edition
is published in the year 2007 by arrangement with
WestBow Press, a division of Thomas Nelson Publishers.

Scripture quotations are from
The New King James Version of the Bible.

The text of this Large Print edition is unabridged. In other
aspects, this book may vary from the original edition. Printed in
Thailand. Set in 16-point Times New Roman type.

ISBN: 1-58547-906-3
ISBN 13: 978-1-58547-906-1

Cataloging-in-Publication data is available from the Library of Congress.

FOR STEVE AND ELAINE

Prologue

I pushed against the spring hinge, cracked open the screen door, and scattered two hummingbirds fighting over my feeder. The sound of their wings faded into the dogwood branches above, and it was there that the morning met me with streaks of sunkist cracking across the skyline. Seconds before, God had painted the sky a mixture of black and deep blue, then smeared it with rolling wisps of cotton and sprayed it with specks of glitter, some larger than others. I turned my head sideways, sort of corkscrewing my eyes, and decided that heaven looked like a giant granite countertop turned upside down and framing the sky. Maybe God was down here drinking His coffee too. Only difference was, He didn't need to read the letter in my hand. He already knew what it said.

Below me the Tallulah River spread out seamlessly into Lake Burton in a sheet of translucent, unmoving green, untouched by the antique cutwaters and Jet Skis that would split her skin and roll her to shore at 7:01 a.m. In moments, God would send the sun upward and westward where it would shine hot, and where by noon the glare off the water would be painful and picturesque.

I stepped off the back porch, the letter clutched in my hand, and picked my barefoot way down the stone steps to the dock. I walked along the bulkhead, felt the coolness of the mist rising on my legs and face, and climbed the steps leading to the top of the dockhouse. I slid into the hammock and faced southward down the lake, looking out over my left knee. I looped my finger through the small brass circle tied to the end of a short string and pulled gently, rocking myself.

If God was down here drinking His coffee, then He was on his second cup, because He'd already Windexed the sky. Only the streaks remained.

Emma once told me that some people spend their whole lives trying to outrun God, maybe get someplace He's never been. She shook her head and smiled, wondering why. Trouble is, she said, they spend a lifetime searching and running, and when they arrive, they find He's already been there.

I listened to the quiet but knew it wouldn't last. In an hour the lake would erupt with laughing kids on inner tubes, teenagers in Ski Nautiques, and retirees in pontoon boats, replacing the Canadian geese and bream that followed a trail of Wonder Bread cast by an early morning bird lover and now spreading across the lake like the yellow brick road. By late afternoon, on the hundreds of docks stretching out into the lake, charcoal grills would simmer with the smell of hot dogs, burgers, smoked oysters, and spicy sausage. And in the yards and driveways that all leaned inward toward the lake's surface like a huge salad bowl, folks of all ages would tumble down Slip'n Slides, throw horseshoes beneath the trees, sip mint juleps and margaritas along the water's edge, and dangle their toes off the second stories of their boathouses. By 9:00 p.m., most every homeowner along the lake would launch the annual hour-long umbrella of sonic noise, lighting the lake in flashes of red, blue, and green rain. Parents would gaze upward; children would giggle and coo; dogs would bark and tug against their chains, digging grooves in the back sides of the trees that held them; cats would run for cover; veterans would remember; and lovers would hold hands, slip silently into the out coves, and skinny-dip beneath the safety of the water. Sounds in the symphony of freedom.

It was Independence Day.

Unlike the rest of Clayton, Georgia, I had no fireworks, no hot dogs, and no plans to light up the sky. My dock would lie quiet and dark, the grill cold with soot, old ashes, and spiderwebs. For me, freedom felt distant. Like a smell I once knew but could no longer place. If I could, I would have slept through the entire day like a modern-day Rip van Winkle, opened my eyes tomorrow, and crossed off the number on my calendar. But sleep, like freedom, came seldom and was never sound. Short fits mostly. Two to three hours at best.

I lay on the hammock, alone with my coffee and yellowed memories. I balanced the cup on my chest and held the wrinkled, unopened envelope. Behind me, fog rose off the water and swirled in miniature twisters that spun slowly like dancing ghosts, up through the overhanging dogwood branches and hummingbird wings, disappearing some thirty feet in the air.

Her handwriting on the envelope told me when to

read the letter within. If I had obeyed, it would have been two years ago. I had not, and would not today. Maybe I could not. Final words are hard to hear when you know for certain they are indeed final. And I knew for certain. Four anniversaries had come and gone while I remained in this nowhere place. Even the crickets were quiet.

I placed my hand across the letter, flattening it upon my chest, spreading the corners of the envelope like tiny paper wings around my ribs. A bitter substitute.

Around here, folks sit in rocking chairs, sip mint juleps, and hold heated arguments about what exactly is the best time of day on the lake. At dawn, the shadows fall ahead of you, reaching out to touch the coming day. At noon, you stand on your shadows, caught somewhere between what was and what will be. At dusk, the shadows fall behind you and cover your tracks. In my experience, the folks who choose dusk usually have something to hide.

Chapter 1

She was small for her age. Probably six, maybe even seven, but looked more like four or five. A tomboy's heart in a china doll's body. Dressed in a short yellow dress, yellow socks, white Mary Janes, and a straw hat wrapped with a yellow ribbon that trailed down to her waist. She was pale and thin and bounced around like a mix between Eloise and Tigger. She was standing in the center of town, at the northwest corner of Main and

Savannah, yelling at the top of her lungs: "Lemon-aaaaaaade! Lemonaaaaaade, fifty cents!" She eyed the sidewalk and the passersby, but with no takers, she craned her neck, stretched high onto her tiptoes, and cupped her hands to her mouth. "Lemonaaaade! Lemonaaaaade, fifty cents!"

The lemonade stand was sturdy and well worn but looked hastily made. Four four-by-four posts and half a sheet of one-inch plywood formed the table. Two six-foot two-by-fours stood upright at the back, holding up the other half of the plywood and providing posts for a banner stretched between. Somebody had sprayed the entire thing yellow, and in big block letters the banner read LEMONADE—50 CENTS—REFILLS FREE. The focal point was not the bench, the banner, the yellow Igloo cooler that held the lemonade, or even the girl, but the clear plastic container beneath. A five-gallon water jug sat front and center—her own private wishing well where the whole town apparently threw their loose bills and silent whispers.

I stopped and watched as an elderly woman crossed Main Street beneath a lacy shade umbrella and dropped two quarters into the Styrofoam cup sitting on the tabletop.

"Thank you, Annie," she whispered as she accepted the overflowing cup from the little girl's outstretched hands.

"You're welcome, Miss Blakely. I like your umbrella." A gentle breeze shuffled down the side-walk, fluttered the yellow ribbons resting on the little

11

girl's back, and then carried that clean, innocent voice off down the street.

Miss Blakely sucked between her teeth and asked, "You feeling better, child?"

The little girl looked up from beneath her hat. "Yes ma'am, sure do."

Miss Blakely turned up her cup, and the little girl turned her attention back to the sidewalk. "Lemon-aaaaaade! Lemonaaaaaade, fifty cents!" Her Southern drawl was tangy sweet, soft and raspy. It dripped with little girlness and drew attention like fireworks on the Fourth.

I couldn't quite tell for sure, but after Miss Blakely set down her cup and nodded to the child, she dropped what looked like a twenty-dollar bill into the clear plastic water jug at her feet.

That must be some lemonade.

And the girl was a one-person cash-making machine. There was a growing pile of bills inside that bottle, and yet no one seemed worried that it might sprout legs, least of all the little girl. Aside from the lemonade banner, there was no flyer or explanation. Evidently it wasn't needed. It's that small-town thing. Everybody just knew. Everybody, that is, but me.

Earlier that morning, Charlie—my across-the-lake-yet-not-quite-out-of-earshot neighbor and former brother-in-law—and I had been sanding the mahogany top and floor grates of a 1947 Greavette when we ran out of 220-grit sandpaper and spar varnish. We flipped a coin and I lost, so I drove to town while Charlie fished off the back of the dock and whistled at the bikini-clad girls screaming atop multicolored Jet Skis that skidded by. Charlie doesn't drive much but, ever competitive, he insisted we flip for it. I lost.

Today's trip was different because of the timing. I rarely come to town in the morning, especially when so many people are crowding the sidewalks, making their way to and from work. To be honest, I don't come to town much at all. I skirt around it and drive to neighboring towns, alternating grocery and hardware stores every couple of months. I'm a regular nowhere.

When I do come here, I usually come in the afternoon, fifteen minutes before closing, dressed like a local in faded denim and a baseball cap advertising some sort of power tool or farm equipment. I park around back, pull my hat down and collar up, and train my eyes toward the floor. I slip in, get what I need, and then slip out, having blended into the framework and disappeared beneath the floorboards. Charlie calls it stealth shopping. I call it living.

Mike Hammermill, a retired manufacturer from Macon, had hired Charlie and me to ready his 1947 Greavette for the tenth-annual Lake Burton Antique and Classic Boat show next month. It'd be our third entry in as many years, and if we ever hoped to beat the boys from Blue Ridge Boat Werks, we'd need the sandpaper. We'd been working on the Greavette for almost ten months, and we were close, but we still had to run the linkage to the Velvet Drive and apply eight coats of spar varnish across the deck and floor grates before she was ready for the water.

Cotton mouthed and curious, I crossed the street and dropped fifty cents in the cup. The girl pressed her small finger into the spout of the cooler, turning her knuckles white and causing her hand to shake, and poured me a cup of fresh-squeezed lemonade that swam with pulp and sugar.

"Thank you," I said.

"My name's Annie," she said, dropping one foot behind the other, curtsying like a sunflower and looking up beneath my hat to find my eyes. "Annie Stephens."

I switched the cup to my other hand, clicked my heels together, and said, "For this relief, much thanks; 'tis bitter cold, and I am sick at heart."

She laughed. "You make that up?"

"No." I shook my head. "A man named Shakespeare did, in a story called *Hamlet*." While most of my friends were watching *The Waltons* or *Hawaii Five-O*, I spent a good part of my childhood reading. Still don't own a television. A lot of dead writers feed my mind with their ever-present whisperings.

I lifted my hat slightly and extended my hand. "Reese. My name's Reese."

The sun shone on my back, and my shadow stretched along the sidewalk and protected her eyes from the eleven o'clock sun that was climbing high and getting warm.

She considered for a moment. "Reese is a good name."

A man carrying two grocery bags scurried by on the sidewalk, so she turned and screamed loud enough for people three blocks away, "Lemonaaaade!"

He nodded and said, "Morning, Annie. Back in a minute."

She turned back to me. "That's Mr. Potter. Works down there. He likes his lemonade with extra sugar, but he's not like some of my customers. Some need more sugar than others because they ain't too sweet." She laughed at her own joke.

"You here every day?" I asked between small sips. One thing I learned in school, somewhere in those long nights, was that if you ask enough of the right questions, the kind of questions that nibble at the issue but don't directly confront it, people will usually offer what you're looking for. Knowing what to ask, when to ask it, and most important, how are the beginnings of a pretty good bedside conversation.

"'Cept Sundays when Cici scoops the live bait at Butch's Bait Shop. Other six days, she works in there."

She pointed toward the hardware store where a bottle-blonde woman with her back turned stood behind the cash register, fingers gliding across the keys, ringing up somebody's order. She didn't need to turn around to see us because she was eyeing a three-foot square mirror on the wall above her register that allowed her to see everything going on at Annie's stand.

"Cici?"

She smiled and pointed again. "Cici's my aunt. She and my mom were sisters, but my mom never would have stuck her hand in a mess of night crawlers or bloodworms." Annie noticed my cup was empty, poured me a second, and continued. "So, I'm here most mornings 'til lunch. Then I go upstairs, watch some TV, and take a nap. What about you? What do you do?"

I gave her the usual, which was both true and not true. While my mouth said, "I work on boats," my mind drifted and spoke to itself: *But I will wear my heart upon my sleeve for daws to peck at: I am not what I am.*

Her eyes narrowed, and she looked up somewhere above my head. Her breathing was a bit labored, raspy with mucus, marked by a persistent cough that she hid, and strained. As she talked she scooted backward, feeling the contour of the sidewalk with her feet, and sat in the folding director's chair parked behind her stand. She folded her hands and breathed purposefully while her bow ribbons danced on the sidewalk wind.

I watched her chest rise and fall. The tip of a scar, outlined with staple holes, less than a year old, climbed an inch above the V-neck of her dress and stopped just short of the small pill container that hung on a chain around her neck. She didn't need to tell me what was in it.

I tapped the five-gallon water jug with my left foot. "What's the bottle for?"

She patted lightly on her chest, exposing an inch more of the scar. People passed on the sidewalk, but she had tired and was not as talkative. A gray-haired gentleman in a suit exited the real estate office five doors down, trotted uphill, grabbed a cup, squeezed the spout on the cooler, said "Morning, Annie," and dropped a dollar in the cup and another in the plastic jug at my feet.

"Hi, Mr. Oscar," she half-whispered. "Thank you. See you tomorrow."

He patted her on the knee. "See you tomorrow, sweetheart."

She looked at me and watched him hike farther up the street. "He calls everybody sweetheart."

I deposited my fifty cents in the cup when she was looking and twenty dollars in the jug when she wasn't.

For the last eighteen years, maybe longer, I've carried several things in either my pockets or along my belt. I carry a brass Zippo lighter, though I've never smoked, two pocketknives with small blades, a pouch with various sizes of needles and types of thread, and a Surefire flashlight. A few years ago, I added one more thing.

She nodded at my flashlight. "George, the sheriff around here, carries a flashlight that looks a lot like that one. And I saw one in an ambulance once too. Are you sure you're not a policeman or a paramedic?"

I nodded. "I'm sure."

Several doors down, Dr. Sal Cohen stepped out of his office and began shuffling down the sidewalk. Sal is a

Clayton staple, known and loved by everybody. He's in his midseventies and has been a pediatrician since he passed his boards almost fifty years ago. From his small two-room office, Sal has seen most of the locals in Clayton grow from newborn to adulthood and elsewhere. Tweed jacket, matching vest, a tie he bought thirty years ago, bushy mustache, bushy eyebrows, too much nose and ear hair, long sideburns, big ears, pipe. And he always has candy in his pocket.

Sal shuffled up to Annie, tilted back his tweed hat, and placed his pipe in his left hand as she offered him a cup. He winked at her, nodded at me, and drank slowly. When he had finished the glass, he turned sideways. Annie reached her hand into his coat pocket, pulled out a mint, and smiled. She clutched it with both hands and giggled as if she'd found what no one else ever had.

He tipped his hat, hung his pipe over his bottom lip, and began making his way around the side of his old Cadillac that was parked alongside the sidewalk. Before opening the door, he looked at me. "See you Friday?"

I nodded and smiled.

"I can taste it now," he said, licking his lips and shaking his head.

"Me too." And I could.

He pointed his pipe at me and said, "Save me a seat if you get there first."

I nodded, and Sal drove off like an old man—down the middle of the road and hurried by no one.

"You know Dr. Cohen?" Annie asked.

"Yeah." I thought for a minute, trying to figure out exactly how to put it. "We . . . share a thing for cheeseburgers."

"Oh," she said, nodding. "You're talking about The Well."

I nodded back.

"Every time I go to see him, he's either talking about last Friday or looking forward to next Friday. Dr. Cohen loves cheeseburgers."

"He's not alone," I said.

"My doctor won't let me eat them."

I didn't agree, but I didn't tell her that. At least not directly. "Seems sort of criminal to keep a kid from eating a cheeseburger."

She smiled. "That's what I told him."

While I finished my drink, she watched me with neither impatience nor worry. Somehow I knew, despite the mountain of money at my feet, that even if I never gave her a penny, she'd pour that lemonade until I either turned yellow or floated off. Problem was, I had longer than she did. Annie's hope might lie in that bottle, and I had a feeling that her faith in God could move Mount Everest and stop the sun, but absent a new heart, she'd be dead before she hit puberty.

Her eyes traveled up me once, then back down again. "How big are you?" she asked.

"Height or weight?" I asked.

She held her hand flat about eye level. "Height."

"I'm six feet tall."

"How old are you?"

"People years or dog years?"

She laughed. "Dog."

I thought for a minute. "Two hundred fifty-nine."

She sized me up. "How much do you weigh?"

"English or metric?"

She rolled her eyes and said, "English."

"Before breakfast or after dinner?"

That stumped her, so she scratched her head, looked up and down the sidewalk and then nodded. "Before breakfast."

"One hundred seventy-four pounds."

She looked at me another second. "What size shoe do you wear?"

"European or American?"

She pressed her lips together and tried to hide the smile again; then she put her hands on her hips. "American."

"Eleven."

She looked at my feet, apparently wondering to herself if I was telling her the truth. Then she straightened her dress, stood up straight, and pressed her chest out over her toes. "Well, I'm seven. I weigh forty-five pounds. I wear a size 6, and I'm three feet, ten inches tall."

My mind whispered again: *O tiger's heart wrapp'd in a woman's hide.*

"So?" I asked.

"You're bigger than me."

I laughed. "Just a bit."

"But—" She stuck her finger in the air like she was checking the direction of the wind. "If I get a new heart, my doctor says I might grow some more."

I nodded slowly. "Chances are real good."

"And you know what I'd do with it?"

"The heart or the few extra inches?"

She thought for a moment. "Both."

"What?"

"I'd be a missionary like my mom and dad."

The thought of a transplant recipient traipsing through the hot jungles of Africa, hundreds of miles from either a steady diet of medication, preventive medical care, or anyone knowledgeable enough to administer both, was an impossibility that I knew better than to hope for or believe in. "They'd probably be real proud of that."

She squinted up at me. "They're in heaven."

I said nothing for a moment and then offered, "Well, I'm sure they miss you."

She pressed her thumb into the spout of the cooler and began filling my cup again. "Oh, I miss them too, but I'll see them again." She gave me the cup, then held both hands in the air like she was balancing a scale. "In about eighty or ninety years."

I drank and calculated the impossibility.

She looked up at me again, curiosity pouring out of the cracks around her eyes. "What do you want to be when you grow up?"

I drank the last sip and looked down at her. "Do you do this to all your customers?"

She placed her hands behind her back and unconsciously clicked her heels together like Dorothy in Oz. "Do what?"

"Ask so many questions."

"Well . . . yeah, I guess so."

I bent closer, drawing my eyes closer to hers. "My dear, we are the music-makers and we are the dreamers of the dreams."

"Mr. Shakespeare again?"

"Nope. Willy Wonka."

She laughed happily.

"Well," I said, "thank you, Annie Stephens."

She curtsied again and said, "Good-bye, Mr. Reese. Please come back."

"I will."

I crossed the street and picked through my keys to unlock my Suburban. Key in hand, I stared through the windshield, remembering all the others just like her and the magnetic hope that bubbled forth from each, a hope that no power in hell or on earth could ever extinguish.

And there, I remembered that I was once good at something, and that I once knew love. The thought echoed inside me: *I am poured out like water, and all My bones are out of joint; My heart is like wax; it is melted within Me.*

A strong breeze fell down through the hills and blew east up Savannah Street. It ripped along the old brick buildings, up the sidewalk, through squeaky weather vanes and melodious wind chimes and across Annie's lemonade stand, where it picked up her Styrofoam cup and scattered almost ten dollars in change and currency across the street. She hopped off her folding chair and began chasing the paper money into the intersection.

I saw it too late, and she never saw it at all.

A bread delivery truck traveling right past me down South Main caught a green light and accelerated, creating a backfire and puff of white smoke. I could hear its radio playing bluegrass and see the driver stuffing a Twinkie into his mouth as he turned through the intersection and held up his hand to block the sun. Then he must have seen the yellow of Annie's dress. He slammed on the brakes, locked up the back tires, and began spinning and hopping sideways. The farther the truck turned sideways, the more the tires hopped atop the asphalt.

Annie turned to face the noise and froze. She dropped the money in her hand, which fluttered across the street like monarch butterflies, and lost control of her bladder. She never made a peep because the tightness in her throat squelched any sound.

The driver screamed, "Oh, sweet Jesus, Annie!" He turned the wheel as hard as it would turn and sent the back bumper of the truck into the right-front quarter panel of a parked Honda Accord. The truck deflected off the Honda just before the flat side of the panel truck hit Annie square in the chest. The noise of her body hitting the hollow side of that truck sounded like a cannon.

She managed to raise one hand, taking most of the

blow, and began rolling backward like a yellow bowling ball, her hat sailing in one direction, her legs and body flying in the other. She came to rest with a thud on the other side of the street beneath a Ford pickup, her left forearm snapped in two like a tooth-pick. The tail end of that easterly breeze caught the bottom of her dress and blew it up over her face. She lay unmoving, pointed downhill, her yellow dress now spotted red.

I got to her first, followed quickly by the lady behind the cash register, who was crazy-eyed and screaming uncontrollably. Within two seconds a crowd amassed.

Annie's eyes were closed, her frame limp, and her skin translucent and white. Her tongue had collapsed into her airway and was choking her, causing her face to turn blue while her body faded to sheet white. Unsure whether her spinal cord had sustained injury, I held her neck still and used my handkerchief to pull her tongue forward, clearing her airway and allowing her lungs to suck in air. I knew even the slightest movement of her neck risked further injury to her spine, if indeed her spine was injured, but I had to clear the airway. No air, no life. Given my options, I chose.

With Annie's chest rising and falling, I checked the pulse along her carotid artery, and with the other hand unclipped my flashlight and lit her pupils. While I watched her eyes, I stuck the flashlight in my mouth, stripped the Polar heart monitor from my chest, and placed the transmitter across her sternum. The pulse reading on my watch immediately changed from 62 to

156. I felt for the point of maximal impulse and then percussed the borders of her heart by tapping with my two hands and discovered what I already knew—her heart was nearly 50 percent bigger than it ought to be.

The lady from the cash register saw me place my hands around Annie's prepubescent chest and slapped me hard across the face. "Get your hands off her, you sick pervert!"

I didn't have time to explain, so I held the transmitter in place and kept monitoring Annie's eyes. Cash-register Lady saw Annie's pupils and her swollen tongue and squatted down next to Annie. She jerked the necklace off the girl's neck, pouring the tiny contents of the pill container across Annie's stomach and sending something else shiny, maybe gold, beneath the truck, lost in the muck alongside the gutter. She grabbed two pills and reached to place them beneath Annie's tongue. Keeping one hand on Annie's neck, and my eyes trained on Annie, I grabbed the woman's hand, clasped my fingers about hers, and spoke calmly. "If you place those in her mouth, you'll kill her."

The woman's eyes lit up and the panic rose, bulging the veins in her neck. She was strong and nearly pulled her hand away, but I held tight and continued to watch Annie.

"Get your hand off me. You'll kill her." She looked at the crowd that had formed around us. "He's killing her! He's gonna kill Annie!"

Two big men in faded overalls and John Deere baseball hats, who had been eating at the café, stepped toward me.

"Mister, you better git yer hands off'n that little girl. We knows Annie, but we ain't knowin' you."

He was nearly twice my size, and this was no time for words, but I was the only one who knew this. Holding tight to the woman's hand, I turned and kicked the bigger of the two squarely in the groin, sending him to his toes and then his knees.

The second man put his huge paw on my shoulder and said, "Fella, tha's my brother and you shouldn'ta done that."

With my free hand, I drilled him as hard as I could square in the gut, which was no small target, and he too dropped, gasping and blowing his breakfast across the sidewalk.

I turned to the woman, who was still screaming and pleading with the crowd. "He's gonna kill her! Annie's dying! For God's sake!"

This was getting worse. I pried open her hand with my other, but made no attempt to take the pills. I looked her in the eyes and said calmly, "Use half—of one."

She looked confused and unable to process.

The bigger brother had made it to his knees and was about to put a hand on me, when I kicked him solidly in the gut, but not hard enough to break a rib.

She looked down at Annie and at the tractor twins at my feet. Her face told me that whatever I was telling her was not equating with what she had either read or been told in the past.

26

"But . . . ," she started.

I nodded reassuringly. "Start with half, then let's monitor. If you place that much nitroglycerin beneath that child's tongue, her pressure will drop so low that we'll never get it back up." I let go of her hand. "Use half."

The woman bit the pill in half, spitting out one half like the top of a musket load and placing the other beneath Annie's tongue. Annie was conscious; her eyes were having difficulty focusing, and her arm hung like that of a string puppet. There was a lot going on around me—people, horns, and a distant siren—but I was trained on three things: pulse, pupils, and airway.

The nitro dissolved and color soon filled Annie's cheeks—the result of expanded blood vessels, increased blood flow, and oxygen to the extremities.

The woman spoke softly. "Annie? Annie?" She patted Annie's hand. "Hold on, baby. Help's coming. Hold on. They're coming. I can hear them now."

Annie nodded and tried to smile. Her pulse had quickened slightly but remained somewhat erratic.

While the siren grew closer, I gauged how long it would take them to arrive, diagnose and stabilize, and then transport. That meant Annie was about twelve minutes from the emergency room.

With Annie blinking and looking at the people around her, I spoke again to the cashier. "Now, the other half."

Annie opened her mouth, and the woman placed the other half beneath her tongue. When that had dissolved, I pulled my own vial out of my pocket, emptied its contents, and handed her one small baby aspirin.

"Now this."

She did as instructed. I unclasped the watch end of my heart-rate monitor and re-clasped it about Annie's wrist. Even on the last hole, it was loose.

While the sirens grew closer, I looked at the woman across from me and pointed at the watch and the transmitter across Annie's chest. "This goes with that. It's making a record of what's going on with her heart. The ER doc, if he's any good, will know what to do with it."

She nodded and pushed Annie's sweat and mud-caked hair out of her eyes and behind her ears.

The paramedics arrived ten seconds later and jumped alongside me. Seeing me in control, they first looked at me.

I wasted no time. "Blunt trauma. Flail segment left chest wall, cleared airway, spontaneous respiration is 37. Felt crepitus, suggesting subcutaneous emphysema, suspicious of partial pneumothorax left side."

The young EMT looked at me with a dazed expression on his face.

I explained, "I think she dropped a lung."

He nodded, and I continued, "Heart rate 155, but irregular. Brief LOC, now GCS 12."

He interrupted me. "She had her bell rung."

I continued, "She's had 0.2 sublingual nitro times two, five minutes apart." I pointed to her midsternal chest scar. "Post open-heart. Possibly, twelve months ago. And"—I looked at my watch—"polar heart-rate monitor in place and recording for seven minutes."

He nodded, stepped in, and began placing an oxygen mask over her mouth.

Behind me, the tractor twins sat wide-eyed and open-mouthed. Having made sense of me, they made no attempt to pull me away. And that was good. Because I had the feeling that had they really wanted to, they could have. Surprise had been my asset, and it was gone.

The medic monitored Annie's pupils, told her to breathe normally, and began wrapping the blood pressure cuff around her right biceps, while the second paramedic returned with a hard collar and a backboard. Two minutes later, careful not to aggravate her arm, they had inserted an IV with saline fluids to help elevate her pressure, loaded her into the ambulance, sat Aunt Cici alongside, and were driving toward the Rabun County Hospital. As they shut the door, her aunt was stroking Annie's hair and whispering in her ear.

While the street cleared and police questioned the driver of the panel truck, the locals milled along the sidewalks, hands in pockets, shaking their heads and pointing up toward the intersection and down into the wind.

I turned to the two guys behind me and extended a hand to help the first up. "No hard feelings?"

The bigger of the two took my hand, and I strained to help him up.

He pointed toward the ambulance. "We thought you 'as goin' to hurt Annie."

My eyes followed the ambulance out of sight. I spoke almost to myself, "No sir. Not hardly." I helped the other to his feet, and the two walked off shaking their heads, straightening their caps, and adjusting the straps on their overalls.

Behind me, an older gentleman, wearing a brimmed hat and Carhartt overalls, and whose boots smelled of diesel fuel, mumbled, "When's that girl gonna get a break?" He spat with precision, a straight stream of black juice into the gutter. "Of all the people in this town, why her? Life just ain't fair. 'Tain't fair a'tall." He spat again, staining the street, and stepped off down the sidewalk.

When the crowd thinned, I crept alongside the curb, found what I was looking for, and slipped it into my pocket. It was worn and had something printed on the back side. The sound of the siren had faded into the distance, and on the air were the smells of cinnamon, peach cobbler, barbecue, and diesel exhaust. And maybe the hint of Confederate jasmine. As I drove away, a line formed at the water cooler jug as people silently dropped in bills on their way back to work.

Chapter 2

Nine months passed before I found the key. She had placed it in the bottom of a wooden box that I'd had since childhood, beneath a tattered and dusty copy of

Tennyson. The name of the bank was printed on the side of the key chain, as was the number of the box.

Charlie and I drove to the bank together. The teller fetched a manager, who checked my ID, led us into a small room with a table and four chairs, and disappeared. He returned quickly with an ashen face and some papers for me to sign. I did, and he disappeared again, reappearing a few moments later with a small locked box. He left, pulling the curtain behind him while Charlie sat quietly, hands on knees, posture perfect, waiting patiently. I inserted the key and turned it. The click turned Charlie's head. I flipped open the top, and inside sat three letters, all addressed to me. The handwriting was unmistakable.

The front of the first letter read *To be opened now.* The second read *After one year.* And the third *After two years.* I held the first in my hands, ran my finger beneath the flap, and pulled out two pages. The first sheet was a copy of the beneficiary assignment page for a $100,000 whole-life insurance policy that Emma's father had taken out on her when she was just a child. Evidently he had acquired it before anyone knew about her condition, and neither of them had ever told me about it. The second page was a letter. I sat down in the chair next to Charlie and started. *Reese, if you're reading this, then it didn't take. That means I am gone, and you are alone . . .*

My eyes blurred, my face grew numb, and I crumbled like a house of cards. Charlie and an older security guard carried me out of the bank and placed me on a park bench where I tucked myself into a fetal ball and shook for nearly an hour.

Later that day, I finished the letter. Then I read it again, and again. Knowing she had written it in advance was a stone in my stomach. At the end of the letter she'd written: *Reese, don't keep this letter. I know you, don't live that way. Set it free. Let it catch a tender breeze and sail away like Ulysses did so many times when we were kids.*

I closed my eyes and could feel her frail, almost translucent, palm on my face, searching to strengthen me—strength despite such weakness.

Obediently I traced and cut a thin pine board, drilled and tapped in the mast—a balsam dowel—folded the letter, threaded the mast through it to form a sail, glued a one-inch candle to the oak board beneath the letter, and doused the board around it in lighter fluid. I lit the candle and shoved it off into the gentle but wide current of the Tallulah. It floated away, fifty yards, then a hundred, where finally the candle burned down, lit the fluid that had puddled around it, and ignited the entire thing. The blaze climbed five or six feet in the air, a thin stream of ash and white smoke climbed higher, and then the small ship turned, tilted sideways, disappeared beneath the bubbles, and sank almost eighty feet, coming to rest on the long-ago buried town of Burton at the bottom of the lake.

I counted the days until the first anniversary, woke before the sun, and flew down to the dock, where I ripped open the envelope, wrapped my face in the letter, and breathed. I devoured every word, every hint of her smell. I imagined the small twitches in the way her mouth would have shaped and formed the words, the tilt of her neck, and the invitation behind her eyes. I could hear her voice, then her whisper, just below the breeze off the lake.

Dear Reese,

I was reading this morning before you woke. The words reminded me. I wanted to wake you, but you were sleeping so hard. I watched you breathe, listened to your heart and felt mine, for the ten-thousandth time, trying to catch the rhythm of yours. Always so steady, so strong. I ran my finger along the crease in your palm and marveled at the power and tenderness there. I knew the moment I met you, and even more now, God touched you. Promise me you'll never forget. Promise me you'll remember. "To bind up the brokenhearted." That's your job. That's what you do. My being gone doesn't change that. You healed me years ago. "Above all else . . ."

Ever yours,
Emma

I spent the day looking out over the lake, running my fingers along the lines of the letter, rewriting it a hundred times, knowing her hand had made the same movements. Finally, at dark, I cut another board, secured the mast, doused the bow and stern, and shoved her off. The single light disappeared into the darkness, finally igniting into a floating inferno almost two hundred yards away. Then, without warning, the flame toppled and disappeared like a flaming arrow shot across the wall.

Another year passed, and I counted down the days like a kid to Christmas—or a convict walking death row for the last time. I didn't need to wake because I hadn't slept, but when morning finally came I walked slowly to the dock, dead man walking, and placed my finger inside the flap. Deliberating. Stuck somewhere between no hope and all hell. If I slid my finger one way, I'd know the last words she'd ever written. One last tender moment alone. A moment we never had. All that separated me from her last words was a little dried glue and a lifetime of closure.

I held the letter up to the sun, saw the faint traces of her handwriting hidden behind the envelope, but could make out no words. I slid my finger out from beneath the flap, recreased the fold with my thumb and index finger, and placed the letter in my shirt pocket.

Another year passed, bringing with it another Fourth of July. The outside of the envelope had yellowed and wrinkled, now smelled like my sweat, and the writing had faded, accentuated by a coffee stain below the flap. Four years had passed since I first found the letters, but seldom had five minutes elapsed that I hadn't thought about her, that day, that evening, or how she'd run her fingers through my hair and told me to get some sleep. How I tried to turn back time, to fly around the earth like Superman, to pray like Joshua or Hezekiah and stop the sun.

But there are no do-overs in life.

Near dusk, a male cardinal perched on a limb nearby, tuned up, and reminded me of my task. I swung between the earth and the heavens, suspended by the sun-faded, wind-torn, and tattered fingers of the hammock. Reluctantly I returned the letter to my shirt pocket and unrolled the newspaper. I tapped the dowel into place, threaded the substitute sail over the mast, doused the base of the ship in lighter fluid, and gently placed the candle atop the deck. Above me, and spread across the northern tip of the lake, a shotgun pattern of fireworks filled the night sky, silencing the crickets. Somewhere south along the lake, little kids screamed and waved sparklers in circles that blurred into golden, burning circus rings where imaginary tigers roamed and jumped.

Five years have passed since I found the key. My only link now to the outside world is a P.O. box in Atlanta that sends all my mail to another P.O. box in Clayton, but not before it's rerouted through a no-questions-asked mail-it center in Los Angeles. If you send me an overnight package, it'll cross the country twice and get to me about two weeks later. For all practical purposes, I don't exist, and no one knows if I come or go. Except Charlie. And what he knows of my secret is safe with him.

In my house, there are no mirrors.

I steadied my small craft, shoved her off, and the silent Tallulah caught her. A gentle breeze wobbled her, she straightened, turned to starboard, and the flame licked the night, climbing upward. The candle burned down, spilling flame across the decks and lighting the sky like a blue shooting star. She blazed, burned herself out, and then disappeared into the silent deep, sounding the echoes of remembrance throughout a hollow and shattered heart.

Chapter 3

Ten minutes in the waiting room of the Rabun County Hospital emergency room filled in many of the missing pieces. Most folks around Clayton, Georgia, had heard the story of Annie Stephens. Parents were missionaries, killed two years ago in a civil war in Sierra Leone; Annie had a twin sister, but she died a year before her parents—from genetic heart complications. Annie now lives with her aunt Cindy and became a viable transplant candidate months ago after the last surgery did little to improve her condition and her ejection fraction dropped below 15 percent—the final straw. Her doctors in Atlanta gave her six months almost eighteen months ago. And because she has no insurance, she's filled that five-gallon water jug seven times, raising over $17,000 to help cover the cost of her own surgery.

I was right when I said she'd never make it to puberty.

Normally, a small hospital like this would not have

a Level 2 trauma center attached to it, but a quick look around told me that Sal Cohen had a lot to do with it. A brass plaque on the wall read *Sal Cohen Emergency Medical Wing.* Around Clayton, the story is legendary. About forty years ago, Dr. Sal lost a kid because the hospital didn't have enough of the right equipment. Two kids, premature twins, and only one incubator. He got mad about it, and two incubators have grown into the best trauma unit north of Atlanta.

Cindy McReedy pushed open the two swinging doors marked *Medical Staff Only* and walked into the waiting room. She stood on a chair, subconsciously picked at the sleeves of her plaid cotton shirt, crossed her arms as if she were cold—or not real good at speaking to groups—and waited while the room quieted down. She looked like she was about six months behind in her sleep and was juggling about eight more bowling pins than she could handle. I'd seen that look before; it would not get better before it got worse. She waved her arms above the crowd, and the tractor twins started telling everybody to "Shhhhh!"

Cindy wiped her eyes and tucked her hair behind her ears. "Annie'll be okay. The arm is a clean break . . . um, snapped . . . but they put her to sleep, set it, and placed it in a cast. She just woke a few minutes ago and asked for a Popsicle."

Everybody smiled.

Cindy continued, "The arm'll heal, albeit slowly. Doc Cohen's with her now, letting her dig through his coat pocket."

Everybody smiled again. Most every hand in the room had dug through that same pocket.

"As for her heart, we won't know for a few days. Annie's tough, but . . . ." She paused. "We . . . the doctors . . . they just don't know. We'll have to wait and see." She folded her arms again and looked over the crowd. She wiped away a tear and half-laughed. "Annie's real lucky that stranger got to her before I did. If it weren't for him . . . well, Annie wouldn't be here."

A few eyes turned to look at me.

Out of the crowd somebody yelled, "Cindy, did you talk with the folks at St. Joe's, and will they finally move her up on the dang list? Ain't she considered critical by now?"

Cindy shook her head. "The problem's not them, but us . . . or rather, Annie. After her last surgery and that whole thing"—Cindy waved her hands as though she were brushing bread crumbs off a picnic table—"Annie won't let them activate her name until she's found the right doctor."

A tall guy next to me spoke up and said, "But Cindy, for the love of Betsy! Override the little squirt! It's in her own best interest. She'll thank you when it's over."

Cindy nodded. "I'd like to, Billy, but it's a little more complicated than that."

It always is, I thought to myself.

Cindy lowered her voice. "Annie's only got one more of these in her. I'm not sure she could make it through another recovery. Everything about the next one has got to be absolutely right because . . . ." She

38

looked at her feet again, then back at Billy. "It'll probably be the last."

The short, squatty woman standing next to the tall man smacked him with her pocketbook, and he shoved his hands into his pockets.

Cindy continued. "Her cardiologist is on his way up here now from Atlanta. Should be here in an hour or so. We'll know more once he's finished with her. After that, we've still got to find a doctor who's good enough and who'll take the risk and operate. We've still got the same hurdles: we need a heart, and not only have we got to find someone who will take Annie, but that Annie will take. Her chances, according to the books, even with the best of doctors, are in the single digits, and . . ." Cindy looked over her shoulder and lowered her voice again. "They're not getting any better."

The room got real quiet. If there had been a consensus of hope, it was gone now.

Cindy looked her age, maybe thirty-five, and I gathered that her matter-of-factness was a product of both personality and life's lessons. Maybe it was how she dealt with it. She'd been through a few battles, and you could hear it in her voice, see it in her face. Sandy-blonde hair to her shoulders, held up in a simple ponytail by a green rubber band fresh off the newspaper.

No makeup. Strong back, long lines. Rigid and stern, but also graceful. Cold but quietly beautiful. Complicated and busy, but also in need. More like an onion than a banana. Her eyes looked like the green that sits just beneath the peel of an avocado, and her lips like

39

the red part of the peach that sits up next to the seed. Her plaid shirt, tattered jeans, ponytail, and crossed arms said she was function over form, but I had a feeling that, like any woman in her position, she hid much of her form because her time was consumed with function. She reminded me of Meryl Streep working the rows of coffee plants in *Out of Africa*.

Beauty is mysterious as well as terrible. God and devil are fighting there, and the battlefield is the heart of man.

She stepped down off the chair, saying, "Any news, and I'll post it on the store window." She looked at an older gentleman who stood off to one side, listening closely. "That okay with you, Mr. Dillahunt?"

He nodded and said, "You just call Mabel, and she'll print anything you want."

As the crowd thinned, Cindy made her way to the Coke machine and started fumbling for coins. She was all thumbs, spilling pennies around her feet and not getting any closer to finding the correct change.

The voices inside my head were at all-out war with one another. While they fought it out inside me, I dug four quarters from my pocket and held out my palm.

She turned to face me and looked like she was trying to hold off a cold shiver. She pushed a few strands of hair out of her face (they immediately fell back where they'd been), took the quarters, and punched the button for a Diet Coke. The circles beneath her eyes told me she was tired, so I unscrewed the cap on the plastic bottle and handed it to her. She sipped, looked across the top of the Coke bottle at me, and said, "Thank you, again." She looked at the floor, dug the toe of her shoe into a worn spot in the terrazzo, and then looked at me. "Doc Cohen tells me I owe you an apology."

I shook my head. "Doctors aren't always right."

"Sal usually is," she said.

We stood in silence a minute, not knowing what to say.

"Annie's got this real good doctor in Atlanta. I just hung up the phone with him, and he said he's anxious to read the information off that strap-looking thing you placed over her heart. He said not many people are walking around with those things."

"They can come in handy."

She crossed her arms, held her chin high, and looked out the window. "Sal told me I could've killed her."

"Reese," I said, offering my hand. "We kind of skipped this step back there in the street."

"I'm sorry." She wiped her hand on her jeans and extended it toward me. "At one time I actually did have a few manners. Cindy McReedy." She pointed through the double doors. "I'm Annie's aunt. She's my sister's daughter."

"Cici. I heard."

We stood for a moment while the room gossiped around us. She pointed to my clothes. "I've met a lot of paramedics in the last few years, and you don't look like any of them. How'd you know what to do?"

A full-length wall mirror next to the Coke machine showed my reflection. She was right. I looked like someone who'd been hanging Sheetrock. To make matters worse, I hadn't shaved in more than five years. Except for the eyes, I was almost unrecognizable to myself.

"When I was a kid, I hung around the ER. Cleaning, doing whatever. Eventually, they let me ride in the fire truck, and we were usually first on the scene. You know, sirens, trucks, big chain saws."

She smiled, which meant she was either buying it or too tired not to.

"Then I worked the moonlight shift during college to help pay for books and classes." I shrugged. "It's like riding a bike." That much was true. I wasn't lying—yet.

"Your memory's better than mine," she said.

I needed to reroute this. I smiled. "To be totally honest, it was the sirens and flashing lights that I liked best. I still keep my nose in it." Again, both statements were true, but they barely skimmed the surface.

"Well . . ." She crossed her arms tighter as if she were getting colder. "Thank you for today . . . for what you did."

"Oh, I almost forgot." I reached into my pocket and held out the small golden sandal that had been looped around Annie's neck before Cindy flung it into the gutter. "You dropped this . . . in the street."

Cindy held out her hand and, when she saw what it held, fought back more tears. I handed her my handkerchief, and she wiped off her face. "It was my sister's. They sent it back in an envelope from Africa once they . . . once they found the bodies."

She paused and let the hair fall over her eyes. This woman had done some living in the last decade, and she wore most of it.

"Annie's worn it since the day it came in the mail." She slid it gently into her pocket. "Thank you . . . a third time." She looked back toward the two double doors. "I'd better get back. Annie's gonna start to wonder."

I nodded, and Cindy walked away. I followed her with my voice. "I wonder if I could come back in a couple of days, maybe bring a teddy bear or something."

She turned, tucked the loose strands behind her ears, and began tying the front of her shirt in a knot at her waist. "Yes, but . . ." She looked around the room and whispered, "No bears. Everybody brings bears. Don't tell anyone, but I've started giving them away myself." She nodded. "Come back, but be creative. A giraffe maybe, but no bears."

I walked to the parking lot, trying not to notice the smell of the hospital.

Chapter 4

My alarm sounded at 2:00 a.m. I slipped down the dock and jumped into the lake. Cold, yes, but it got the blood flowing. After my swim, I juiced some carrots and apples, added a beet, some parsley, and a piece of celery for what has been called "protective measure," and then followed it with a baby aspirin. By three I had added enough temporary hair dye to turn my light brown hair almost totally black and then accented my sideburns and beard with enough gray to add twenty-five years to my profile. A little before three thirty I drove out to the road, looking like no one I'd ever met but in plenty of time to beat the traffic and make my 5:30 a.m. flight out of Atlanta.

I sat at the gate in B concourse waiting for the flight attendants to call my row. I don't like airports. Never have. When I find myself wondering what hell must be like, I'm reminded of the terminals in Atlanta. Thousands of people, most of whom don't know one another, crammed into a limited space, all in a hurry and trying desperately to get out. No one really wants to be there because it's simply a mandatory delay, a non-place—you're not home and neither is anyone else. Everybody's just passing through. In some ways, much like a hospital.

We landed in Jacksonville, Florida, and I drove a rental car to the Sea Turtle Inn at Jacksonville Beach, where the conference started promptly at 8:00 a.m. I checked in, slicked my hair straight back, added more gray around the edges, splashed some Skin Bracer on my face, and tied a double Windsor knot that shortened my tie to two inches above my belt. My coat was too small, sleeves too short, and my pant legs were hemmed at noticeably different lengths. The pants and jacket were both navy but mismatched, from two different suits I had bought at the consignment shop, and my wingtips were double-soled and twenty-five years out of style. I slid on my thick, horn-rimmed glasses, which contained no prescriptive benefit whatsoever, kept my eyes to myself, and steadied myself on an old worn cane.

I stayed in the bathroom until after everyone had left, walked in after the announcements had been made, sat in the back, spoke to no one, and gave no one the opportunity to speak to me. *And, after all, what is a lie? 'Tis but the truth in masquerade.*

The keynote speaker was a man I'd read much about, who had also written much and who was now considered one of the leaders in his field. I'd heard him at a few other conferences around the country, but despite my interest, and the fact that he was just slightly wrong in a few areas, my mind was elsewhere. The window to my left looked out over the Atlantic, which was calm, rolled with sets of small waves and dotted with pelicans and the occasional porpoise or surfer. By the time I looked back at the podium, the group had recessed for lunch. I can't tell you what the man talked about, because all morning I had been thinking about a little girl in a yellow dress, the taste of that lemonade, and the engraved reference on the back side of the sandal.

These conferences served two purposes: they kept guys like me current on the latest information, the practices and techniques that don't make it into the journals but take place every day; and they brought colleagues together so they could catch up and pat one another on the back. I know lots of these people. Or, rather, *knew*. Even worked pretty closely with a few. Fortunately, they couldn't recognize me now even if they sat down beside me.

Which is exactly what happened just after lunch. I was sitting two rows from the back in a sparsely populated and poorly lit area of the room when Sal Cohen shuffled down my row and pointed at the seat next to me. *What in the world is he doing here?*

I nodded and kept my eyes pinned forward. The slide show continued for almost two hours wherein Sal fluctuated between deep interest and deep sleep accompanied by a slight snore.

At three in the afternoon, a new speaker mounted the podium. He had performed about four years of research on a new procedure, now called the "Mitch-Purse Procedure," which had become the new buzzword among most of the men and women in this room. It was especially fashionable now that a doctor in Baltimore had been the first person to successfully pull it off. I had no interest in his discussion and really didn't care if somebody had figured out how to make it work, so I excused myself and bought a cup of coffee in the lobby. Shortly after five in the afternoon, they concluded the one-day conference, credited my attendance, and I drove back to the airport for my flight home. And yes, I was a bit worried that Sal had booked the same flight home. I checked the flight roster before boarding, and Sal's name didn't appear. If it had, I would have missed the flight and found another carrier.

We landed in Atlanta, and after a few delays and a wreck in the northbound lane of the Beltway, it was after midnight when I got home.

Across the lake, Charlie's house was dark, but that meant little. His house was often dark. I heard the faint sound of his harmonica echoing through the walls. A few minutes after I arrived, the sound stopped and the night fell quiet. All except the crickets. They tuned up and sang me to sleep—which took about thirty seconds.

Chapter 5

I cracked the boathouse door at 5:00 a.m. and smelled Noxzema. Charlie didn't like a sore butt, so he rubbed Noxzema on the chamois of his shorts before we got into the boat. It was dark, but I could see his stumpy form sprawled across the boathouse floor, stretching. I could also see the wet footprints shining through the dark, showing me where he'd climbed out of the water and into the boathouse. He had been doing Pilates for years and could pretty well hook his heel behind his head when he wanted. Most limber human being I'd ever met. Also one of the strongest.

Next to him sat Georgia, his yellow Lab. He never went anywhere without her. Her tail flapped the wooden floor and let me know she was happy to see me.

The wood floor creaked below me, telling Charlie of my arrival, but I imagine he'd heard me coming before

I cracked the door. The edge of the lake lapped the rock bulkhead below and sounded off the hollow chamber of wood three feet above it. I turned on a fluorescent light above one of my workbenches, and Charlie smiled but didn't say a word.

On one side sat the two-man scull. I tapped it, and Charlie nodded. It weighed only about eighty pounds, but at over twenty-five feet long, it took two of us to get it into the water. Charlie grabbed the bow and I the stern. He backed down the ramp and slid his end into the glassy, still water.

I pulled the boat alongside the dock and patted Charlie on the shoulder.

He said, " 'Morning to you too."

He grabbed the ladder, found the boat with his toe, and climbed down, strapping his feet into the bindings in front of him. I grabbed the oars and slipped carefully into the seat up front. I strapped on my "spare" heart-rate monitor while Charlie tapped his fingers on the oars—Morse code for *I'm ready to go now!* We pushed off, dipped the oars in, feathered as the water droplets from the blades painted the lake in half circles, and pulled out of the small finger that accented the northern tip of Lake Burton.

The silence hung warm around us. Charlie whispered over his shoulder, accompanied by a half smirk, "You had a long day yesterday."

"Uh-huh." Another dip, another pull, another feather.

The muscles in Charlie's back rippled down from his

48

neck, around his shoulders, and into his ribs in a con-cert of taut human tissue.

"What'd you wear?" he said, now with full smirk.

"Same thing," I said.

Charlie shook his head and said nothing more as we folded and unfolded into a rhythmic pulse.

Tip to tip from Jones Bridge to Burton Dam is nine miles. Most mornings we do all of it. Down and back. Charlie and I are a pretty good match. I'm taller and leaner, he's thicker and stouter, but I'd never cross him in a dark alley. Whereas my VO_2 max is greater—meaning I have a larger heart and lung capacity and can consume more oxygen over a longer period of time—Charlie's got another gear in his body that's not subject to the laws of physics or anatomy, the kind that's buried deep down and allows ordinary people to do extraordinary things. Like win a state wrestling championship by pinning the number-one-ranked wrestler in the country—twice.

It was a double-elimination tournament, and since his opponent had never lost in high school matches, Charlie had to wrestle him twice. The first time he pinned him in the second period, and in the second match he tied the guy in a knot like a pretzel and pinned him in the first minute. What made it even more impressive was that while his opponent was a senior, Charlie was a sophomore. Starting with that one, Charlie won three state championships and never lost another match in high school.

With the current of the Tallulah pushing us along,

Charlie sank his oars in, pulled hard, and shot us southward. The jolt told me he was feeling pretty good and that today would hurt. And if it hurt this much *with* the river, it would hurt that much more coming back against it.

Canoeing or sculling the river can be tricky after 7:00 a.m. when the motorboats appear, so we go in the early morning. Sudden changes in weather are as common as the sun, but nobody knows when to predict them. Because of the surrounding mountains, unexpected gusts and tornadoes can rip across the lake and sink any- and everything. In 1994, some years before we moved up here, a "supercell" of tornadoes known as the Palm Sunday Killer ripped through here, and everybody remembers not only the sound but all the debris that floated down the lake for days afterward. The bodies that once lived in the homes didn't float downstream, because most of them were so full of holes from flying limbs and shingles that they sank to the bottom where the old town of Burton used to sit.

Rowing is a sport unlike any other. On the surface, it's the only one where you don't constantly look ahead. More often than not, where you've been—your hindsight—tells you where you're going. In track and field, sprinters and hurdlers look like locomotives at full speed—their arms and legs pounding the track and air like rods and pistons. In football, players spin about like battering rams or bumper cars. And soccer is an anthill of players caught between a ballet and a bullfight. But in rowing, the man in the scull is something of a spring.

To understand this, open the back of a wristwatch while the coils of the hairspring open and close. In rowing, the body falls into a groove, albeit a painful one, whereby the rower repeats exactly the same pulse over and over and over again. He crouches into a spring, knees tucked into his chest with arms extended, having sucked in as much air as his lungs will allow. He digs in, pushing with his legs and starting the long pull with his arms, expelling air throughout the pull. He reaches full extension, spent, and gorges on air as deeply as his lungs will let him. At the top of his pull, the rower lifts his blades and pulls his knees into his chest once again, sucking in air the entire way back down the boat, only to return and unselfishly empty himself once again.

It is much like the beating of a human heart. So demanding is the action of rowing on the human body that some rowers pump half again as much air through their lungs during the course of a race as most any other athlete in the world. That's why rowers tend to be giants with broad wingspans and lungs like zeppelins.

Which is a good picture of Charlie. If he were a bird, he might be a condor. Or better yet, an albatross.

The joy of rowing comes in the movement. The scull is long and narrow, so it glides across the water at terrific speeds. The combination of blades, outriggers, and gliding seat combine like a percussion section to create a clink-clunk-hiss noise that sounds a rhythmic tempo across the water. Even though you sit backward, you're somehow aware of your surroundings, guiding the bow with the eyes in the back of your head. Steering is as much a feel as it is a response. Every few pulls you look behind you to print the panorama like a photograph in your mind. Then, turning back, you watch the wrinkling line where your keel has cut the water and the big round pools of ripples poked into the lake by your blades. With every successive pull, the pools you're making grow and grow until eventually they overlap and combine.

We settled into our rhythm and glided through the mouths of Dick's Creek, Timpson Creek, and Moccasin Creek. Beads of sweat cascaded off my nose. My heart-rate monitor told me I was near the tip of my target zone, and Charlie's sweat-soaked back and expanding lungs told me he was too. The feeling of rowing in concert with another, soaked in sweat, painful but comfortable with your own effort, is a feeling unlike any other. It's the "runner's high" times two. Maybe three.

Just because I sit in front and am technically responsible for steering doesn't mean that Charlie doesn't know where he is. We had passed Murray Cove and Billy Goat Island and pulled past Cherokee Creek when Charlie asked, "You see the dam yet?"

"Five or six more pulls."

"We're getting slower. We'd better pick it up if we're gonna try to win the Burton Rally this year. I hear those Atlanta guys are coming back."

The Burton Rally was a bridge-to-dam race that Charlie and I had competed in for the last four years, placing third the first year and second every year since. Our nemesis was a duo of ex-Olympians from Atlanta. They were good, but we were gaining. Or at least they were letting us think we were. Their advantage, aside from the fact that they were just better, was a Kevlar boat that weighed about half as much as ours. But we liked our boat. For one race a year, the HMS *Emma* managed just fine.

Charlie pulled hard and jolted us forward.

I asked, "You feeling rested this morning?"

Charlie leaned in closer and placed one finger in the air. "I am only one, but still I am one. I cannot do everything, but still I can do something. I will not refuse to do the something I can do."

I smiled. What Shakespeare did for me, Helen Keller did for Charlie.

Gliding atop the water is a freeing experience—it's all future, all possibility, where the record of the past lasts only a few seconds and then is gone forever. At the dam we sat up, coasted, and drank the air. The only sound was the alarm on my heart-rate monitor telling me I was outside my target zone. Charlie heard the alarm and smiled, but said nothing because his alarm was sounding too. I turned us as sunlight began to light the water and burn off the morning steam. Spirals like miniature tornadoes rose in swirls all around us, forming little clouds and adding to the warm sweat that draped us like a liquid blanket.

It was a common sight, and one that reminded me that, despite all the ugliness and all the horror, beauty survived, and Emma would have loved it. It reminded me of another such morning, when I woke early, boiled the water, brought her a cup of tea, and then helped her down to the bank. She sat with her knees tucked into her chest, hugging me with one arm and her cup with the other. I wrapped her feet in a fleece blanket while she just shook her head at the sight in front of her. Taking a sip of tea, she kissed me, leaned her head on my shoulder, and whispered, "That which we cannot speak about, we must pass over in silence."

At the time I had not read Wittgenstein, but I have read him many times since.

Charlie felt me pause and whispered over his shoulder, "A pretty morning."

"Yeah." I paused, drinking it in again. "She would've loved it."

Charlie nodded and sipped from the air as the water and history slid beneath us.

Back at the dock, he climbed out of the scull and felt his way along the sides of the boathouse until he got his bearings.

"You got it?" I asked.

"Yup, I'm good. Just seeing where I am."

Charlie sees mostly with his hands and ears because his eyes are useless. Other than lightning during a storm, fireworks on the Fourth, or looking directly into the sun, he's as blind as a bat. That too happened five years ago, but we don't ever talk about it. The reason for his sudden blindness is well-known between us, but the reason behind the reason is not.

And this explains Georgia. She's a seeing-eye dog that I got for him as a Christmas present, once we were certain his sight wasn't returning. I tucked her under the tree, and Charlie agreed to keep her, quickly falling in love. She's supposed to lead him, but it seldom works out that way. Charlie also owns a walking stick, a white one with a red tip, but he rarely unfolds it. It stays in the corner of his house or folded up in his back pocket. As blind as he is, he's just not that blind. As for me: *No, I'll not weep: I have full cause of weeping, but this heart shall break into a hundred thousand flaws or ere I'll weep.*

Charlie found the edge of the dock and lowered himself to the guide wire. Starting to pull himself across the forty yards of water to his home, with Georgia swimming close alongside, he turned and asked, "You still having that dream?"

"Yeah."

"You figured out what it means?"

"Not really."

"You need an interpreter?"

"Think you can?"

Charlie shook his head. "No, but if you sleep any less, you'll turn into an owl."

"Thanks."

Charlie smiled, treading water. "Well, every time I get up to pee during the night, I can hear you over here tinkering with something."

"Yeah . . . well, school taught me a few things, and how to live without sleep was one of them."

"Yeah, but that ain't healthy. It's twisted."

"Tell me about it."

"I don't know how she ever put up with you."

"Thanks. Don't let that shark bite you."

Charlie hummed the theme song to *Jaws* and began pulling again. He wanted to say more, I knew, but he let it go. It was often what Charlie *didn't* say that spoke the loudest.

Chapter 6

I grew up in a hundred-year-old house just a few blocks from the Vinings town square. It was a no-frills, two-story wooden house that rose up out of the earth, tall and narrow, like it had been squeezed during construction. It was surrounded by two wraparound porches—one on each floor—and framed by eight magnolia trees that provided shade regardless of the time of day. From the street, you could barely see the house.

It wasn't large, only three bedrooms, but had almost as much square footage in porches as it did inside. The huge, sprawling limbs of the magnolias spread about the house like giant arms. When the trees were in bloom, my mother opened every window and reversed the rotation of the attic fan, sucking in the outside air and the scent that emanated from the canopy under which we lived. Some of the limbs swayed and bent in under the porch or rubbed up against it—house and trees almost like an old married couple who had grown comfortable with each other's company. We spent a lot of time playing in the coolness on the porch or climbing along the miles of magnolia limbs.

My father hung bird feeders in every tree, making bird-watching easy. From finch to cardinal, mockingbird, blue jay, crow, hummingbird, martin, and even the occasional owl or red-tailed hawk, our life on the porch was an education in the flying, singing, nesting, and mating habits of every common bird in northeast Georgia. The most common were the cardinals; at one time we counted eleven nests. The laser-bright male stood proudly and protectively alone against the dark green and brown backdrop, never far from the darker, more blood-colored female with whom he would mate for life. Come nighttime in the spring, the walls of our house echoed with the concert of male and female cardinals, sending out their voices like submarines sending sonar pings from the dark depths of the ocean's floor.

Emma and I met on the playground in second grade. I had just crossed the jungle gym without touching the ground and was still hanging there when I spotted her watching me. She was the new kid, had just moved to town, quiet, usually drawing something in a sketch pad and always watching everything out of the corner of her eye. She was small for her age, maybe even a bit frail, and during recess, when the other kids were playing kickball or climbing on the jungle gym, Emma would sit at the picnic table, open her sketch pad, and take pictures with her pencil. What she could do with fifteen minutes, a pencil, and a blank sheet of paper was almost uncanny.

One day at the end of recess, she nonchalantly handed me a sketch and returned to her seat on the far side of the room. It was me, dangling like a monkey with a silly look on my face. And she was right, I had been trying to show off. Her sketch had captured that. The next day during lunch, she offered me her chocolate chip cookie, and I gave her my milk. The following week, we moved our seats together in Mrs. Wilson's music class, and I even skipped a kickball game to watch her sketch. At the beginning of our third-grade year, her folks moved into a brick home around the block from us, so I had to walk past her house on the way to school. Most mornings I'd bump into her and her little brother, Charlie.

Charlie was four years younger and had unusually big arms for a kid his age, which explained why Emma affectionately called him Popeye. Charlie loved to build things and, even more, beat stuff with a hammer. And due to the size of his arms, he could swing it too. He was also real protective of his big sister, and for the first couple years he too watched me out of the corner of his eye.

Charlie was adventuresome and didn't always think things through, so when he tried to swing from one of our magnolias using his Stretch Armstrong action figure as the rope, he ended up with an ugly amputation and a real mess. Lying in a pile of magnolia leaves next to the porch with Stretch's arm in one hand and Armstrong goo leaking everywhere, Charlie looked to me for help.

"Curious" and "plays well alone" defined me as a child. From the time I learned that Legos snapped together, I had transformed my room into a maze of my own private construction projects, forcing my mom to all but give up on getting me to clean it. Model airplanes hung from fishing wire pinned to the ceiling, Lincoln Log houses five and six stories high stood in the corners, toothpick forts like the Alamo rested on overstuffed bookshelves, and houses of cards held together with glue took up too much space on my desk. I had taken apart wrecked Matchbox cars and rebuilt new ones with pieces from fifteen different cars; built my own slingshots out of surgical tubing; improved the cranks, gearing, and brakes on my own dirt bike; increased the high speed on the fan in my room; and improved on the rate of twist in a Slinky so that it actually would cascade down a series of steps the way the commercial touted. In short, I liked to tinker, and what's more, I had an insatiable need to know and understand how things worked.

Especially the human body. If buildings and vehicles were interesting, even fascinating, then the human body was an all-encompassing obsession. The walls of my room were covered in posters and diagrams demonstrating everything from bone structure and muscular growth to organ systems and the electronic neural pathways of the brain. Because my hands played a large role in educating my mind, by the age of seven I had already dissected and sewn back together two giant frogs, one fish, a neighbor's cat, an armadillo, and a long black snake—all of which were dead, or quickly dying, before I got hold of them.

At that age, my dissecting could more accurately be described as digging around, but my sewing showed promise. In order to improve, I practiced. I sliced the skin of an orange and then sewed it back together, careful not to spill the juice. When I had mastered oranges, I graduated to French bread, because the skin is delicate, brittle, and tears easily.

Having seen my work with at least one frog and the neighbor's Siamese cat, Charlie offered me his limp hero, and I set to work reattaching his arm and then forcing the goo back in so it would regain its shape. After I tied my final knot, I painted the stitching with superglue to seal the wound. Ugly, yes, but it worked, and Stretch survived to be a hero another day. I handed him back to Charlie, who yanked and pulled and then said, "Thanks, Stitch." The name stuck, and so did my friendship with Charlie.

Chapter 7

The morning of the last school day before Christmas break in third grade, I was walking past the O'Connors' house thinking about how much I wanted a Red Ryder BB gun when Charlie hopped out of the bushes and told me that Emma had had a "spell" and his folks had taken her to the hospital. I listened to him tell me what had happened, and then I said, "Charlie, I'm not going to school. I'm going to see Emma. What're you gonna do?"

He looked back toward the house, then down the street toward school, threw his backpack into the bushes and said, "I'm with you."

We ran all the way to the hospital and into the emergency room, where I didn't see anyone I knew. Acting like a lost kid, I told the lady at the information counter that I couldn't find my mom and sister and could she please tell me where they were. She bought it.

Charlie and I got off the elevator on the third floor and found Emma's mom leaning against a Coca-Cola machine, crying. She walked me down to Emma's room, but Emma was secluded behind a plastic tent. She waved at me and smiled, but they wouldn't let me any closer. That's where she spent Christmas. Me too, except for Christmas morning.

Just before the New Year they brought her home, and I had to throw rocks at her window to show her my new rifle. Emma eventually got better and returned to school a few weeks into the spring quarter, but from then on her walk was slower, her breathing different, and her parents treated her like their good china.

One afternoon when the three of us walked in from school, Emma went upstairs to get some sleep, and her mom pulled me aside and handed me a pill container. "Emma's got to take these. They're like vitamins, and . . ." She paused. "They're real expensive, but . . . Emma's got to have them." She gently put her hand below my chin, and I looked up. Her eyes were tired and red, and the bags beneath them were almost as big as her eyes. "Honey, every day at lunch, you make sure Emma takes her pill."

I wrapped my fingers around the container and nodded.

"You got to promise me."

"Yes ma'am, I promise."

Each day at lunchtime, I'd open the container and hand her one. Emma would run her fingers across her lips like she was zipping her mouth shut, cross her arms, and shake her head.

I'd wait patiently.

Between gritted teeth and zipped lips she'd say, "That's a horse pill. Makes me gag every time I try to swallow it."

To make it easier, I'd cut it in half with my Swiss Army knife and then ask the lady behind the cafeteria line for some chocolate pudding or soft yogurt. It was easier to get down that way.

She'd look at me, and I'd whisper, "Emma, I promised."

She'd put the pill in her mouth, take a bite of pudding, and mutter, "Yeah, but I didn't." Threatening not to swallow, she'd say, "Take back your promise."

I shook my head.

"Take it back, Reese."

"I can't."

"Can't or won't?"

"Both."

Emma's eyes would burn red and she'd swallow. She stopped speaking to me for almost a month, except for our lunchtime fights. From third grade on, I turned into the pill patrol, and Emma hated me for it.

Or at least I thought so.

Chapter 8

It was after I found the key that I started having the dream. It faded in, imprinted me, and has been there ever since. Like all dreams, mine are odd and don't always make perfect sense. This one doesn't have a crisp beginning and ending, but it is consistent and shows up every time I close my eyes.

I am standing in an eighteenth-century home. Stone walls, wood floors, fireplace, and on the table before me lies somebody, maybe the owner of the home, who has been mortally wounded in battle and is gasping for breath. He is in horrible pain, dying a slow and terrible death. I think I've been in the battle too, but not as a soldier. And probably not a medic. Maybe a flag bearer, but I can't really say why I think that other than that I'm draped in a flag.

In my hands is a pitcher of water. The pitcher is cracked and chipped, and when I hold it upright it leaks like a sieve. Water is pouring everywhere. I haven't got enough fingers to plug all the holes, so the floor is a puddle of his blood and my water. But when I turn the pitcher over and pour, it stops leaking. And though I pour it completely over, it never runs out of water. I stand over this person I've never met and pour water over his body. Despite my pouring, I cannot determine what is wrong with him. I'm frantically trying to find out where he is wounded, but he shows no visible signs. All I know is that when I pour, he can breathe and seems to be getting better. But the more I pour, the heavier the pitcher grows, and pretty soon, despite the feeling that I am using both my hands and all my strength, I am unable to hold it any longer. Exhausted, I collapse to the table where the wasted water leaks, spills around me, and the person on the table begins screaming and dying once again.

Every night it is the same, and just before the dying man takes his last gasp of air, I wake up, drenched, cramped, suffering from muscle spasms in my hands and arms, thirsty beyond belief, my ears ringing with his screams and wrapped in the fear that he is dying from something very simple. Something everyone should have seen by now, but no one has. Something I can't see, because I too am blind.

Chapter 9

At the far end of Emma's backyard ran a creek about ten feet wide, usually only ankle-deep, though it varied with the rain, and flowing with a gentle current over sand and rounded baseball-sized rocks and marble-sized pebbles. The creek collected in the mountains, wound through the low-lying hills, and then passed

Emma's house on its way to a lake. At times we'd see small trout, even caught a few with a butterfly net, but mostly the creek formed the barrier of her backyard.

One of our favorite activities was building sailboats out of board and newspaper and then setting them afloat, and afire, down the creek. Charlie would cut several flat boards, the belly of the ship, and then we'd drill and tap wooden dowels into the front and center of the boat to serve as our masts. We'd empty the trash can looking for the morning paper and then take an entire section and fold it several times, giving us a sail that was about twenty sheets thick, making it sturdy and self-holding. We'd cut a slit at the top and bottom, slide it down the mast, and then douse the bottom of the boat with kerosene. We'd light a small candle, place it in the stern of the boat, and set it afloat in the creek. The ship would gently roll downstream while we followed in our bare feet. A hundred feet downstream the candle would burn down, light the kerosene, and ignite the entire ship. We built and burned entire fleets as the years went by.

I was waiting in the kitchen while Emma dressed upstairs. Her mom stood over a griddle, busily flipping pancakes. I sipped a glass of orange juice, trying to get my nerve up. I had rehearsed my question enough times that I thought I could get it all out at once. Finally I said, "Miss Nadine?"

"Yes dear?"

"Can I ask you something?"

"Sure."

"Well, why is Emma always taking those pills?"

Her mom put down the spatula, teared up, grabbed a tissue off the kitchen counter, and sat down next to me at the breakfast table. She wiped her nose, looking for the words. "Emma has a hole in her heart."

That struck me as incredibly wrong, so I thought about it for a minute.

"Is that why she sleeps more than other kids? And why she doesn't ever play any sports with the rest of us?"

Emma's mom nodded.

Learning had always come easily for me, especially when it came to books. I could read most anything once, even just skim it, and if you asked me to regurgitate that same information a year later, I could give it back almost word for word. But what I knew in my head stayed up there, swirling about the other ten zillion things I had retained. That knowledge informed my actions, what I did and how I did it.

What Emma knew filtered from her head down into her heart and informed who she was—what I have since come to call the Infinite Migration. If my wonderings about life were scientific, bent toward examination and physical discovery, Emma's all leaned toward matters of the heart. While I could understand and explain the physics behind a rainbow, Emma saw the colors. When it came to life, I saw each piece and how they all fit together, and Emma saw the image on

66

the face of the puzzle. And every now and then, she'd walk me through the door to her world and show it to me.

I thought for a minute. "Can't the doctors just sew it shut?"

Her mom shook her head. "They don't know how. It's . . . it's complicated."

I looked up the stairs, listened to Emma's light footsteps as she scurried about her room, and then back at her mother. Somewhere in that moment, thunder clapped in my head, and life became real simple. Singular in purpose and in vision.

"Miss Nadine," I said, nodding. "I can fix it. I mean, I can fix Emma's heart."

Her mom wiped the tears off her face and patted me on the knee. She waited a long minute and then said, "Son, if I ever met a kid who could, it's you. You have gifts I've never seen in other people. So . . ." She closed her eyes a long minute, then opened them on me. "You do that, son. You do that, you hear?"

Nobody needed to tell me that Emma was special. Even at eight she had a rare ability to express on the outside, whether through word or action, what her heart felt on the inside. While I got all bottled up and couldn't get out my mouth what my heart felt, Emma had no such difficulty.

That afternoon, beneath the maple tree in her front yard, while the sun hung dusk on the fencerows, Emma grabbed me by the hand, pulled me close, and hid us beneath the shadow of its branches. She sniffled, checked the windows over her shoulders, and behind her eyes I saw something that had not been there that morning. Years later I would recognize it as the seeds of hope.

She checked the windows again and said, "Heard you talking to Mama today."

I nodded with my head while my heart noticed something different. Emma placed her hand along my cheek, leaned closer, and kissed me on the corner of my mouth. And when she did, the veil lifted.

From then on, making sure she took her pill became something I did out of protection and not obedience.

Chapter 10

I slipped through Ingles to pick up a few groceries, then drove west on Highway 76 past the civic center, library, elementary school, and the hospital. I needed to stop in, deliver something other than a teddy bear, and pick up my heart-rate monitor, but that would wait. I drove past The Well, Davis Stipes's bar, and took in a deep whiff from the grill, but I didn't have time for a cheeseburger.

Davis serves the coldest beer and the best cheeseburgers in the state of Georgia. His menu is printed on the wall and lacks any frills. From the "Slight Murmur" with its single patty and slim trimmings to the "Persistent Palpitation" with its three cheeses and sautéed onions to the "Carotid Clotter" with its two patties and chili and jalapeño slices to the "Cardiac Arrest" with its one-pound patty wrapped in smoked bacon and covered with three types of cheese to the heart-stopping "Quadruple Bypass" with its four succulent patties just dripping with saturated fatty acids and Davis's secret sauce to the "Transplant," which is a large platter mounded high with all of the above, Davis's burgers are nothing short of a heart attack on a plate. And I eat one every Friday night whether I need to or not.

Around the corner from The Well is a double ess called Harley's Curve that has taken more than its fair share of prisoners. About seven years ago I was driving through on my way back to Atlanta—intent on buying a big Harley motorcycle—just after a guy on a Japanese crotch-rocket had failed to navigate both turns. He was faceup in the street with blood oozing out his nose and ears. I knelt and attempted CPR, but halfway through the first chest compression I realized his entire chest cavity was nothing but mush, and the only purpose his helmet served was to keep his brains from spilling onto the asphalt. I never bought the Harley.

I passed The Well, zigzagged through Harley's Curve, and headed home, where I was sure that Charlie had given up on me. Home was cold when I arrived, and Charlie was nowhere to be found, but I could hear him across the lake blowing on his harmonica. He was getting pretty tuned up, so I knew it wouldn't be long before he started tapping his foot and really breathing.

From bluegrass to classical, he knows hundreds of songs, and he can transition seamlessly through all of them.

Lake Burton is my backyard. Rich with history, Burton was once a prospering town, but they flooded it to generate hydroelectric power for the rest of the state. The locals didn't care. They took the money, moved their stills, and watched the water level rise and cover the sidewalks and the stones in the cemeteries.

In the early 1800s, after the departure of the Cherokee Indians, Burton grew into a thriving gold-rush town situated at the intersection of the Tallulah River and Moccasin Creek. Relatively untouched by the Civil War, the town became one link in the chain of the great railway explosion of the 1880s and 1890s. By the turn of the century, Rabun and Habersham counties held the largest tourist attraction in the country, second only to Niagara Falls. The Tallulah Gorge, called the "Niagara of the South," attracted wealthy tourists as well as Georgia Power.

The sheer rock walls that fell for hundreds of feet made a perfect place to construct a series of dams to generate hydroelectric power. In 1917, Georgia Railway and Electric Company bought up the town of Burton—which by then boasted three general stores. They built a dam and began flooding the surrounding land on December 22, 1919. The eighty-some-odd homeowners, whose homes had just been flooded, hopped into their canoes and runabouts and watched the lake rise up beneath them. When the lake topped out, the tips of the sixty-foot-tall pines were some thirty to forty feet below the surface of the water, which was as clear as green ice. In a sense, Burton became a flowing cemetery—a lot had been buried up there. Tucked in nooks and crannies all around the lake are more than a dozen cemeteries, some with stones dating back to the 1700s.

At its highest point, the cliffs at Tallulah Gorge drop twelve hundred feet to the bottom. Twice men have ventured across the chasm. Professor Leon made it across on July 24, 1886, and Karl Wallenda retraced his steps eighty-four years later on July 18, 1970. Once the dams were built, the engineers squeezed the mighty Tallulah down to a trickle. Old men in nightly bathroom runs now pee more liquid than she flows at this point. But all that backed-up water has to go somewhere, so thanks to that trickle, the lake has a surface area of more than twenty-seven hundred acres and sixty-two miles of shoreline. Today Rabun County is home to five hydroelectric lakes, consuming about 2 percent of the county's 377 square miles.

Burton didn't really get famous until Elliot Wiggington wrote his *Foxfire* books, and then Jon Voight climbed out of the gorge in the movie *Deliverance*, and the state of Georgia constructed Highway 400, so romantically depicted in the many chases of the Burt Reynolds classic, *Smokey and the Bandit*.

Today Burton is the weekend vacation spot for the millionaires from Atlanta and their kids—every one of whom owns a Jet Ski. Rising up out of the oak, pine, hemlock, and mountain laurel, most every inch of shoreline is covered with somebody's dream second home. When it's not being run over by the Jet Ski crowd, the lake is home to migrating mallards, buffleheads, mergansers, and loons. Come springtime, cardinals, finch, and mockingbirds sport their mating colors and nest all around the lake. Local year-round residents are the hummingbird, osprey, bald eagle, kingfisher, and a few great blue and green herons. And twice a year, the monarch butterfly migrates through.

In my front yard—which could be my backyard, depending on your point of view—I feed deer, turkeys, squirrels, chipmunks, raccoons, rabbits, and a black bear I've named George, because he's curious. And I am told that, thanks to the Lake Burton Hatchery, the lake is full of rainbow, brown, and brook trout. All told, there are some forty-two species of fish in these waters—including bluegill, red-breasted sunfish, largemouth bass, and yellow perch—although I've never caught a single one despite hundreds of hours of trying and Charlie's tireless encouragement.

Oh, I can see them. I can see them just fine, but getting them to take my bait is another matter entirely. Most folks, including Charlie, use crickets. Which is the heart of the problem. I won't fish with crickets. But despite my inabilities and eccentricities, Charlie still asks me to tie his knots because I'm pretty good at it. I've had a lot of practice with knots.

The roads around Burton are a plethora of Norman

Rockwell's Americana—apple orchards, dilapidated gristmills, craft stores, comb honey, smoked bacon, Coca-Cola, the Marlboro man, and cold beer at every turn. Vintage cars painted in rust dot the pastures that flow with creeks, cows, and horses. All summer long, hay bales rolled into one-ton mounds sit big as shacks, covered in white plastic like melted snowmen until the winter cold sheds their coat and feeds them to the livestock. And farmers, those whose lives are connected to the lake yet uninterested in it, sit atop green or red tractors beneath dusty brimmed hats, roll cigarettes, and pull at the earth for one more year like a pig suckling the hind teat.

And God? He's in these hills because we are. No matter how far you run, you can't shake Him. Maybe Davis and I know that best, but Emma knew it first, and Saint Augustine said it best: *You stir man to take pleasure in praising You, because You have made us for Yourself, and our heart is restless until it rests in You.*

Chapter 11

It was clear, growing cooler late one summer evening. I could smell the rain coming. Dark clouds first, followed by the strong, moist winds that rattled the magnolias and then the overwhelming aroma of a coming rain. At first, light drops fell softly, then larger drops smacked as they intersected the hand-sized, waxy magnolia leaves on their way to earth. Emma and I were sitting on the second-story porch outside my bedroom door, taking turns looking through the telescope pointed out into the Milky Way before the clouds blocked our view.

Beneath the tripod legs, a collage of jigsaw puzzles spread about the floor in front of us. For me, stars were a fascination and jigsaw puzzles a hobby. While I was piecing together seven puzzles simultaneously, she spent her time reading or sketching. Amid the stereophonic birdsong that surrounded us, Emma read *Great Expectations* and sketched the birds that perched nearby.

I had taken all seven thousand puzzle pieces, thrown them into the same basket, and then mixed them together like numbers in a bingo game. Then I dug my hand in and began forming the outlines of seven different pictures. I would need two weeks to put them all together, but it was the process that I enjoyed. One jigsaw was difficult enough, but add the other six, and that's when it started to get fun.

It was, I believe, my introduction to the scientific process. With each piece, I'd reason: if not here, then here, and if not here, then here, and . . . so on. Puzzles forced me to look at something from several angles before I moved on, to look again, and again, and possibly again because each piece—no matter how small or seemingly insignificant—was critical to the whole. With the outlines scattered about me, I let my hands and eyes work the floor while my mind wandered beyond the boundary of the porch and over the surface of the farmer's moon, which was full and had risen early.

After the storm, which was preceded and followed by a good bit of wind, I heard a cardinal singing. But the singing was different from the usual; the sound was hollow and haunting. I looked out my window to see a male cardinal standing on the porch next to the fluttering form of his mate. Apparently she had fallen or been thrown during the storm and had either broken or severely bent her wing. Our neighborhood was pretty well armed with cats so, given time, she wasn't long for this earth. And all her flopping around was only making matters worse—almost like fishing with live bait.

The male stood over her, next to her, encircling her, singing and calling at the top of his lungs. When I walked outside, he hopped up on the railing and eyed me with anger and suspicion—the feathers rising to a point on the top of his head and back of his neck. And when I cupped her in my hands, he flew in circles, just a foot or two from me, between the porch and the branches.

"It's okay, girl," I said. "Let me get you inside where I can take a look at you."

The male cardinal flew up to a branch, changing his tune to alert and alarm. Halfway through the door, I turned and said, "Don't worry, sir. I won't hurt her. You can look inside my window if you want."

I took her inside, placed her under my magnifying glass, and immediately saw the problem. Somehow during the storm, debris had blown through her wing, bending a few feathers, marring the skin, and placing a deep cut in one wing. The fine bone wasn't visibly distorted, but I'd have bet my microscope that it was fractured. I cleaned out the fine debris and then taped her wing closed, but not so much that she felt trapped. I pulled my birdcage off the shelf, filled the water bottle, and placed her inside.

All the while, watching me like a hawk, her fire-engine-red mate was sitting outside my window, singing at the top of his lungs. I knew that cardinals mated for life, so he wouldn't be going anywhere. "Don't worry, sir. She'll be okay. I'll take good care of her."

The loneliest sound I have ever heard is that of a male cardinal calling out for a female who does not answer. And he will stand on that limb and sing at the top of his lungs for days.

Emma whispered, "He's crying."

"You sure?" I asked.

"I know," she said matter-of-factly.

"How? How do you know? Doesn't sound like crying to me."

She looked back at the cardinal and said, without feeling the need to prove it, "That's 'cause you're listening with your ears and not your heart."

"What do they do when they find each other?"

"They sing together."

Emma slid across the floor, sat Indian-style, and bumped knees with me. She raised an eyebrow and whispered, "No man is an island, entire of itself . . ." She placed a finger on my nose. "Any man's death diminishes me, because I am involved in mankind . . . therefore never send to know for whom the bell tolls . . ." She tapped me twice. "It tolls for thee."

I have since come to believe that the cry of the cardinal, heard at random across the planet, out every bedroom window or screened back porch, is the sound of the multitudes pleading for the one.

I set the birdcage on a small table near my second-story window so the female could see her mate and he could see her. I changed the tape every few days, careful not to ruffle her feathers, and let her stretch her wing. And every day, that male cardinal stood like a sentinel at Buckingham Palace, singing for her. Most afternoons I'd collect some seeds, place some in her cage and on the sill, and let them eat together. They seemed to appreciate it, because they didn't waste any time. Eventually, he would fly to the windowsill and then onto the cage, where she'd peck at his feet. He'd flutter to the side of the food tray, and they'd peck beaks through the cage.

After three weeks of recuperation, I took the tape off completely and let her stretch inside the cage. Then I opened the cage door and turned it out toward the window. "Go ahead, girl. It's okay."

She flew gracefully out the door and lit on a small branch next to the male. Those two stayed in that nest outside my window throughout middle school and high school. And every day they sang their love song to each other. Emma used to tell me, when they'd come back to the window, that they were singing for me.

Chapter 12

My piece of property faces Charlie's. We own the opposite sides of a little finger off the eastern side of the lake. My view is of his house and vice versa, although he owns a little point that allows his guests— if he had any—a more panoramic view of the lake.

My house is a two-story, four-bedroom cedar shake with a red tin roof and heart-of-pine guts. Emma and I bought the land, an old fish camp, seven years ago after Charlie saw both lots come up for sale. We thought it'd be our weekend getaway, maybe some- place where I'd take a leave of absence and help nurse Emma back to health after her surgery. Emma thought we'd spend more time here, teaching our kids to swim and water-ski on the lake. She had big plans, and with her gift as an artist, she sketched them in detail.

Emma's plan called for three structures—a house, a dock, and a workshop. About five years ago, Charlie and I started construction on the workshop. Given Charlie's condition, much of the actual work was left up to me, but don't think Charlie was uninvolved. Born with power tools in his hand, I'm convinced he was a carpenter in Herod's workshop in a past life. While I sweated, grunted, and smashed my thumb with each whack of the hammer, he stood beside me running his fingers across the grain and cut of the wood, sensing the way it joined, held fast, or trimmed off a room. We subbed out the electrical because I know my limits, but anything having to do with running water or sewage, or with the cutting, sanding, shaping, or fashioning of wood, we did. I guess it goes along with my carpentry and plumbing roots.

Countless times Charlie made me redo something I'd already cut two or three times because he didn't like the way it joined together, the way it made a seam, or because it left a gap. As a result, I got better, but I'll stop short of saying respectable.

My property slopes down to the lake at about a thirty-degree angle, so when we first bought it we hired a guy with a front-end loader and asked him to flatten the fish camp and then haul out about two stories' worth of rock and dirt. When he finished, we had a flat spot about ten feet above the level of the water that cut seventy feet into the side of the hill, where it met a huge rock wall like the kind you see along highways. We dynamited the wall, flattening it, and then built up from there.

On the last blast, we pulled away the rubble and discovered a small L-shaped cavity in the rock. It was about large enough to drive my truck into and tall enough to stand in. Nearly flat and level, we cleaned it out, hung a lantern or two, and then built a bunk along either side. During the hottest months of summer, we slept in our "cave," where the rocks kept it from getting too hot. It made for a silent and safe retreat.

Half the first story of the workshop sat underground, while the second story rose out of and above it. The fact that half of it was surrounded by dirt meant that after we installed the potbellied stove, we stayed pretty warm in cool winters. And because those hills stay cold long after daylight, we kept cool in the summers. The workshop opened up through two sliding doors that, when opened, allowed you to drive two cars side by side straight through.

Charlie could tell you more about tools and construction in five minutes than I will know in a lifetime, but like a lot of other good teachers I've known, he taught me at my own pace. Once we finished the structure of the workshop itself, he left the finishing details to me.

We covered the walls in solid cedar and hung an exposed steel beam from the ceiling, running front to back, that would allow us to lift and move heavy and large objects like boats using a system of rolling pulleys. We installed four ceiling fans and recessed lighting, shoved the potbelly into the corner, and wired surround sound through ten speakers, indoors and out.

I made several dozen more trips to Home Depot, Lowe's, and Sears and started stocking the shelves with tools of every kind and brand. I bought two band saws, a planer-jointer, three disk sanders, several rasps, files, rubber mallets, wood mallets, clamps, a case of Titebond glue, two ninety-degree drills, a Dremel, two jigsaws, a punch saw, a handheld power planer, two entire sets of hand tools like screwdrivers, end wrenches, ratchets, and sockets, four rolling three-piece tool chests standing almost six feet tall, and every voltage of cordless power tool they offered. In short, when I made it to the checkout counter with four hourly employees pushing or pulling five overstuffed carts, every man standing in line stood with his bottom jaw at his toes.

While I enjoyed the tools, Charlie loved them. But, like Georgia, they did little to ease my guilt.

I spent three days thinking about placement and organization. Everything had a place and everything was in its place. Once organized, each tool was either within arm's reach or just a few steps away. Meaning we wasted little effort once work began.

As a finishing touch, I hung a dozen or so rolls of duct tape on well-placed hooks scattered about the workshop. Used by the Allies as a treatment for wounds in World War I, duct tape started as a medical dressing and has since grown to having several thousand uses—and it seemed like a day never went by that we didn't find a new one.

While I finished off the inside of both the workshop and the dockhouse, Charlie hired a team of talented laborers to help him build the stone bulkhead and steps that led from where the house would be down to the dock. Dropping a plumb line from the corner of the original fish camp, I staked out the slab for the rest of the house, called in the concrete trucks, and managed the guys pouring concrete while Charlie oversaw the stone team. At night we compared notes.

Charlie told me that every good house was built around a fireplace, so when his crew finished the bulkhead in a week, Charlie set them to working on the fireplace in the den, just off the kitchen. Before they left, the crew chief looked at Charlie and then at the leftover rock and said, "You got enough stone for a pit; you want one?"

Charlie knew what he was talking about. "Yeah." He pointed. "Put it right there."

The crew cleared a twelve-by-twelve flat between the house and workshop, poured their own slab, and built a barbecue pit big enough to smoke an entire pig and all the chickens and Boston butts you could manage.

With the workshop up and running, I turned my attention toward the dock. During the winter, when the lake was low, we sank twenty-four pilings and strung them with two-by-six stringers. Although we didn't own any boats at the time, we were planning ahead, so we built a two-story, three-bay, drive-in dock with remote-control garage doors and electric lifts. Off to the side we put a large platform three feet above the summer's normal water level, and dotted it with six rocking chairs. The second story was open, covered with a green aluminum sheeting roof, surrounded by a railing and centered with a huge picnic table. Next to the table hung Emma's hammock. It gave one of the best southward views on the lake. From my perch atop the dockhouse, I could see nearly five miles down the lake before it turned southeast toward the dam.

Having cut our teeth on the workshop and the dock, both admittedly allowing for more raw workmanship than the house, and with a cured slab and stone fireplace standing all alone, we started looking over Emma's sketches of the house. Her plan called for incorporating the old two-room fish camp into a two-story lake house. So, staying true to the plans, we kept the original kitchen, den, and porch.

Charlie was a big believer in overbuilding, so when we started framing the house, he studded it with two-by-eights, just ten inches center to center. Overkill, yes, but why not? Charlie was happy, and so was I. We only planned to do this once. Emma's painting was growing off the canvas, and we intended to give it all the texture and color we could imagine.

With the framing up, we walked through the empty inside of an unfinished house, and Charlie reminded me of what Emma had said as she stood over that bare ground and painted with her hands. *Every time I walk in here, I want to feel as if a candle were lit in every corner. The rooms should glow . . . with a golden hue.* She had pointed to the old pine floors in the original kitchen. *Like those floors.*

"How do we get a 'golden hue'?" I asked.

"Pine," Charlie said, pointing down at the floors. "Old pine. Preferably the heart, and you can't get it at the lumber store. At least not the good stuff. The kind you want . . . like that"—he pointed again—"has been setting up a few hundred years."

So we got in the Suburban and spent six months

scouring old Georgia highways and farms, knocking on doors and asking suspicious farmers if we could disassemble their rotten barns and leaning shacks and haul off the timber. Most nodded, bolted the door, and pulled the shotgun down from the mantel while we pitched a tent in whatever field was available and spent three days pulling apart boards and studying the craftsmanship of men who'd worked almost two hundred years ago.

With lumber starting to pile up, I bought a warehouse off the Clayton courthouse steps. The abandoned warehouse was located just a few miles up in the hills, so Charlie and I trimmed away the vines, swept out the floors, and started stacking our lumber in racks up off the ground where the moisture couldn't reach it. After six or eight more months, we had enough for my house and a couple of others. Everything—floorboards, walls, trim, ceiling, even the plate rack in the kitchen—we built from wood that we had resurrected from barns and shacks throughout pecan groves and oak stands in Georgia. There's a gold mine in salvageable wood draped in kudzu, pine needles, and acorns if someone is willing to peel back the vines and plane the wood. It's a slow process, and you're bound to uncover a few snakes, but maybe life is like that—you never know when something that's been hidden is going to rise up and bite you, or glow with a golden hue.

After eighteen months and more sore thumbs than I care to count, I handed the air hammer to Charlie, and he drove the final nails into the ceiling trim. We unplugged the compressor, hung up our tool belts, blew the sawdust out of the workshop, split a beer, and stepped back to "look" at our work. Charlie ran his fingers along the walls and trim like a man searching a cave in the dark, his hands spread out across the wood and his nose close enough to smell it. When he finished, he nodded and said nothing.

A few days shy of Easter, I spread my sleeping bag across the floor, lay down in an empty house, looked out through the window, and noticed for the first time that I was surrounded by dogwood trees. The next morning, they were in bloom. I lifted the window of our second-story bedroom, poked my head out into the branches, and shook my head. Emma had known all along.

Chapter 13

We were swimming in the stream behind the O'Connors' house when Emma hit puberty. I was twelve, she was eleven, and Charlie just eight, which might explain his reaction. Emma was floating around like a seal in about a foot of water, not a care in the world, when the water around her started changing color. I probably don't need to paint you a picture. Scared and surprised, she stood up, and that's when it became apparent that Emma was bleeding—a lot.

Charlie ran up the bank and started screaming, "Mom! Mom! Emma's dying! Emma's dying!" which probably wasn't what his mom needed to hear. I wasn't quite sure what was going on, but I had a pretty good idea she wasn't dying because she seemed fine, and when she stood up, she looked just as surprised as we were.

Charlie disappeared inside while I helped Emma up the bank and tried not to look at her legs. She was scared, and my staring wouldn't help matters any. I turned my back, and she slipped off her suit and wrapped herself in my towel. Then I held her hand, and we just stood there. She didn't want to sit down for fear of staining the towel.

"You okay?"

She nodded and tried to smile.

"You sure?"

She nodded again, squeezed my hand tighter, and looked cold. Miss Nadine came running outside, half-scared out of her mind, thanks to Charlie. She saw the suit, Emma's legs, and the two of us standing there quietly. It didn't take her long to put two and two together. She quit running, took a deep breath, put her arm around Emma, and smiled. "Sweetie, you'll be okay."

"But, Mama," Emma said, "I don't really feel bad."

"I know, honey, it's just part of life."

Miss Nadine put her arm around Emma and walked her inside, only to reappear a few minutes later with a hand towel tossed over her shoulder. She sat down on the porch bench, called us over, and put her hands on our knees. "I want to tell you two something . . . ."

Charlie was shaking, sniffling, and looked worried.

"Emma's fine, but . . ." She looked for the word. "She's . . . a woman now."

That night, I dug into my books and spent hours reading about women's bodies and the way things worked. Sure, at first I was titillated by it, every young boy is. Emma didn't look like those pictures, but I knew that in order to fix her, in order for her to live, I had to get past all that. So I did. I read on and found out that her medication had brought on the early onset of her cycle—a common side effect in young girls.

It would not be my last such revelation.

Chapter 14

During the last several months, Charlie had learned how to use a hammer and nails and was putting them to good use. The O'Connors' backyard was covered by a huge live oak, which Charlie began filling with scrap lumber he had pulled from construction Dumpsters and neighbor's trash piles. For the last several months, it had become his all-encompassing obsession, and every afternoon he would remodel and expand his Swiss Family Robinson tree fort. It was three stories tall, not including the crow's nest, had several ladders and poles to climb up or slide down, and with his dad's help, working windows, two ceiling fans, lights, and running water.

It really was an entire world unto itself, and he was never finished with it. Finished wasn't a concept Charlie understood when it came to that fort.

Emma had missed a little more than a week of school, and I was starting to worry. I stopped in to see her one afternoon with Charlie and found Dr. Hayes and his nurse, Miss Lou, whispering with Emma's parents. When they finished, Miss Lou took Charlie into another room. Then Miss Nadine got on the phone with my mom, whispered some more, said, "Thanks," and hung up.

A few minutes later, the nurse called me to the back room where I saw Charlie holding a tissue over the end of his finger and looking confused. Miss Lou bent down and explained that she wanted to prick my finger to determine what type of blood I had.

"Type O negative," I told her.

She looked surprised. "You sure?"

"Positive, but"—I held up my finger—"suit your-self."

She nodded, looked askance at me, and gently pricked my finger.

Blood is an amazing thing. A fluid miracle. Like us, it's a living organism filled with living cells, and if you take it out of its carrying container—us—it dies. The average adult carries five liters in his or her body. There are four types of blood, but only one—type O—that can be given to every other person on the planet. People with type O are called universal donors for obvious reasons. On the flip side, there's only one type that can receive from every other person on the planet: type AB positive, the universal receivers. As it turns out, Emma's blood type was AB positive, which was both good and bad. Good for Emma, but bad for Charlie and me.

I had never given blood before, but I had an idea of what was going on. So I stretched out in a chair and laid my arm up on the side, and sweet Miss Lou started the whole rubber-band-and-alcohol-swab routine. Charlie wasn't too sure about all the needles and whispering, so he started to shake a good bit and ran out back to his fort.

Miss Nadine talked him out of the fort and back to the house, where she sat the two of us down to talk. Apparently, the added strain on Emma's body caused by the monthly loss of blood had been exponentially compounding Emma's problem. It weakened her, made her less able to fight infection, and started her on a downward spiral that she never really quite recovered from month to month. The doctors felt that if they could supplement Emma's blood supply with outside blood every couple of months, they could increase her chances of healing with less stress on her own body. Sort of like blood doping in reverse. But rather than taking a finely tuned athlete to the next level, it would just barely bring Emma up to normal. The theory was good, and it helped Emma—almost like a three-week caffeine hit—but even they knew then it was only a Band-Aid.

But Charlie didn't really get it. He understood forts and hammers much better than he did people and their blood.

Dr. Hayes had come back in while Miss Nadine was explaining, and he knelt down next to Charlie.

"Son," he said, "your sister is real sick. Your blood could help her live better. Especially right now when she needs it. See . . ." He gently took Charlie's arm, patted it, and then pointed inside. "Your blood has these little dump trucks in it called red blood cells. They carry stuff your body needs all around your body like cars on a racetrack. Do you have a racetrack?"

Charlie smiled and nodded his head.

"When you lose blood," the doctor continued, "or don't have enough in your body, or have a weak heart that can't fill up those dump trucks with enough gas to make it around the track, then you get a sickness called anemia. Right now Emma has a pretty bad case. " He looked Charlie in the eye. "Will you give her some of your dump trucks?"

Charlie glanced toward the stairway that led to the second floor, and I knew he was picturing his sister, pale and weak, too tired each day even to climb up to his fort and see his latest improvements.

"Emma needs more dump trucks?" he asked.

The doctor nodded.

Charlie looked to his mom, and she nodded too as the tears drained through the deep, dark pits that had swelled beneath her eyes and where all the eye makeup now puddled. She looked like a raccoon.

Charlie rolled up his sleeve. "Can I just give her all of them?" he said.

Three days later, Miss Nadine was still crying.

Chapter 15

Annie lay sleeping when I cracked the hospital door late Friday afternoon and walked into her room. Through the lone window I saw a cow pasture spotted with manure and dandelions and split by a small creek trickling down out of the hills. The cows had all huddled around the hay feeder except for one old bull who stood like a sentinel in the middle of the creek.

Cindy sat an arm's length from Annie, feet propped on the bed, head fallen to one side, still wearing yesterday's clothes, asleep with a book resting on her chest. The book had a plastic cover and was stamped with a library binding. It was titled *How to Make Big Money in a Small Business*. Scattered about the floor were five or six books and pamphlets, all wrapped in that same public-library plastic and all to do with obtaining loans and money management. On the desk next to the bed sat a red folder. Scribbled across the top in a female's handwriting were the words *Burton Bank and Trust, Loan Application*.

On the air I smelled Sal's lime-scented aftershave, telling me he'd just been here. The two mints sitting next to the phone confirmed it. I set the green stuffed frog on the bed and turned to tiptoe out when Annie whispered, "Hey, Sh-sh-shakespeare." Her speech was slow, unsteady, her lips thick with medication.

Cindy sat upright, wiped the drool off her chin, and started toeing the books and folders into a pile beneath Annie's bed.

I turned and patted Annie's feet. "When you've known him as long as I have, it's Billy."

Annie's eyes were heavy and glassed over. Undoubtedly, her doctors, in both Clayton and Atlanta, knew she was high-strung and needed rest, so they had kept her pretty well sedated over the last couple of days. I would have.

I placed the volleyball-sized frog closer to her and took out a small box that the lady at Rovers Hardware had wrapped for me. Annie smiled a doped-up smile and with her one good hand pulled the bow while I held the box and untied the ribbon. She lifted the top and pulled out a large copper bell that looked as though it had once hung around the neck of a cow.

"Thought that might help business," I said. "Maybe get folk's attention."

She smiled, rang the bell once, and blinked slowly. "I think I already got that." She looked back up at me. "You got any more pretty words for me?"

I scratched my chin and looked out the window. Sitting down next to the bed, I picked up the bell and said, "Tell me where is fancy bred . . . in the heart or in the head? How begot, how nourished? Reply, reply. It is engendered in the eyes, with gazing fed; and the fancy dies in the cradle where it lies. Let us all ring fancy's knell: I'll begin it—ding, dong, bell."

Cindy sat up and began studying me with new curiosity.

"Is that more Hammmmmmlet?" Annie asked, trying

hard to get her lips to sound the *M*.

"No. It comes from a little story called *The Merchant of Venice*."

She closed her eyes, fell silent for a few minutes, and faded off into the wonderful world of drug-induced sedation. Cindy watched with apprehension as Annie breathed.

"It's the medicine," I reassured her. I glanced at the machines above Annie's bed, all tracking her progress. "Pressure looks good, pulse is stronger than I had expected, and her oxygen saturation is not bad, given what she's had to deal with." I patted Annie's toes again. "She's tough."

Cindy nodded, but eyed me with more curiosity. I could see the questions beginning to swirl, and my Sheetrock disguise was crumbling.

Annie woke and, after two trips around the room, her eyes found me again. "Doc says I can leave in a few days."

"I heard. That's good. You probably miss your own bed."

"Tell me about it." She waved a shaky hand around the room. "You ought to see all the stuffed bears I've got."

I looked around the room, which was spilling over with flowers, Get Well balloons, and ten to fifteen stuffed animals—mostly bears.

"I see."

Cindy broke in. "Annie and I've been talking, and we'd like to have you for dinner." She covered her eyes with her hand and shook her head. "I mean, have you *over* for dinner."

"I got it." I smiled.

"It's the least we can do." She turned to Annie, who nodded slowly. "Annie's a pretty good cook and was just talking about fixing you some peach cobbler."

Annie nodded again. "No kidding," she said with her eyes closed, "I really can cook. Although"—she held up her left arm, thick with a plaster cast—"I'm gonna have a hard time rolling the biscuits."

Annie sounded as if she'd just left the dentist after having four cavities filled.

It'd been a long time since I'd accepted an invitation to dinner. And even longer since it'd been with a female.

I nodded. "Then I'll only come if you'll let me roll out the biscuits."

"You can cook?" Annie asked, surprised, her head bobbing to one side as if it had just fallen off its perch.

"No, but I learn quickly."

"Folks around here say you build a pretty mean boat," Cindy said. "That true?"

"I restore them more than I build them. I just improve on somebody else's design."

"From the way people gossip, you're pretty good at improving. Houses too. I thought you looked like you were in construction."

"Oh, it's like anything," I dodged, thankful that she had blanketed me with the construction tab. "Once you learn how, it's not all that complicated. The right teacher, good tools, a little patience, and you could do it."

"I doubt it," Cindy said. "I can barely change a light-bulb without help from Annie."

"Well, sometimes a good team can make all the difference."

Cindy sat upright and began tightening her ponytail with several loops from a second pink rubber band. Her curious eyes had become assertive; the hallway talk had given her little information and raised as many questions as it answered. "Sounds like you know what you're talking about." She was digging again.

Annie's eyelids were falling down, giving me an easy exit. I whispered to Annie, "You get some sleep, and I'll come see you next week for dinner."

Annie unconsciously reached up and clasped the sandal now hanging on a chain and resting just above the tip of the scar on her chest. Her thumb gently rubbed the back as she nodded off to sleep.

Cindy looked embarrassed, like she had pushed too hard and too fast. She walked me to the door, fiddled with her hair, and said, "I think she likes the frog. Thanks."

I waved her off as if to say, *Don't mention it.*

Cindy handed me my heart-rate monitor and said, "Annie's doctor downloaded some really good information off here. He said you were right to put it on Annie. Said it helped him understand the strength of her heart under strain and . . . how long we have to find another one."

The sight of Annie plugged in to every outlet on the wall, beeping, flashing, and monitored by two to three nurses down the hall, brought back a lot. Everything was familiar. The smell of antibacterial soap, the temperature in the room cold enough to hang meat, the way the clear tape circled the IV and held the needle to Annie's arm, the constant monitoring of every aspect of life. I opened my mouth and spoke from my heart before my head had time to tell it to shut up.

"Does Annie like the water?" I asked.

Cindy looked confused. "Yeah, she can see it from her bedroom window, but she only gets in it to bathe."

"How about if I take you guys for a ride in a boat next week? Charlie, my partner, and I ought to have it finished by then, and I'll need to take a test run before the owner picks it up in time for next month's show."

Cindy smiled and looked back at Annie. "I think she'd like that. Just as long as it's not too rough and her doctor thinks she can handle it." She chewed on a cuticle and held one finger in the air. "You better let me get back to you on that." She nervously tucked the hair behind her ears again. "Transportation is . . . sometimes a problem." Her admission was painful.

"That sounds like a long story," I said, trying to ease her apparent embarrassment.

"It is, and it begins with the high cost of health care."

The heart has its reasons which reason knows nothing of. I stepped through the door, beginning to feel uncomfortable as the reasoned voice in my head filtered down to my unreasonable heart.

"No worries. I'll pick you up." I scribbled on the back of a pizza coupon that had been taped to the door and said, "Here's my number. Check with her doctor and call me Tuesday morning to let me know if she's up to it."

Cindy nodded and shut the door behind me. Just as the door clicked shut, I spotted Annie's chart stuffed in the hanger on the wall outside her room. Without thinking, I slid it from the sleeve and began thumbing through its pages.

A nurse spotted me and yanked it out of my hand. "May I help you?"

Her hair stood a foot off her head in a tightly wound beehive, and she had plucked every last hair of her eyebrows. Her entire posture said, *Don't mess with me!*

I didn't.

"Uh . . . no. Thanks. I was looking for . . ."

"What?" she said, one hand propped on her hip.

"Pizza coupons," I said, trying my best to act stupid.

Without taking her eyes off mine, she reached in her multicolored shirt and pulled out a coupon for two large pizzas. "Now, what else can I do for you?"

She was probably an excellent nurse. I shook my head and waved the coupon. "Thanks."

She watched me as I walked out.

I unlocked the Suburban and sat for a moment while it warmed up. It was Friday night, time to head for The Well. I could already taste the Transplant.

Chapter 16

Because Dr. Hayes had been so bent on getting Charlie's and my blood, I went to the library and checked out every book I could find having anything to do with the human heart. If they wanted our blood, then there must have been some secret to it, so when I found a book that even mentioned the heart or blood, I read it. And that meant I read a lot of books.

One day as I sat in the library, surrounded by almost a dozen books, some pretty severe acne covering my face, Ms. Swayback, the librarian, tapped me on the shoulder and asked me, "Son, do you really intend to read all those books?"

"Yes ma'am."

"You mind if I ask you why?"

"I'm studying the heart."

She shook her head and put her hands on her hips. "Son, I wasn't born yesterday." She shook her head again and smiled a knowing smile. "Now, you mind telling me?"

"I'm gonna fix Emma. Figure out how to sew shut the hole in her heart."

"Oh, well, that sure explains it." She readjusted her hips, using them as shelves to prop her hands up. "Listen here, you little squirt, don't you get smart with me. And you better read every one of those books and then put them right back where you found them. I'm not wasting my time reshelving all those books just 'cause you're looking for the nudey pictures. I know your type."

I wasn't quite sure what she was talking about, but I said, "Yes ma'am," anyway. A week later, after I had actually read all those books, put them back exactly where I'd found them, and proved I wasn't going to be the trouble she thought, Ms. Swayback would help me find any book I wanted, even getting them on loan from libraries as far away as Florida.

She wasn't my only initial critic. My parents thought I had lost my mind, but when my science grade improved from a C– to a B+, they quit questioning me and even offered to let me stay late at the library when Ms. Swayback would drive me home.

People marvel at the genius of Mozart because he supposedly wrote "Twinkle, Twinkle, Little Star" at the age of three and composed his first symphony at the age of twelve. And yes, of course he was a genius, but another way to look at it is that he just discovered early what it was God made him to do. That's all. For some reason, God gave him a little extra, or a little something different, and Mozart found out what that was and then got a head start on using it. Of course he was brilliant, but that's not the point. The point is he knew, and then he got to work.

I was no Mozart, and I had to work at it, but I never doubted what God made me to do. Not till much later.

The thought of Emma and her pitifully pumping heart got me out of bed in the mornings and kept me up late. Soon I was doing more work outside of school than in. I learned everything I could about how the heart and circulatory system worked: dark, sticky bluish-black oxygen-poor blood flowed into the heart, which immediately shot it back to the lungs where the carbon dioxide was taken out and fresh oxygen was poured in, turning it a bubbling, slippery purplish-red. Then, charged up and busting with pressure, it was returned to the heart, which again immediately shot oxygen-rich blood back to the body, which was starving to be fed.

And this occurred not once, but more than one hundred thousand times a day. I thought about this a long time. And when I understood this process, not only the physical anatomy of it, but the idea of it, what it did, the fact that when it worked, you lived, and when it stopped, you died, I shook my head and cried at the simplicity of it.

As early as 3000 BC, the Chinese had named the heart the Emperor of Organs. Since then, people have spent their whole lives looking for the Holy Grail, the fountain of youth, or the center of the universe. Why look so far away when it's right there in the middle of every human on the planet? The more I understood this, the closer I thought I was getting to fixing Emma.

I placed my hand on my chest, looked inside myself, and whispered, "Life is where the blood flows."

One day a kid in my class brought his dad's *Playboy* to school and passed it around during recess. I took one look, and it struck me as completely wrong. It made me feel dirty, like I wanted to take a shower. Deep down, I knew that whoever had done that to those girls, taken all those pictures, must be a pretty sick person. My heart told me that.

I handed it back. *That could be Emma,* I thought.

Don't let me sound like some saint. Of course I wanted to see naked women, but beneath the part of me that was intrigued was another part, the part that knew better, the part that knew I was here to fix Emma. That part of me, where my soul lives, convulsed, vomited, and spewed disgust across the glossy centerfold.

Walking home that day, I was quiet. Even embarrassed. When Emma asked what was wrong, I told her. When we got to her steps and I had finished my story, she pulled me close and kissed me on the cheek—one heart speaking to another in a language that only the two of them speak.

Emma had the sickest heart of any human I'd ever met, but out of it flowed more love than from any other ten hearts put together.

Soon my teachers could no longer answer my questions, so I spent more and more time in the library soaking up everything to do with the human body. By the end of eleventh grade I had read several major text-books for undergraduate premed students and even a few on Harvard's recommended list. I could quote them and see the diagrams in my head. But in all my study, I began to notice one problem: if I was going to science to find life and understand how to bring that back to a dying, diseased human heart, I had gone to the wrong place.

To science, the heart was just something to be dissected, labeled, and put on a shelf in pickle juice where a kid with glasses and a mouthful of braces could say, "Ooh" and "Ahh." The scientific approach was cold, unfeeling, and even the way they talked about it was sterile. As if the heart were nothing more than cells linked together by other cells.

Most books said it simply: The heart is a two-fist-sized organ divided in half by a muscular membrane called the septum. Each half has a thin-walled muscular collecting chamber called the atrium and a more muscular ejecting chamber called the ventricle that pumps blood through the lungs. Blood pours into and out of ventricles through valves, the tricuspid and pulmonary valves in the right ventricle and the mitral and aortic valves in the left. In the lungs, blood is reoxygenated, exchanging oxygen for carbon dioxide, sent back to the heart through the pulmonary veins, and then fired through the body via arteries where the process is repeated more than one hundred thousand times each day, resulting in the movement of more than two thousand gallons of blood. Smoking, high blood pressure, birth defects, and elevated blood cholesterol can all damage the heart's ability to pump blood.

All the descriptions were so sterile. The books talked about it as if it were a sump pump stuck down in the muck and mire of somebody's backyard. Never in all my scientific reading did I encounter anything that talked about a broken heart. Never did I read anything about what the heart felt, how it felt, or why it felt. Feeling and knowing weren't important, only understanding. After all I had read, I was starving for someone to talk about the heart as if it were alive, not dead. Someone who wrote about the kind of heart I had found in Emma.

Emma knew this.

As I struggled with the library, diagrams, and Latin descriptions, she noticed the pained look on my face. We sat at a large table, separated by our stacks of books. Emma's physical activities were somewhat limited, so going to the library was something to which she looked forward and which we did almost daily. On my side of the table sat dozens of scientific books and manuals written by professors, PhDs and MDs, all known as experts in their fields. And on Emma's side sat dozens of old books, most written by men long since dead: names like Coleridge, Wordsworth, Milton, Keats, Tennyson, and Shakespeare.

Seeing my frustration, she put down *Paradise Lost*. From her backpack she pulled out a wrapped gift— about the size of a thick book—and put it behind her back. She led me from the table and pulled me between the rows of bookshelves where the librarian couldn't see us. Surrounded by thousands of years of knowledge stacked high on either side, the best that the Western world and modern medicine could accumulate, Emma tapped me on the sternum and showed me that she—who had never read any of them—knew more than all of them added together.

She brushed my hair out of my eyes and placed her palm flat across my chest and said, "Reese, your books might not tell you this, so I will. Every heart has two parts, the part that pumps and the part that loves. If you're going to spend your life fixing broken hearts, then learn about both. You can't just fix the one with no concern for the other." She smiled and placed my hand across her heart. "I should know."

She pulled the book from behind her back and held it to my chest, then she walked away and left me holding the gift. I peeled off the wrapper to find the complete works of William Shakespeare.

In the months that followed, Emma made sure that we read aloud from my copy of Shakespeare. Eventually, we began speaking to each other in the lines we remembered. Emma was much better at it than I. We did it so much that even Charlie—who was sick of hearing us speak the King's sixteenth-century English—learned to play.

One Saturday afternoon the three of us were going to a movie. When Emma saw me coming, she threw up her hands and said, "O Hamlet! Thou hast cleft my heart in twain."

Charlie looked over his shoulder and said, "Oh, brother!"

Without skipping a beat, I hopped up on the front steps and knelt, taking her hand in mine, and said, "O! Throw away the worser part of it, and live the purer with the other half."

And to this day, I wish the same.

Chapter 18

Four neon beer signs hung in the window of The Well in full Friday night glow. Atop the apex of the roof, a neon strip of lights outlined a well-endowed woman wearing nothing but high heels and a cowboy hat.

The Well is an anomaly in Clayton. As out of place as a baseball in a football game, or a poker chip in church. The structure itself was built from huge stones pulled from the shoreline around Lake Burton. Some of the stones are as big as beach balls. They've been squared, mounded together, and piled atop one another to form walls that at a minimum are two feet thick. The roof is built from huge rough-cut cedar timbers and draped with cedar shakes that are nearly covered in moss. The moss hangs down, accenting the huge front door that was once the loading door on a steamer in the North Sea. The door is six inches thick, nearly eight feet square, made from planks that are almost a foot in width and held together with three thick iron straps. It hangs on runners and must be slid open and closed by a very strong person.

The place was built in the fifties by a hermit who must have been afraid of nuclear war with Cuba, because the cellar was just as stout as the building above it. Dug down into the rock, it became the county's fallout shelter after the hermit hopped on the Appalachian Trail one afternoon and walked to Maine with his dog, never to be seen or heard from again. Due to its stone construction, The Well stays cool all summer, and thanks to its six-foot-wide fireplace, warm all winter.

It sat vacant for years until Davis Stipes got hold of it. And Davis, or Monk, as we call him, is as much a mystery as the former owner's disappearance. Davis is forty-something and likes Hawaiian shirts, cut-off jeans, flip-flops, and the fact that very few people suspect him of holding a doctorate in theology. In truth, he holds two. A military brat, he was born in England where his dad was stationed with the SAS. He's traveled more than most anyone I know, attended universities and seminaries all over Europe, dropped off the radar screen for most of his twenties, spent five years in a Spanish monastery where rumor has it he took a vow of silence—and kept it—and has never married. Although he says he's open to the possibility.

The details of his lost decade are a little fuzzy, but people with secrets in and around Clayton are nothing new. There are a lot of secrets both above and below the surface of Lake Burton. Davis's mother and father died while he was studying in the Spanish monastery. He buried them in London, along the river Thames, and when he read his father's will, he discovered his folks owned a little ten-acre tract on Lake Burton. Obviously, they'd had hopes of building a retirement home. Davis flew back to the States to put it on the market, but when he drove around the lake and pulled onto the gravel drive next to the Burton Campground, he changed his mind.

When The Well came up for sale, Davis was on his way to the Clayton hardware store to pick up some more bolts for the extended dock he was building. He drove through Harley's Curve, saw the sign, inquired about the price at the real estate office in town, and was told to make an offer. The city wanted to be rid of the headache, so Davis canvassed a few friends, sketched out a business plan on a napkin, and told them what he wanted to do.

"One of my favorite stories is when Jesus meets the woman at the well. Imagine that moment. She was a 'loose woman,' known around town, and in the flash of a second, He knew everything about her: her five husbands, current boyfriend, everything she'd ever done wrong—He knew it all. Yet He spoke to her and loved her despite all the baggage she brought with her. Something about how He treated her was magnetic, because she wanted to be there. Like all of us, she was thirsty, and when He pulled that bucket up just spilling over with clear, cool water, she shoved her whole face in it and sucked it dry.

"The people who are really thirsty aren't going to church on Sunday. They're driving around this lake, running from their secrets, looking for a good, quiet, fill-your-stomach place to eat. Trying to fill that God-shaped hole with a bigger house, another boat, a second mistress, whatever. So let's take the bucket to them. Speak to the heart, and the head will follow. And the fastest way to the heart is through the stomach. I want to get in the business of making God-shaped cheeseburgers."

The silent four nodded, pitched in, and the five of them bought it off the courthouse steps for $100,000. After about six months' renovation, Davis opened the doors. The first day, the wait at the door was an hour, and it's been overcrowded ever since. For the last three years, seven days a week, Davis has pounded out the burgers and tended bar. On his days off, which are few, he disappears into the mountains.

The Well is not your local biker hangout. Above the door is a small, barely noticeable sign that reads: *As for me and my house, we will serve the Lord.* And that's just the beginning. The entire place is one well-disguised billboard for God. The cocktail napkins are printed with Scripture from Genesis to Revelation, there's a Bible on every table, the mixed drinks are labeled after the twelve apostles, and chalkboards around the bar are covered with everything from the Ten Commandments to the Sermon on the Mount.

And while the jukebox is filled with rock-and-roll titles, all the records have been replaced with gospel music. G5 may read "Hell's Bells" by AC/DC, but when the quarter's dropped in and the unsuspecting bar hopper sits back with his beer to combat the writing on the walls with some good old hard rock, he's greeted by the Atlanta Gospel Choir singing, "Ain't No Rock Gonna Cry in My Place."

Most of the servers are kids from church, and on Tuesday, Thursday, and Sunday mornings, Davis fills the room with recovering junkies, admitted adulterers, and struggling soccer moms in his morning Bible study. Right now they're working their way through the Gospels, and focusing on the words in red.

Davis lets his bar speak for itself. It's neither his podium nor his pulpit, but he's always listening, and he'll speak up if you ask him the right question or look like you need a friend. And while he may serve both beer and mixed drinks, I've never seen him touch either one, although he is partial to his own cooking. Between the environment and the food, people can't stay away. This includes Charlie and me.

And talk about successful restaurants. An armored truck makes two pickups a week. With that much money flowing through here, you're probably asking yourself, *Yeah, what about the money? Sounds like a scam . . . like maybe he's using all that religion and Scripture quoting to pad his own pocket.* Problem is, we all know better. Davis got his investors to oversee the finances so he could concentrate on what he did best—hoisting up the bucket. As a result, Davis never touches a penny; he's paid a reasonable salary with a quarterly bonus based on net income and couldn't steal from himself if he tried.

The parking lot was half-full, and Davis's enormous Harley, chromed from stem to stern, sat to one side of the front door when Charlie and I arrived. I parked next to Sal Cohen's decade-old Cadillac, and we walked in. Four guys stood in the back propped between pool cues and baseball caps, talking above squinty eyes and the cigarettes dangling from their lips. The cloud of smoke hanging just above their heads swirled slightly from the single ceiling fan that sucked the air around the inside of the bar. The stacks of quarters lined up along the green velvet rail told me they'd be there all night.

Upside down on the wall above the bar hangs the world's largest armadillo. At almost three feet long with a pre-roadkill weight of twenty-five pounds, he was three times bigger than any armadillo I'd ever seen. All the locals called him Leppy, because armadillos are known to carry leprosy, but I just called him Gross, because he was.

An out-of-town couple sat at a table against the wall, clutching hands and wearing slick biker leathers, unscuffed Dingo boots, bandanna do-rags, and black T-shirts they had bought at Bike Week the year before. They were what the locals call "weekend warriors from Atlanta."

Davis stood sweating in a white, grease-stained apron, flipping a griddle full of burgers with one hand and pounding out patties with the other. As we walked through the door, he waved his spatula at us. Charlie tapped the floor with his walking stick, checking the location of the chairs between him and the bar.

"Hungry?" Davis asked over his shoulder.

"I could eat the butt end of a horse," Charlie replied.

"Ahh." Davis smiled and shook his head to avoid the smoke. "A man after my own heart."

I spotted Sal, patted him on the back, and we took a seat at the bar next to him. Davis poured me a Sprite from the fountain while he made Charlie a St. Peter— Johnny Walker Black Label with soda.

Davis had no problem with you drinking if he detected it wasn't an issue for you. If it was, and he did, then he'd serve you, but you might not enjoy it very much. Drinking had never been an option for me. Occupational hazard, you might say. And after I left my occupation, I just never picked it up.

On our left sat Sal, making his way through a cheese-burger—which, as slowly as he ate and as much as he chewed, would take the better part of an hour. And on my right slouched a greasy, skinny stranger staring at three empty glasses of beer and trying to make sense out of the Scripture verses printed on his cocktail napkins. Davis had loaded him up with popcorn, peanuts, and napkins, apparently working him over pretty good.

As for the empty glasses—he hadn't really drunk three whole beers. He thought he had, but the alcohol content had been altered somewhat. Actually, it'd been altered a lot. To strangers that are "of legal age," Davis gives what they ask for. Real beer. At least until they demonstrate a need for it. After that, he waters it down a bit, mixing regular with an unleaded version like

O'Doul's. It's mixed beneath the bar and comes out the tap looking like real beer, so the guy drinking it has no idea. It's a little frothy but settles quickly. For the folks that are "not yet of legal age," which Davis can spot a mile away, he serves them the nonalcoholic stuff straight up.

The stranger next to me was a perfect example. Davis had spotted him the moment he walked through the door, and the look on the kid's face told me he was starting to get worried. Normally, three beers should have had some buzzing effect, but tonight something was different.

"How's the boat?" Davis asked, slicing tomatoes.

Sal perked up, bent an ear our way, and forked his food around his plate while his jaw moved in rhythm with the slow-tempo gospel spilling out of the jukebox, like a cow chewing its cud. Sal had one speed—his—but at his age, nobody seemed to mind. It might have been slow, but it was effective. And one other thing, you could count on it. Everybody did.

"Coming along," Charlie said. "We're just a few days away. That is"—he threw his thumb at me—"if I can get Captain America to keep his eye on the ball."

Davis flipped a burger and looked at me. "I heard you were the center of excitement in town the other day. Heard you were wearing your cape too."

Between the naked-woman weather vane atop the roof, the "We Bare All" and "Adult Toys" signs in the windows, and Davis's unadvertised beer-pouring practices, you might think he's misleading people, showing them one thing and giving them another. Lying, to call it what it is. Because there are, in fact, no naked people in Davis's bar; no one bares any skin other than Charlie, who sometimes does a belly-button routine on open-mike night. The only adult toys are a pool table and a few dartboards. And chances are pretty good that when you buy a Budweiser, you're not getting 100-percent Budweiser.

Davis will admit all this if you ask him, but he's zeroed in on his target audience and knows what appeals to them. I'm not saying he's right or wrong, and I'm not suggesting the end justifies the means, but he's passionate about getting people to heaven. And judging by his Bible study attendance during the week, it's difficult to argue with his results. If it means titillating people's sin senses and hoodwinking them on their beer, he's comfortable standing before God and telling Him he did it that way. That's just Davis.

If he'd lived in Germany during World War II, he'd have been one of the people who answered the knock at the door and told the SS soldier there were no Jews in his house, while his basement was bursting at the seams with eight or ten families whose fathers' names were Hananiah, Azariah, and Mishael.

Bottom line, Davis is not interested in the people who aren't attracted to the promise of big bosoms, cold beer, and the possibility of having both. And for that reason he's targeting the folks who think they can't live without them.

Davis refilled the glass of the kid next to me, gave him a fresh napkin, and stepped back to the grill where six or eight burgers were sizzling through medium rare. The stranger smiled at Davis, shot an eye toward me, and started reading his napkin.

I grabbed a toothpick and stuck it in my mouth. The three big-screen televisions hanging behind the bar were tuned to two baseball games and one middleweight boxing match.

When Davis's back was turned, the skinny stranger leaned toward me and swore. "Hey, dude, is this a real bar or what? I think this dude is whacked. Sounds like a preacher. And what's the deal with these napkins and all this religious mumbo jumbo written on the walls?"

I didn't know the first thing about him, but the stranger cussed like someone who was making up for inadequacies someplace else.

I nodded, pointed toward Davis, and whispered, "Monk's got a pretty clear picture of what his job is, but don't let it get to you. You tried the burger yet?"

The stranger shook his head.

"Try one. It's worth whatever verbal abuse you have to endure from the owner."

"I heard that," Davis said over his shoulder.

The stranger smiled and said, "Barkeep, I'll have what he's having."

Davis sidestepped the griddle smoke again and said, "Three Transplants, coming up."

Swiveling on a bar stool, Charlie and I small-talked

the stranger, who, as it turned out, was a sixteen-year-old kid named Termidus Cain.

"But," he whispered, "everybody calls me Termite."

He looked twenty-five and had the stubble, knuckle scars, and fake ID to prove it. Problem was that his eyes gave him away. He said he'd just moved to town looking for work and running from some woman's husband down at Lake Lanier. His nose was long, pointed, and moved like a mountain road across his face. At some point it had been broken—badly—and now traveled like an *S,* making the base almost an inch to the right of the pinnacle between his eyes. Soaking wet, I doubt he weighed 125 pounds. And he had a habit—probably acquired recently—of looking over his shoulder.

"Termite," Davis interrupted, shoving a platter in front of him, "eat up."

Termite attacked the plate like a guy breaking a three-day fast.

I noticed his hands, which were thick with calluses and stained with grease. Compared to the rest of his scrawny body, the size and strength of his hands were out of proportion. I swallowed and waved my fork at him.

"What do you do when you're not drinking beer, eating cheeseburgers, and running from angry husbands?"

He looked quickly over his shoulder, saw no one, stuffed another enormous bite in his mouth, and muttered, "Engines."

"You build them?" I asked.

He shrugged his shoulders. "Whatever."

"You any good with marine engines?" Charlie asked.

He looked at us with nonchalant cockiness. "Any engine. Don't matter none what kind. I s'pose my specialty is Jet Skis, motorcycles, and cigarette boats, 'cause I like things that can go fast." He waved his fork in the air and squirted some more mustard on his burger. "But it don't matter none."

I pointed south toward Charlie Mountain Road. "If you're any good, the guys at Anchorage Marina are always looking for mechanics. Seem to pay pretty fair too. And this lake's loaded with rich kids tearing up their daddies' Jet Skis, Ski Nautiques, and eighty-year-old boats."

Termite nodded and registered this tidbit without looking up. He didn't seem to need to prove he was any good with engines, which probably meant he was. Obviously, engines were not an area of inadequacy.

In ten minutes he had consumed most of a dinner that normally takes me the better part of forty-five minutes if I pace myself. He scraped his plate clean and then tapped his beer glass with his fork like a seasoned drinker.

Davis served him his sixth "beer," and Termite drank with all the confidence of an underage, cocky kid who needed redirecting before he ended up in some cell with a bunkmate named Butch who can bench-press five hundred pounds and likes to call people "Sue." When he finished his beer, he thumbed a cigarette from the pack in his shirt pocket, hung it James Dean–style between his lips, then lit it with a silver Zippo lighter, which he slammed shut on his thigh in a public and prerehearsed fashion before slipping it back into his pocket.

Over the course of the last four years, Davis had prodded and probed enough to know that I had a secret and that Charlie knew what it was. After about three years' worth of digging at me and realizing I wasn't talking, he was kind enough not to dig too much further. Although that didn't stop him from getting in his jabs when he could.

"So . . ." Davis leaned over the bar and stuck his nose about three inches from mine. "How're we doing today?" He dropped a napkin on top of my food and waited for me to read it.

I picked it up and held it toward the light. *1 John 1:8, 9*. I knew this one because Davis had dropped it here before.

Termite tapped me on the shoulder, leaned in like he was trying to steal the multiple-choice answers from my test, and whispered, "What's yours say?"

I placed it on the bar and sipped my Sprite. Without looking at either him or the napkin, I said, "If we say that we have no sin, we deceive ourselves, and the truth is not in us. If we confess our sins, He is faithful and just to forgive us our sins and to cleanse us from all unrighteousness."

Termite slammed back the rest of his beer, wiped his mouth with his sleeve, and said, "You guys need to take a dang chill pill."

Charlie just smiled and shook his head. Sal smiled, stirred his food, nodded in agreement, and chewed in equal rhythm.

I forked the mound of food on my plate into smaller bite-sized portions while Davis opened himself a bottle of water and winked at Termite, who wasn't quite sure about this whole thing.

I wiped my mouth with the corners of the napkin and kept my eyes on my food. "Monk," I said, "my sins are many and well-documented, but they'll die with me."

Davis leaned in closer. "Let's see, the last time we left off you were telling me about where you went to high school."

I had done no such thing, and Davis knew it.

Charlie leaned toward Termite and said, "Pal, don't let Monk wink at you. He spent time in a monastery with about a hundred other men dressed in robes and . . . well, you know what they say."

Termite looked at Davis. "No kidding?"

Davis nodded but never took his eyes off his burgers, which were getting close to perfect. "About two hours outside of Seville, up in the mountains."

Charlie's little wink and comment did two things: it got me out of having to brush off Davis, and it gave Davis an intro. In a sense, Charlie was watching my back. I wondered if he'd do that if he knew the whole truth.

"A monastery," Termite repeated. "Why'd you want to do something stupid like that?"

Davis turned and chewed on his answer before he spoke it. "I was arguing with God."

Charlie spoke up. "Which is a lot harder when you don't speak for five years."

Termite looked confused.

"He took a vow of silence," I explained.

Termite's eyes grew big, he looked at the floor, at all of us, then back at Davis. "You didn't say a single word to another human being for five years? Not even a whisper?"

"It's not exactly like that. There are times and places for talking. It's more about living in an atmosphere of silence. But, yep, I did. For five years, four months, three days, eighteen hours, and . . ." Davis thought for a moment. "A couple of minutes."

Termite was starting to get interested, but he gave us a look like he knew better than to let somebody pull the wool over his eyes. "So when you could finally just talk again, what's the first thing you said?"

Davis looked off into the distance, then said, "Excuse me, do you have change for a twenty?"

Termite laughed, lit another cigarette dangling from his lips, and slammed the lighter across his thigh. Over the next ten minutes, Davis told him the abbreviated version of his story, as he'd done to a hundred other Termites. The amazing thing about Davis's story was how unlike it was from every fish story I'd ever heard. It didn't grow with each telling. It remained true. A testimony to Davis's belief that the truth is good enough.

Termite liked all the parts about world travel, exotic,

faraway places, and how Davis backpacked bootleg Bibles behind the Iron Curtain when there still was one. Termite thought for a minute. "You was in Spain, right?"

Davis nodded.

"That near Italy?"

"Pretty close."

"Did they have nude beaches?"

Davis nodded. "Yes, although I can't speak from experience."

"You mean to tell me that with all that travel, you ain't never been to no nude beach."

Davis shook his head.

"Well, don't you think they need Bibles too?"

"Yes, but there's probably a way to get them to those people while they still have their clothes on." Davis slid a bowl in front of him and said, "Try some onion rings."

While Termite engulfed the onion rings, Davis told him the story of how he was running through the Alps trying to get away from the East German police, about returning safely and then burying his parents, of flying here, buying this bar, his silent investors, his morning Bible studies and—Davis tapped Termite's glass with his spatula—his nonalcoholic beer.

Termite looked around him, took it all in, looked down at the seven empty beer glasses in front of him, then looked at Charlie and me, who had heard the story dozens of times. He pounded one fist on the bar. "You guys' eyes is turnin' brown."

120

Somewhere in Termite's head, there was a disconnect between what he was hearing—the story of a man risking his life to take Bibles into a communist country—and where he was hearing it—a strip bar. Between the big-busted weather vane atop the roof, the neon signs in the windows, the pool tables, the ashtrays, the Harley at the front door, the promise of cold beer and naked women, Termite was having a difficult time. He looked at us and raised his hands. "This is a joke, and pretty soon I'm gonna see some really big breasts bouncing across the pool table and start feeling drunk, right?"

Charlie put his arm around me and broke in, "Pal, the only breasts you're bound to see around here is if Reese or me raise our shirts. But"—he tapped the bar with his folded walking stick—"I'll dance on the bar if it'll make you happy."

"Yeah," I said, "you really haven't lived until you've seen Charlie here paint his stomach with lipstick and do his one-man belly-button routine."

Termite sat back and his eyes grew big as Oreos. "You guys tellin' me . . . you don't like women?"

Charlie hugged me around the neck and kissed me square on the cheek.

"I ain't dadgum believing this. I'm in a dang queer bar. The guys back home ain't never gonna believe this." Termite stood up and put the bar stool between himself and us while his eyes scanned the bar for a more portable weapon. "I need to take me a whiz. A long one." Termite walked to the bathroom, looking over his shoulder. "And don't none of you sweet girls foller me, neither."

Termite disappeared into the bathroom, and we all started laughing. Even Sal, who looked at Davis and said, "I think your unorthodoxy just got you in a jam."

Davis smiled, shrugged his shoulders, and wiped down the bar. After a second or two he said, "People dying of thirst in a desert will do just about anything for even one sip of water. And that kid"—he pointed toward the bathroom—"is parched."

A few minutes later, Termite walked out of the bathroom with nervous eyes. His shirt was tucked in and his belt cinched up tight. He walked to the other end of the bar, pulled a wad of one-dollar bills out of his pocket and said, "Yo, quiet man, what I owe you?"

Davis kept wiping the bar. "Let's see, for one Transplant and seven beers . . ." Davis looked at the ceiling and appeared to be calculating. "That comes to one Tuesday morning."

"What?" Termite looked confused, then backed up and pointed at all of us, waving his finger like a pistol. "See, I knew you guys was gay."

"Kid," said Davis, "for you, there's no charge. But if you're interested, I teach here every Tuesday, Thursday, and Sunday morning. We're walking through parts of the Gospels, studying the words in red, and you're invited. I'll give you one free meal every time you come back." Davis held up a glass and smiled. "And all the beer you can drink."

Termite shook his head. "Nah, red words or not, I'm

paying my dang bill. I ain't owing you sorry Betsies nothing. Y'all trying to get me back here for some queer fest on Tuesday. I seen this kind of thing on *Cops*, and I ain't falling for it. Getting you hooked on the beer and food, and the next thing I know you've slipped me a Mickey, and I wake up wearing a dress and posing for pictures."

Termite started throwing one-dollar bills on the bar and counting as fast as his fingers would let him. "Here. Here's thirty dollars." He looked at Davis. "We square?"

"Kid, you don't need to pay me."

"I ain't your kid and I ain't your girl. Now, are we square?"

Davis nodded. "We're square."

Termite walked backward out the propped-open door. We watched from the bar as he cranked his Camaro and spun gravel out the drive, Lynyrd Skynyrd's "Sweet Home Alabama" blasting out his open windows.

Davis shook his head. "I always did like that song," he said.

Charlie tried to cheer him up. "He'll be back. You saw the way he scarfed down that Transplant."

Davis nodded. "That's probably a good kid who, like all of us, has come to a fork in the road. He's just a few decisions away from turning down a road that's real steep and difficult to climb back up once he sees it's a dead end."

Charlie and I dropped twenty dollars on the bar, and

I said, "We're under the gun to get Hammermill's boat ready so he can give the boys at Blue Ridge a run for their money."

Davis poured me a to-go cup of Sprite and then started pouring beers for three regulars who had walked through the door just after Termite ran out.

"What's his problem?" one of the guys asked Davis as he pointed in the direction of Termite's cloud of dust. "You show him his reflection in the water?"

Davis shrugged his shoulders and looked square at me. "Didn't need to. I think that's what he's running from."

I pulled up next to the guide wire that looked like an electric fence leading to Charlie's front door, but he didn't really need it.

He turned toward me. "You heard from that woman yet? The one with the little girl? I think her name was Annie."

"How'd you know about her?"

"Stitch, I'm blind, not deaf."

I shook my head. "No," I said. "I told her to call me next week and I'd take them out in Hammermill's boat."

"You think she will?"

"How should I know?"

Charlie smiled, got out of the car, and turned around, finally saying what he'd been wanting to say all day. "The Fourth is just a few days away."

"I know," I said quietly.

"Got your nerve up?"

"Working on it."

"How many years has it been?"

"You know better than that."

Charlie nodded and looked out over the lake as if he could see it. He pulled his walking stick from his back pocket, threw it like a yo-yo to extend it, and then tapped the car door. "Letters are supposed to be read, you know. That's why people write them."

"I know," I said, looking down into my lap.

Charlie smiled. "You want me to read it for you and tell you what it says?"

I dropped the stick into drive and said, "Hey, Georgia left you a nice steamy present just outside your front door. Good luck finding it."

Charlie stuck his nose in the air, smiled again, and walked off. His questions had said enough.

I pulled out of his drive and turned away from my home. Minutes later, I pulled into the hospital parking lot where one yellowish street lamp lit the entire lot. I parked off to the side and spotted a janitor wringing out a mop next to a side door. I waited until he finished, saw my chance, and slipped in behind him just before the door closed. Hospitals are busy places, and you can get by relatively unnoticed if you look like you know what you're doing. If you hesitate, they'll pounce on you.

Passing an empty lounge, I felt behind the door and found a white coat hanging on the hook. I pulled it on and found a stethoscope rolled up in the pocket. I hung it around my neck, stepped into a bathroom to slick my hair back, and walked confidently, yet not too quickly, down to Annie's door. I wanted to look busy, but not too busy. Sort of "relaxed busy."

I slid the clipboard from its sleeve and kept walking, almost as if I had been sent to pick up outgoing mail. I passed the nurses' station without so much as a hello, then turned a corner and disappeared into another bathroom. I locked myself in a stall and thumbed through Annie's chart. Three minutes of flipping pages told me all I needed. I returned Annie's folder to its hanger and disappeared out the same side door I'd come in.

Back home, I went to my closet and pulled out the old engineer's transit case stored there. When we were kids, Emma and I had found it in the attic, dusty and empty, and the leather strap used to carry it had a small cut in it. The tag on top of the wooden-hinged lid read *Circa 1907*. It was mostly weatherproof and offered plenty of room for the things I valued—like books.

I took out her letter and walked to the dock, holding the letter close against my chest. I placed it beneath my nose, breathed, and lied to myself for the ten-thousandth time. When I opened my eyes, I noticed I was still wearing the white doctor's coat.

Chapter 19

In preparation for Christmas one year, I bought an old two-person rowing shell that had seen better days. I set it up on two sawhorses in the garage and spent nights steaming and replacing the ribs, the planks on the bottom, the seats, oars, locks, anything that moved or served as a stress point. Essentially, I built a new boat using the old as a model. It was a learn-as-you-go project. I had never rebuilt a boat, but I knew a thing or two about rowing, and I thought maybe it would give Emma and me something to do that might help strengthen her heart. On Christmas Day we followed the creek down to the lake. There I blindfolded her and walked her up to the dock, where I had set the shell. On the side I had stenciled HMS *Emma*.

We gently set off; she'd row as long as she could, which wasn't very far, and I'd watch her back, the way her short, thin hair fell along the lines of her shoulders, and the obvious, ever-apparent struggle between her soul and the vessel that contained it.

I knew her heart was weakening. Her color and breathing told me that. Soon our rowing became more of a sketching cruise for her, and twice the exercise for me. That paid off for me, because I joined the rowing team and learned that, unlike Emma, I did not have a weak heart. My heart worked just fine. Better than most, actually. The added weight of pulling her around the lake worked wonders on my own heart and lungs, not to mention my arms, back, and legs. That spring I placed third in the one-man shell at the state finals. But while I benefited greatly from pulling her around the lake, I often looked at her back, looked inside her chest, and knew the disease was worsening.

Chapter 20

As Emma's condition and physical appearance changed, her mom grew increasingly frustrated with modern medicine and its practitioners, which meant she was more liable to try anything. Emma and I would sit in her room and listen through the air vents as her parents whispered about her chances and, despite her dad working two jobs, the bills that kept piling up. Their twice-monthly trips to Atlanta grew less frequent, and their zeal over experimental medications waned. Having exhausted both medicine and their bank accounts, they next sought tent-revival religion.

The Reverend Jim Tubalo was a self-proclaimed healer who traveled the Southeast with a three-piece suit, shiny watch, long white hair, longer purple bus, and a "whatever you can give" attitude toward finances. He, his entourage, and their tents made a biannual "here for three nights only" run through town, and Emma's parents had us out the door before five. Opening night found us front and center with Emma's mom leading her to the head of the line. I was scared, but I followed—to protect Emma from both her mom and the guy with the white hair.

Under the bright lights, loud music, and louder screaming, Rev. Jim laid hands on Emma and promptly scared her half to death. He gripped her by the shoulders, then started screaming into her ears and smacking her on top of the head with his Bible. This went on for about thirty seconds while Mrs. O'Connor held Emma's arm and Mr. O'Connor tried to figure out if this was helping or hurting matters. The preacher went to hit Emma on the head one last time when her dad, a rather big man himself, reached up and took hold of his arm.

"Sir, I don't mean any disrespect, but you hit my daughter one more time with that Bible, and I'll make you eat it."

Rev. Jim closed his eyes, raised his hands, and screamed, "Thaaaaaank yooooouuuuuuu, Jeeeeeeeeesus! She's healed." He paraded around the stage looking like he was trying to scrape bubblegum off the bottoms of both his shoes while the congregation clapped and music blared.

He looked at Emma's mom and dad and said, "The Lord has spoken to me." He nodded, shook his head, humming to himself, and then turned back to Emma's folks. "He just told me your little girl's healed. The infirmity, the vile sickness, has left her body."

Emma's dad gently took her hand, said, "Come on, darling. I'm sorry," and led us off the stage while Rev. Jim reported to the congregation that there'd been another healing.

We sloshed through the parking lot, which smelled a lot like a cow pasture, and loaded up in the back of the O'Connors' block-long station wagon, where Emma and I got caught in the cross fire of her parents' heated conversation. Her mother was trying to convince her dad, who wasn't buying the whole parade, that the man really could heal people.

Her dad listened and then looked in his rearview mirror. "Honey, don't get me wrong. I'm not saying the Lord can't or doesn't heal people, but if and when He does, I'm not sure He wears a three-piece suit and a shiny watch, or asks for a whatever-you-can-give-thousand-dollars when he's walking out the door."

Her mom looked incredulous. "He didn't ask you for a thousand dollars!"

"Right back there." Her dad pointed over his shoulder with his thumb. "That nice man who helped us to the door said, 'Rev. Jim's regular fee is a thousand dollars, but feel free to give whatever you can. Two thousand is fine too.'"

Her mom got real quiet, and I nodded because I had heard him. Emma too.

Emma spoke up. "Mama, God doesn't need the Reverend Tubalo to heal me. He can do it whenever and wherever. I know that."

Her mom glared toward the backseat and pointed her finger at both of us. "Don't you two take his side. Y'all shush."

I could feel the fabric of her family coming apart at the seams. Emma held my hand and swallowed her pill. By the time we got home, she was sleeping with her head in my lap. Her dad led her upstairs, put her into bed, tucked her in, and got ready to clock in at the bank downtown where he served as the weekend night watchman. Her mom checked on Charlie and started a pot of coffee.

I watched from behind the bushes as Mr. O'Connor drove off to work and Emma's mom walked back in and wiped away her tears. I walked around back, climbed the magnolia tree in the dark, straddled the limb outside Emma's window, and watched her sleep under the moonlight.

About midnight I crept to the window, slid it open, slipped inside, and stood next to Emma's bed. Watching her breathe, I knelt and placed my hand over her warm heart. It was pounding, struggling, and working almost twice as hard as mine.

"Lord, I'm not too sure about tonight, and I really don't think that Jim fellow has any kind of special deal with You. But I know the people in this house are running out of ideas. So, what I'm trying to say is . . . if You're all out of options, then let's give Emma my heart. It's a good strong one."

The moonlight bathed her with a bluish hue, making her look even more cold and sickly.

She opened her eyes and looked at me, and I saw the tear that had formed in the corner of her eye. One hand came out from under the covers, and she curled her right index finger.

I knelt by her bed. She pulled me close, where her breathing swept across my cheeks, and then slid her hand across mine.

"You can't give what you don't have."

"But—," I protested.

She shook her head and put her finger to my lips. "You already gave it to me."

Chapter 21

Charlie and I spent Monday putting the final touches on Hammermill's Greavette. Hammermill was chomping at the bit to get her in the water, and called three times from Atlanta to check on our progress. We polished the topside and ran our fingers over the smooth surface just admiring her beauty. We wanted a day with her to ourselves because she was our best work yet. We had replaced the keel and ribs with white oak, attached a deep red mahogany skin with stainless screws, and then brushed on almost fifteen coats of spar varnish. She was gorgeous. The guys at Blue Ridge Boat Werks, who in truth can run restoration circles around us, would salivate at the sight of her.

We began restoring boats after we'd finished the house, because that had been Charlie's intention from the start. I really didn't care. I just wanted to do whatever he wanted to do. If he'd wanted to build pianos or rocking chairs, I would have joined him.

First thing we did was to take a roundabout drive up north in search of a HackerCraft in need of some TLC. After about two weeks of searching newspapers and boat traders, we found it. A fellow named Dyson had advertised an "old wooden boat" in the classified ads, so we gave him a call and went to see. He led us through his garage past twenty-five years of pack-ratting, pulled back a canvas, and wiped a quarter-inch of dust off the mahogany bow of what was once a triple-cockpit beauty. Nothing cuts the water like a Hacker. We paid cash on the spot, trailered her home, and have been tinkering away ever since.

If you take one look at her, you'll notice we haven't been in a hurry. We'll work a few weeks, put her aside to take on a paying customer, and then come back to it when our energies are recharged. Right now, she'll float, and from a distance even looks like a Hacker, but up close it's apparent we're only halfway finished. The bow, side rails, and basically everything that you see from above is in need of about fifteen coats of spar varnish and some fine sanding. Her chrome needs redipping, and the glass could use replacing. Also, the seats are pretty hard. While she may not be the prettiest boat on the lake, she purrs like a kitten. Even in her disheveled state, she's got it where it counts. When we brought her home, Charlie ran his hands along her lines and asked, "You mind if we call her *Podnah?*"

The restoration process is simple, really. That is, the process is simple, not the workmanship. Workmanship is acquired, and Charlie has a good bit more than I do. The first thing boat makers do is to lay the keel, the backbone of a boat. When you restore, you follow right along. From keel to ribs, then the bottom surface, up the sides, top, then the cockpits. Most of the support wood is white oak. It's heavy, strong, moderately affordable, and bends well when enough steam is applied. The surface pieces are crafted from one of the more than five hundred types of mahogany, preferably Honduran. Mahogany is the king of woods, which explains its disappearance from the planet. It's dense, impervious to bugs, and due to its knotless grain is a woodworker's dream. Along the way, you either custom-fit or replace all the mechanical pieces: engine, transmission, steering linkage, fuel lines and tanks, etc. It's not unlike disassembling several Matchbox cars and putting a few back together using the best pieces. The only difference is that the pieces are larger, they actually work, and they cost a good bit more.

Hammermill's Greavette is a Canadian boat, built in 1947 by naval architect Douglas Van Patton up near Ontario. The boat is twenty-four feet, cigar shaped, with a triple cockpit and built for speed and looks. It's sort of a souped-up version of the HackerCraft, which, in everyone's estimation, is the most sought-after and classic wooden boat ever made—especially those made in the midtwenties. Anything from '25 to '29 is a pretty hot commodity. Hammermill really wanted a Hacker, but when one wasn't to be found, he landed on the Greavette. Whereas the Hacker is known for its crisp, classic, clean-cut lines, the Greavette has more rounded edges, giving it the cigar-shaped look for which it is famous. But sitting side by side, the Greavette is no match for a '27 Hacker.

Hammermill's no dummy. He paid a little over $30,000 for the boat in its rotten, disheveled condition. He then paid Charlie and me, over a ten-month period, about $40,000 to restore it. That may sound like a lot for some wood that floats, but now it's worth about $100,000 to the right buyer.

Many restorers try to recapture the original mechanics of the boat, but that often requires constant maintenance and finding parts that no longer exist. So for the Greavette we found a used Dodge 360-cubic-inch engine from a wrecked Durango that had only about five thousand miles on it. We bought a new Velvet Drive 1:1 transmission, meaning for every turn of the engine you'd get one turn of the prop, and custom-fitted two stainless gas tanks alongside the second cockpit. The result gave us about twice as much horsepower as originally intended and the ability to carry about three times as much gas. Some of the finishing touches included an external rudder, new gauges, green leather seats that we had made down near Lanier, and beveled glass in the windshield. Hammermill would love it.

Charlie met me at the boathouse Tuesday morning at eight, just itching to fill the tanks and get it floating. We set her in the water, popped a cork, poured champagne across the cutwater, launched, and I let him drive. It was one of Charlie's greatest joys.

Even blind, Charlie knew the lake better than most who could see as they drove around it. Since it was a weekday and traffic would allow, I sat in the copilot's seat and gave him directions above the hum of the Dodge: "Easy to three o'clock," "Back off and hard to six," "Straight up and level," "Jet Ski to starboard," "Cruiser to port," or "No wake."

Charlie simply listened and then turned the wheel or adjusted the gas depending on my directions. It got fun when I'd tell him, "Nautique with sunbathers at eleven thirty." He would sit on top of the seat back, lift his hat, and wave as if he had seen them all along.

"They're waving," I'd say, and the smile would spread across Charlie's face like he really could see it.

With a little help, Charlie docked at the marina and started pumping gas. I tapped him on the shoulder and said, "Be right back." Three pumps over, wearing an Anchorage uniform with a name patch ironed onto his shirt, sat Termite, sucking on a piece of beef jerky and with his face buried in—*Newsweek*? I walked up behind him and tapped him on the shoulder.

He shut the magazine and looked at me over his sunglasses. "Oh, no, not you again. Look, I ain't like you guys."

"What're you reading?"

Termite held up the *Newsweek* carefully to keep the edges of both magazines even.

"Termite, I wasn't born yesterday. I went to school with guys pulling that little trick in class long before you were even a thought in your parents' minds."

He grinned, pulled out the girlie magazine, and held it up like a calendar.

"See?" Termite smacked the glossy paper with his index finger. "That's what I'm talking about."

"What exactly is it that you're talking about?"

"That!" Termite pointed. "I'm gonna get me some of that."

"Let me see."

Over the weekend, Termite had shaved his beard, trimmed his hair, and even tucked in his shirt, but his face had erupted in acne. His chin had a natural dimple like Kurt Douglas, and he might be a good-looking kid if he'd gain twenty pounds, lay off the beer, start taking some multivitamins, and bathe. He checked the board-walk behind him that led into the marina bait shop and office, then handed me the picture.

It was a centerfold of some nineteen-year-old sili-cone beauty pictured in a pose that no girl had ever struck without being paid. I took the two-page spread and folded back every portion of the picture except the part that showed the girl's neck and face. When I held it up and gave it back to Termite, I said, "Let me see if I got this right."

He looked confused. I sat down next to him and dan-gled my feet over the boardwalk.

"You see that girl?" I pointed to the face. "She's probably named something sweet like Amanda or Mary. She's from some small town in Wyoming or Texas, and her daddy used to pay for dance lessons and coach her softball team when she was in grammar school. He put Band-Aids on her skinned knees and brushed her hair out of her face when she had bad dreams and couldn't sleep."

Termite's face turned sour. "You're starting to ruin this for me."

"Termite," I continued, "that is somebody's daughter. She's somebody's little sister, and someday, she might even be somebody's mother."

Termite spat, pushing a long stream of spit between his two front teeth. It arced into the water. "What's your point?"

"My point is that there's more going on here than exposed skin and a few wild facial expressions." I unfolded the picture. "This is the vaginal canal. It leads to the uterus and two things called ovaries, and for about a week every month it's not that clean a place."

"I know where babies come from."

"Yeah? Well, a woman giving birth is a thousand times more beautiful than this picture, and yet you're settling for this. This," I said, pointing again, "is something you ought to wait and let your wife show you instead of trying to buy it from a little girl who once took piano lessons before her feet could touch the pedals."

Termite took back the magazine and closed it. "Well, I didn't take the picture. And it don't hurt to look."

"The mind is a pretty amazing thing. Almost as amazing as the heart."

"I don't follow you."

"Your mind imprints images, especially that kind, on the heart, so that ten and fifteen years down the road, when you're married and trying to make something out of your life, they come drifting back, bubbling up and reminding you how much greener the grass is outside of your own bed."

Termite smiled and nodded, holding the jerky like a cigar. "Sounds like you know what you're talking about."

"Termite, I have loved one woman in my lifetime. During seven years of marriage, she was kind enough and loved me enough to give me, among other things, my own pictures. She's been gone five years, but"—I looked out across the lake and lowered my voice— "I've got enough memories to last a lifetime, and I wouldn't sell you a single one for every picture in every magazine around the world. And you know something—the ones where she has her clothes on are worth just as much as the ones without."

Termite got real quiet and chewed on his fingernails, spitting the pieces into the lake.

Charlie topped off the tanks and hollered, "Come on, Stitch. Hammermill's probably ringing the phone off the hook."

I stood to go. "Termite, you're young, and I'm not sure you're going to understand what I'm about to say, but here's the nugget: Without the heart, nothing else matters. She could be the Goddess of Love, you could have all the mind-blowing sex you could physically handle, but when the shooting is over, and you're starting to think about getting a bite to eat, smoking a cigarette, or what you do with her now, you're just lying in bed with a woman who means little more to you than the remote control for your TV. Love is no tool; neither is a woman's heart. What I'm talking about, you won't find in that magazine."

Termite scoffed and shoved the last bite of jerky into his mouth. "How would you know? You just said you've only loved one woman. I think you need to test-drive a few cars before you buy one."

"You can buy that lie if you want, but if you're working for a bank, you don't study the counterfeit to know the real thing. You study the real thing to know the counterfeit."

I untied the bowline and shoved off. Termite stood on the dock trying to figure out what I had just said. He pitched the stub end of the jerky into the lake like a cigarette butt. It flew through the air, spinning end over end like a football that just left a kicker's foot in a field-goal attempt, and landed in the water where a bream or bass quickly sucked it off the water's surface.

I pointed at his magazine and then the bait shop. "And if that guy in the office sees that magazine, he'll fire you for sure. He doesn't put up with that stuff around his docks."

Termite dropped his shoulders like he knew he was about to start looking for another job. "You gonna tell him?"

I shook my head.

"You sure?" he asked again.

"I won't need to."

"What? Why's that?" he asked.

"Because of something my wife read to me that I have since found to be true."

Termite dropped his shoulders as if he knew he was about to get another sermonette. "Yeah? What's that?"

"From out of your heart, you speak." I pointed at the magazine. "You put that crap in your heart, and you can't help but find it coming out your mouth. It'll color and flavor your whole person. Pretty soon, it'll eat you up."

"Yeah, well . . . I still want to get me some of that."

"Termite, every man does. It's in our makeup. Something would be wrong with you if you didn't. That's why they sell so many."

Charlie and I drove Hammermill's boat the long way home. He smiled over every ripple, wake, and current. I just wanted him to keep the thing moving. Despite my affinity for working on boats, I don't always like riding in them. I have a tendency to get a little woozy. As long as we're moving, I'm great, which is why rowing is no problem. But the moment we stop, and that boat rocks the least bit, I'm about three minutes from hanging my head over the side.

We docked, lifted the boat up out of the water, and Charlie said he was taking the rest of the day off. He slapped me on the back and started feeling his way down to the dock while practicing his steps.

"Dance class tonight?"

"Yup," he said, looking like Fred Astaire dancing with a walking stick. "We're learning the mambo. Probably end with a waltz."

"Charlie, you're a piece of work."

"You ought to see the instructor. She's French and . . ." Charlie smiled and continued dancing across the dock. Clicking his stick down the stone steps, he said, "It's Tuesday. You know what you're doing?"

I knew what he was asking, I just wasn't sure how

to answer him. "Not really."

"I can tell." Charlie spun around. "Holler if you get stuck."

"Thanks."

He felt his way along the side of the dock, lowered the sandbags that raised the guide wires we had strung underwater from his dock to mine, and he took a flying leap off the dock.

The last couple of days, I'd had a nagging feeling that my promise of a boat ride to Cindy might have gotten me in over my head. Charlie's question had pretty well convinced me that I had, but I didn't have time to worry about it too much because the phone was ringing when I walked in the back door.

"Hello?"

"Reese? Reese Mitch?"

"Speaking." I knew who it was.

"You still want to take two girls for a boat ride?"

"What makes you think I'd change my mind?"

"Experience."

"Sounds like a story there."

"You might say."

I laughed. "Just filled up with gas. Tell me where you live."

Chapter 22

By our senior year in high school, our physical activities together had become somewhat limited. We could go to the movies or dinner or shop through one or two

142

stores, but we couldn't stroll the mall or a park for four or five hours unless we rented a wheelchair, and Emma hated to be seen that way.

Her forced idleness told me the clock was ticking, so I continued to read every scientific book I could get my hands on that dealt with the human heart. But the more I read, the less I understood why textbooks treated the heart like Humpty Dumpty. Medicine and science—thanks in large part to Aristotle and Descartes—had divided the body into systems and parts. As well they should. How better to understand it? But I was learning that getting well and finding healing are two very different things.

We were walking home from school one day when Emma took me by the hand and pulled me through old man Skinner's apple orchard. She had grown more quiet and idle, sketching less and seldom leaving the house without me. She looked brittle and pale, and a sadness had crept in behind her smile. It was as if the oil in her lamp were running low.

She sat me down beneath a big apple tree, surrounded by fallen fruit, and handed me a box wrapped in a red bow. The sun hung low and lit the gray streaks that had recently appeared above her brow and above her ears, highlighting her brunette hair. I untied the ribbon, and inside sat a small gold medallion, about the size of a quarter, clasped to a gold chain. On the front was engraved *Above all else, guard your heart* . . . And on the back . . . *for it is the wellspring of life*. Thirteen magical words. She hung them around my neck, and we sat beneath the tree, surrounded by green grass, apples, and uncertainty, her listening to the beat of my rower's heart, and me concerned with the weakening and distant beat of hers. I stroked her hair, breathed deeply, and whispered inside myself, *I knew it was love, and felt it was glory.*

That afternoon many of the pieces fell into place, and it struck me that doctors can help people get well, even prolong their lives, but they cannot heal them or make them whole. That's something else.

Chapter 23

I opened the boathouse door, eyed my two choices, and dropped the lift. I knew Hammermill's Greavette would make a better impression, but I guess I'm just a fan of works-in-progress. Finished boats don't need me, and *Podnah* still did. Once she had floated clear, I cranked her up and backed out of the boathouse. I cleared the slip, slid into the Tallulah, and turned south to pick up Cindy and Annie.

They lived in a two-room cottage along one of the finger creeks that fed the lake. Much like the fish camp Emma and I had first slept in, it was long on character and short on everything else.

When the engineers flooded the town of Burton, the waters rose up the sides of the small Appalachian Mountains and formed what are now fingers where people built houses, or shacks, depending on their budget. On one of those fingers is Wildcat Creek Cove.

The farthest reaches of the creek are narrow and over-hanging with trees where more than one rope swing has been hung.

Somewhere in the fifties, Cindy explained, her parents had bought what they called their "Sugar Shack"—a summer vacation spot and weekend getaway. The creek that led to their walking path and small dock was narrow, about three times the width of the Hacker, but looked deep, so I dunked the paddle in the water and checked, then eased up to the dock.

From the boat I could see Cindy standing over the sink in the kitchen and Annie hovering in the shade near the back door. The girl I had met on the sidewalk was now more frail, less bouncy, wearing a faded baseball cap on her head and a bulky cast on her left arm and walking with small, unsteady steps. She was engulfed in a blaze-orange life vest and looked like a floating fish bobber.

I tied off the boat, and Annie waved me closer. She placed a handkerchief over her mouth, coughed quietly, and smiled. She'd developed that fragile eggshell exterior that most kids have when they get pretty sick. I'd seen it a hundred times. It grew out of uncertainty and the realization that life is not open-ended. I had seen it in Emma. On days when she felt worse or just plain lousy, she'd try to cheer me up by telling me what she'd learned from King Solomon. She'd raise her chin, which usually brought on a cough, and stick a finger in the air and quote, "A joyful heart is good medicine, but a broken spirit dries up the bones."

Annie needed some good medicine.

She was standing by a box about two feet square with walls maybe two and a half feet high. It had been built out of junk wood, so none of the pieces matched. It stood on four legs that lifted it off the ground, and the inside walls were covered in wire mesh except for the top six inches, which were covered in slick nylon. The box had no cover or top.

As I walked closer, I noticed that it smelled. Almost rotten. I looked inside and saw three or four half-eaten chunks of potato, a few vegetable slices, and ten thousand crickets.

Annie whispered, "This is my cricket box."

I nodded and watched as the bottom of the box moved: crickets crawling on crickets crawling atop other crickets.

"I grow them here and then sell them to the bait shops. I sell them at $2 a dozen and they sell them for $4."

"I never knew there was such a high markup on crickets."

She nodded. "Folks around here like to fish with them. So me and Aunt Cici built this box and started growing them about a year ago."

I nodded again, just getting used to the smell and the sight of so many crickets crawling across one another.

"I sell about ten dozen a week during the summer. Sometimes fifteen. That's twenty to thirty dollars a week, and I really don't have to do anything." She looked up at me and smiled. "Pretty easy work, huh?"

"Yup."

"I've made almost $600 this year just in crickets alone. If these make it, I've probably got another couple thousand in here."

"That's an expensive box."

She nodded and looked inside. "Tell me about it." We both studied the chaos crawling below us. "Sort of weird when you think about it."

"What's that?"

"That I'm selling crickets so I can buy somebody's heart."

I nodded. "I guess that's one way to look at it."

We walked down the steps, and Annie's hands shook as we neared the dock. I cranked the engine and then watched Cindy run out the back door drying her hands. I lifted Annie in and pretended to straighten her life vest with one hand while the other felt gently for a radial pulse.

When Annie looked up at me, she also lifted her eyebrows. Her chest followed suit, and the result filled her lungs with air. It was a purposeful filling, like when Sal placed his stethoscope on her back and listened. Only this time, nobody had asked her to. I listened, knew she was struggling, and remembered listening to Emma do it ten thousand times. She breathed out and floated above the satisfaction of two seconds of just-enough air.

I cut the engine and spoke: "I shot an arrow into the air, it fell to earth, I knew not where; for so swiftly it flew, the sight could not follow in its flight. I breathed

147

a song into the air, it fell to earth I knew not where; for who has sight so keen and strong, that it can follow the flight of a song? Long, long afterward, in an oak, I found the arrow still unbroke, and the song, from beginning to end, I found again in the heart of a friend."

Annie raised her eyebrows, sucked in again, and then sank once again inside her life vest. "Shakespeare?" she asked, smiling.

"No," I said. "Longfellow."

Cindy smiled, climbed into the boat, and drank deeply of the air. The only difference between her breathing and Annie's was that Cindy looked like she was hooked up to an oxygen tank and Annie wasn't. She sank down in the middle cockpit, letting her hair spill across the mahogany top and her sunglasses reflect the sky.

I looked in the rearview mirror and noticed that last week's utilitarian dress of function over form had been replaced. In jean shorts that looked like she'd hemmed them herself, sandals, a white cotton button-up, Georgia Bulldogs baseball cap, and sunglasses, Cindy was doing a respectable job of revealing the form that had been disguised by work and necessity. With her head titled back, I hoped she hadn't observed my double take. She looked like anything but the cashier at the hardware store.

The Velvet Drive transmission has only three settings: forward, reverse, and neutral. As with most boats, the speed was obtained by revving the rpm's of the engine, not shifting to higher gears. The stick used to engage any one of the three stood in front of Annie's knees like a lever working a secret trapdoor, so I pointed and got her to help me.

"We need to go forward, so pull in that hand lever and push the whole thing forward."

Annie gripped the handle and squeezed with both hands, but noticed she needed a little more oomph. So she closed her eyes, squeezed harder, and pushed. The engine slipped into gear, and we idled out of Wildcat Creek.

We motored past a few larger homes that had grown up along the creek in the last decade and approached the open waters of the lake. Annie looked excitedly at Cindy and then at me. "I've never been out here."

How can you live on this lake and not get out on it? I wondered, then felt guilty for thinking it. Dumb question.

"Where would you like to go first?"

Annie pointed south, and I turned as directed.

The shoreline of Lake Burton is a monument to big houses, most of which are the second or third home of those who stay there. Each new construction is an attempt to outdo the neighbor next door. Owners brag, letting the practiced names and descriptions roll off their tongues like memorized poetry. Oh, so-and-so was our architect. It's a such-and-such home from this-or-that period. I know because after I had put them back together again and they had gotten off my table, every single one of them invited me to their second home in Vale, Aspen, or Bermuda . . . or Lake Burton.

For some, it was a way of saying thank you.

Everywhere Annie's curiosity pointed, I turned the boat. For two hours we rode the creeks and shoreline of Burton. The smile and amazement never left her face. Dick's Creek, Moccasin Creek, Old Murray Cove. And when I showed her the dam, her eyes grew as large as half-dollars. Cindy, too, looked relieved, like she was glad to see Annie smiling but also grateful for the adult company. As we rode north, Annie placed her head on Cindy's lap and napped beneath the rumble and hum of the engine. Knowing she'd do well to sleep, I motioned to Cindy and asked if she was comfortable. She nodded and I motioned again at the lake, wanting to know if she'd like to keep going. She smiled, tipped her hat back, and we drove another hour around the lake.

It was almost five when Annie woke at the north end of the lake, up near the YMCA camp, just beyond the bridge. As we passed southward under the bridge, I pointed east toward Charlie's and my little creek-with-no-name and said, "I live down there."

Annie perked up. "I want to see."

I hadn't thought about that. I was hoping to point and pass by, not point and stop in.

Cindy motioned behind Annie's back, trying to let me know it wasn't necessary. Annie's face told a different story.

"I don't have any lemonade," I said to Annie.

She smirked. "That's okay. I don't drink it anyway. Too sweet."

I turned into our creek and idled up alongside the dock. Cindy helped me tie up and hang the bumpers alongside. I cut the engine and lifted Annie onto the dock, and their jaws dropped. They took in everything: the boathouse, the workshop farther up the hill, and then the house, barely visible through the dogwood trees.

"This is yours?" Cindy asked, as if she were afraid the real owners would appear any minute with a shotgun, telling her to get off their property.

I led them up the walkway, where Annie instinctively grabbed my hand. Her hand was small, cold, a little uncertain—a feeling my hand knew well. *What the hand dare seize the fire, and what shoulder and what art, could twist the sinews of thy heart? And when thy heart began to beat, what dread hand, and what dread feet? When the stars threw down their spears and water'd heaven with their tears, did he smile his work to see? Did he who made the Lamb make thee?*

We had stepped onto the stone walkway that led up to the house when Charlie called out from across the lake, "Stitch? That you?"

"Yeah," I hollered back. "Brought my little cruise in for a tour of home. Charlie, meet Cindy McReedy and Annie Stephens."

Charlie waved his white stick while Georgia sat ready at his side. "Hi, ladies. You two look lovely. Just lovely."

Cindy looked at me, a little confused.

Charlie then turned side to side to show off his suit.

151

He buttoned the top button and snugged up his tie. "I'm off to my dancing lesson. How do I look?" He wore a blue and white, three-button seersucker suit with white and black penguin wingtips. Add a top hat, and he'd have looked like Chaplin.

"Charlie, you look . . ." I smirked at Annie. "Just great."

"I know it," Charlie said, dusting his shirtsleeve with the back of his palm. "Let's just hope the ladies do too. Preferably, ones that smell good." He smiled, grabbed the cable that acted as a guide wire up the steps and into his house, said, "Ladies!" and then disappeared beneath the trees.

"Who is that?" Cindy said with a smile.

I took Annie's hand and began leading her up toward the house. "Oh, that's my brother-in-law, Charlie. He's . . ."

I heard Cindy stop and take a short, quick breath that sounded like the end of it was squeezed off due to a constricted airway. Then I thought about what I'd just said.

I turned and held up my hands. "My wife, Emma, was Charlie's sister. She died almost five years ago."

Annie's hand tensed in mine, and the questions in Cindy's eyes disappeared, only to be replaced by twice as many more colored by shades of shared pain.

"I'm sorry," I said. "I . . . Charlie will always be my brother-in-law."

Cindy's chest rose and fell as another deep breath filled her lungs, and the muscles in her face relaxed.

"We work on boats together, and he helped me build this house."

Annie was now holding my hand with both of hers. She pointed behind her. "But he's blind."

"I know," I said, my eyes following Charlie's suit up through the tree line. "Just don't tell him that."

She smiled and followed me up the steps. Halfway up she said, "Did he call you Stitch?"

I nodded and, opening the door and letting them into the back porch, told her the story of Charlie swinging like Tarzan with his Stretch Armstrong rope. Cindy turned her head as though she'd caught a whiff of something she liked to smell. "What's that?" she said, pointing her nose in the air.

"One of three things." I pointed at the green shoots sprouting up between the house and the lake that covered the underside of the trees like a bed of tall grass. "That's mint. Emma planted it here when we bought this place about seven years ago, and it spreads like kudzu. No weed whacker in the world can tame it."

They smiled.

"Or second, it's that rose-scented geranium at your feet. I bought it at your hardware store a few weeks ago because I liked the smell."

Cindy rubbed the leaves to activate the scent and then smelled her fingers.

"Or third"—I pointed toward the open window of my second-story bedroom—"bachelors don't always do their laundry on time. Please tell me it's one of the first two."

Cindy smelled again. "Mint. It's the mint."

"Pick some, and I'll make tea," I said.

Cindy picked a few shoots while Annie and I put on a kettle to boil.

While the tea steeped, I gave them a tour. Annie noticed the many charcoal sketches and oil paintings decorating most every square inch of wall space in my home and asked, "You like art?"

"Some."

"These are really good."

I nodded.

"Is this somebody in New York or L.A.?" Cindy asked.

"No." I shook my head. "My wife."

Cindy folded her arms, looking cold again, while Annie examined everything. I gave them a tour including every room in the house save one: my office. I keep it locked and seldom go in except when necessity requires.

Cindy noticed one of Emma's early sketches of the lake and said, "That early morning, swirling-tornado look that spins across the lake just after sunup is one of my favorite times of day out here." She studied the painting some more. "She was talented."

I grabbed three glasses and began filling them with ice, then pointed a glass toward the shop. "Would you like to see the workshop?"

Annie nodded while Cindy poured tea and gave everyone a sprig of mint. We walked to the workshop, I turned on all the lights and punched Play on the CD player—Mozart.

"This is where you work?" Cindy asked incredulously.

I nodded. "Pretty nice, huh?"

"I'll say so." Annie looked over the tools while I explained how Charlie and I worked.

"And Charlie really helps you?" Cindy asked.

"You ought to see his chain-saw carvings. He's really pretty good."

"You're kidding."

"I promise," I said, pointing to the beam and hoist in the ceiling. "Charlie has great hands. He'd have made a great surgeon except for the fact that he liked working with wood."

Cindy looked at me and stepped closer, letting out one of the questions that had first pricked her fancy in the hospital. "You know a thing or two about surgeons?"

I smiled. "Only what I've read."

Cindy looked around her at the tools, the organization, the cleanliness. "This looks more like an operating room than a woodshop."

Chapter 24

The human heart is remarkable in that it is designed to pump continuously for a hundred and twenty years without ever needing to be reminded what it was meant to do. It just does it. In all my reading and study, I have come to know one thing without any shadow of doubt: if anything in this universe reflects the fingerprint of God, it is the human heart.

While it pumps more than a hundred thousand times a day without stopping, funneling hundreds of gallons of fluid around the body, it derives no benefit from the blood it pumps, making it the most unselfish of organs. In order to feed itself, it siphons from its own flow then reroutes it through three main arteries that loop back around the outside of the muscle to feed itself. Two of these arteries feed approximately half the heart, and the third, largest artery—also known as "the widow-maker"—feeds the other half. If it becomes blocked with plaque, a condition known as coronary artery disease, the heart stops.

If caught early, this condition can be corrected with a stent or a bypass—taking an artery from another place in the body, like the leg or inside the chest wall, and rerouting the siphon.

If you've ever bought an old house with iron plumbing, you have some idea of how this works. Rather than remove all the old, you simply snake it to dislodge the clog—a temporary fix—or add new pipe to bypass it altogether—much more permanent. Following such surgery, it is not uncommon for an individual to leave the operating room with four or five bypasses and a rather expensive medical bill.

In the womb, a baby gains oxygen through its mother's lungs, which she sends, along with everything else the baby needs, via the umbilical cord. Baby's heart doesn't need to send blood out to the lungs to be reoxygenated; Mom has already taken care of that. To prevent the needless flow of blood through those tender, developing lungs, God created a small hole between the right and left atria—the top portions of the heart—that allows it, in utero, to bypass the lungs. At birth, a hormone called prostaglandin causes the hole to close and begins routing the blood into and out of the lungs. When that doesn't happen, and the hole doesn't close, it's called an atrial septal defect.

For most of us, things work pretty well until genetics, what we've eaten, or how we've lived catches up with us. Usually, that "catching up" is called a heart attack, which is nothing more than plaque clogging an artery and stopping blood flow to a portion of the heart. Anyone who's ever run the quarter mile knows what I mean. The first three hundred yards can be relatively fun, but by the last turn and final straightaway, the human body is so oxygen-deprived the muscles are beginning to lock up, making the runner feel as if rigor mortis has set in. Experienced runners call the last fifty yards "the bear" because it often feels as if one has jumped on your back.

In truth, the muscles in the runner's legs have burned far more oxygen than the heart and lungs can supply. Extremely fit sprinters can minimize this through aggressive training, as can rowers, cyclists, marathoners, and others, but training has its limits. It cannot overcome genetics. The physical limitations of aerobic exercise are established by the volume of oxygen and blood the heart and lungs can send throughout the body.

God gives most of us mortals normal hearts and lungs. To others, He gives a little more. A slightly larger heart and lungs. Studies of long-distance athletes confirm this. And yet to other people, like Emma, He gives a little less. One thing my education never taught me was the reason for this.

When the human heart has suffered an attack, often the area that's been shut off from blood flow will die. Amazingly, even half-dead, the human heart still pumps. People can survive and live somewhat normal lives with only part of their hearts functioning, though it changes their lifestyles substantially. The heart is not only the most unselfish of organs, it is also the most courageous and faithful.

Emma's problem was not the buildup of plaque, but that her embryonic hole had never closed, causing a continual partial bypass of blood to her lungs. Many people walking around the planet right now suffer from the same problem, have no idea of its existence, and will never suffer a day for it. It's almost as common as a mitral valve prolapse—a common heart condition in which the last valve of the heart doesn't close all the way, allowing something of a backwash into the heart. Emma would have continued to lead a completely normal life had one thing not occurred. Her hole enlarged, resulting in a continual flow of oxygen-depleted blood coursing through her veins.

As the hole enlarged, it further crippled her heart, causing the onset of the disease that would further enlarge it—a natural result of a muscle working overtime. The enlarged muscle fills up the cavity in which it lives and works, creating more pressure against the walls that house it, thereby decreasing the space it has to work in and, once again, causing itself to work that much harder and that much less efficiently. It's called dilated cardiomyopathy and is often described as increased volume in the heart, causing the muscles to dilate like an overinflated balloon. It's a problem that worsens exponentially rather than incrementally. It's like gaining forty pounds at the waistline while trying to wear a belt with only one hole. You can buy a bigger belt, but you can't enlarge your chest.

From the moment we are born, every human on the planet is dying. Emma was just dying at about six times the rate as the rest of us. And if during that slow death she looked perpetually tired, she was. Emma lived her entire life feeling as if she were running the last hundred yards of the quarter mile, always behind and never able to catch her breath.

My reading had taught me that Emma's heart was diseased, big and flabby, inefficient, and inherently weak. Nothing anyone could do to her present heart would do her any good. It was beyond repair and, after so much deterioration, had lost most of its elasticity. The very real danger that Emma faced was the popping of her balloon.

The heart, brittle, inelastic, and frail, will pop or tear, causing a hole in the side of the ventricle, through which blood will pour out into the pericardium, the nearly bulletproof sac surrounding the heart. The blood, now on the outside of the heart, fills up this sac, which is so tough it won't bust. This, in turn, places increased pressure on the heart, in effect suffocating it. In doing so, it places more pressure on the heart than it can pump, a condition known as pericardial tamponade.

In emergency situations, when there is no time to open the chest, the only way to alleviate the pressure is through pericardiocentesis—a doctor inserts a heavy-gauge needle through the sternum at about a thirty-degree angle to the patient, trying to avoid the lungs and pierce the pericardium to allow the blood to exit through the needle and decrease pressure on the heart. The problem now is that the patient has a hole in both the heart and the pericardium and is losing body fluids at a fantastic rate, which is dropping the blood pressure and further compounding the stress on the heart. It's a downward fall that can quickly spiral out of control.

The good news is that the heart is still able to pump. The bad news is that the heart is a lot like an old well pump; it works great as long as the prime is retained, but once that prime is lost, it's a devil to get going again. So, following the pericardiocentesis, the trick is getting the patient open and sewing up the holes while keeping the blood pumping and the body's fluid levels up.

And if I had known all this about the heart as a kid, I would have ripped open my chest, severed my own arteries, and given Emma mine.

Chapter 25

It was nearly dark when we made it back to the dock. I had probably kept them out too late. Annie had dozed again, so while Cindy tied off the boat, I lifted Annie into my arms and she wrapped hers around my neck— a familiar sensation. One I missed. I walked slowly up to the house. As we neared the cricket box, raucous with noise and nighttime chatter, Annie raised her head.

She looked down, and the crickets fell quiet, making a low, almost inaudible chatter, as if they obeyed or observed something I knew nothing about. It was like a song you could hear only if you weren't trying to listen, or a far-off star that you could see only when you weren't focusing, and then only out of the corner of your eye.

She put her finger to her lips and whispered, "Shhhh."

I listened. "What are they doing?" I asked.

She looked at me as if I should already know. "Why . . . they're crying."

I leaned in and tried to hear, but couldn't. I shrugged my shoulders.

She whispered in my ear, "Only if you listen closely, and you want to, can you hear when crickets cry."

I leaned in again and turned my head, almost pointing my ear downward.

She whispered again, "No, no, no. You don't hear

them with your ears." She poked me in the chest gently with her finger. "You hear them with your heart."

I almost dropped her. Recovering, I tried to change the subject. "Why do they cry?"

Annie thought for a minute. "Because they know."

"They know what?" I asked.

She looked at me as if it were so simple. "They know that if Dr. Royer doesn't find a heart, and Aunt Cici doesn't find somebody who can put it in me, and I don't stay healthy until then, and we don't find the money to pay for it, then . . . I won't be here next year to talk to them." She put her head back down on my shoulder and closed her eyes. "And . . . because they know it's their life for mine."

In my arms, Annie weighed ten thousand pounds. "How do they know all that?"

She smiled like I was teasing her. "Because I tell them, dummy."

O! the world hath not a sweeter creature; she might lie by an emperor's side and command him tasks.

Cindy unlocked the door and showed me the way to their room. I placed Annie in her bed and stepped back as Cindy tucked her in. The concrete-block house was small and had only two rooms: a bedroom complete with one dresser and two single beds, and another room that served as the kitchen, living room, and den. Two pictures sat atop the mantel. Scattered across the kitchen table, which was a wobbly card table covered by a red plastic tablecloth, were all the finance books and loan applications I had seen at the hospital.

Cindy caught me looking at the pictures. "The one on the left is Annie with her mom and dad, almost three years ago. The other is last year's school picture."

Annie favored her dad, although her smile looked more like her mom's. They were suntanned and vibrant. I wanted to ask questions, but figured I'd stayed long enough and wasn't sure I wanted to get into that conversation. The school picture showed Annie in front of a blue canvas backdrop, holding the handlebars of a red bicycle and smiling. Printed on the front of the picture at the bottom, partially covered by the frame, was the word *Proof.*

In the other room, Annie coughed again, evidence that the cough had sunk into her lungs.

"Has her doctor listened to that?"

"Yes." Cindy nodded. "Sal was here this morning. He said I should keep her away from other kids and out of Sunday school for a few weeks. It'll take a while."

"Sal's a good man. A good doctor."

"The best. He's never sent me a bill, and there's no telling how many thousands of dollars I owe him." She fumbled through some pots in the kitchen. "You want some coffee?"

I squinted one eye and considered. "You got any tea?"

"Sure." She pulled the kettle off the stove and began filling it under the sink faucet.

I turned my back and appeared to be looking out the window while my eyes continued scanning the house for any sign that a boyfriend was soon to come charging in the front door. In the background, I heard Cindy pull a knife from the drawer.

"You want lemon in your tea?"

"Yes, thanks."

Cindy cut the lemon one time and then screamed, "Oh! Ouch!"

I turned as Cindy dropped the knife and reached for a towel, dripping red blood across the kitchen floor. By the time I took eight steps and grabbed her hand, it was covered in red and splatter had painted the kitchen floor.

I held her hand and studied the cut while Cindy held her hand out, chest high, and covered her eyes with the other hand. Her face turned ashen, and I knew she was about to buckle. "The sight of blood make you queasy?"

"Only my own," she muttered as her knees crumpled. I caught her midfall and carried her to the couch. I wrapped her hand in the towel she'd been holding and then returned from the kitchen with some peroxide. I emptied my pockets onto the table beside Cindy, washed my hands, and then her cut, which was deep into the meat of her left palm. I had the feeling she wouldn't make a very compliant patient when I started wielding a needle and that if I could get to work before she came to, I'd be a lot better off. I pulled the flashlight from my belt, turned it on, and held it over Cindy's hand using my teeth as a vise. I threaded a needle and, by the time she opened her eyes a minute later, I had already completed my fourth stitch. She looked at me and then grasped her cut hand with the good one, fighting the urge to yank it back to her chest.

"Oh, my!" she said closing her eyes and putting her head back down on the couch. She tried to control her short, deep breaths and then opened her eyes, studying me through one eye while I quietly tied the sixth stitch. "This is a good one," I muttered around a mouthful of flashlight. She didn't say a word but tried not to look at her hand. Cindy looked over my shoulder and appeared to see someone. I heard small footsteps, and Annie said, "Aunt Cricket, you okay?"

"Yeah, sweetheart. Fine." She nodded and tried to wave Annie off. "Go back to sleep." Annie walked up behind me and leaned over my shoulder. When she did, her thumb-worn sandal dangled around my collarbone. It sparkled with each turn. Annie looked at my work and then at Cindy. "You cut yourself?" Apparently, Annie had no problem with either blood or needles.

Cindy's color had partially returned, but she wasn't about to move off that couch. Not only was she linked to me via eighteen inches of purple monofilament stitching, but there was still too much blood in sight. "Yeah, just a silly little cut. You go back to sleep." She closed her eyes and winced as I looped the needle through her skin.

I held the flashlight and whispered to Annie, "This cut here"—I pointed with the needle and shone the light so Annie could see—"is almost to the bone, slicing a goodly sized vein here." I pointed closer with the needle. Annie studied it and then looked at her own hand for comparison. I continued, "Cricket did a doozey on this one. I think eight stitches should do, and judging by the looks of the nice rusty knife over there, she's going to need a tetanus shot."

"Oh, great!" Cindy closed her eyes and began forcefully breathing deep and slow.

Annie whispered in my ear, "She doesn't like shots."

I looked at Cindy's face, which had faded white again. "I gathered that."

I tied off the last stitch, turned to Annie, and nodded my head toward the small snips lying on the table beside me. "My hands are full. You mind cutting this for me?" Annie grabbed the snips, inserted her small fingers into the holes, and gently leaned forward. "Right up next to the knot," I said. I held out the stitching like an umbilical cord, and Annie cut it with all the care and concern of a first-time father. Annie snipped it and studied her handiwork. I nodded and said, "Can you get me a washrag?"

Annie returned with a faded and tattered green washrag and handed it to me. Cindy saw it and spoke up, "No, honey, not our good ones. Get those old white ones with the spots on 'em. Next to the washing machine." Annie fetched the washrag, and I doused it in hydrogen peroxide and gently padded Cindy's hand and stitching.

Cindy looked at me, "What? You don't have a shot in there too? I'm afraid of what else might be in those pockets."

I smiled. "No shots." I applied pressure to the

166

stitches, helped her sit up, and placed her hand above her heart to slow the bleeding, which had all but stopped. Annie sat down next to Cindy, covering her mouth when she coughed. Cindy looked at her. "I'm okay, sweetie. You get some sleep." Annie yawned and rested her head on Cindy's shoulder. Cindy looked at me for help. I scooped Annie off the couch and carried her to her bed, pulling the covers back up around her neck. I think she was asleep before I ever left the room.

Cindy sat on the couch, fighting the nausea and studying her hand. She looked at me. "I have a feeling you've done this before."

"Just a time or two," I said, offering nothing more. The kettle on the stove began to whistle above the boil, so I poured two cups of chamomile, and we sat in the silence, hovering our mouths above the steam rising from our cups.

Silence crept in and made me uncomfortable. I started looking for an exit. "You're tired; I should probably get going." It was a lie. She did look tired, but she also looked like she could use some adult company as well as a week's worth of sound sleep. The circles beneath her eyes told me she didn't sleep much at night. Despite her reaction to the sight of her own blood, she was a tough woman. I had seen those same circles before under my own eyes.

Cindy stood and opened the door for me. "Hey," she said, still holding her wound at collar level, "I know this is forward, but I'm going to ask anyway. And, admittedly, it's as much for me as it is for Annie."

She waited for me to tell her it was okay to ask whatever she was about to ask me. "Okay," I said beneath the porch light.

"We're going to Atlanta tomorrow afternoon. To see Annie's doctor at St. Joseph's. Would you have any interest in going with us?" She smiled and leaned against the door. "We could take your car, see the doctor, and then I could buy you a really healthy hot dog at the Varsity."

Annie coughed again, this time longer, and I could feel something pulling at the layers of scar tissue that had encircled my heart. The thought of driving to St. Joe's and hanging around was not something I looked forward to, although I knew enough places to hide, but . . . Annie coughed again.

I nodded. "What time can I pick you up?"

"We need to be there at three."

"I'll pick you up at one."

She nodded and I stepped off the porch. I turned, almost afraid to ask the question because I already knew the answer. "Just curious, what's the name of her doctor?"

Cindy cleared her throat. "Dr. Morgan. Royer Morgan."

I steadied myself on the doorframe.

"You know him?" she asked.

I shook my head. "Just curious. That's all." I tipped my hat. "G'night. And"—I nodded again at her hand—"Advil will help the throbbing."

"Thanks. 'Night." Cindy shut the door behind me,

and I hurried down the narrow walkway.

When I reached the lake, I leaned over the dock, steadied myself on *Podnah*, and then found my reflection on the moonlit lake. My face was distorted. Losing ground, I bent over, opened up, and vomited all over my reflection in the water.

The next morning at daylight, I stood next to my Suburban pumping gas at the station not far from my house. About the time I topped it off, an old Cadillac pulled alongside me. The muffler had a hole in it, and the car was dirty.

Sal Cohen rolled down the window and said, "Just came from Annie's house where I gave Cindy a tetanus, cleaned a wound, and was amazed to find that you had sewn it up." He scratched his chin and looked off through the windshield. "Some of the finest stitching I've ever seen. I doubt it'll scar."

I shrugged. "It's like riding a bike."

Sal leaned his head out the window and probed, "And just where did a builder of boats learn to ride that bike?"

"Long time ago. I worked the trauma truck in college."

He tipped his hat, let off the brake, and said, "I'd like to meet the paramedic who taught you that."

I watched him drive away and had one thought: *I need to get out of town immediately.*

Chapter 26

Thanks to rapid advances in medication, Emma's condition stabilized somewhat during college. She didn't try to graduate, just took every literature class they offered and painted constantly. Looking back, I think those days were some of her happiest times—times when she breathed the deepest.

To satisfy our folks, we dated through two years of college before marrying in our third, just after I took the MCAT. We had a small, low-key ceremony in her parents' backyard, and spent our wedding night wrapped up in a fleece blanket somewhere in an old cabin tucked back in the Smokies.

The tenderness and honesty of our wedding night are things I think of often. We just stood there, two kids who'd grown into adults and married. Nothing hidden, nothing to prove, just us. We flew to New York, and for two weeks we rode old trains and stayed in bed-and-breakfasts from there to Canada. I had never seen Emma more excited, more free from the past than I did on that train ride. With every mile of track, her shoulders fell and her smile spread.

When we returned home for my senior year, I opened the mail to my MCAT test scores. I scored a 45—meaning I aced it. Pretty soon, I began receiving *Dear-Reese-We-are-pleased-to-inform-you* letters from every med school in the Southeast. Most awarded full scholarships and promised coveted research positions, but everything outside my singular study wasn't even a blip on my radar screen. I wanted to know one thing: What can you teach me about the human heart?

During my interview process, most panels, filled with white-jacketed and plaid-bow-tied doctors, stumbled through the answer or balked at the very idea that I would ask so insolent a question. I wasn't being prideful. I simply knew my purpose, and I didn't have time to wait for them to figure it out. I needed to hit the ground running.

Things changed when I interviewed at Harvard. As one of three finalists for an endowed fellowship, I sat in front of an eight-person panel and was encouraged to ask questions of my own. I respectfully said, "I have one."

They raised their eyebrows and waited.

I asked, "If I join your program, could you tell me in one sentence what you will teach me about the human heart?"

Dr. Ezra Trainer—bow tie, tweed jacket, gray beard, laser pointer, and a handful of M&Ms, which he was popping one at a time into his mouth—raised his finger, lowered his glasses, and said, "Guard your heart, for it is the wellspring of life."

I nearly jumped out of my chair.

Chapter 27

Dr. Trainer began the first day of anatomy class with three simple rules: "Drink unsweetened iced tea—the tannic acid is good for your heart, as is the absence of refined sugar; take an aspirin every day, as it causes your arteries and veins to become less sticky and less apt to catch plaque; and never take the elevator when there's a stairwell nearby." He patted the jar of M&Ms on his desk and said, "Oh, and take care to control your addictions."

Some things are so simple.

He ended class by saying, "Remember, ladies and gentlemen, you will learn many techniques and procedures, but the best tool you'll ever work with is the one that fits between the earpieces of your stethoscope." When the laughter quieted he held up a finger and said quietly, "Never forget, the best is the enemy of the good."

But I already knew this, because I had read Voltaire.

On our first day, we met our cadavers. My team and I were given three people, all blue, wrinkly, and very much dead, whom we would work on throughout the semester. While most teams labeled their cadavers with numbers or something technical like Alpha, Beta, and Delta, we named ours.

We knew we'd dissect everything from their big toes to their medulla oblongatas, but to keep us humble, Dr. Trainer insisted, "These folks were walking, talking people at one time. They loved, spoke, and dreamed. Dead or not, I think we ought to treat them that way."

The first was a seventy-something man who had apparently smoked himself onto that table. We named him Winston. And when they say that tar sticks to the lungs, they're not kidding. His looked like a road map of tiny tar highways.

The second was an Asian lady in her forties who, we would discover a month later, died from a heart attack. We named her Cathy, because she reminded one team member of his aunt.

The third was a man in his midsixties who'd suffered a massive stroke—judging from the calluses on his hands, probably on the golf course. We named him Scotty because we thought he would have looked right in some sort of Scottish plaid. And when those same people say that plaque actually connects to the sides of the arteries like Velcro, they're not kidding. Two months later, we dissected Scotty's carotid artery—the one that allows blood flow from the heart to the brain—and found his 99 percent blocked.

That first night, I brought Emma into the morgue, a large, cold room filled with sixty tables and just as many bodies, and pulled back the sheets. Most folks saw blue bodies, contorted lips, and shriveled body parts, devoid of human fluid or function. Some sick trick out of a midnight horror movie. Not Emma. To Emma, the human form was a divine reflection. She walked between the tables and said, "That makes us pretty special."

While I filled our home with books, journals, diagrams, and set my face like flint toward learning everything known about the human heart, Emma poured her heart onto canvas and filled our lives with color and expression.

Except for Emma, who really did know everything about me, I had never told anyone of my future plans. I figured I could talk all I wanted, but talk mattered little. Actions spoke. Despite that silence, when we began cutting Winston's sternum, intent on dissecting his heart, everyone turned to me and said, "You should."

We split him from his sternum to the base of his esophagus with a cordless Stryker saw, inserted a stainless rib spreader, and gently cranked opened his chest. Beneath the pericardium—the sac that protects the heart—sat his "wellspring"—diseased and long since affected by years of smoking. I looked around, the others nodded, so I reached my hand in and wrapped my fingers around it. It was cold and hard.

This is why you're here. This is the starting point. Learn this, Reese. Learn everything about it.

Toward the end of my first year, Dr. Trainer brought me into his office and sat me down across from him. He pointed at me with an unlit pipe. "Reese, any fool can see that you're a bit different from most students." He pointed toward the wall behind me. "I'm your adviser, so you might as well choose early. Basically, you've got three options."

I knew this, and he knew I knew this, and he knew that I knew that he knew, but there was more going on here than a simple conversation between teacher and student. He pointed his laser at a diagram on the wall, which showed a tree with three branches.

"Electrophysiologists are the electricians of the heart. Primarily, they put in pacemakers and play gin at the club on Saturdays. They send their kids to private schools, drive foreign cars, and ski two weeks in Utah during the winter."

He moved his laser to the right side of the diagram. "Invasive cardiologists are plumbers. They put in stents and then play golf with the guys who don't play gin rummy. Their wives carpool with these guys' wives"—he flashed his laser back at the electrophysiologists—"and they probably buy time-share condos in the Bahamas where they spend two weeks fly-fishing in the summer."

Slowly he moved his laser to the middle of the diagram, the trunk, and began running it in circles. "Cardiothoracic surgeons." He said it slowly, with reverence and emphasis. "We're the carpenters, the builders. We perform bypass surgeries and transplants and do things that the golfers, the guys playing gin rummy, and the fly fishermen only dream about. We work too much, seldom ski, get paid a lot less than we used to, and most of us are bastards. In truth, we're the end of the line, the last stop before either the pearly gates or the fiery pit."

He tossed me the laser pointer. "Choose."

I had known my place on that poster since I made my promise to Emma's mom. I may not have known what to call it, but I knew my place. I sat back and pointed at the trunk. "Here. Always have been." I clicked off his pointer and quietly set it on the front of his desk.

He sat back and folded his hands, and the springs in his chair accentuated his nod. He hung his pipe over his lip, considered a moment, and said, "Good. That is good." He scratched his chin, and his eyes narrowed on me. "You need to know from the beginning . . ."

"Yes sir?"

"It's an amazing organ, truly the emperor, but not all hearts start up again after they've been stopped." He looked out through a window and somewhere out into a now-foggy past. "Remember that."

During internship, Dr. Trainer inevitably turned to a few select individuals in the class and asked them to assist in an afternoon bypass. It was one of the perks of med school. The infamous question had long ago placed Dr. Trainer on a mythical pedestal. For weeks, the classroom chatter had been, *How will you respond when he calls your name?*

Toward the end of my second year, Dr. Trainer turned to me one day and said loudly before the class, "Doctor, are you busy this afternoon?"

I never even blinked. I had waited my whole life for that moment.

I scrubbed, joined him in the OR, and watched him peel the mammary artery from beneath the rib cage of Jimbo, a forty-something construction worker who was ninety pounds overweight and about three beats away from a flatline. I stood across from Dr. Trainer and next to Dan, his PA, who was cutting with a Bovie and pulling an artery from Jimbo's leg for the second and third bypasses.

Dr. Trainer inserted the artery, completing the first bypass, and then looked at me with a queer expression pasted across his face. His face turned red, his eyes rolled back, his knees buckled, and he passed out cold, hitting the tile floor with a thud. With Jimbo lying on the table, chest open, heart stopped, living off a pump, the OR went into a frenzy.

Dan dropped the Bovie and began hyperventilating, bumping into sterile tables and slinging stainless instruments all over the place. The head nurse removed her sterile table from Dan's reach and paged Dr. Trainer's partner, Jack Metzo, but he was thirty miles from the hospital and stuck in traffic. Problem was, Jimbo didn't have time for Dr. Metzo to navigate the interstate and the ensuing downtown Boston stoplights.

While a nurse started screaming at Dr. Trainer in high-pitched annoying shrieks, Dan started mumbling incoherent mumbo jumbo to the techs and nurses scattered about the room. I looked at the anesthesiologist, who held up his hands and looked at both me and the perfusionist and said, "I'm not scrubbed."

I looked at the perfusionist, who looked at me, held up her hands, and gave me a blank, unscrubbed stare.

I turned to the head nurse, held out my hand, and said, "Needle-driver."

She looked at the floor, at the patient, then at me, and placed the threaded needle into my palm. I had seen it done a hundred times, performed several dozen "successful" cadaver bypasses, read about it a thousand times, and dreamed about it every minute of every day for twenty years. In my mind, I had walked through every stitch and every second.

I asked the anesthesiologist to raise the table, because I'm about three inches taller than Dr. Trainer, reached my hands into Jimbo's chest, and then did what God had made me to do. I fixed his heart.

Several stitches into the second bypass, I looked down at Dr. Trainer who, evidently, was playing possum. I picked up on this because I caught him looking at me through one eye and watching the video monitor with the other. When he winked at me, I realized he had this whole thing planned, and everybody was in on it but me.

No matter. In twenty minutes, I had rerouted the circulation around Jimbo's heart with three new arteries, one from his chest and two from his leg, pulled him "off pump," and watched his heart fill with blood and turn deep red. With blood filling the cavities, I reached my hand in, wrapped my fingers around his heart, and squeezed.

It beat. And then it beat again. And Jimbo didn't die.

After I had sewn up the pericardium, run three drain tubes out the wall of his stomach, wired his chest shut, and stitched and stapled the skin above his sternum, I stepped back.

Dan shook his head and laughed. "Seventeen times we've done this, and you're the only one we've ever let finish. Usually Dr. Trainer's back up in two minutes, after the guy in your shoes soils his scrubs or screws up an already screwed-up heart." He pointed to Jimbo. "Good work too. Almost as good as him." And he pointed behind me.

I turned around, and Dr. Trainer was looking over my shoulder, taking M&Ms from a nurse who was feeding him one at a time.

Dr. Trainer nodded and said with a smile, "Maybe." When I pulled off my gloves and apron, he winked. "Just maybe."

Chapter 28

The only original item of furniture that I kept from the fish camp was an oversized, lion-footed, iron bathtub. The thing was waist-deep and looked like something out of a brothel. Charlie said it weighed three hundred pounds, and Emma absolutely loved it. She'd get the water warm but not too hot and let the tub fill up while she plucked her eyebrows in the mirror above the sink. After she quit sneezing, she'd slide in, sit for a long time, run more warm water as needed, and read. She must have read a hundred books in that thing. Bubbles, wet towel behind her head, feet propped up.

Sometimes I'd poke my head in the bathroom and ask, "You want some company?"

And every once in a while, she'd look at me from around her book, move her bookmark, and nod. I'd climb in and lean back, and she'd read to me while I rubbed her feet. We'd step out looking like two raisins.

I kept the tub when Charlie and I built the house, to remind me of those moments. If I wanted to get rid of it now, I'd have to blow up the house. The thing was so heavy that we'd had to reinforce the bathroom floor to hold it plus the water, plus whoever was in it. While Charlie stood at the bottom of the stairs, I paid two other guys to help me carry it upstairs. We placed it against the wall, facing a window that overlooked the lake.

Charlie just shook his head and said, "Suit yourself, but I don't know why you're keeping that old thing."

I ran the water, making it as hot as I could physically stand it, and then soaked myself. The moon lit on the lake like a single headlight, and a light breeze ruffled the trees outside. I cracked the window, turned off the light above me, and sat in the dark, waiting.

Pretty soon they started. It didn't take me long to drift off. When I woke, the crickets had fallen silent, having finished their serenade. It was past midnight, the water was cold, and I stepped out, pruny and withered.

I don't know how many times Emma and I sat in that tub together. And the memory of her stepping out of that tub, hair pulled up, water dripping from her earlobes and fingertips and toes, is one of those images that I'd not sell to Termite for all the tea in China, or all the magazines in the world.

Chapter 29

Med school taught me many things, but one thing kept coming back over and over again: it is incredibly hard to kill the human body. People do all sorts of things to themselves; they smoke like chimneys until their lungs look like Winston's, drink like fish until their livers are pickled, eat like pigs until their hearts and kidneys are fatty and three chins hang off their faces, sit around like slugs until it hurts to walk . . . and yet the human body takes all that punishment and keeps right on ticking. This gave me hope, because if people can voluntarily cause that much abuse to normal systems, and those same systems still give them seventy or eighty years of life, then I figured people like Emma who involuntarily live with a defective and abnormal system ought to at least get half that amount of time. This meant that while the clock was ticking, I had time to learn what I needed, and Emma had time to wait for me.

I finished Harvard Medical School in three years. Then, thanks to Dr. Trainer's recommendation, I was fortunate enough to be selected for a five-year general surgical residency at Mass General.

Mass General taught me a lot. On call seven out of every fourteen days, I learned that sleep is a weapon and we can do with much less than we get. I often worked three days and two entire nights without one second of sleep. After nearly seventy blood-soaked and tissue-cutting hours, I'd drop into bed next to Emma, sleep four to six hours, then get up and do it again.

And I wasn't the only one. The twelve of us who made up the surgical residency team at Mass General had been handpicked from the best schools around the world. We were called "the best" because we were. Our record proved it. I justified the long hours away from Emma by telling myself that every hour spent in the hospital was one more hour in pursuit of perfecting my craft. One more hour credited toward her healing.

With my time completed at Mass General, I got a call from one of the best transplant surgeons in the world, asking me to spend eighteen months under his wing at Vanderbilt learning the art of transplantation. We accepted, moved to Nashville, and I fell in alongside this tall, lanky, mild-mannered country physician who, despite his humility, just happened to be the number one or two best transplant surgeon the world had ever known. Despite his credentials and the aura that surrounded him, he insisted that we call him "Billy." We did, but behind his back we called him "Sir."

Whereas Mass General had taught me to survive and think on my feet, Vanderbilt taught me to heal. Transplantation wasn't difficult; the mechanics of it have been around for years. Cut the old heart out, stitch the new heart in, sew the patient up. The hard part comes next, after surgery, when you literally force the human body, via powerful drugs, to accept a foreign organ. To do so, you selectively weaken parts of the immune system so that it can't attack itself due to the fact that

John Doe's heart is now sitting center stage amid a body it was never meant to power. It's a delicate walk. To force acceptance and ward off rejection, transplant recipients take an average of fourteen pills a day at specific times.

Thus, being a transplant surgeon makes one by default an expert on infectious disease. You train yourself to recognize symptoms that others don't, tuning in to even the slightest variation in a person's blood count or chemical makeup. The way a cough sounds, the color of the eyes or the skin, the smell of the breath.

Unlike other surgeons, who often operate on someone they have never met and then see that same patient once in two weeks for a final checkup, transplant surgeons meet their patients months in advance, know their stories and family histories, and then endure along with them the agonizing process of waiting for a heart. Following surgery, they see their patients weekly, then monthly, for years afterward. They are linked by this indescribable act whereby one takes another person's heart and places it in a living person's chest, where it instinctively beats again. Few doctors share so close a bond with their patients.

After eighteen months at Vanderbilt, I got a call from St. Joseph's in Atlanta. They were trying to start a transplant program and wanted me to head it. Billy gave me his blessing and cut me loose. I shook his hand and said, "Thank you, sir," and Emma and I drove home to Atlanta.

By this time I carried two cell phones and two pagers

and had been on call 24/7 for about seven years. I was thirty years old, and people were coming from all over to meet me. I'd never lost a patient who wasn't already dead, never been sued, and never not had a success, so word of my ability was spreading.

After my second year in practice, Charlie—who'd gone into the construction business north of Atlanta—called us to say he'd found some property for sale on the northern tip of Lake Burton. Two lots, one containing a one-room fish camp with a porch, faced each other across a narrow finger of the lake.

The three of us met the Realtor late on a Sunday afternoon when my surgery schedule was clear, and walked the property. The existing structure was sparse but clean and would work as a weekend getaway until we could build what we wanted. From the moment we set foot on that soil, Emma began imagining the kind of home she wanted. On the ride back, she began putting her ideas on paper. We made an offer from the phone driving south on 400 and signed the papers later that week.

One afternoon, after four simple bypass surgeries and one thoracotomy, I walked into my office to meet an elderly man from China. Doubled over and leaning on a cane, he raised his head and greeted me. I stooped to shake his hand and make eye contact. Even though we didn't speak the same language, I knew what he wanted. *I want to live* in any language means *I want to live*. The eyes say it as clearly as the lips.

I turned around, scheduled the OR, and that night, he began living again. When they saw I could work with small, frail tissue, that's when they started bringing the children to see me. The steadiness of my hands and my ability to sew fine stitching in small places with dangerously thin tissue was much sought after among parents whose children's small, frail hearts needed miracles wrapped in the disguise of modern medicine. And when I saved the eight-year-old who'd had three previous surgeries and was unable to come off the four machines that were keeping her alive, that's when they started calling me "the miracle maker."

Emma just smiled and continued to hope.

The life of a transplant patient is no painless ordeal. Following surgery, patients endure a long stay in the hospital during which they sleep little, are probed and pricked often, and endure several rather uncomfortable tubes poking into or out of different bodily orifices. Within a short period of time they suffer their first episode of inevitable rejection when the body's immune system attacks the alien threat, the thing in the center of the body that's not supposed to be there.

Then begins the time-consuming search for the right combination of drugs to regulate the body's immune system. Then the frequent biopsies, when a doctor runs a tiny pair of tweezers down a tube stuck into a vein of the neck and clips off five little pieces of heart muscle to study and analyze. Then follow weeks of physical therapy and weekly and then monthly checkups.

Finally, patients must accept and comply with a life-long regimen of diet, take a dozen different medications daily at just the right times, and pay inordinate attention to every cough, sneeze, and sniffle, each cut or sore that appears on the body, and the most minuscule variation in temperature. But despite all that hardship, and all that pain, people line up to endure it.

Then there are the doctors. The honest ones will tell you that few of us are immune to a bit of a God-complex. The system itself breeds the problem. Unlike CEOs, who receive feedback from their stockholders or boards of directors, doctors receive little to no correction. We feed off control. And in the operating room we are in total control; everyone is subservient to our smallest command. No argument. No negotiation. No question or protest. We prescribe, and people do. We extend a hand, and people jump. And with every saved life, we are affirmed. "Nice job, Doctor." "That was good work, Doctor." "Well done, Doctor."

Our mouths might say, "Oh, it was nothing, really," but in our minds we're saying, *You bet it was good work.* We feast on our own pride and are gluttons for our own self-promotion. And don't think we leave it inside the OR. Because most of us have an overdeveloped sense of self, we treat most relationships the same way, which explains why we work twenty hours a day and have no home life, leave a wake of failed marriages, and send Christmas cards to our kids.

I escaped this complex not because I was a better man than those around me, but because I couldn't afford to fall victim to it. I came home every night and climbed into bed with a woman whose breathing had me running scared. I began working twenty hours a day not because I fed off the affirmation, though I wasn't immune to it, but because I hoped that God would remember all my good deeds and spare Emma.

Often I'd walk in the door after two nights and three complete days at the hospital and lie down in bed, my eyelids heavier than I could hold up. But sleep was the enemy, and I did whatever I could to hold it off because all I wanted to do was listen to my wife breathe. Doing so held my doubts at bay.

Many nights she'd turn over, see my open eyes, and brush my cheek with her thumb. "Hey, you."

I'd smile.

"You're not sleepy?"

I'd shake my head.

She'd smile and touch my lips. "You're lying."

I'd nod.

She'd tuck herself under my arm, find my feet with the tips of her toes, close her eyes, and drift off. Each time I wanted to say, "Wait, no, don't go. Stay. Just a few minutes longer." But before I could get the words out, she'd be asleep.

So I'd lie there, my heart racing, and inside my arms her weak chest would fill and then empty itself. The urge to sleep was powerful, but I stood amid the storm, the waves crashing over my bow as I fought to command the rudder. But I had no more control over this ship than I'd had over the boats we built and floated down the creek as kids. We might glide across the surface, row in perfect, clean strokes, or swim discreetly in the shallows, but in the end, the water carried us. *It was the best of times, it was the worst of times . . . it was the spring of hope, it was the winter of despair, we had everything before us, we had nothing before us.*

When I was sure she was asleep, I'd place my stethoscope against her frail back and listen. Hours later, the storm raging in my ears, the waves crashing down on my mind, my hands weary on the tiller, I'd still be listening. Finally, when I was weakened and unable to stand any longer, a final wave would break, shatter my hull, and tumble me to shore. An hour later I'd wake to the sting of sunlight and the pang of uncertainty. A castaway.

I understood that Emma's case was more complicated than anything I'd ever faced. While the transplant surgery itself would be delicate and complex, it was the postsurgery that had me guessing. With so many years on powerful drugs to slow the degeneration of her heart, her immune system was already weakened. The trick would be to continue to selectively weaken her immune system so that it accepted the new heart, while also strengthening the rest of her immunity so that we could grow old together. While I was hopeful, her time was running out. Emma had told me that she didn't want me to perform her surgery because if something went wrong, she didn't want me walking around with that albatross draped around my shoulders the rest of my life.

While Emma's ejection fraction continued to fall and close in on 15 percent, I began thinking about the team I'd need to operate. I needed a good pair of hands. I wanted someone who was as good as I was. Dr. Lloyd Royer Morgan was a fifty-something surgeon who had performed his fair share of transplants, making him one of the top surgeons in the eastern half of the U.S. Royer often operated out of St. Joseph's, so we frequently rubbed shoulders.

Royer was a teddy bear. Six-foot-eight and with hands like bear paws, he was a gentle giant. Due to the sheer size of his hands, he was limited in what he could do with children, but he was everybody's all-American when it came to adults. If my heart failed and I needed a heart surgeon, I'd want Royer's hands in my chest.

Emma and I took him to dinner at Chops in downtown Buckhead, where he drank red wine, nibbled at a steak, and listened to our story. At the end of dinner, I asked him to be my hands. He looked at Emma, she nodded, and he said yes.

We began the multitude of tests that certified her ready for surgery. We also listed her. About midnight on a Tuesday, I entered Emma's information into the national transplant data computer, also known as the UNOS database, and formally registered her as a waiting recipient. I called her, and she began to cry. She didn't like having to wait for someone else to die so she could live.

Chapter 30

Wednesday would be a warm summer day; the breeze off the lake told me that. I was up early because my dreams wouldn't let me sleep late. Actually, they didn't let me sleep much at all. I wore a flannel shirt with a collar that I could pull up if needed, put on my sunglasses, and pulled down my baseball cap. To make myself look even worse, I had not trimmed my beard. In my faded gray Suburban covered with Georgia red clay, which looked nothing like the Lexus I once drove, I felt I could escape detection at St. Joseph's.

The narrow graveled road winding down to their house was carved from gullywashers and a chronic lack of maintenance. I pulled into the drive and saw Cindy and Annie sitting on a bench, reading. Annie was wrapped in a blanket and wearing a purple fleece beret; Cindy wore a knee-length skirt that was not new and a sleeveless cotton sweater that had worn thin in spots.

There is a look, a hollow, thinning, wasting look shared by people who are chronically ill. The eyes are sunken; skin color is pale, glued over a blue translucent base; veins are exposed and appear brittle; hair is not something you'd see on a Revlon commercial; and movements are slow, as if the body were walking through water or the feet blistered from the sun. The medical term is *cachexia*. The more common expression is "death warmed over." Whichever you prefer,

Annie was beginning to have the look. And beneath it was the faint suggestion that more and more vibrancy, more and more life, was slipping away.

She hopped off the bench, walked up to the passenger-side window, and said, "Hey, you, guess what we've been reading?"

I got out, walked around, and opened the door for her. "Oh, do tell," I said.

"*Madeline*."

"You don't say."

Cindy spoke up. "Yeah, we thought about Dr. Seuss, but figured you'd get tired of three-letter words."

Highway 400 south was uneventful, and we pulled into St. Joseph's twenty minutes early.

Cindy shook her head. "You must have been here before. It always takes me an hour just to find the right entrance."

I smiled and said, "The Internet is a wonderful thing."

"Yeah, but they charge you twenty bucks an hour to use it at the Internet café."

"Come to my house. You can use my connection anytime." As I said it, I made a mental note to move my laptop out of my office.

I parked around back in patient parking that few patients know about.

"Wow! We can park here?"

I tried to look curious. "I think so. That sign says we can."

Cindy shook her head and opened Annie's door.

"You coming up?" she asked.

"No, I think I'll stay put. I try not to go to doctors' offices unless absolutely necessary."

She smiled and held Annie's hand as they entered through the electronic door. I sat in the car, staring at the cover of *Madeline* and remembering how Emma's mom had read it to her.

Thirty minutes later, a tap on the window woke me up. A security guard motioned to me with an imposing-looking black stick. "Excuse me, sir, can I see some ID?"

Mike Ramirez had been the nighttime security five years ago. His parents were natives of Old Mexico, which explained his dark, tanned skin and dark hair. I can't say how many times Mike met me at the door after midnight and made sure my car would start and that nobody jumped out of the bushes and took my wallet, watch, or life.

Mike and Sofía had two kids and were hoping for more. He always carried pictures and said his goal was to send them to private school. As soon as he made Director of Security.

He knew Emma because of all her trips to the hospital and had followed her progress religiously. At her funeral he sat two rows back, crying like a baby.

In the five years since I'd last seen him, Mike had rounded a bit more in the middle and his hairline had receded. I had always liked Mike, always liked talking with him and always looked forward to seeing him when I finally clocked out of the OR and began the short trek to my car. But the last thing I wanted to do was show him my ID.

When I looked up, he tapped the glass again and said, "Sir, I'm sorry to bother you, really am, but security is pretty tight around here, and if you'd be kind enough . . ."

I rolled the window down and reached for my back pocket. My wallet was there, but I didn't let him know that.

"Ummm . . ." I stalled, hoping Cindy and Annie would miraculously appear. I pointed toward the electronic door without looking at him. "I gave it to my sister and niece so they could get a bite. They're just inside. A checkup at Dr. Morgan's office."

He paused. "Oh . . . so you're waiting on a patient?"

"Yeah, little girl, 'bout this tall, wearing a purple thing on her head. You know how little girls are. All trying to be the Cover Girl model." I tried to sound as backward and country as I could, but I wasn't sure he was buying it.

"Yeah, tell me about it," he said. "Got two of my own."

That meant he and Sofía had four kids now—the first two were boys. I glanced at his badge. *Director of Security*. Good. I knew it made him proud.

"Uhh . . . sir," I said, trying to sound stupid but willing, "if you need me to move, I can. But I really need to be here when they come back down."

I cranked the car, but Mike put his hand on the window frame and said, "Hold on just a second."

I put my foot on the brake, but kept the car in drive.

Mike turned his head, grabbed the little radio transmitter hanging on his shoulder, and said, "George, call up and ask Mary Jane in Dr. Morgan's office if—" He looked at me and whispered, "What's her name?"

"Annie."

He spoke into the radio again. "If Annie, a little girl wearing a purple thing on her head, has had her appointment."

Mike scanned the area around us, ever vigilant, watching the parking lot but training his ear on the radio. A plane flew overhead, garbling the transmission. He depressed the Talk button and said, "Come again, George."

"Yeah," George returned. "She's on her way down now."

I breathed a little easier.

George spoke again. "You might want to meet them at the door, 'cause Dr. Morgan's bringing them down."

"Ten-four," Mike said, straightening a bit.

I rudely waved at Mike, rolled up my window, and readjusted my disguise. Mike walked to the door just as Royer walked through it, pushing Annie in a wheelchair, followed by Cindy. He had a large envelope tucked beneath his right arm. The films.

I looked straight ahead, turned the radio on so I couldn't hear them, and didn't offer to help. Royer opened the rear passenger door, lifted Annie off her chair, placed her on the seat, and buckled her in. Cindy let herself in the front door and sat, deflated.

Royer kissed Annie on the forehead and shut her door. She leaned against the seat and closed her eyes. Cindy rolled down her window and leaned her head out the window. Unable to hear Royer, she turned off the radio and said, "Thank you, Dr. Morgan."

Royer handed her the films and then looked into the backseat where Annie sat breathing short, shallow breaths with her eyes closed. "Cindy," he said, holding up his hands, "God gave me good hands, but He gave me big hands. I could perform her surgery, but she needs somebody special. Somebody gifted. I can't physically get my hands into the places she presents, and I can't physically sew stitching that fine. We'll have to find someone else." Royer stopped and looked off into the distance.

"I knew a surgeon who could pull this off . . . we called him the miracle maker. But I haven't been able to find him for a few years . . . Well." He snapped back to the present and patted the films. "You keep these. We'll keep Annie a priority on the list. Her ejection fraction now puts her close to the top. Worst case, I'll do it. But . . ." He looked back at Annie. "It's time to start praying for a miracle. We need it."

Cindy wiped away a tear and whispered, "Thank you." She rolled up the window and sat with her hands in her lap.

I placed the car in reverse and was just about to touch the gas when she rolled the window back down and said, "Dr. Morgan?"

Royer turned and came back.

She took a deep breath and changed hats, from mother to provider. "I'm behind in my payments to your office. Next month I think things will change. A bank I've been talking to . . ."

Royer lifted his hand and waved her off. "Later," he said. "Surgery first. Then, when she's back in school, running around on the playground, chasing boys, and asking you to help her paint her fingernails, then we'll worry about other stuff."

Cindy choked back a sob.

Royer patted her on the back. "Let's keep our eye on the ball. Get Annie well, let her get married, have kids, be a wife, a mom, a grandmother. All this is possible, but we've got a few hurdles to overcome." He looked again at the films. "Don't lose those."

For the first time, Royer looked inside the car. At the driver.

I was looking straight ahead, but I could see Royer studying my hands as they sat poised on the wheel.

Serious oversight on my part. I pulled my sleeve down to cover my watch—the Blue Seamaster Omega diver's watch Emma had given me on our first anniversary.

Royer leaned down to see what he could of my cheekbone and face. I never looked his direction. His eyes narrowed, and he looked at Cindy, then at me, back at Cindy, then back at me. He spoke slowly and deliberately, looking all the while past Cindy at me. "Miracles still happen. Despite what some people think, miracles still happen."

We drove out of the parking lot, and Cindy put her hand on my shoulder. "Thanks for bringing us. I don't think I could have done this alone."

"You've been doing pretty well thus far," I said.

"Appearances can be deceiving," she said, looking out the window as we drove into traffic. Annie was asleep so we skipped both the Varsity and Starbucks and rolled back onto the northbound ramp of 400.

I was quiet, lost inside the questions that hounded me, and I guess Cindy picked up on my mood.

"You've been quiet since we left the hospital. You okay?"

"Oh, yeah, sure, just umm . . . thinking about Annie."

Cindy nodded. "Join the club."

Annie slept the whole way home. We pulled into their drive after dark. The motion-sensor spotlights came on and comforted me. I left the Suburban running, carried Annie inside, patted Cindy on the shoulder, and walked myself out as Cindy softly called "Thank you" from Annie's bedside. I climbed into the car, and there on the passenger's seat lay the envelope.

The two sides of me competed for control.

I looked again at the envelope, then picked it up and slid the contents out. I found pictures; computer disks that no doubt held the ultrasound images; the video of the heart cath, which would show the dye injection and overall performance and strength of the heart; and, finally, a CT scan. I held the scan up to the dome light and studied the contours of Annie's heart.

Royer was right.

I carried the envelope to the door, slid it between the weather stripping and the wood, and drove home. I parked the car, walked up on the porch, and listened to the crickets. The noise was raucous.

Chapter 31

It was the weekend of July Fourth, and I knew the lake would be crowded with people, boats, and the noise of Jet Skis, but I needed to get Emma out of the house. She'd been bedridden for months and, if she'd had the energy, would have gone stir-crazy weeks ago.

I was keeping her alive with almost daily intravenous injections of dopamine—sort of an adrenaline kick for the heart. It forced her heart to artificially beat stronger and with more regularity, but it also decreased the life of it. Since Emma was near the top of the transplant list, Royer and I agreed that the increased strength caused by the drugs would help her, so we fitted her with a PICC. The "peripherally inserted central catheter" looked like an IV in Emma's left arm, but in truth it was attached to a tube that traveled up her arm and extended all the way to her right atrium, allowing the drugs to dump directly into her heart where they could mix with the optimum amount of blood. It kept us one step ahead of the dark night that was nipping at her heels.

Emma was thin, looked deathly pale, spoke little, mostly at a whisper, and blinked slowly. Her hair was thin, nails brittle, and mouth often filled with cotton balls. She had neared the top of the list, but with other names still taking precedence, I knew we had the weekend to ourselves. So I packed the car with enough Plasmalite and IV fluids to continue her daily dopamine injections and three bottles of liquid oxygen, which I had been using nightly to help her sleep. The increased O_2 count eased the workload on her body, allowing her to rest. It was like putting energy in the bank. After a transplant, the body made huge withdrawals. The oxygen brought back some of the color to her face, and she enjoyed moments of relative excitement. Just in case a heart became available, I called the guys at Life Flight, gave them the exact GPS coordinates of the house, and told them there was a parking area a hundred yards away that could accommodate the helicopter.

Emma, the nasal cannula hooked over her ears and pumping oxygen up into her nose, put her head on my shoulder, and we drove to the lake. We were excited. After waiting so long, after so much study, so much hoping, we knew we were within weeks of a totally different life.

I had cleared my surgery schedule for two days, something I'd not done since I'd been in practice, and spent the day on the phone receiving updates from nurses and consulting with other doctors about past and future patients. After lunch, I even went for a row—something that for years had been confined to a daily 5:00 a.m. explosion on a stationary machine in the doctors' fitness center at the hospital. From her perch above the lake, Emma sketched, slept next to a cup of tea, and watched the wakes from the boats crash along the bulkhead.

That night a twenty-year-old on a motorcycle in Daytona, hyped on a cocktail of beer and amphetamines, revved his café-style racing bike to somewhere north of eighty miles an hour and tried to jump an entire intersection before the adoring eyes of a few dozen fellow thrill-seeking kids. He hit the ramp, had the distance, the speed, and, unfortunately, the height—because at the pinnacle of his jump, the power line he had failed to allow for nearly decapitated him. His bike landed without him, the power company pulled him down, and he was declared brain-dead upon arrival. He was only kept alive while the attending physician talked with the parents about organ donation. The hospital in Daytona listed the heart, and the national computer declared it a perfect match with two patients.

The great thing about the UNOS database is that it removes from the equation any situation in which a doctor is asked to play God. The only possible exception to the no-assign rule is when your transplant program has grown rather large, and your network of listed patients has grown. Even then, the chances of a perfect match for more than one of your patients is about like your odds of being struck by lightning and attacked by a shark on the same day. The network system administrators affirm the match through a system of double checks before any phone calls are made, and then they make the two phone calls to the physicians listed as responsible for both patients. That afternoon, both phone calls came to me.

"Hey." It was Royer. "We got . . . an opportunity."

His tone of voice told me something else.

"We got a heart."

"And?" I asked.

"It matches Shirley . . . and Emma."

Six weeks prior, Shirley Patton had come to see me. She had just turned forty, had two kids, thirteen and ten, a husband of fifteen years, and had one wish: "I want to see my children graduate college."

The only problem was, her heart wasn't going to let her do that. Her son had wheeled her into my office, and when I asked her to stand, she couldn't. She had heard about me and my team, about Royer's experience and my cutting-edge abilities, and had driven up from Brunswick to ask me to cut out her heart and put a new one in.

I saw the way she looked at her son, the way her daughter cared for her every need, and heard how her husband had worked three jobs just to give her the baseline of health care she needed.

She pushed her chair over to where I leaned against my desk, took off her reading glasses, and grabbed my hand. She turned it over in hers, studying every crack and callus, and then looked up at me.

"I've heard you have a gift," she'd said. "Will you share it with me?"

Given her condition, we admitted her into the apartments owned by the hospital that sat adjacent to the trauma center. Shirley had weakened to the point that she'd never leave the hospital. Either we'd get her a heart or she'd die waiting for one.

Royer continued, "It's entirely your call. We can have Emma up and walking around in three days, and then get on the phone and get the word out about Shirley."

I shook my head, and Emma ran her fingers through my hair. Without ever hearing the conversation, she knew. Somehow, she knew.

"It's okay," she said. "I'm okay."

I studied her eyes, shelved the doubts that were screaming at me from behind her eyes, and said, "I'll be there in ninety minutes. Get Shirley ready."

Royer swallowed, said, "I've got . . . 9:14 a.m. . . . now." He hung up and boarded a plane while I showered, kissed Emma, and called Charlie to babysit.

Emma led me with her hand, a forced smile, and hoarse whisper. "Go on. Give Shirley a hug for me."

I broke most every posted speed limit en route to Atlanta while Royer flew to Daytona. He returned, opened the cooler, and there, standing over Shirley, handed me a perfect heart.

I did what I needed to do, sewed the last stitch, and took Shirley "off pump." Her new heart filled with blood, turned bright red, and beat like a drum. I spoke with her husband and left him in the waiting room with their kids, where they'd been talking about, of all things, college. I returned home after dark, thanked Charlie, and turned to Emma.

She reached up and ran her finger along the dark lines that had permanently found a home below my eyes. When she saw my face, she smiled. She knew Shirley was well and would make it. Talking had become more difficult, as had whispering, so she scribbled a note and pointed with her pencil. "Why don't you get some sleep."

With my phone not ringing and my beepers not beeping, with no patient awaiting my arrival, and with no heart en route via a Learjet, I carried my wife to our bed, lay down next to her, placed my arm around her thin and bony waist, and closed my eyes. She locked her fingers inside mine and placed the warm skin of her back against my chest, and then the sleep crept in. When I woke in the darkness hours later, beneath a booming umbrella of Fourth of July fireworks, Emma wasn't there.

Chapter 32

After dinner, some brown rice covered in Worcestershire sauce and a piece of grilled salmon rubbed with cayenne pepper, garlic salt, brown sugar, and molasses, I drove up into the hills to my warehouse. I pulled back the dusty tarps, studied the stacks, pulled twelve suitable heart-of-pine planks and four four-inch-square timbers off the top, and drove back home, where I spent the night in my lakeside OR covered in sawdust and varnish.

By the time Charlie appeared at 5:30 a.m., intent on a row, I had turned the legs, built and snugged the skirt using mortise and tenon, screwed and glued on the top, and was ready for the second coat of varnish.

Charlie shuffled over, gingerly walked the perimeter, ran his fingers along the edges, and said, "Nice table."

"It'll do," I said, critiquing my own work.

"You expecting company?"

"No," I said, not looking up.

Charlie smiled and said, "You gonna make some benches to go along with it?"

"Hadn't thought about that."

"Well," he said, scratching his chin, "where's she gonna sit?"

That got my attention. I looked up and saw him smiling. "I don't know."

For some reason Charlie was in high spirits, meaning the row was hard, long, and fast. I kept pace but only with difficulty. My mind was elsewhere. An hour later, we hung the boat up in its rack and Charlie patted me on the back, just before he dived off the end of the dock.

With one arm he grabbed the guide wire and with the other he pulled himself through the water. Georgia sat on the opposite dock, whimpering, her paws hanging off the edge, watching Charlie's ballet dance through the water. He reached his dock, rubbed her ears, and then made her walk behind him while he led her to the cabin for some breakfast.

The phone rang, and rang a second time before I picked it up. "Hello?"

"Hey, I've got a business proposition for you." Cindy sounded perky, which meant she'd been up all night thinking. In the background I heard people talking and a cash register ringing.

"Okay." I tried to sound upbeat.

She spoke to someone else. "I came in early to take care of the purchasing. Frank said I could use his phone. I'll be off in just a second. Sorry."

I could see her sitting up straight and chewing on her bottom lip. I heard a woman's shoes walk off across a hollow wooden floor.

"Okay, sorry. I'm back."

She paused, and I could practically hear her push her hair back behind her ear the way women do when they're thinking, nervous, or both.

"I grew up on this pecan farm just off I-75, north of Tifton and south of Macon. About fifty acres in trees. We sold off the house years ago, but still own the groves. Unfortunately, most of the trees are dead or have been hit by lightning. Anyway, where was I? Oh, yeah, we've got this old barn." She paused to let *old barn* sink in. "It's about two hundred years old. I don't really know what I'm talking about, but it's pretty big and I think there's some good wood in it. If you'll pull out what you can, I'll split it with you fifty-fifty. I'll even help, if you'll tell me what to look for and what to do."

I figured the transaction in my mind, but the economics of it had nothing to do with money. I was silent a moment, so she filled in the space.

"I just thought that maybe with your expertise, well . . . the money would really help . . ."

Annie coughed in the background, a deep, mucousy cough, and I heard Cindy whisper, "Annie, honey, cover your mouth. And don't put your pencil down, you get busy on that schoolwork." Annie said something I couldn't hear, and Cindy responded, "I don't care what that teacher says, you're not that far behind, and you're making it to the third grade next year."

I spoke up. "I'd have to see it first."

"Well, with enough notice I can get the weekend off."

"Is today enough notice?"

"Maybe. I'll ask." She lowered her voice. "Boss isn't in the best of moods today, but she never is this time of month. She's got the worst PMS of any woman I've never known." She paused, then spoke normally. "That's probably more information than you needed."

I smiled. Cindy had a wonderful way of thinking out loud. Annie coughed again, this time longer, eventually dislodging some of the mucus draining through her chest and bringing it to the back of her throat. I had heard that cough ten thousand times before. And every time, the picture that went with it returned.

"See what you can do about work, let me talk with Charlie because we'll need him too, and then we'll shoot for Saturday morning, early. That okay with you?"

She was quiet for a minute. In my mind I saw a lady sitting in a borrowed office talking on a land line because she couldn't afford a cell phone. I saw a lady who'd been working two, sometimes three jobs, trying desperately to break the vicious cycle she was in. I saw her take a deep breath, I saw her smile, I saw her shoulders rise and relief fill the aching cavity beneath. And, as I'd seen in hundreds of patients who had come through my office, I saw a glimmer of hope return from somewhere deep, rising like a phoenix out of the ashes of defeat and impossibility.

In a whisper I was accustomed to, she said "Thank you" and placed the phone quietly in the receiver.

Chapter 33

Friday night came and found me famished, but I had resigned myself to a microwave dinner. Apparently, Charlie had not. At 5:30 p.m. he appeared on his dock, dressed to the nines.

"Hey, Quiet-Boy! Boy-Who-Won't-Answer-His-Phone! Boy-Who-Don't-Need-to-Be-Building-Boats! Get your butt over here and pick me up. It's dinnertime."

I locked my office, where I had spent most of the day, grabbed my keys, and drove the dirt road that circled the little finger of the lake around to Charlie's front door. He stood there with Georgia, tapping his foot. He climbed in, told Georgia to "Kennel!" at his feet, and with a smile on his face said, "Go that way," which was opposite The Well.

"Where we going?"

"To pick up some friends of mine. I'm taking all of us to dinner."

I pulled over and put the stick in park, then turned to Charlie and raised my eyebrows.

He looked at me and said, "Yeah, doctors don't really like being told what to do, but you're not my doctor. Besides, if we're going on a little trip tomorrow with these people, I just thought I ought to get better acquainted with them."

We rolled down into the drive where Cindy and Annie sat waiting, looking as if it were the first time anyone had invited them out to eat in their entire lives. Their smiles were worth the price of ten dinners.

I walked around and opened Charlie's door. "Cindy, Annie, you met my brother-in-law, Charlie, the other day. This is his girlfriend, Georgia."

They laughed, and Charlie aimed his face in our general direction. He held out his hand, oddly pointing at Cindy, and she took it, looking at me.

"It's okay," I said to Cindy, "don't worry. Charlie can't see you, but he's already figured out what you look like."

Charlie smiled, closed his eyes, and hummed like he'd just eaten a chocolate-chip cookie. "And I love Beautiful," he said with his nose in the air.

Cindy blushed and ushered Annie forward. Annie

looked up at Charlie, not quite sure what to do, and Charlie turned his ear toward her. Her breathing sounded like that of a chronic asthmatic. Charlie stepped from the car, knelt down, and placed his right hand gently on Annie's face.

She stood, hands at her sides, beret flopped to one side, while Charlie traced the contours of her face with his fingertips and then found her hand and shook it gently. He placed his face very close to Annie's, moving his eyes as if trying to find any light or reflection whatsoever. When he finished "reading" her face, he took Annie's hand again and said, "I once knew a girl who looked a lot like you." He held her hand with both of his and said, "I hear you have a special heart."

Annie smiled and unconsciously rubbed the sandal about her neck.

Charlie listened, placed his fingertips around both the sandal and the nitroglycerin pill container, and asked, "What's this?"

Annie beamed. "That was my mama's. It's a sandal."

Charlie leaned in, placing his ear closer, like a safe-cracker at work. His fingers tried to read the letters: *Ez 36:26.*

"It's from Ezekiel," said Annie.

Charlie nodded and let it dangle once again at the base of her neck. He spoke in a low, reverent whisper. "I will give you a new heart and put a new spirit within you." He placed his hand flat across the top of Annie's chest. "And I will take the heart of stone out of your flesh and give you a heart of flesh."

Annie looked surprised. "How'd you know that?"

Charlie smiled. "My sister liked that verse. She always had a book in her hand. She and Romeo here," he said, thumbing his hand at me, "were always memorizing stuff and then talking to each other in the phrases they remembered. Some of it rubbed off on me, and I've been trying to get rid of it ever since. Guess I hadn't gotten rid of that one."

"Can I meet her?" Annie asked.

Charlie smiled and stood, taking Annie's hand and leading her to the front seat. "Yeah, in about eighty years."

I dropped them off at the front door of The Well, let Charlie and Georgia guide them inside to a table, and parked. The time alone would allow me to get my story straight so that I could lie with precision when we got to the question-and-answer period.

Just as I reached the door, a light rain started falling. The dark clouds above told me that more than light rain would fall tonight.

I found them in the corner where Davis, wearing an apron that read *Women Want Me and Fish Fear Me,* was evidently entertaining Annie with stories. I stood in the shadows and watched her light up the room. Even pale and drawn, she had a smile that cast a daylight glow not even a blind man could miss.

And Charlie didn't. His face caught it, warmed beneath it, and, like the moon, reflected it back to the rest of us. Davis took their drink orders while I slipped behind the tables to my seat between Annie and Cindy.

"What's good?" Cindy asked me.

I opened her menu, leaned over, and pointed at the burgers. "Anything off this 'medical' section here. Davis makes the best burgers this side of anywhere."

She looked at me. "What're you getting?"

I looked at Annie, then back at Cindy. "The usual. A Transplant."

Annie dropped her menu, smiled, and pushed her beret out of her eyes. "Yeah, me too." She threw her hands at us as if to say, *It's no big deal.* "I been needing one anyway."

The laughter felt good. Actually, the laughter felt great. It was cleansing. And if anybody needed it more than I, it was Cindy. Davis reappeared and took our order: "three Transplants with an extra plate." He disappeared behind the griddle and started pounding ground meat into burgers.

While we talked, the local band began setting up for the Friday night live entertainment. Sasquatch consisted of four guys from Atlanta who had left their insurance and brokerage jobs to drive two hours north and lose themselves in acoustic and Southern rock.

While we waited on our food, Cindy directed her questions at Charlie, who was all too happy to answer them. I sat on the edge of my seat, listening, wondering, and worrying. Charlie launched into our childhood, spinning wild and true tales about all the trouble we got into and keeping the girls laughing. Thankfully, he avoided the other half of the story.

Twenty minutes later, Davis delivered our food, and

we started to eat beneath the single bulb that lit our table. Just as I was picking up my fork, Annie spoke up and said, "Mr. Charlie, would you say the blessing?"

Charlie smiled and whispered, almost to himself, "From the mouths of babes . . ." He stretched out his hands, holding Cindy's and Annie's, who in turn held mine, and bowed his head.

"Lord, You're the only one here who knows what You're doing, so we ask that You come hang out with us a bit. Be the guest of honor at this table. Fill our conversations, our time, and our hearts. For"—Charlie pointed his voice in my direction—"they are the well-spring of life."

Cindy's grip on my hand unconsciously grew stronger, as if she were responding in the left hand to Charlie's grip in the right.

"And, Lord, we thank You for Annie."

The bar grew quiet. At other tables, heads bowed and people nodded behind closed eyes.

Charlie continued, "We all know she needs a new heart; it doesn't take a rocket scientist to see that, but that's what You do. You fix broken hearts. So, fix those at this table that need fixing." He paused and let the words sink in. "I don't pretend to know more than I should, but You said in Jeremiah that You know the plans You have for us, plans not to harm us, to give us hope and a future." He paused again. "Because, Lord, I have a feeling that this little girl deserves it. And I know nothing is more dear to You than a little child."

Cindy's hand shook. At the table behind Charlie, a

lady sniffled, and the man with her offered her a tissue. Charlie raised his chin. By now everybody in the bar was listening, and most eyes were not dry.

"Lord, thank You for this food, for Davis, and for my brother Reese. I pray You bless him . . . keep him . . . and make Your face shine upon him. Amen."

I looked up and saw Davis kneeling behind Annie. His eyes were closed, he was praying, and his scarred and mangled knuckles moved like giant waves across Annie's thin back. She sat quietly, eyes closed, her lips moving. Another minute and Davis stood, walking slowly back to the grill.

From the corner of my eye I saw a young man sitting by himself in the corner, smoking a cigarette, intently watching our table. Termite leaned forward, out of the shadow, and snuffed his cigarette in the ashtray on his table. I nodded at him; he nodded back and then let out a long, smoke-filled breath.

As we finished dinner, Sasquatch stepped to the mike and started with their signature song, a Southern rock/country tune called "Jump-start Me, Jesus, My Batt'ry's Runnin' Low."

Annie and Cindy loved it. They clapped throughout the song, singing the chorus when the lead guitarist, Stephen George, got back to it.

Davis dropped the check on the table, at which point Cindy reached into her purse. Charlie heard the jangle and shook his head. "No, ma'am, not here. This is my date, and I'm paying for dinner. But not before I have just one dance with this lady right here." He stood up, found his way to the corner of the stage, and whispered in Stephen's ear.

Stephen nodded, stepped on some electronic panel at his feet, which did something to the amp behind him, and set down his guitar. He stepped behind the piano and started playing Billy Joel's "She's Got a Way."

Charlie took Annie's hand and bumped his way again between tables and chairs out onto the dance floor. Annie followed, one giant smile. Charlie dropped onto two knees, Annie's head just slightly above his. He placed one arm around her waist, the other he held chest high to the side. Annie placed one hand in his, the other atop his shoulder, and beamed her way in circles around the dance floor.

Midway through the song, every eye in the restaurant was trained on those two. When I looked down, Cindy was holding my hand. She just shook her head and watched both everything and nothing all at once.

That dance was one of the most beautiful things I have ever seen.

Looking for an excuse to get my hand back, I gave Charlie's money to Davis and folded my hands in my lap. Cindy looked embarrassed and fumbled with her napkin. On the opposite side of the restaurant, Termite lit another cigarette, dropped some money on the table, finished his soda, and walked out.

I cut the engine, and Charlie and I walked them to their door. Annie hugged Charlie's legs and said, "Thank you, Mr. Charlie. I had a lot of fun."

"Good night, Annie."

Annie put her finger to her lips and squinted one eye as though she wondered whether or not to ask a question.

Charlie waited, read the silence, and said, "Something on your mind?"

"Mr. Charlie, I was just wondering . . . is it hard . . . not being able to see?"

Charlie sat down Indian-style on the porch and gently placed both of Annie's hands in his. She sat down across from him and pressed her knees up against the tops of his shins. The porch light was weak, but it reached down and feathered their shoulders.

"Annie, about two thousand years ago a blind man named Bartimaeus lived in a city called Jericho. Every day he sat outside the city gates, because everybody passed there. If you were blind and needed to beg for money or wanted to get someone's attention, you'd go there."

"You mean like the men at the stoplights holding those cardboard signs?"

"Sort of." Charlie smiled. He had taken a red handkerchief from his back pocket and folded it methodically across his thigh. "Bartimaeus had been there for years, just sitting at the gate, blind as a bat. Most everybody knew him, and I bet they were tired of him screaming all the time. But what else is a blind man to do? If he didn't rant and rave a little bit, he'd die."

Now he held the handkerchief gently against Annie's eyes. "Okay, you hold that, and I'll tie the back."

Annie placed her fingers over it and then squinted her eyes closed. Charlie reached around her and gently tied the blindfold around her head. He continued his story.

"So there's old Bartimaeus, begging, screaming, just being a regular old pain in the tuchus."

Annie interrupted again. "What's a tuchus?"

Charlie laughed. "You're sitting on it."

I watched the exchange and smiled: *Blessed are the pure in heart, for they shall see God.*

Cindy stepped closer to me, her shoulder touching mine.

"One day he hears this crowd coming. Now, Bartimaeus knew most everything going on those days. He was sitting at the city gate. You might say he was like the anchorman for FOX or CNN. So when this crowd starts getting closer, Bartimaeus stands up, waves his arms, and yells at the top of his lungs." Charlie paused. "You know what he was yelling?"

Annie shook her head.

"Well . . ." Charlie's voice had fallen to an excited whisper. "He knew a crowd that big could only mean one thing. So he starts screaming, 'Son of David, have mercy on me! Son of David, have mercy on me!' That might not sound like a big deal to you, but in those days it could get you killed. It was a signal to all the other Jews standing around that at least one person thought the Man coming their way, who happened to be Jesus, was the Messiah—the king they were waiting for. Anyway, old Bartimaeus, he's sick of the gate, sick of being blind, so he ain't waiting any more. And he don't care if somebody kills him or not. He knows the stories, he's heard the news, he's convinced. So he starts jumping up and down, yelling for all he's worth." Charlie painted the air with his hands.

"The locals, not wanting Jesus to think their town is full of a bunch of nuts and weirdos, tell Bartimaeus to shut up! But not Bartimaeus." Charlie shook his head. "People been telling him that for years. He's not about to shut up. Meantime, Jesus has gotten close enough to hear, and He stops the crowd and says, 'Bring that man to Me.' So now the crowd rushes over to Bartimaeus, brushes him off, and says, 'Come on.' Now, I imagine his clothes were dirty and tattered, and chances are pretty good he needed a shower."

Annie smiled and pinched her nose between thumb and index finger.

"So they bring the blind beggar to Jesus, and I imagine Bartimaeus falls flat on his face, his eyes level with Jesus' toes. I mean, if you really believed the whole 'Son of David' bit, then on your face would be just about the only place you'd be. And Jesus says to him, 'What do you want Me to do for you?' And Bartimaeus, lying in the dirt, looks up and says, 'I want to see.' So Jesus dusts him off, straightens his clothes, and says, 'Go. Your faith has healed you.' And just like that"—Charlie lifted the blindfold off Annie's face, and she sat blinking and adjusting to the porch light—"just like that, Bartimaeus could see."

Annie smiled, and Cindy covered her mouth with her fingers. Then Charlie stood up and helped Annie to her feet. "And that's pretty cool, but what happens next is even more interesting."

"What's that?" Annie asked, rubbing her eyes.

"Most of the blind folks Jesus healed ran off home and told everybody they could see. 'Bingo! Hello, Mom! I'm back in business!' A natural reaction. But Bartimaeus, he walks over to the city wall where he's been hanging out for years, picks up his jacket, and follows Jesus along the road." Charlie knelt down and placed Annie's hands and fingers along his eyes. "Annie, the best and most beautiful things in the world cannot be seen or even touched; they must be felt with the heart."

"Did Barta . . . Bartimay . . . Bartimmam . . ." Annie gave up.

"Bart," Charlie said.

Annie smiled. "Did Bart say that?"

Charlie shook his head. "Nope, another one of my heroes did. A lady named Helen Keller."

Annie said, "Oh, yeah, I've heard of her."

Charlie held out his hand. "Annie, I had a wonderful date."

Annie hugged his neck, careful not to knock him in the head with her hard plaster cast.

"I may be blind, but I can still see." He turned in my direction. "Sometimes, I see better than those who still have their eyes."

When Annie let go of his neck, her mouth said,

"Good night, Mr. Charlie," but her tone of voice said *Thank you.*

Charlie responded to the meaning beneath the surface. He was good at that. "You're welcome, Annie."

Cindy hugged him, held Annie's hand, and the two walked inside.

Annie was almost through the door when she turned and walked back over to me. "Good night, Mr. Reese."

" 'Night, Annie."

Annie walked inside, and I heard her shut the bathroom door.

Cindy looked at us both and just shrugged her shoulders. "Thanks, guys. See you tomorrow, but . . ." She looked inside and then lowered her voice. "We'd better make it a late start. I have a feeling Annie's going to need her rest."

Charlie kissed her on the cheek, said, "G'night," and we loaded up.

When I placed my hand on the ignition, Charlie placed his hand on mine. "Wait a minute." He placed his finger to his lips and rolled his window down. Georgia lay below him, curled up on the floorboard. Her wagging tail made a rhythmic thumping on the mat. Charlie tilted his head, listening, and when I placed my hand on the ignition again, he took the keys and held them in his lap.

A minute later, Cindy turned out Annie's light, and we heard a door squeak. Then Annie coughed. Deep, low, and loud. It was getting worse. A few seconds passed, and she coughed some more. This time, more spastic, almost twenty times in a row.

Charlie looked in my direction and said, "You hear that girl coughing?"

I knew what he was asking.

He shook his head and smacked me hard in the chest with an open palm. "I asked you if you heard that little girl coughing."

I sat back, looked ten thousand miles through the front windshield, and took a deep breath. "Yes, Charlie, I hear her."

Charlie nodded and handed me the keys. "I hope so." He looked out the window and crossed his arms over his chest. "For your sake, for that little girl's sake, and for Emma's sake, I hope so."

Chapter 34

The sound of breaking glass jolted me off the pillow. "Emma?!" I looked toward the kitchen and the sound. "Emma?!!"

I heard a rustling, and then a muted moan. Emma was lying faceup on the kitchen floor, her nightgown twisted around her. Her eyes were open, and she was gripping her chest. Her face was a picture of excruciation. I hit my knees, felt her carotid and distal pulse, and knew she had about three minutes before her heart stopped.

"Charlie!" I screamed out the back porch while digging through the drawer of kitchen utensils. "Charlie! Call 911! Charlie, call 911!"

If I was to give Emma any chance whatsoever, I had to alleviate the pressure on her heart. The only way to do this was to draw off the blood, and the only thing I had that would do it was the meat injection syringe in the kitchen utensil drawer. I found the six-inch needle, the width of a pencil lead, screwed it onto the syringe itself, and kept screaming for Charlie the whole time. Emma's eyes had closed, and her carotid pulse told me her systolic pressure was now less than 80. She was unconscious, from either the pain or the lack of blood flow, but that was good because I didn't want her to remember what I was about to do. I turned the O_2 canister on *Full* and ran the tubes to her nose. Her neck veins were bulging, meaning pressure was backing up in the system.

At this point, the brain-damage clock started ticking. I spread her out flat on her back, stretched her limp arms above her head, angled the needle, and pressed it into my wife. The tip pierced the pericardium; I drew on the syringe, started the flow, and unscrewed it from the needle. The result allowed a free-flow stream of oxygen-depleted blood to spray across me and the opposite kitchen wall. Almost a liter of blood painted the kitchen walls and floor before the flow slowed and began to pump with the now-regular beat of Emma's heart.

As the pressure subsided and the flow continued up her throat, Emma's eyes opened. This did not mean she was necessarily conscious, but it did mean that oxygen was reaching her brain. If I could get to her heart, sew up the hole, and Life Flight got here in time, we could make it to the hospital, where I could place Emma on a machine that would keep her alive for twelve hours while we found a heart. It was all possible.

I never doubted. I had done it a hundred times. All I needed was enough fluid and to keep one lung expanded and her heart pumping. I looked her in the eyes and said, "Emma, I'm here. Stay with me."

She nodded, closed her eyes, and faded again.

Charlie rushed in with a cell phone held to his ear, and his eyes grew as wide as silver dollars. "What are you doing?!"

I cut him off. "She's okay, but we've got about two minutes."

As his eyes scanned the scene in the kitchen, he screamed wildly into the cell phone for Life Flight.

I put my finger over the end of the needle, stopping the flow, hoping to force some volume out into Emma's body, and said in as calm a voice as I could, "Charlie, IV fluids and toolbox in the trunk."

He looked at me, unsure whether I was helping or hurting. I said it again, calmly, "*Now*, Charlie."

Charlie flew out the front door, emptied the trunk, and came tearing back into the kitchen. As he did, his heels hit the wet, slippery blood on the linoleum and sent him airborne five feet. His feet flew toward the ceiling while his head aimed directly for the doorjamb. Rather than protect his head, Charlie consciously cradled the fluids in his arms and broke his fall with his head. He should have been out cold, but the adrenaline kept him going. He sat up, turned his head as if he were trying to see with one eye, and held out the IV fluids.

I rigged a drip, handed it to Charlie, and said, "Squeeze this as hard as you can."

I pulled an intubation tube from the emergency kit I kept at the house and ran it down Emma's throat, clearing the airway.

Charlie wrapped his strong hands around the IV bag and began force-feeding the fluid into Emma's heart. His gaze was lost somewhere above her face. As he pumped fluid into her arm and, hence, her heart, the fluid coming out the end of the needle turned pale, and at times, clear.

"Razor blade and wire cutters," I said to Charlie.

Charlie dug one hand through the tool bag and came out with a large pair of Channel Lock wire cutters and a box of regular razor blades.

I turned Emma on her right side, stretched her left arm over her head to pull apart her rib cage, and switched the Plasmalite bag for Charlie. Just before I cut her I looked at Charlie and said, "Turn your head."

He said, "Do what you got to do."

I handed him an eight-ounce bottle of Betadine from the kitchen counter, held out my hands, and said, "Cover me."

Charlie did as he was told and painted my hands and forearms brown. I smeared the over-pour across Emma's chest and ribs and then had Charlie douse the razor blade. Timing my touch with Emma's inhalation, I felt for the radial pulse. It disappeared completely

223

when she breathed in, a symptom called *pulsus para-doxus*—meaning "paradoxical pulse."

I pulled the pouch from my pocket, threaded a needle, and laid it across Emma's bare chest. Then I cut an eight-inch incision horizontally between ribs four and five, snipped a six-inch section of the rib with the wire cutters, and placed a rolled kitchen towel at either side to both sop blood and hold the ribs apart. I sliced the pleura—the sac that holds the lung— deflating the lung, and pushed it out of the way. I reached in, saw the pericardium, touched it with the tip of the razor, and blood and water flowed.

Peeling away the tough sac exposed Emma's heart and showed me what I was looking for—a transmural rupture. I stuck my finger in the hole, stopping the flow. The heart had begun a ventricular fibrillation. In short it's called V-fib, meaning it had stopped beating and was now quivering. This was both bad and good. Bad in that it had stopped beating, but good in that it would be easier to sew and wouldn't need much help to get going again.

Charlie had emptied his second bag and figured out how to rig the third himself. He closed his eyes and squeezed his palms together, his neck straining under the pressure. He was in pain, the back of his head was bleeding a good bit, and he was both screaming and crying at once. I couldn't tell if his body hurt, his heart hurt, or both.

I placed my flashlight between my teeth, pointed it inside Emma's chest cavity, and stitched an eight-hole purse string—a stitch that does exactly what it sounds like. When I pulled it closed, the tissue tore in three places, so I had to reach farther across the tissue of her heart and start over. I pulled again, and it held.

Something outside of me told me I was hearing a helicopter, but whatever it was lied to me. With the stitches holding, I reached in and palpitated Emma's heart with my hand, easy at first, then harder. That's when I realized she had quit breathing.

No problem, I told myself. *Sometimes the body just needs reminding.* With my hand still palpitating her heart, I breathed forcefully through the intubation tube and filled Emma's lung. The heart took its cue and began beating on its own. I pulled my hand out, Emma breathed by herself, and I checked the carotid pulse. Low but present. The clock was ticking. We were only seconds ahead of the Reaper, but we were ahead.

Charlie finished his third bag, and we were still a long way from getting to the hospital. I propped Emma's feet up, hoping to drain whatever fluid I could into her chest, and checked her pulse again. This time there was none. I turned her again, massaged her heart, and kept breathing into the tube coming out her mouth.

Charlie was covered in red, screaming at the top of his lungs, and looking toward the ceiling. Whatever he was looking for, he couldn't find. Inside myself, I knew we still had time.

As I was leaning over to breathe again, a young paramedic dressed in blue and wearing rubber gloves came flying through the front door. He looked at me, saw nearly five liters of blood and fluid splattered and puddled across the kitchen, and his jaw dropped.

I screamed, "I need two pads and charge to 200! Now!"

He shook his head as if dazed.

"Charge to 200! Now!"

The paramedic dropped his bag, pulled out two pads attached to long wires, and stuck them to Emma's chest and back. I massaged, breathed again, and he charged the machine. When the green light told him we were go, he said, "Clear!"

I pulled my hand, and he shocked Emma. Her body stiffened, relaxed, and I felt for a pulse. Nothing.

I reached in his bag, pulled out what I needed, and said, "High-dose epinephrine! Shock at 300!"

The paramedic, now joined by the driver, had connected a fresh IV bag and was continuing to force-feed Emma. He did as he was told. I expunged the air bubbles, slammed the syringe into Emma's heart, shot in the entire dose, and pulled my hand away. The paramedic yelled, "Clear!" and I watched Emma's chest rise and fall.

Nothing.

"High-dose epinephrine and shock at 360!"

"Clear!"

Nothing.

Charlie began screaming, "Emma! Emma! Emma!"

I looked at the paramedic and screamed, "Shock at 360!"

He said, "But sir . . ."

"Shock at 360! Now! Do it now!"

He looked to his partner, who had quit squeezing on the bag and was just looking at me.

The driver said, "Sir, the patient is asystolic. By protocol, we're in the V-fib algorithm and—"

I grabbed him by the throat and squeezed as hard as my hand would allow. "The patient is my wife! Charge and shock at 360!"

I shoved him out of the way, charged the machine, shot in more epinephrine, and shocked Emma at 360. She convulsed one last time, her arms twitching almost as if she were hugging herself or trying to keep warm, and fell limp.

I was charging the machine and pounding on Emma's chest with both my hands when Charlie tackled me off her, slamming me to the floor and sliding us across the linoleum where he pinned me and held me down.

I fought to free myself from Charlie's grip, but no matter what I did, I could not get him off me. He buried his head against mine and screamed, "Stop it! Stop it! You hear me? She's gone! Reese, Emma's gone!"

The words reverberated in my head without meaning.

The paramedic walked out of the kitchen, talking into his shoulder radio. "We've got a situation here. I've never seen anything like it. The patient's thoracic cavity is cracked open . . ." He lowered his voice. ". . . with hand tools, kitchen utensils . . . via the rib cage. We've given high-dose epinephrine—intracardiac, shocked each time to 360, and . . ." He paused and looked back into the kitchen. "She's not coming back."

For several minutes Charlie and I lay on the floor, Emma's head on my chest. I didn't know anything was wrong with Charlie until he pulled his face close to mine and said, "Tell me what this looks like. I want to know." That was the last image Charlie ever saw.

An ophthalmologist later confirmed that when Charlie had fallen, he detached his right retina and injured the left. If he had stopped there he'd still be able to see out of one eye, but as he squeezed and strained to push fluids into Emma's body, he saw the curtain come down over his left as the other retina came fully detached.

The paramedics gave a full report of my heroic attempt to save Emma's life. Several hospitals heard about it and sent doctors to interview and research. In a vain attempt to exonerate me, the professionals in my field coined what happened that day the Mitch Procedure. Three years ago I read in *Chest* that an unnamed doctor in Atlanta, Royer no doubt, had hired lawyers to remove a description and accompanying history of the Mitch Procedure from all future medical textbooks, citing inconclusive evidence.

He was unsuccessful.

Chapter 35

It was midnight when the rains came down in force. The winds blew in first, rattling the house; then the lightning lit the night sky like an angry woman shaking her fist. I stood on the porch, face hovering over a cup of tea, watching the wind tear at the trees and water. I looked across the lake and in the lightning flashes saw Charlie's dock. I strained my eyes against the now-sideways rain. What I saw did not surprise me.

Charlie stood on his dock, dressed in boxer shorts and skin, facing the rain. The waves were crashing against the corner dock post and soaking him from the waist down. The rain took care of everything else. He was dancing in place, waving at the rain, and his face was upturned, scanning the sky for lightning. Every time it cracked a tree and sent flames skyward, Charlie roared in delight, threw his arms in the air, and screamed at the top of his lungs.

"Hah! I saw that!"

The thunder rocked again.

"Hah, hah! I can see! I can see!"

Lightning cracked again, this time longer with five or six flashes. It hit another tree nearby, and the percussion sounded so loud it rolled through the house like an earthquake. Charlie stepped nearer the edge of his dock. The wind whipped through our cove and pulled at him; he wrapped himself in its arms and danced with the storm.

Lake Burton is known for its violent storms that pass as quickly as they come. The storm cracked another time, then blew northward and, like a jealous lover, left Charlie standing alone and mostly naked on his dock. Georgia came running out of the house, whining, licked his shins, and the two climbed up the walk to his house. Dance over.

In the quiet that followed, the slow, mournful melodies of Charlie's harmonica filtered through the leaves and cried a lonely tune. Charlie was the eternal optimist. Life was always sunny, always half-full, but at times his soul cried. And when it did, it did so through that instrument. If you wanted to know what he was really feeling, what his heart might say, you needed to listen to him breathe through that harmonica.

I walked down to the dock, stepping over fallen limbs and more leaves than any backpack blower could handle. Across the lake, the shoreline was spotted with an irregular pattern of house lights, suggesting that the power was out up and down the lake. The water had returned to its dormant, black-glass state. The clouds had blown through, ten billion stars shone down from above and, east over my shoulder, a lazy half-moon appeared. It looked like it had kicked back and was watching a ball game.

I sat down in my favorite chair, an Adirondack, propped my feet up on a makeshift ottoman—a planter holding no plant—and leaned my head back. The storm had cooled the night air, but it was not cool. Sort of a warm summer blanket that you didn't mind wearing.

I thought of Royer, his kindness, and how much I missed him. Of working alongside him in the OR, discussing cases, sharing successes. Together, we were good.

I thought of Annie, her cough, the purple beret that was too big, her yellow dress and Mary Jane shoes, the water jug that was almost full, and her gentle, trusting eyes.

I thought of Cindy, the weight on her shoulders and her outer frail facade that was so close to cracking. I didn't know how much longer she could keep it up.

Then I thought of Emma and how much of her I saw in Annie.

"Son of David," I whispered, "I want to see."

Chapter 36

Like the scalpel I was so accustomed to working with, Emma's death severed me. I watched my heart roll through the dirt like a discarded piece of rotten fruit, beating outside myself.

My whole life, everything about my existence, had led to one singular moment, but that moment had come and gone and left me alone. All my preparation had been in vain.

I wanted nothing to do with medicine, with surgery, with my past, or with sick and hurting people ever again. I tried to forget all I had learned, all I had become, all the faces and hearts I had helped heal, to push Delete and blank the tape that had become my mind and walk away.

After the funeral I packed one bag, listed our Atlanta penthouse with a Realtor, called the Vietnam Veterans to pick up anything they wanted, and drove north.

Somewhere around the I-285, I threw my pager out the window. Another few miles and I tossed out the second. Once on State Road 400, I pitched the first of the cell phones into oncoming traffic, where a semi-tractor flattened it. Soon I followed it with Emma's cell phone, which hit the asphalt and shattered into pieces. When I got to the lake, I walked to the end of the rickety old dock and threw my second, and last, into the water.

Hours later, I walked into the house and unplugged the ringing phone. I looked around, locked the door, and drove out the driveway.

Eight months later I returned. I can't really tell you where I went. It's not that I'm ashamed, but rather, I just don't remember. On more than one occasion, I had to look at the cover of the phone book just to tell myself what city I was in. At one point in the first couple of weeks I remember looking down at the odometer, and five thousand miles had clicked by. Three months later, the trip set had turned over, and I calculated the mileage at around fifteen thousand.

A couple of things stand out. I remember seeing the Atlantic, I remember seeing the Canadian Rockies, I remember seeing the Pacific, and I remember being encouraged to turn back at the Mexican border. Other than that, I can't tell you much. I guess my credit card and ATM receipts would tell the real story.

When I finally showed up at the lake, Charlie was just returning from a "school" where they teach blind adults how to live after losing their sight—most by violent accidents. We walked around each other for a couple of days like the same ends of two magnets turned to repel rather than attract. It's not that we didn't want to talk, we just didn't know how or where to start. I mean, how do you talk to the brother of the wife you couldn't save?

Finally he just walked over, put his hand on my shoulder, and said, "Reese, you're the greatest doctor I've ever known."

Maybe that hurt most of all. I hugged him, we cried some, never really said more, and then just started picking up the pieces, which by that time had scattered all over the place. Every now and then we'd find one. Still do. Sometimes together, sometimes alone. Building the house, the boathouse, and then boats just became our own group therapy. We've been regular attendees ever since.

Chapter 37

Cindy called and said Annie was too tired to make a trip south of Macon. "Besides," she said, "I couldn't get the day off."

I thought for a minute. "Would you mind if Charlie and I went without you?"

" 'Course not." Cindy sounded surprised. "If that's okay with you. It's great with me."

I wrote down directions, and Charlie and I drove south pulling a trailer down 400, then I-75. In Atlanta we stopped at the Varsity, where Charlie ate a not-so-healthy lunch of two chili dogs, onion rings, and a Coke, and then pulled back out on the highway. I drank some orange juice and ate a banana.

We arrived at Cindy's place about two o'clock, and she was right. It was run-down and needed about six months of TLC. Most of the trees were dead, the grass was overgrown and weeds rampant, the house caked and peeling and in need of a sandblasting and then three coats of paint. But she was right about one other thing. The barn was a gem.

Charlie and I walked the premises, me describing and him pulling back the kudzu and reading with his hands. Then we walked inside the barn, where I led Charlie to the timbers and his eyes really lit up.

"This is a gold mine," he said, smiling. There was no use driving home empty-handed.

We pitched camp outside the barn—a pup tent, card table, cooler, and propane stove—set up a portable shop that included a planer and a table saw, and set to work. Charlie pulled the boards, ripped them out of the two-hundred-year-old home, and handed them to me so I could pull any nails and then fed them through either the planer, table saw, or both, depending on the character of the wood.

I would have described each piece to him, but his hands could tell him far more than my mouth, and I didn't need to rob him of the discovery. He was having too much fun. Georgia watched us from her perch atop the trailer. Never far from Charlie, she'd occasionally hop down to come check on me.

By dark, we had thirty or forty boards loaded in the trailer, all eight to twelve inches wide and maybe two to three inches thick. Good planks that would bring good money. I figured we had two more days of plank-pulling and then we could get to the timbers, the mother lode.

I called Cindy after eight, when I knew Annie would be asleep. She answered the phone as if she had been connected to it. "Hello?"

We small-talked, I asked about Annie, she asked about the drive, and then I told her what we had found. "Your barn is in good shape. Charlie and I think we'll be here two, maybe three more days, and we can bring home some lumber. Maybe even a good load."

I knew she was afraid to ask, but she must have been paying bills because she was wearing her business hat. "How much do you think we can make?"

I had done some figuring, measuring linear feet, and I had a pretty good idea of the wood's value, but I didn't want to get her hopes up. I threw out a conservative number. "Maybe twenty-five thousand."

There was a stunned silence, followed by a "Wow."

"Yeah," I said, "it really depends on what we find in those timbers. If they're in good shape, each one could bring fifteen hundred to two thousand. But we'll have to see. We still have a lot of wood to uncover before we get to them."

"Do you guys need anything?"

"No," I said, peeling back a blister. "Charlie's serenading me now, so we're in pretty good shape."

I hung up, and Charlie quit acting like he wasn't eavesdropping.

"Hey, Stitch?"

"Yeah."

"What's it look like around here?"

"Well," I said, looking around, "we're sitting in a big pasture amid what looks like about a hundred or so mostly dead pecan trees that were once really big."

"Are all the rows straight?"

"Yeah, pretty much."

"I mean, how far can you see down the nearest row?"

"Couple hundred yards for sure."

He stood up, tightened his belt, and tied his shoelaces tighter. Then he looked at me. "I want to run flat out."

"What do you mean?" I asked.

Charlie pointed down what he thought was a row of trees. "I mean, I want to run as fast as I can, as long as I can . . . until I give out."

I was tired. "Right now?"

"Yup. And if you don't go, I'm going by myself."

I knew he was serious. I stood up, grabbed a six-foot stick that would allow Charlie to stay in constant contact with me, handed him one end, and said, "Turn left half a step."

Charlie turned.

"If you run straight that way, you won't hit anything for what looks like a half mile.

"And at a half mile?"

"Well . . ." I studied the landscape. "If you're moving

fast enough, looks like you'll cut yourself in half on some sort of fence."

"Barbed wire or just plain?"

I looked at him. "Charlie, it's a half mile away."

Charlie smiled and licked his lips. "You gonna keep up with me?"

"You keep this up, and I'm liable to run you smack into the nearest pecan tree."

Charlie nodded. "Waiting on you." He stood poised like a cat.

"Nope," I said, standing even with him, waiting for him to jump and yank the stick that linked us together, "on you."

Without so much as a warning, Charlie sprang forward, taking huge strides, floating over the earth as though gravity didn't affect him the same way it did the rest of us. His left arm was pumping up and down like a piston, while his right hand clutched the stick held between us. The sound of his lungs taking in and expelling air was like a train moving uphill.

Charlie was a blur, and when I finally caught up enough to turn and look at his face, he was smiling ear to ear. By the end of the night, we had made eight trips to the fence and back.

Chapter 38

The next morning, we started at dawn. By noon the double-axle trailer was half-full, and I knew my dollar figure to Cindy had been low. Heart of pine brought a fair price on the open market, but heart of pine this old and in this good shape would bring a premium. By the following afternoon, we had stripped the barn down to its bare framing. What we didn't keep we had been mounding in a huge pile nearby.

Now the only thing remaining was the timbers. And we were in luck. Not only were they pristine, outside of the usual nick and scar that simply gave more character and drove the price up, but also there were almost twice as many as I had originally calculated. We might need a bigger trailer. It took us an extra day because the timbers were ten to twelve inches square and some were almost sixteen feet long. Wood like that just didn't exist anymore. We were sitting on top of some real money.

At daybreak on Wednesday morning, I called into the park service and requested a burn permit. Charlie tossed a match into the bonfire, and we backed up. That wood caught in a matter of seconds and burned hot and high until almost noon. The cloud of black smoke rose over a mile into the air.

Charlie stood close enough to singe his hair and asked me, "What's it look like?"

"It looks like a meteor that's just hit the earth."

He nodded and crossed his arms, and the glow lit up the sweat on his face.

We pulled out of the field, the truck engine whining under the weight of an incredibly overloaded trailer, and started the slow return north. I knew Cindy would rather not wait for the money, so an hour north of

Atlanta, we pulled into a lumberyard where Charlie told me most custom-home builders from all across Georgia bought special-order lumber.

We pulled in, were met by a builder, and struck up a conversation. He nearly jumped out of his skin when we pulled back the tarp. Knowing what it would bring in Atlanta, he offered us a fair price, and we even helped him unload the timber. We had close to four thousand linear feet of planks that averaged seven dollars a foot, plus the sixteen timbers that averaged fourteen feet apiece. Each one of those brought more than $2,000. After it was all unloaded, the man cut us a check for $58,000. I would say that's not bad for five days' work, but it's all relative.

We pulled onto Burton Dam Road, the southern road around the lake, and I said, "You thinking what I'm thinking?"

Charlie nodded, and the smile spread. By the time we reached their drive, it had stretched ear to ear.

When we eased down the gravel drive, the two were eating dinner. Cindy met us at the door dressed in short flannel pajamas, which looked more like something a man would wear than a woman, and a red baseball cap. Charlie and I looked like two coal miners and smelled even worse. We were in desperate need of some Lava soap, a razor, five or six ounces of aftershave, and some real strong deodorant.

Charlie handed Cindy the check. She looked at it, and her eyes widened. She read it a second and a third time, and then erupted. She jumped up, threw her entire body around me, and squeezed me so hard I couldn't breathe.

Charlie heard all the commotion and said, "What about me? I was there too."

Cindy, now almost under control, let go of me and gave Charlie a bear hug and a wet kiss on the cheek. She showed the check to Annie, who gulped and then said, "Wow, that's a lot of lemonade and crickets."

Above our protests, Cindy served us bowls of black beans and rice, dotted with a few pieces of chicken for flavor, while Annie poured us each a glass of milk. We sat at the kitchen table for an hour while Charlie told war stories of the last five days.

As we were standing at the door, saying our good-byes, Cindy disappeared to her bedroom and reappeared a moment later with a check made out to me for $29,000.

Charlie heard her tearing the check from its binding, and his ears pricked up. "What's that?"

I read the check and looked at Cindy. "Charlie, I'm not real good with my figures, but I think this is equal to about four or five days in the ICU." I handed it to Charlie, who pretended to read it, and said, "Wouldn't you say so?"

Charlie nodded as if he could read every word and then handed it back. "Yeah, maybe six."

I tore the check in half and handed it back to Cindy.

Charlie smiled, shook his head, and said, "It's just that high cost of health care."

Cindy picked up Annie, who looked taller in Cindy's

arms, and sat them both down, rocking Annie sideways and brushing her thin hair out of her tired eyes. Cindy closed her eyes and shook her head, kissing Annie's cheek.

"That's all right," Charlie said, gesturing with his hand. "Sometimes I even leave me speechless. Happens all the time. Especially with a few of the women at bingo who just love me."

Cindy managed a half whisper. "I don't know what to say."

"How 'bout saying you'll fix us dinner tomorrow night at Reese's place? He loves salmon. Boy eats it all the time."

Cindy smiled and nodded. She tried to say something, but just stuck a finger in the air and nodded again.

Charlie smiled. "Cindy, honey, life is either a daring adventure, or it is nothing."

Cindy bit her lip.

Annie looked at me and whispered, "Does he know Shakespeare too?"

I nodded. "Yes, but that's not Billy. It's Helen Keller."

"Oh, yeah, I remember her."

I dropped Charlie and Georgia off at their front door. After Charlie shut the car door, he felt his way around to my side, put his hand on my shoulder, and patted me. "Thank you," he said. "I needed that."

I nodded. "Yeah, me too."

I took my foot off the brake, but when Charlie turned

around, I stopped, and he leaned inside the car. He thought for a minute, then pointed his face in my general direction. "You looked in the mirror lately?"

"No."

He paused and rubbed his chin. "Ought to."

"What am I looking for?"

"Something that ain't been there in a long time."

Chapter 39

When the phone rang a few days later, I was buried beneath the middle cockpit of the Hacker trying to repair some electrical lines. I placed a greasy hand on the receiver and said, "Hello?"

The high-pitched screaming from the other end almost burst my eardrum.

"Aaaaaahhhh! Oh—Ohmy . . . Aaaaaahhhhhhhhh!"

I knew two things: it was Cindy, and she was out of control.

"Cindy?"

"Aaaaaaaaaaaahhhh!"

"Cindy!" I heard the phone drop, but the screaming continued.

"Is it Annie?" No response. I heard things crashing and breaking in the background.

I didn't wait for the answer. I jumped off the boat and hit the dock running. "Charlie! Put her in the water!"

Driving in a car would take me fifteen, maybe even twenty minutes because I'd have to circle the lake. *Podnah* could get me there in five if I pushed her. I bounded into my office, grabbed the backpack stuffed into the top of the closet, and shoved the cell phone in my pocket on the way back out the door.

When I reached the dock, Charlie had her in the water, engine running. I jumped in, rammed the stick into reverse, and planted Charlie against his seat with the thrust from the propeller. We banged both doors on the way out, putting deep grooves in the wood. When clear, I slammed the stick forward and pushed down on the throttle, moving it from one o'clock on the steering wheel to almost six o'clock, where it stopped. The boat dug in, made the turn, and shot out of the water. Within seconds we had planed and I was dialing 911 on the cell phone.

The noise from the wind kept me from hearing too well, but when I thought they had picked up, I handed the phone to Charlie, who began talking as best he could given the speed and bumps. We flew into the creek, where we were met by every overhanging limb in north Georgia, and turned hard to starboard. I flew off the bow, hooked a loop around the first piling I came to, and bounded up the steps and past the cricket box.

The crickets were quiet. The house was not.

The back door stood open, and the inside of the house looked like it'd been hit by the Tasmanian devil. Stuff was everywhere. If somebody had been looking for something, they'd evidently not found it. Brooms, kitchen utensils, pots and pans, and every magazine or book within arm's reach littered the floor. Cindy stood on the kitchen countertop holding an iron skillet in one hand and a very frightened Annie in the other.

I grabbed Annie, sat her down on the countertop, and began monitoring her eyes, her airway, and her pulse. It took me about three seconds to assess that, other than an elevated pulse, she was fine. I was about to place my heart-rate monitor across her chest, but she looked at me like I was just as crazy as her aunt. When it registered that Annie was relatively okay, and not in need of the man I once was, I looked at Cindy, whose eyes were trained on the far corner of the room.

Meanwhile, Charlie had crawled up the walk and made it to the back door with the cell phone up to his ear. When he poked his head in, he said, "Talk to me, Stitch! They're en route."

"Cindy?" I asked. I pulled on her jeans leg. "Cindy, what's going on?"

She pointed an iron skillet to the corner, but still didn't look at me.

I turned to Annie. "Can you tell me what's going on?"

Annie whispered, "There's a snake in the house. Over there."

I looked up at Cindy, then back at Annie. "She called me because of a snake?"

Annie nodded.

"So, there's nothing wrong with you?"

Annie shook her head. "Nothing other than the usual."

I leaned against the wall and slid down, coming to

rest on the carpet, my head in my hands. I felt my own heartbeat returning to somewhere close to the normal range and the color returning to my face. Then I walked over to Charlie, who stood looking as disbelieving as I felt, still holding the phone. I grabbed it, apologized to the lady on the other end, and hung up.

With two hands, I gently took the skillet from Cindy and placed it in a drawer. Then I fetched a shovel from the garage, walked over and around the objects Cindy had flung in the general direction of the living room corner, and found a five-and-a-half-foot pine snake coiled up, hissing, scared halfway out of his mind. I scooped him up with the shovel, walked out the back door, and released him in the fern about fifty yards from the house.

Then I leaned the shovel against the back door, walked back inside, helped a shell-shocked Cindy off the countertop, and then sat down on the couch.

Charlie spoke first. "Somebody want to tell me what's going on?"

Annie was the first to laugh. A low giggle, which pretty soon grew into an all-out howl. She sat on the couch, kicked her heels, and laughed hysterically.

"It's not funny," Cindy said. "That thing could've . . . could've . . . eaten us."

"Charlie," I said, starting to laugh, "come on in, but walk slowly because most of the house has recently been tossed into this general area."

Cindy grabbed a loose pillow and threw it at me. I

threw it back, and five minutes later the air in the house was full of floating feathers. Charlie shuffled over, tripped over a couple of pillows, felt his way along the countertop, and then Annie took his hand and led him to a seat on the sofa.

I looked around and said, "So, I guess you really don't like snakes."

Cindy looked up at the ceiling, closed her eyes, and took a deep breath. "I need a vacation. A long one. Somewhere on a beach in an easy chair with an umbrella in my drink and little men in grass skirts bringing me refills." She looked around the house and then at me. "But wow! You got here fast."

"Yeah, well . . ." I pointed at Annie. "I thought you were calling about her."

The realization finally hit her. Cindy put her hands to her face and covered her eyes. A minute or two passed while she put herself in our shoes. Then she said, "I'm sorry, Reese, I just didn't think . . ."

She pointed around the room, apparently following what had been the path of the snake. "I was looking at that snake. It was hissing, and I was running out of things to throw."

I laughed again. "Evidently."

"It's not funny. I almost wet myself when that thing started crawling across the living room straight for us, doing his little tongue in and out, bobbing his head back and forth and hissing. To me it looked like an anaconda or something."

"I'm not sure who was more scared, you or him."

"I think I lost ten years off my life."

"You know, a pine snake won't hurt you. We want those around. They eat other snakes."

"Well, excuse me, Mr. Zookeeper," Cindy said, smiling. "I just failed to ask him for his license and registration when he walked in the door."

We helped them clean up, then ambled down the walk toward the boat, which Charlie had fortunately remembered to turn off. We loaded up, and Cindy threw us the bowline. She sank her hands into the front pockets of her jeans and looked a bit embarrassed. "Sorry, guys."

I held out my hand. "Don't even think about it. You did the right thing."

I bumped the stick into drive, and Charlie purposefully bumped it out.

"Hey, we're doing a pig on Saturday and wanted to know if you guys want to join us."

I looked at Charlie. "We are?" He elbowed me, and I said, "I mean, we are. Right, we've been planning it a long time."

Cindy smiled. "What do you mean, 'doing a pig'?"

"Ohhhhhhh." Charlie licked his lips, ran his fingers along his belt line, and did his best Ray Charles imitation. "That's where we take this whole pig, usually about a hundred pounds, and cook it all day, low and slow, and then spend the evening pulling off some of the best pork you've ever tasted. Essentially, it's a mountain of sin on a plate, and most folks don't eat for about a week afterward."

"About like that Transplant you guys made me eat."

"Something like that." Charlie nodded.

Cindy thought for a minute, no doubt running her work schedule through her mind. "What time you want us?"

" 'Bout noon. And bring your bathing suits."

Cindy looked at Annie, who was nodding. "See you at . . ." She slapped her forehead with her open palm like she had forgotten something and said, "Oh! Dang!"

Charlie heard the smack, the change in tone of voice, and said, "What?"

I interrupted her. "Don't worry. I'll pick you up, right here. Noon."

Cindy smiled, put her arm around Annie, and walked back up the walkway, keeping one eye on us and one pointed in the general direction of where I had released the snake.

We revved the engine, idled down the creek, and emptied into the Tallulah where we skirted the no-wake zones. As we pulled into the boathouse, Charlie put his hand on my shoulder and smiled. "Looks like you better get to town and buy us a pig."

"Yeah," I said, turning the wheel, lining up with the lift, and then cutting the engine. "I gathered that."

"Oh, and . . ." He turned around with a huge grin on his face. "Don't forget the grass skirts."

Chapter 40

I walked down Main Street Tuesday afternoon carrying a plastic bag overstuffed with two drugstore grass skirts that were spilling over the edges. Walking up the sidewalk en route to Vicker's Meat Market, I saw a lady wearing a baseball hat walking directly toward me, led by her husband and two children. When I saw her face, something snatched the air out of me and left me standing like a man with no skeleton.

Shirley. Her son had grown two feet. He was handsome and strapped with muscle. Her daughter had long hair, had turned beautiful, and had long legs like her dad. Harry was barrel-chested and walked proudly down the street, his name printed on his shirt.

I stopped, looked for an exit, and couldn't find one. The street was too open, the shops to my left too confined, and it was too late to turn around. Shirley's eyes passed over me. Something in her brain registered, and she looked again. She let go of Harry's hand and started toward me. I stopped next to the newspaper machine, pulled down the bill of my cap and fumbled for two quarters, hoping the earth would open up and swallow me.

Shirley eyed me with suspicion, looked past the hat, the long hair, and the beard, and then her face lit up like a bulb. "Dr. Mitchell?" she whispered.

I spilled a dollar's worth of change across the sidewalk.

She touched my shoulder as if she were touching a ghost. "Jonathan?"

I turned slowly, the quarters circling my feet like swirling water, and looked at Shirley's face—she'd gained weight, which was good—and saw the tears welling in her eyes.

I took off my sunglasses and hat and ran my fingers through my almost shoulder-length hair. I took her hand in mine, felt a strong distal pulse, and said, "Hey, Shirley. You . . . you look great."

She wrapped her arms around my neck as the rest of her family gathered around. I shook Harry's hand and marveled at their son who was taller than I was. Shirley said, "He's been awarded an appointment to the Academy."

She studied me while the silence that surrounded us spoke volumes.

"I heard about . . . about Emma." She put her hand across her heart as the tears fell off her face. "And I heard what you did. About me, I mean. I'm so sorry."

She hugged me again, and I felt how strong her back had become. Shirley had made it. She was a survivor. And based on the look of things, she'd live to see her grandkids.

She let go, and I tried to break the tension. "Royer treating you well?"

Harry spoke up. "Yeah, next to you, he's the best." He looked at Shirley and then back at me. "No kidding, he's taking great care of us."

Shirley smiled and wrapped her arm around Harry. "I

can run three miles without stopping." She patted Harry on his flat stomach and said with a smile, "I'm not setting any speed records, but we're healthy and . . ." She choked back the emotion. "And we're good."

She wrapped her arms around my neck a second time, as if I'd disappear if she didn't, and squeezed as hard as she could. Her children edged in closer, put their arms around me, and even Harry joined the group hug that they were staging front and center in downtown Clayton.

Harry handed Shirley a white handkerchief from his back pocket, and she tried to laugh.

"Whoever had this heart before me must have been a real crier," she said, "because I didn't used to be this emotional."

It had belonged to a twenty year old, but I never told Shirley that. She needed to be able to live, not feel guilty for doing so. And I don't know how she'd ever heard about my phone call with Royer. Sometimes it's hard to keep stuff like that quiet. Even in hospitals.

I looked down at Shirley's daughter, who reached up and hugged my neck. She kissed me on the cheek and said, "Thank you, Dr. Jonathan . . . for saving my mom."

My name echoed in my ears and sounded strange, stiff and starched, though I knew it was stained.

I nodded and put my sunglasses back on while I still had control over my eyes.

Harry saw I was having a difficult time, so he herded them in front of me and said, "Okay, okay, we've embarrassed the doc enough for one day. You guys get going. Our reservation won't wait forever."

Shirley kissed my cheek and as she did, her tears ran down my face. They tasted salty and sweet.

The four of them leaned on one another and walked off down the sidewalk while I steadied myself against a lamppost and looked inside the shell of me. A minute or so later, I felt a hand on my shoulder.

Sal Cohen stood smiling at me with a curious look spread across his face. He pointed down the sidewalk and said, "Friends of yours?"

A tear slipped out from beneath my glasses. I looked down at Sal, nodded, and whispered, "Yeah. Old friends."

Sal took off his hat, wiped his brow with his handkerchief, and let his eyes follow them down the sidewalk. He gave me a knowing look. "Feels good, don't it?"

I watched them walk away and nodded. When I caught myself nodding, I looked back at Sal, but he was gone.

Chapter 41

I sat in the tub for almost two hours, soaking, sleeping, sipping some red wine, and thumbing through the last month's *Chest*. It was nearly 3:00 a.m. when I dried off, dressed, and walked into my office and shut the door. Charlie would be on the dock in a little less than three hours and, if my passwords still worked and could get me the access I needed, I had some work to do. There was always the possibility they had locked me out, but if I knew Royer, he'd have made sure they kept my accounts and codes active. I'd probably be leaving a trail that could lead Royer right to my doorstep, but I'd take that chance.

After a daylight row with Charlie that left me spent but feeling temporarily clean, I left him rolling around on the dock with Georgia and returned to the house to put on a pot of coffee. The voice-mail light on my phone was flashing. Even before I punched the Play button, I had an idea who it was. The tape rewound and then clicked forward. Background noise filled the air, and Royer's voice launched in without even a hello.

"Hey, Doc, although to be quite honest, I'm being a bit liberal with the term. Our IT people called me pretty early this morning and said somebody'd been playing with my confidential files. Said whoever'd done it knew all my old codes and most of the short-cuts. Poked around a good bit, read several active files, and then left without stealing or rearranging a thing.

"Well, almost. The person did do one very interesting thing. Wrote a note in Annie Stephens's file to request a TEE. That was my first cue that I wasn't dealing with some twisted computer hack hell-bent on deleting my files. But anybody who suggests a transesophageal echocardiogram for Annie knows two things: the risk is too great, and she can't pay for it.

"Then, just as I was about to call financing and argue

the cost of the test to give a little girl one shot in a thousand, I got another rather unusual call. Wonder of wonders, financing called me and told me that Annie's account, which had been a little more than $18,000 in debt, had been paid up. And what's more, whoever called had paid in advance for a TEE. They wanted to know if I had ordered such a test.

"Jonny, you've been gone a while, and there's a few things you might not know. Annie's pretty well-known around here. Makes most of us smile most all the time, and whenever somebody starts tinkering with her file or her care, we get our dander up."

Royer's tone was harsh. I expected nothing less. A bear can be either a teddy or a grizzly, depending on the need.

He took a deep breath and continued. "So, naturally, I faked a page and said I needed five minutes. I checked the file; they were right—as are you—and so I've scheduled Annie. But you know as well as I do that she'll have to be sedated, and she's not going to like that, and Cindy is running the narrow ridge as it is and liable to crack any minute. And when you throw all that together, you've got a pretty good recipe for disaster."

Royer thanked a nurse who had evidently brought him a cup of coffee. He took a long sip while the machine continued to record.

Swallowing hard, he said, "The test is next Friday—that's ten days from now, in case you can't find your calendar. Now, you started this ball rolling, so here's the deal. I'll run the test, but if I don't see you here Friday morning, wheeling that little girl down the hall, I'm spilling the beans. And Jonny, that's not an idle threat."

Another pause, and I could practically hear Royer deliberating.

"Guess that gives you a little time to chew on your dilemma. So while you're chewing—and I got to be honest, I hope you choke on your own self-pity—I just want to ask you one question . . ."

I hit the Stop button and walked toward the kitchen, where I found Charlie leaning against the doorframe, Georgia at his feet, both looking in my general direction.

"You don't want to hear the question?" he asked, his palms opened toward the machine like he was inviting someone into his house.

I walked past him out onto the back porch and wondered how far I could get by nightfall if I got in the car and started driving.

"Well, I do." Charlie clapped his hands and rubbed his palms together. "I rather miss that old son of a gun." The sarcasm grew thick. "Gee, I wonder what the old devil might ask you?"

Charlie felt his way along the wall and walked to the machine. He ran his fingers across the buttons and pushed the large one in the middle, and Royer's voice returned. It crawled through the house, over the rafters, through the floorboards, and out the screen onto the back porch. It found me on the landing at the top of the stairs where I stood holding on to the railing, steadying myself before the blow.

"Jonny, tell me something, if you don't mind." His voice cracked. "If I could call Emma and tell her about Annie, what do you think she'd say?"

Charlie rewound the machine and then felt his way across the hallway to the kitchen. He rummaged through the coffee mugs, poured two cups, and shuffled his way slowly out of the kitchen and onto the back porch, where he found me weak-kneed and white-knuckled atop the stairwell. He offered me a mug and I took it.

"Thanks."

We stood in silence a few minutes, letting the smell of coffee beans mix with the smell of lake water and mint.

Finally Charlie nodded his head back toward the machine and spoke. "What was he talking about?"

The taste of fresh beans filtered down my throat and warmed my cold stomach. The lake was starting to turn under a light breeze, and somewhere a boat was approaching at what sounded like half-throttle. Somewhere behind it, several kids were screaming with laughter.

"A TEE is when you insert a probe down the mouth and into the heart of a . . . a sedated patient. It uses sound waves to look at the chambers."

I held the cup between both hands, asking myself if Annie's heart could handle the stress and if the risk was worth the information.

I continued, "The heart is divided by a wall in the middle, called the septum. Before we are born, we have an opening called the foramen ovale. Because our moms are doing all our breathing for us, there's no need for our blood to circulate through our lungs. At least not yet. So this opening allows the blood to bypass that step. When we're born, prostaglandins release and the hole closes, forcing our lungs to start working on their own."

The wrinkle above Charlie's eyebrows grew deeper. "And if it doesn't close?"

"The blood jumps straight across the heart rather than through it."

"What's that mean . . . for Annie."

"It means that most every day of her life, she feels like she's running the last turn of the quarter mile and never able to catch her breath."

Charlie stood next to me and "looked" out over the lake. "Like my big sister?"

Seconds passed, and I didn't answer. Finally he put his hand on my face and read the wrinkles. Something he had not done since Emma died. He asked again, "Like Emma?"

I nodded.

Charlie pulled his hand off my face. "Can it be fixed?"

"If caught in time. If not, the ripple effects are far-reaching and permanent. My thought was that if Royer saw an opening, he could close the hole with a catheter and a balloon. It'd be a short-term fix, a Band-Aid, but

Annie'd never know it, and that might buy her some more time. And right now . . ." I lowered my voice. "Time is the enemy."

"How much has she got?"

The breeze off the lake was cool. A few mallards screamed overhead, circled, and then glided down the water near Charlie's dock where a drake was hiding beneath a rhododendron. Georgia tore down the steps in search of some fun. "Not much."

Charlie shuffled his way through the door and into the house. He was gone several minutes. I heard him in my office rummaging through my closet. Obviously looking for something, but sometimes it's best to just let Charlie do his own thing.

A few minutes later, he returned carrying the transit case. He appeared in the kitchen, holding both handles. He dropped the box in the middle of the floor and pointed at it. "Drink up."

He found his way to the back door and used the railing to guide himself down the steps. Two more minutes and he was midway, following the "dry" guide wires around the back end of the creek.

I walked into the kitchen and sat down next to the dust-covered box. The lid squeaked as I fingered my way through twenty years of history. At some point in our lives, Emma had read every book in here several times, many of them out loud to me.

At noon, my head was splitting. With every page I turned, the picture in my head of her doing the same grew more colorful and detailed. Surrounded by books, I lay down on the kitchen floor and ran my fingernail along the grooves of the wood. Deep inside, caked along the grooves and the cracks between, were small, almost pinhead-sized flecks of red.

Life's but a walking shadow, a poor player that struts and frets his hour upon the stage, and then is heard no more; it is a tale told by an idiot, full of sound and fury, signifying nothing.

Chapter 42

I was on the road early Thursday morning, saying good-bye to no one. By daylight I was just a few hours from Hickory, North Carolina. At a quarter to eleven I pulled into the gas station and parked in front of the public phone. Leaving the car running, I rummaged through the rain-swollen phone book and found the number I was looking for.

After three rings, he answered. His voice resonated through the phone, kind and confident, but weaker now. It'd been more than ten years since we'd spoken. The picture in the alumni newspaper showed him and his wife arm in arm in their "getaway" in Hickory. Wearing a plaid vest, his pipe tucked inside his right hand, he looked content, living out what remained of his life with his wife, who, like many doctors' wives, had spent most of her life sharing him, with first the hospital and then the university. Now was her time. He had promised her that.

"Hello?" he said.

"Hello . . . um, sir?"

Silence followed. Ten seconds or more. I heard his pipe slide from one side of his mouth to the other, and then the rattle of his teeth as he bit down again.

"I've often thought of you," he said at last. "Wondered how you're getting along. And if."

"Yes, sir, well . . . I was in Hickory and wondered if we might have lunch."

The pipe moved again, and his tone of voice told me he was smiling. "You mean you drove all the way over here from wherever you've been living because you wanted to talk with me?"

I smiled. He had weakened, his voice told me that, but a weak body did not equate to a weak mind. "Yes sir."

Fifteen minutes later, I parked in front of his house. One look in the rearview mirror told me that he might not recognize me. In fact, I might scare him. It was a good thing I had called first.

I slipped my sunglasses into my shirt pocket, walked up the lawn, and rang the bell. Soon I heard the shuffling sound associated with old men who wear their slippers until afternoon.

He opened the door and stood a moment while his eyes adjusted to the sunlight. He pulled the pipe from his lips and nodded. "Doctor," he said, extending his hand.

I extended mine. "Sir."

We sat on the back porch, and Mrs. Trainer poured us tea while we watched their cat tear at a ball of red yarn.

He stirred, occasionally looking at me, but didn't say a word. I had come to him, so, ever the teacher, he would wait on me.

"Yes sir, well . . ." I fumbled with my tea bag and eventually dripped it across my lap and laid it on the saucer. "Um . . . sir, like I said, I was just driving through and knew from the alumni bulletin that you had retired here." I sipped, looking for the words. "So how do you like retirement?"

He shook his head. "Hate it." He pointed his pipe end toward the kitchen, where somebody was washing dishes. "We both do."

"How's that?" I asked.

He wrapped his tea bag around his spoon, squeezed the dark juice out using the string, then carefully laid it and the spoon on his saucer. He sat back, sipped, looked out over the backyard, and said, "My whole life, I've been one thing. Doctoring is what I do. It's who I am. Retirement doesn't change that. So now I'm spending three days a week giving physicals down at the indigent clinic."

"So you're staying active?"

He looked at me, and inside his eye I caught sight of a flicker, almost a fire. "Jonny, don't talk to me as though I were an old man. My body may be frail, shoulders not as broad . . ." He ran his fingers along his plaid vest. "My coats may not fit as tight as they used to, and I may take more medication than I ever have, but one thing remains . . ." He nodded, looking past the backyard over his, and my, past. "You may take me out of doctoring, but never the doctoring out of me."

We sat quietly, sipping, while the cat played. Finally he set down his cup and said, "I followed your story. Read it in all the papers. A few even called to interview me, but . . ." He held up his hand. "I declined." He leaned back, his chair squeaking. "I've often wondered what happened to you, where you went."

He packed his pipe and lit it. The plume of air filtered out of him, surrounding us with the sweet smell. It reminded me of school, of endless days of discovery, of him, and of Emma. I breathed deeply and then held it a long time.

He turned to look at me again, squinting beneath the smoke. He pulled a white handkerchief from his back pocket, blew his nose, and then refolded the cloth and returned it to his pocket. "Now, you want to tell me why you're here?"

"Sir," I said, turning my chair at ninety degrees to his, making eye contact easier on us both. "I've got a . . . situation."

"Well . . ." He raised and lowered his chin and scratched a day-old beard. The cat jumped onto his lap, laid its head on his thigh, and purred. He looked at me, raised both eyebrows, and nodded. I had learned that very trick from him. That nod was how I told a patient to go on, without actually saying it.

"Well . . . sir . . . ," I stammered.

"Jonny," he interrupted, "at my age, I never know how long I have. You better get your story in now, while I can still hear you and can sit up long enough to respond intelligently." He smiled and sat back.

I took a deep breath, scratched my head, and started in. Every word. Beginning from the moment I'd left medical school, on through my residency and specialization in transplantation, through Nashville and then our choice to head to Atlanta. I told him of our practice, of Royer, of Emma's decline, and then of our last weekend at the lake. I also told him the one thing I'd never told anyone.

When I finished, he sat quietly for some time, puffing on a cold pipe. His eyes had narrowed and he wrinkled his forehead. The cat purred, his hands stroked its silky black hair, and his feet sat wrapped in fur-lined slippers. He pointed to an orange tree that hung over his fence.

"I knew a farmer once," he started, staring out over the fence. "Think his name was James. Had an orange tree, a lot like that one. It hadn't bloomed in several years and wasn't looking too good. Still had green on it, but not much. One morning I caught him standing next to it, sizing it up and murmuring to himself. In one hand he held a hammer, and in the other he held three twelve-inch spikes. When I asked him what he was doing, he told me to stand back, and then he drove one of the spikes into the trunk, about knee height. That nail split the thin skin on that tree, and the farther in he drove it, the more white ooze seeped out around the head of the nail. He drove a second at waist level and a third about here." He raised his hand level with his collarbone.

"Why?" I asked.

"That's exactly what I asked him. You know what he said?"

I took the bait. "What?"

"He said, 'Sometimes trees forget they were meant to blossom and just need to be reminded.' I looked at the three spikes and asked, 'Why not ten spikes?' He shook his head and eyed the tree. 'Nope, three is a good enough dose. Don't want to kill it, just remind it.'"

We sat for almost thirty minutes, letting the quiet breeze filter through the trees, ruffle the cat's hair, and roll the red yarn about the back porch. He dozed once, then woke only to doze again. Finally, he began to snore quietly.

I stood just loud enough to wake him but not so loud as to startle him. He stood with me, looped his arm around mine, and we walked arm in arm to the door.

He leaned on me and I leaned on him.

I walked through the front door and turned to say good-bye, but he cut me off. He tapped his chest with two fingers. "After more than sixty years of medicine, I'm still amazed at this little thing. Fist-sized, it sits in the center of us, never stopping to take a break or even pause. So simple, yet so complex and so utterly unknown." He raised his hands in front of him, almost as if he had finished washing in the sink outside the OR and was waiting for the nurse to hold gloves while he inserted his fingers. "I have held more than a thousand hearts in my hands. Hardened arteries, plaque, small flutters, all signs of disease. To this day, I can close my eyes and run my fingers along the left and right main and tell you if there is disease or not." He closed his eyes and rubbed both index fingers along the tips of his thumbs.

He paused and blew his nose again. "In all my study, all my practice, all my teaching, I never met another doctor as gifted as you. Your skill, personality, and ethic made for a great combination, but it wasn't those things that caught my eye that day at your interview with our board."

"Sir?" I said.

"You had something very few applicants ever have."

I studied his face, not sure where he was leading.

He placed his hand on my chest, palm flat against the sternum. "If I could get away with it, I'd strap you to a gurney, charge the paddles to a thousand, and shock you until your toes curled and your hair straightened."

"Sir?" I said, confused again.

"You need reminding, son."

His wife walked up from behind, put her arm around him, and tucked herself under his shoulder. He looked tall again. He continued, "If God ever made one man to do and be one thing, it was you."

I turned, pulled my sunglasses from my shirt pocket, and slipped them over my nose. "Sir?" I asked. "What if . . . what if I've forgotten how?"

He shook his head. "Son, that well won't ever run dry."

Chapter 43

Saturday morning found Charlie and me leaning over a dead pig, rubbing seasoning into the meat. Three things make great barbecue: preparation, heat, and the pit itself. Our preparation involved a dry rub of our secret recipe, which is heavy on garlic salt, pepper, and cayenne. We had lit the coals about 7:00 a.m., and would add more as the day passed, but the secret for good barbecue is "low and slow." You've got to be patient, take your time, and cook the meat slowly over ten to twelve hours, depending on the size of the pig— and you've got to keep your eye on it. If you don't enjoy that aspect of it, or the constant maintenance the fire requires, you might as well not get started.

Perfectly cooked meat occurs within a rather short window. Admittedly, our best asset in this whole parade was Charlie's nose: he could smell "not yet," "just right," and "too late." He was better than one of those little white pop-up things they stick into the Thanksgiving turkey that lets you know when it's done.

We built the fire on one side of the pit, which generated heat and smoke that then wafted up and across an iron grate that held the meat before spilling out an eight-foot chimney. We controlled the airflow at two places: the door to the fire pit and the chimney. Too much airflow, and the fire would burn too fast and cause the meat to turn tough; too little, and the fire wouldn't generate enough heat and would die, causing the meat to sour.

Since Charlie couldn't see the smoke coming out, we had bought a large thermometer, secured it to the iron lid, and taken the glass panel off the front. Charlie then read the thermometer with his fingers and adjusted the flow accordingly. Because we're talking about relatively low temperatures, say between 180 and 200 degrees Fahrenheit, Charlie was allowed some wiggle room. We messed up a couple of pigs before he finally got it right, but I'm not interested in a perfectly cooked pig. To be honest, if it made Charlie happy to tinker with it, I'd eat it anywhere from raw to cremated.

Cindy phoned in the morning and said her boss had called her in for half a day, so she'd be at the hardware store until noon. She asked me to pick them up at Annie's lemonade stand after she clocked out about twelve thirty.

I parked three blocks down the street and started a slow walk up Main. Things were quiet, including Annie. Her "Lemonaaaade!" call had been reduced to the tarnished cowbell, slow, deep, and hollow. It fit Clayton.

Annie wasn't pacing the sidewalk, soliciting customers, but sitting in her chair in the shade, wrapped in a tattered sweater that undoubtedly belonged to Cindy. I wondered if her inactivity would have an effect on people's giving. As I got closer, I could see that it had, but not in the way I'd anticipated. Her cup was spilling over.

"Hi, Annie."

"Hey, Reese," she said, jumping out of the chair and running over to hug my leg.

But still the heart doth need a language . . .

She wrapped her left arm—still thick with plaster casting—around my waist and pointed toward the window of the hardware store. "Aunt Cici will be out in a minute. She's pulling some crickets for a man who's going fishing."

Since Charlie had organized our little get-together at my place, I wasn't quite sure how we'd pass the time. Hospitality just isn't one of my gifts. But Annie's comment gave me an idea.

I looked down at her. "Do you like to fish?"

"Never been."

I mouthed the words, but made no audible sound: "You've-never-been-fishing."

Annie shook her head and laughed that beautiful, tender laugh I'd begun hearing in my sleep.

"Even with all those crickets in that box at your house?"

Annie raised her eyebrows and shook her head again.

I walked into the hardware store and found Cindy leaning over the cricket box. "I'd like . . . um . . ." I looked down in the box. "Three dozen crickets, please."

She looked up at me, rested an elbow on top of the box, and said, "You're kidding, right?"

"No," I said, studying her face, "should I be?"

Cindy stuck her hand back in the box and started chasing crickets. "It's just that these things don't always sit still while you try to lasso 'em."

I looked into the box again and then out the window at Annie. This time I whispered, "I want as many crickets as will occupy her, you, Charlie, and me for most of the afternoon."

Cindy smiled, nodded, and handed me a tube made out of wire mesh and capped with two cardboard ends. "Here, hold this."

I held the tube while she wrestled the crickets. Every so often, she'd hold up her hand, I'd lift the lid, and she'd drop in a few before the others crawled out. It was a delicate dance, but we managed not to get out of time, and I never stepped on her toes. I paid, she clocked out, we moved Annie's stand inside and stashed her money in the store safe, then walked toward the truck.

I held the door while they climbed in. When I got in myself, Cindy looked at me and asked, "Your wife teach you that?"

"Teach me what?"

She elbowed the door. "To hold the door. Every time we go anywhere with you, you're always holding the door. I'm not sure if I'm beginning to like it or if there's something wrong with me. I'm thinking about racing you to the next one."

I thought for a minute and realized that maybe, somewhere in the residue of what was once me, I wasn't all that different from Annie. Maybe my inner emotions still had expression, still made it to the surface and bubbled out. Maybe I wasn't dead after all.

"Yes, I guess she did. I've never really thought about it. And no, I don't think there's anything wrong with you."

Cindy smiled, and Annie inched closer to me, rubbing her shoulder and leg against mine.

Because it wasn't too much out of the way, we detoured past the marina, where I found Termite pumping gas for the weekend warriors. He looked disgusted.

"Hey, Termite."

He almost stood up but caught himself before seeming excited to see me. Instead, he nodded that cool-kid nod that says, *I'm doing just fine here on my own private island, and I can do with or without you. Your presence doesn't change things a bit.*

Termite wasn't a very good liar. He was in bad need of some friends. "What time you get off?" I asked.

"Couple of hours."

"You got dinner plans?"

He looked at me suspiciously and even took a step back. "Why?"

I shook my head and smiled. "You really don't trust people, do you?"

"Nope." He looked around the marina and waited for me to carry the conversation again. He spun his Zippo lighter across the thigh of his cut-off jeans, spending energy and time.

I obliged him. "Because Charlie and I are cooking a pig, and we're having a few folks over. Thought you might enjoy it."

"What time?"

"Whenever. Nothing's too formal. It'll be ready whenever you get there. If it's not, it will be soon enough."

Termite looked out over the marina again. "I might stop by for a few minutes."

"Well, if you can fit us into your busy social schedule, drive north to the bridge and then turn back six houses. We're on the southeastern side. You'll smell the fire."

A Jet Ski was parked nearby, painted in flames. Down the side someone had airbrushed *The Rocket*.

"That yours?" I asked.

He nodded.

"You build it?"

He nodded again.

I patted him on the shoulder, which caused the hair on the back of his neck to rise like a pit bull's. "See you, Termite."

He looked toward my car and saw Cindy and Annie. He said, "Hey, Doc, they be there?"

His question stopped me. I turned around. "What'd you say?"

"I asked if those two would be there."

"Why'd you say 'Doc'?"

Termite shrugged and stuffed his lighter back into his pocket. "Dunno. Guess 'cause you're always checking on people, and you remind me of this doctor I had back home."

I looked at the car then back at Termite. "Yes, they'll be there."

"Okay." Termite nodded almost to himself. I drove out of the marina parking lot, and Cindy asked, "Wasn't that kid in The Well the other night? Sitting at the bar by himself?"

I nodded. "Termidus Cain is his name."

"What?"

"Uh-huh, that's why he goes by Termite."

"I'm not sure which is worse."

"He's new around here. Running from something. Needs some friends and maybe a hot meal too. Besides," I added, pointing my thumb over my shoulder and out the back window, "I was hoping he might bring his Jet Ski."

Cindy looked as if she wanted to say something, but let it go. We drove the last few miles in relative silence.

We pulled off the hard road, down the gravel drive, and back into the woods where my house sat tucked into the edge of the lake. Charlie was sitting next to the fire, snoring, when we drove up. His chair was leaning against a tree, his Atlanta Braves baseball cap covered his eyes, and Georgia lay at his feet, her nose pointed toward the pig.

The girls changed inside while Charlie and I fed more coals to the fire. I had raked the beach below my house and placed two beach chairs facing southward along the lake.

Cindy saw the setup and made a beeline for the beach, her flip-flops smacking her heels as she walked across the cool sand. She wore a two-piece suit. The bottom looked like a normal girl's bathing suit while the top looked more like a tank top. If she were tanning, she wouldn't have to put lotion on her stomach or back, because they were covered. When she spread her towel across the seat, I saw a four-inch, horizontal scar just above her belt line. About where her kidney was. Or used to be.

Annie skipped down to the beach wearing a little girl's two-piece. It was a mixture of orange and green neon colors and was too big, hanging loosely about both her hips and chest. It looked like one of those suits little girls wore when they wished they were more grown-up.

Her chest incision had healed well. Staple holes dotted the sides of the scar, which was red and raised somewhat. But for the most part, Annie had not scarred badly. Which was good. And the fact that she wasn't afraid to let the world see it meant she hadn't scarred too badly on the inside either. Both would make the next surgery less difficult for whoever did it—cutting her open and sewing her up would take less time, not to mention the fact that she'd be less conscious of it for the rest of her life.

Cindy read while Annie began working on a sand castle, but her energies were low. So I set up an umbrella, and she napped for a couple of hours while Cindy finished a novel.

When she placed it on the beach next to her, I asked, "Any good?"

She shrugged. "It had its moments."

"What else you bring?"

Cindy readjusted the towel behind her shoulders and said, "Nothing. What you got?"

"Not much. Most of the folks I read are dead or so boring they ought to be."

"What about all those people you're always quoting?"

"You sure?"

She shrugged again. "Why not?"

I ran inside, picked *Robinson Crusoe* off my bedside table, pulled out my bookmark, and then made a pitcher full of raspberry fruit smoothies on my way back out the door. When I passed Charlie at the fire pit, he held out his hand. I placed a glass in it, and he placed his other hand on my shoulder and whispered something.

When we both arrived on the beach a few minutes later, dressed in grass skirts and carrying fruit drinks decorated with little umbrellas, Cindy howled with laughter.

She read and sipped her drink while I tied a clothes-line from the beach back up to the barbecue pit. Charlie objected to my fussing, but the string helped. Annie and I worked some more on her sand castle—which was short on sand and long on rocks—and around four o'clock I heard a Jet Ski coming north up the lake. Termite, seated atop his flame-covered two-seater, was holding a rope and towing a second three-seater Jet Ski—one I'd never seen before.

He beached both and hopped off, sniffing the air. "You were right. Smells good too."

Termite's acne had erupted again, and the few tattoos scattered across his arms and back made him look dirty and in need of a shower. He was all skin and bones, and looked like one of those mangy dogs that live around a Dempsey Dumpster in some back alley. He'd been brought up hard and looked that way.

Despite this, I didn't doubt his courage. This kid had *not gonna quit* written all over him. If life had dealt him a bad hand since birth, his gumption had gotten him this far. You transplant enough hearts, and you begin to be able to recognize this sort of thing.

Termite didn't wait for introductions, but followed his nose to the pit where Charlie raised the lid and explained the process to him. When he walked back down to the beach, his stomach was growling. I introduced him to Cindy and Annie, and when I did, Termite took a long look at Annie's scar. Then he looked at me but didn't say a word.

I knew he was waiting on me to ask about the second Jet Ski, so I obliged. "You always tow a second Jet Ski around with you?"

"Nah," Termite said flippantly while nervously turning his lighter inside his pocket. "Some folks out of Atlanta burned up the engine a few weeks ago, so I replaced it. Brought it along 'cause it needs breaking in before they get back here next weekend just raring to burn up another one."

"How'd they burn it up?" Cindy asked.

"They drained the oil out trying to save some money on an oil change, but then forgot to put oil back in it before they went screaming off down the lake."

Cindy nodded. "Yeah, I can see where that might mess things up."

"Yeah, well they messed up about two thousand dollars. I tell you, doctors may be smart, but they ain't always bright. Most of them are long on book sense and short on common sense." Termite spat across the beach.

His tongue looked like it was starting to fish around the edges of his mouth for a cigarette. He looked at me and waved an elbow at the Jet Ski without too much enthusiasm. "I brought it along thinking you might want to take it for a spin or something."

It was the first olive branch Termite had ever offered me. I took it. "You show me how it works?"

Termite educated me on the Jet Ski, giving me way more than I needed, but I kept quiet. I listened while he talked me through everything from the firing sequence of the spark plugs all the way to throttle response. When he was finished, I could have taught a class.

We pushed it out into the water and cranked it up, where it sat idling and purring like a kitten. While I wrapped and taped a plastic bag around Annie's cast-heavy arm, Cindy stood up, which brought another long look from Termite, and then walked down into the water. She climbed on and sat in back. I helped Annie into the middle seat, and then I sat in front. Termite hopped aboard his machine and then looked at me but pointed at Charlie. "He want to go?"

"He's blind, not deaf and mute. Ask him yourself."

Termite looked at Charlie and then back at me. "What'd he say his name was?"

"Charlie."

"Hey, uh, Charlie, you want to go?"

Charlie smiled and turned his hat around. "Only if you let me drive."

Termite looked confused, while Cindy and Annie laughed. "But, uh . . ." He looked at me and whispered, "But he's blind."

"Yeah, I know," I said. "Just don't tell him."

Termite slid back on his seat and helped Charlie aboard.

By definition, adults who become blind have to become, if they aren't already, touchy-feely people. It's how they navigate the world. So when Charlie climbed aboard the Jet Ski, placed his hands on the grips, and then patted his stomach like he expected Termite to wrap his arms around him, Termite flinched. He looked at me, then at Charlie.

Charlie sensed Termite's hesitation and said, "Termite, unless you want me to run this thing in circles like a one-legged duck, you better figure out how to help me steer."

Termite slid closer, now maybe only a foot from Charlie.

Charlie said, "Here's the deal. You pull on my arms when you want me to turn. Right arm is right turn. Left arm, left turn. One pull is a slight turn, two pulls is a harder turn, a long solid pull is just that—all the way. And as for speed, you squeeze my arm while you're pulling back. The harder you squeeze, the faster I go. Got it?"

Termite nodded, and Charlie asked him again, "Got it?"

Termite nodded again, then realized his mistake. "Yeah, I got it. But I still like girls."

Charlie smiled and said, "Me too."

Termite lit a cigarette, and then started pulling on Charlie. He looked like a kid who was milking a cow for the first time—a lot of work with little result. It took him about ten minutes to figure out how to steer Charlie. But once he got the hang of things, they managed to keep it off the beaches and away from the docks.

The five of us headed north under the bridge and up beyond the YMCA camp. We drove slowly, letting Annie get comfortable with the bumps.

After a few minutes, she tapped me on the shoulder. "I can't see."

"You want to sit up front?"

She nodded, climbed over me, plopped down in front and held on to the insides of the handlebars. That didn't bother me as much as what happened next. Cindy scooted up behind me, wrapped her arms around my waist and lightly pressed her chest to my back. She poked her head around my shoulder and said, "Onward, James."

I'm not sure who was more uncomfortable, me or Termite, but between Termite's tattoos, Charlie's blindness, Annie's scar, and our grass skirts, we made quite a sight.

We drove the lake for over an hour. Everywhere Annie pointed we went, and every time we passed a boat, Termite told Charlie, who then waved like the president on parade. Eventually even Termite started waving. The picture of Charlie grinning and waving, and Termite shaking his head in disbelief, was one of the funnier things I had seen lately. I laughed so much my stomach hurt.

At six thirty, we were all pretty hungry, so we beached the Jet Ski. Cindy and Annie searched the kitchen for paper plates while Charlie, Termite, and I flipped the pig over. I handed Termite a thick pair of insulated rubber gloves and began pulling long pieces of pork from around the ribs, then from the buttocks and shoulders. Termite did what I did, and when I finally bit into a piece, he did too.

The juice smeared across his lips, oozed out the corner of his mouth, and ran down his chin. "Dang, that's good."

"Uh-huh," I said.

"Nah, I mean, that's goooooooood. You two ought to go in business or something."

"That'd take the fun out of it," Charlie said.

We carried a tray to the top of the boathouse, where

the girls had spread a red-and-white-checkered table-cloth across the picnic table. After everybody had been served, Charlie sat at the head and extended his hands. Termite, who was about to stuff three handfuls of pork into his mouth, put down his food, took a deep breath, and closed his eyes. We all held hands and Charlie began, "Lord . . . ."

Annie interrupted him. "Mr. Charlie?"

Charlie looked up.

"Can I say it?"

Charlie nodded again, bowed his head, and waited.

Annie wasted no time. "God, it's been a good day. I had fun. I think everybody did. Thanks for letting us go for a ride, for keeping us safe, and for my new friend Termite and his two Jet Skis. Thanks for this food, thanks for Charlie and Reese fixing it, and Lord . . . ." Annie paused.

I opened my eyes and saw her head tilted as she considered how to say what she was about to say next.

"Whoever's got the heart You're gonna put in me, well . . . if they need it more than I do, let's just let them keep it. But if You're ready for them up there with You, well, then please help them take care of it until Dr. Royer can find somebody to help put it in me."

I was ready for the *Amen,* but she kept at it.

"And Lord, wherever that man is, please . . ." Annie paused again, looking for the words. "Please let him know that I really need him. Amen."

Charlie said, "Amen," but didn't let go of my hand.

When I pulled gently, he pulled back, bringing my eyes to his. Charlie's eyes were lost somewhere above the top of my head, and when he blinked, a tear trickled off his right cheek and landed on our hands.

He asked me to pour him a glass of tea and then asked me for the bread basket, which contained slices of overly buttered garlic bread. He passed it to his left, saying, "Cindy, have some and pass it on."

Cindy placed the basket down next to her, peeled away the napkin, and jumped four feet in the air, spilling her tea and screaming for all she was worth.

All of us but Charlie froze; he started laughing so hard that he knocked his chair over.

Cindy eyed Charlie, looked slowly back inside the basket, realized that the snake was plastic, and slapped him as hard as she could on the shoulder. "Charlie! I can't believe you did that!"

By this time Charlie had rolled out of his chair and onto the floor. Annie lit up with smiles, her face almost as covered in pig grease as Termite's.

Charlie pulled himself up, took the wiggly snake out of the basket, and said, "Did you all know that this is a china snake?" He ran his fingers along its length and pointed at the words stamped on its belly. "See, made in China."

The laughter felt good. And after Annie's prayer, all of us needed it.

Cleanup on a pig is almost as involved as the process to cook it, but between the five of us, we had everything cleaned and the extra meat bagged in about thirty minutes. Then, while Charlie showed Annie and Termite our workshop and boathouse —where Termite paid particular attention to the Hacker—Cindy and I sat quietly atop the boathouse watching the sun roll behind the green hills on our right.

Cindy sat in a rocking chair, reading, while I rocked myself in the hammock. After I got my nerve up, I asked the question I'd been wondering about all day. "Where'd you get that scar?"

Cindy looked up from the book, and I pointed at her back. "The one where your kidney used to be."

"Oh." She looked down and appeared to be reading again. "I gave it to somebody who needed it."

I laughed and said, "What? You sell it on E-bay? Make a quick ten to fifteen thousand?"

"No." She shook her head, not looking up.

I realized then she wasn't kidding. "You really donated it?"

Cindy nodded and kept her eyes on her book.

"To whom?"

Cindy looked down at Annie, who was leading Charlie by the hand up the steps. He didn't need her hand, but she didn't know that and he was kind enough not to tell her.

"Stacey, my sister . . . Annie's mom. When we were much younger." She smiled. "I guess you might say that organ donation just runs in the family."

We helped Termite load his Jet Skis with enough leftovers to last him a week. Maybe two. He hopped up on the seat, turned back at me, tipped his chin, and then rode off down the river pulling the second Jet Ski like a pack mule. I think that was his way of saying thank you.

We drove the girls home, and I carried Annie to her bed while Charlie waited in the car. Next to her bed sat a baby monitor, the kind that flashes a series of red lights whenever a noise cues the mike. For years, Emma's parents kept a similar monitor next to her bed.

I pulled the covers up and then walked out while Cindy told Annie good night. I stood in the kitchen, growing a little uncomfortable with the idea that I was no longer uncomfortable around Cindy. I wouldn't go so far as to say I was comfortable, but it really didn't matter. Either way, my sense of betrayal grew in equal measures.

I leaned against the countertop and bumped into a plastic speaker-looking thing plugged into an outlet in the wall. The other end of the baby monitor. Speakers had changed since Emma's time. First, this one was smaller, and second, the reception was much better.

I heard Annie's voice first. "Aunt Cici, did you have a good time today? . . . Do you like Reese?"

Cindy must have been nodding in answer to these queries, because I heard no reply.

Annie asked another question. "Do you think he likes you?"

This time Cindy responded, "Honey, I'm not sure. Grown-ups sometimes have a lot going on inside their hearts and . . . I think Reese has a hurt heart."

"Like mine?" Annie asked.

"No," Cindy answered, "not like yours. More like he gave it away a long time ago, and when his wife died she took it with her."

"Oh," Annie whispered. "Can he get it back?"

"I don't know," Cindy said. "I don't know if he wants to. Sometimes the memory of love is so strong that it edges out most everything else." A few seconds passed. "He's waiting, honey, so you better start and I'll finish."

"Dear Lord," Annie started. "Thanks for today. Thanks for all those people who bought lemonade this morning, thanks for Reese and Charlie and Termite, and for letting me live one more day." Annie paused. "Please be with Reese and . . . heal the broken places in his heart."

Cindy sniffled and said, "Good night," and Annie protested, "But you didn't finish."

"Sometimes, you say all that needs saying. Now, good night, and go to sleep."

Cindy walked out Annie's bedroom door, and I set the monitor down. She met me at the front door, and I saw that she'd been crying. She looked embarrassed. "Sometimes that kid prays the darnedest things."

I nodded and walked out the door.

She tugged on my shirtsleeve and stopped me. "Can I ask you something?"

My mouth and my heart had two competing reactions, but my mouth spoke before my heart could stop it. "Sure."

"Dr. Morgan called today, said he wants to run another test on Annie sometime next week. She'll have to be sedated. We'll probably be in the hospital most of the day, and I was wondering if . . ."

I stopped her. "Yes." My answer sounded harsh, almost medical. I softened. "Sure. I can drive. When?"

"I'm not sure. Can I let you know?"

I nodded and walked toward the car. "Good night."

She walked up behind me again and put her hand on my shoulder. When I turned, she leaned in and kissed me on the cheek. But it was a double kiss. The first part landed on my cheek, and the second part landed more on the corner of my mouth. "Thank you for today," she said.

"It was noth—" I started.

But she put her hand to my lips and said, "It was everything to that little girl in there, and because of that, it was much more than nothing. Both . . . to her and to me. Thank you, Reese."

I nodded again. " 'Night."

Charlie and I started out the drive. We didn't get too far before he decided to get in his two cents' worth. "Those baby monitors really are something, aren't they?" He turned a bit in his seat and adjusted his seat belt. "They seem to pick up every little sound and . . . man! They can project too."

I just shook my head. "You don't miss much, do you?"

"When it comes to sound, no, I don't."

"I'll say. That's bionic."

Charlie turned, smiled toward me, and said, "I'll trade you."

We drove for a moment in silence, a few winding uphill turns followed by a short downhill and then a long uphill straightaway. The Suburban downshifted into low gear and began making a grinding climb. When the road leveled, I pulled off to the side.

"Charlie," I said, wrestling our past and looking for the words, "if I could give you my eyes, I would."

Charlie sat a moment, his thumbs climbing over and diving under each other. "I don't want your eyes," he said, his face pointed out the front window, "but you could use my ears."

When I climbed into bed somewhere after midnight, I replayed the day in my mind. Charlie had been unusually quiet, which, once again, told me more than his speech, and Termite had enjoyed himself—I think even letting the rest of us cast anchor somewhere near his island. Somewhere in there, I realized we had not gone fishing. Somehow the time had passed without my worrying about it.

Trapped in their mesh tube on the porch, the crickets chirped up and sounded like a freight train sawing through the floor of the living room. I carried the wire tube outside, slid off the lid, and watched each one jump to freedom. Within seconds, the cage was empty. I returned to my bed, closed my eyes, and listened. They hadn't gone too far.

Chapter 44

The outskirts of the lake, away from all the tubers, knee-boarders, and skiers, lay peaceful against a backdrop of hilltops and cemeteries. A century ago, when people learned that Burton was to be drowned beneath some hundred feet of water, the locals began burying their loved ones atop the hillsides, where the edges of what would become Lake Burton would never reach them. Others dug up those who had been buried and moved their thin boxes with mules and wagons. Confederate soldiers, kids wiped out from some epidemic, women who died in childbirth, all re-laid to rest in the cool air and sunshine along the ridges.

As a result, the current developing sprawl had grown up around and now encircled most of the cemeteries, making it difficult to drive around the lake—in either boat or car—without passing half a dozen graveyards. I turned the boat lazily, following my curiosity, and everywhere I went, the ducks seemed to find me. The glassy green water spilled off the sides of the cutwater like the drips off the magnolia leaves that hung over the porch where I grew up.

When Emma and I were thirteen, I once asked her mom if I could take her roller-skating.

Miss Nadine put her hand on her hip, looked out through the kitchen window where Charlie was shooting bad guys from the crow's nest of his fort, and then put her finger to her mouth. "Just don't let her get overextended," she finally said. That was her way of saying, "Watch out after her, and don't let her expend more energy than she should."

Sometimes I think that every time Emma looked out upon her life, she did so through the prison bars and barricades that others had welded around her. *Don't let her get too . . .* was a daily phrase, uttered in defense of her as if she might break. I'm not accusing anybody in particular, we all felt that way. Afraid that she might chip or break, like a dainty china cup, so we put her on a shelf, and it was there that she lived. Most days, I wonder if we kept her from ever pouring water.

Her mom dropped us off at the skating rink, and we bought our tickets, laced up our skates, and waited on the bench until the DJ switched to slow music, the kind where couples were invited out onto the rink. Then I led Emma onto the floor. She turned around, then faced me, a little wobbly on feet that rolled. She placed her hands on my shoulders, fearful yet trusting, and smiled for eight tenuous laps while the DJ played a love song.

When the couples skate was over, the tempo picked up and the kamikaze kids erupted back out onto the floor. I led Emma over to a bench, and she sat breathing heavily, yet smiling as I'd seldom seen her. She was winded, would need a good nap, and she was finished for the day. But the look in her eye told me that more good had occurred inside her than would result from the medication she'd take all month. There was a slight sparkle that told me her hope hadn't died, but was still simmering beneath the surface. As I untied her skates, she tapped me on the shoulder and then placed her palms around my cheeks. She lifted my face to hers and kissed me. I don't mean she just pecked me the way you do when you kiss your mom good-bye before school; I mean, Emma spoke to me. Her lips were wet and soft, and her hands trembled slightly.

We turned in our skates, bought a Coke, and waited on her mom outside. I remember that day for two reasons. First, the kiss. If I close my eyes, I can feel it still. Even after we married, Emma didn't let a day pass that she didn't place her palms on my cheeks, force my tired and worrying eyes to meet hers, and then place her lips to mine.

And second, I learned something that all my reading and all my studying and all my professors would never teach me. Hope is not the result of medicine or anything that science has to offer. It is a flower that sprouts and grows when others pour water upon it. I think sometimes that I spent so much time worrying about how to protect and strengthen the flower—even going so far as to graft in a new stem and root system—that I forgot to simply water it.

When I pulled into the finger creek that led to my house, Cindy and Annie were sitting on the beach where they had taken up residence in their beach chairs. Annie looked like she was in between naps, looking out between the bars that framed her life, passively watching the activity on the lake, while Cindy had her nose buried in *Robinson Crusoe*. Judging by the speed with which she was flipping pages, and the few that remained, she was nearly finished.

When I stepped out of the boathouse, she sat up and hollered at me. "Sal came by to check on Annie, so we thumbed a ride when he left. We won't bother you—we just couldn't pass up a day like this"—she waved her arm out across the lake—"without sitting in chairs like these."

"Make yourself at home. I'll be working on the Hacker for most of the afternoon. Get whatever you need; the house is yours. Holler if you need me."

I went upstairs to change into some work clothes and make sure the office was locked. That done, I tiptoed back down to the workshop. A few minutes later, bare feet shuffled on the sawdust behind me. I was putting the finishing touches on their table, but I wasn't quite ready for them to know that yet. I had hoped it would be a surprise.

Annie eyed the power tools lining the wall and unconsciously began running her fingers up and down the vertical scar on her chest. "Reese?" she said, almost in a whisper.

I threw a tarp over the table, walked around the bench, and stood in the doorway where the breeze touched my face. "Yes?"

Her bathing suit looked as if it'd grown bigger. "You ever been sedated?"

I shook my head and sat down on an empty upside-down five-gallon bucket. "No, I haven't, but," I assured her, "I've heard you can't feel a thing and you really don't remember much."

She took a few more steps, eyeing the sanders and cordless drills. "I have," she said flatly.

On the wall above her hung a Bosch jigsaw and Milwaukee Sawzall. Both were handheld saws made for cutting complicated cuts in tight places—a lot like a sternal saw, which is used to cut through the sternum before a spreader is placed in and cranks open the human chest.

"And I remember a lot of it."

"You were probably just dreaming," I said, trying to shrug it off and change the subject. "Anesthesia can give people weird dreams."

Annie walked down the row of tools, studying each one, and said, "Yeah, but I wasn't dreaming."

Her tone caught me, and I began listening more intently now.

"Before we met Dr. Royer, I went to another doctor in Atlanta. He was always real busy. We'd wait a long time to see him, and then he was always in a hurry. I didn't like him very much."

Annie talked like a seasoned patient, no longer a kid. Somewhere in that distant memory, the girl in the yellow dress selling lemonade had been whisked away on the same wind that spilled her Styrofoam cup.

"He did a surgery to give me a few more years to wait on a heart. I don't know how many operations they were doing that morning, but it felt like that barbershop where Aunt Cici takes us to get our haircuts.

Always a big line of customers." She began rubbing the back of the sandal wrapped around her neck.

"Somewhere during the surgery, the anest . . . the anesth . . . the—" Annie shook her head. "The person who put me to sleep was shuffling between two or three different surgeries, and must of forgot to check up on me. At least she didn't come back when she was supposed to, and I sort of woke up."

I almost fell off the bucket. Pieces of the puzzle were falling into place, and the emotional wall I used to protect myself was crumbling like Jericho. If Annie had knocked on my city gate that day at the lemonade stand, then she'd just splintered it with the battering ram that was her heart.

"I remember being kind of fuzzy, and all I could see was blue. I thought maybe I had woken up in heaven, but then I focused a little and saw that the blue was a sheet taped up over my face. I didn't know where I was or why all these tubes were jammed down my mouth and nose or why I couldn't move my arms and legs. I could see a bunch of lights, and somebody standing over me was talking to somebody else, but I couldn't understand what they were saying, and I remember feeling a lot of pressure in my chest and then being real cold."

I sat still, remembering the horror of other such stories I'd either read about or been told firsthand by patients around the country. For each of them, their worst nightmare had come true. And for each of them, going back under the knife was the most difficult thing they'd ever done. Many refused.

"Then this nurse looked under the sheet, sort of just checking on me, and there I was, looking right back at her. I don't know who was more scared, her or me."

Annie walked out on the dock, where the sun's reflection off the lake lit her pale frame, making her look like an angel who'd flown too close to the ground. She turned deliberately and said, "Dr. Royer wants me to go have some test on Friday. He says he needs to know something about my heart, and the only way he can know for sure is to put me asleep and then run this wire camera down my throat and next to my heart."

I nodded. She walked over and sat on my lap. Her legs were bare, like she'd just shaved them, but I knew she never had.

She looked around the lake again, up at Charlie's dock and house, and then at me. "You think I should let him?"

For a girl who was literally wasting away before my eyes, she felt heavy. The weight of her pressed my leg into the ground and pinned me to the earth like a tent peg. "Yes," I said, offering nothing more.

She looked down at the dock and the two large carpenter ants that were circling her foot. "Would you?" she said, while her eyes followed the ants and her thumb unconsciously rubbed the backside of the golden sandal hanging around her neck.

I took a deep breath. "I don't know, Annie. I can't answer that."

She hung her arm around my neck, like she would a

teammate on her softball team while they watched the last inning, win or lose. She nodded and blew a baseball-sized bubble with the wad of bubblegum filling her right cheek. Finally she looked at me. "Could you come with us?" She looked out the door toward Cindy, then back at me. "I'm not sure how much more of this Aunt Cici can take. The last bank just turned down her loan request."

I nodded. "Yes."

She hopped off my leg and walked over to the steps leading up to my hammock. "Can I nap in your hammock? I won't mess it up."

I nodded one final time, and she began a slow climb to the top of the boathouse. Halfway up the first flight of steps, she stopped to look for fish below and catch her breath. I carried up a fleece blanket and pillow, but when I got there, she was almost asleep. I covered her, propped up her head, and watched her elevated heart rate rhythmically pulse through the carotid artery on her neck. After counting her pulse and watching her quick, short breaths only partially fill her lungs, I returned to my bucket where the sun was beating down.

I don't know how long I sat there, looking out over that water. However long it'd been, it was long enough for Annie to fall asleep, for clouds to block out the sun, and for Cindy to finish *Crusoe*. When I looked up, a lizard was climbing across my feet and shins. Cindy was standing in front of me, leaning against the door-jamb, arms crossed, looking out over the lake.

Too skinny, eyes sunk too far back in her head, Cindy was starting to show some wear and tear, but she could not hide the fact that beauty lurked just below the surface. It struck me that was the first time I'd thought such a thing about anyone since Emma. And that thought in itself scared me.

Cindy had wrapped a towel around her waist, but had evidently grown comfortable walking around me in her bathing suit. As bathing suits go, it was conservative, same halter top and bikini bottom, but it was still a bathing suit. And bathing suits and underwear are basically the same thing; we just wear them in different settings. When you boil it down, the deciding factor is geography.

She didn't look at me but just stood quietly, as if doing so was comforting and had become easy. That too scared me. Finally she spoke. "You said make yourself at home, so I went looking for some aspirin. Found it in the upstairs bathroom. I love the tub. 'Magine your wife did too."

I nodded, wondering about my locked office door.

"I finished your book." She pointed toward the chair, then looked back out over the lake. "I can't imagine what it must have been like to be him." She shook her head and pointed her big toe at an ant that was walking around her feet.

I didn't follow. "What?"

"Crusoe."

"Oh."

"One minute he's sailing along, not a care in the

world, the next his ship is going down, he's tossed about like Jonah, and then . . . the island." She wrapped her arms tighter about herself.

I stood from my bucket and hung it on the wall behind me. My signal that this conversation was about to be over. I don't know why I said what I did, other than that I'd had a long time to think about it, and maybe because I was starting to remember. "Cindy?"

She looked at me.

"We are all shipwrecked. All castaways." I took a few steps forward, toward the boat launch and the edge of the dock. I dug my hands in my pockets and then turned, my eyes meeting hers. "One day, we all wake on the beach, our heads caked with sand, sea foam stinging our eyes, fiddler crabs picking at our noses, and the taste of salt caked on our lips." I turned slightly, glancing up at the shadow of Annie's frail frame swinging gently in the hammock, rocked by the wind. "And, like it or not, it is there that we realize we are all in need of Friday to come rescue us off this island, because we don't speak the language and we can't read the messages in the bottle."

I walked out to the edge of the dock, the corner closest to Charlie's house, and sat on the ledge, dipping my feet in the water. Moments passed before Cindy sat beside me. She sat down close, her shoulder and thigh rubbing against mine. She was entering my personal space, suggesting that, at least in this moment, it was space that we shared. More *ours* than mine or hers. Her touch was friendly and knowing, not invasive. But it was also terrifying.

She wiped her eyes, which were red and wet, and would not look at me, but studied the water below us. Our feet looked green and distorted. Below them, bream sped past followed by two good-sized bass.

"Did your wife teach you that?" she asked quietly.

"No," I said, shaking my head, "her absence did."

Chapter 45

Friday morning I woke early, got on the water with Charlie long before the sun was up, and left Royer a voice mail telling him when we'd be at the hospital. I also told him a couple of other things. Actually, I asked.

I asked that he perform Annie's procedure in one of the rooms near an exit and not on the cardiac floor— preferably the children's floor, where the walls were painted to look more like a child's room and less like a hospital. The less stress we inflicted upon Annie, the better.

There was an obvious benefit for me too, but I addressed the root of that one with my next question. I asked him to use nurses and other staff who had never met me. His staff, our staff, was loyal, and according to the records I'd been snooping into, I still knew most by name. In spite of my haggard appearance, they'd recognize me much the same way Shirley had in town. I wasn't ready for that, and I knew he'd understand. Finally, I asked him to check with accounting, and said he'd understand why once he did.

I picked up Cindy and Annie at their house just after daylight. They both slept most of the way to Atlanta. When I drove through Starbucks and ordered a latte, Cindy held her hand up, and her two fingers made the peace sign. I changed my order and asked for two.

Royer himself met us in the parking lot. He was standing behind a wheelchair, smiling. Inside the seat of the chair sat three stuffed animals: Winnie the Pooh, Tigger, and Eeyore. Annie stepped out the car and promptly hugged him, a sight that caused me to remember that Royer was everything good in a doctor.

Cindy grabbed her purse and introduced me to him. We shook hands, his engulfing mine, and exchanged formal pleasantries. Then he led us into the service entrance, up the elevator, and off at the children's floor, where we were met by bright walls, butterflies, and a hallway that looked like the yellow brick road. Annie lit up.

Royer steered us down a short hallway and into a large room in a corner of the hospital. It was perfect: a couch, an easy chair, a television with VCR, and a window that looked out over the northwest side of Atlanta. The room had been painted to look like the Hundred Acre Wood and Pooh's house.

Annie hopped up on the bed and grabbed something. "Look," she said, pointing it to Cindy, "our own remote control."

Cindy looked at us, embarrassed, and shrugged her shoulders. "The simple pleasures in life."

Royer pulled Cindy to the doorway and whispered just loudly enough for me to hear him above the cartoons Annie had selected. "Nurses will be in shortly to get her IV line in and take her vitals. I'll be back in about thirty minutes to drip some sleepy stuff down her arm."

Cindy crossed her arms and nervously scratched the outsides of both.

Royer continued, "The procedure might take all of fifteen minutes; then we'll let her sleep it off and spend the day parked in front of that TV." He put his hand on her shoulder and said, "Don't worry. Hang in there."

Cindy nodded and pulled on the tattered sweater she'd been carrying since the car.

I grabbed a magazine, tried to look dumb, and kept my glasses on until I was certain I'd never seen the nurse before. As other nurses came in, dressed in clown-printed scrubs and colorful plastic shoes, each talked with Annie. If Annie was nervous, she didn't show it. They got her into a gown, helped her put on her big red Clifford slippers, and swabbed her arm with alcohol.

She winced when they inserted the IV needle, and a tear slipped out of her left eye and down her cheek. Cindy, biting her own lip, caught it, and sat on the other side of the bed holding Annie's hand. I stood against the far wall, pressing my back hard against the window for fear that I might launch myself across that room and start acting like the someone I used to be.

They began a fluid drip to keep her hydrated and brought her a cup of ice, which they told her she could chew on. She didn't touch it, but quietly watched the television above us. After a few minutes of cartoons, she mashed the power button on the remote and then pressed the button on the side of her bed to raise her head. The mechanical bed raised her to a sitting position, and then she looked at me. "Reese?"

"Yeah," I said, prying my back from the wall and pulling up a chair next to Annie's bed.

"You be here when I get back?"

I nodded, afraid to speak for fear that my voice might crack.

She held out her hand, and I placed mine in it. She leaned closer and twitched her head, pulling me closer as if she wanted to tell me a secret. I leaned in, and Annie's eyes darted to Cindy, "Don't let her sit here and worry while I'm gone. There's a really good café on the third floor, so get her a piece of chocolate-raspberry cake with the yummy raspberry dressing."

I nodded and smiled.

"Oh, and—" She raised her hands around her neck and took off the sandal necklace. She unlocked the clasp, slid it from around her neck, and then laid it in my open palm. Her hands were shaking. "Hold this for me 'til I get back."

I looked down and held the small sandal in my hand. I ran my fingernail through the edges of the letters and raged against the torrent of tears that was spilling over the dam inside me. *I will give you a new heart . . .*

"You know what my mom told me when she gave it to me?"

I shook my head.

"She told me she had a dream where she saw my surgery and the doctor putting a new, strong heart in me. In her dream it was raining outside, and the clock on the wall read 11:11 and the doctor had a Band-Aid on the inside of his elbow."

"She tell you how it turned out?" I asked.

Annie smiled. "Nope. Said she woke up before we got to that part."

Royer walked in, sat down across from me, and took Annie's other hand. "Okay, big girl, here's the deal." He held up a syringe and eyed the line running out of her IV bag. "I'm going to shoot this sleepy stuff through that valve called the piggyback. Then, once you're good and snoring, we'll roll you down that hall while your aunt and your kind chauffeur sit and wait on you."

Annie liked him calling me her chauffeur. She also liked the part about her snoring.

"Then I'm gonna take a look at your heart. When I'm done, I'll roll you back in here and let you wake up at your leisure." From his pocket he pulled a small silver bell that looked like the kind the Salvation Army rings at Christmastime, and laid it in her lap. "If you need me before, after, or during, you ring this. You got it?"

Annie picked up the bell and rang it a few times. Royer stood and walked around my side of the bed, so I walked to the corner of the room and held up the wall.

Royer emptied the syringe into Annie's IV and said, "Okay, waiting on you."

Royer was walking out when Annie said, "Dr. Royer?"

He turned.

"You're forgetting something."

"Oh, yes, yes." Royer walked back over, knelt next to Annie's bed, and grabbed her hand. He closed his eyes, she closed hers, and Cindy sat on the end of the bed and held Annie's feet that were cozy beneath the sheets.

After a second of silence, Annie looked up at Royer and said, "You want to ring and I hang up?"

Royer shook his head. "You ring."

"God?" Annie said, as if He were sitting on the edge of the bed. "Please help Dr. Royer to see what he needs to do. Help Aunt Cici not to be scared and let her know that I'll be right back . . . and . . ." She paused, and her voice told me she had cracked into a large smile. "Thank You for my own personal chauffeur."

The single light above painted her in white, the monitors next to her flashed red and blue, and Royer looked huge kneeling next to the bed.

She looked to Royer and whispered, "Your turn."

Royer cradled Annie's tiny hand between his huge paws. He kissed her hand, pressed it against his forehead, and said, "Lord, You're the only one here who really knows what He's doing, so we're planning on You taking charge. You promised Annie something, and we're holding You to it. Forgive us if that's too

302

bold, but we don't have time to be timid. I got a feeling You're not finished with this one, not hardly—You're just barely getting started, so . . . bottom line, You're needed. It's time to clock in. Let me see what I need to and . . ." Royer paused, and his voice grew low and more steady. "Give this girl sweet dreams in the process."

I whispered "Amen" and watched as Royer kissed Annie on the forehead.

"See you in an hour or so."

Annie nodded; her eyelids had grown heavy, and she tried to speak, but her words were all connected and run together. Another minute, and she was asleep.

The nurses pushed the bed down the hall, leaving Cindy and me sitting in the room wondering where to start.

I took a stab. "How 'bout that chocolate cake?"

Cindy nodded, tucked her hands tighter under her armpits, and we walked out into the hall. When I pulled my hat down and put my sunglasses on, she raised an eyebrow but said nothing. She and Annie had warmed to my eccentricities, partly from kindness and partly just from having too much going on with themselves to figure someone else out. We walked to the café, and I kept my eyes to myself.

During the day, a hospital is an intense place. It's a cauldron of emotions, struggles, and people with short fuses facing few options. Peopled with nurses, doctors, patients, social workers, administrators, and family members, everybody is bouncing off one another like atoms in a centrifuge rapidly transiting between some-where and somewhere else.

But at night, while most of that remains true, a serene quiet falls along the halls that seems more in touch with not the gravity of life and death but the imme-diacy of it. No less critical but somehow more man-ageable. I always preferred working at night.

As Cindy and I walked the halls, the hospital was alive, pulsing with the smell of disinfectant, the sound of hushed tones and unguarded laughter, and the feel of unending possibilities. I loved this, the feeling of absolute and eternal optimism, the feeling that no matter how bad or no matter how dire the circum-stances or predictions, that until death has been declared and the sheet rolled up over the patient's eyes, that even beyond the flatline, anything is possible. Beneath the undercurrent of even the direst predic-tions, hope lives here. It creeps along the corridors, hangs from every corner of every room, and speeds down every gurney in search of a soul in need.

I ran my finger along the seam of the wallpaper and remembered one afternoon after Emma had undergone a round of tests and lay in her bed, recovering. I'd stop in and check on her every ten minutes or so, and about two in the morning, I asked her how she felt.

She opened heavy eyes, tilted her head, and said, "Reese, hope lives here, and death can't kill it."

Cindy bumped into me as a nurse passed by. I took a deep breath, as deep a breath as I'd taken in a long time, and filled every inch of me with the smell of what was so good and so familiar. It filled me, and I knew in part what I had not known in a long, long time—the doctor's high. The surge of all that I had missed, all that I had come to know and love, jolted through me like a thunderbolt at dawn. Then the image of Emma, cold, still, and unbreathing on the floor of the kitchen, passed across my eyes, flooded through my heart, and my mind only had one thought: Annie.

Cindy grabbed my arm and attempted to steady me as I swayed and banged my shoulder against the wall that led to the nearest nurses' station. "You okay?"

I didn't answer.

She placed her hand on my face, forcing my eyes to find hers. "Reese? You okay?"

The intercom overhead paged a doctor. I heard his name, I heard that he was needed in the OR, and I heard, "Stat!" When all that registered in my mind, and the pieces fell into place like a giant game of Tetris, something deep within me stirred. "Yeah." I nodded. "Just hungry, I guess."

We small-talked en route to the café, but our minds were elsewhere. Cindy, I knew, was trying not to think about Annie lying on that table with instruments probing her heart. I could think of nothing else.

I knew what Royer would be looking for, I knew how and where he'd look, and I knew how long it would take. And if I knew Royer, he'd make a video of the entire procedure under the guise of showing Cindy what he had done while I just happened to look on.

The café was brimming with people. I pulled the collar up on my unbuttoned flannel shirt, pulled my hat down, and we sat in a corner. If Cindy thought me curious, she didn't let on. We ordered chocolate cake and both nibbled.

On Emma's last visit to the hospital for some routine blood work, we had come here, sat two tables over, and ordered a milk shake. She had sipped, I had not, and we talked about life after the transplant. She had laughed easily, held my hand across the table, looked skinny beneath clothes that were once not so baggy, and tried to hide the eyes that were set so deep and so dark.

Every few minutes, doctors and nurses who knew us both would come to the table and wish her well. They'd pat her on the shoulder, shake my hand. Everyone just knew that we'd be having fun and laughter-filled conversations in the months to come. Nothing was more right, more deserving, more ordered out of a Norman Rockwell painting—Emma would live, and we would too, together, as it should be.

"Reese?" Cindy shook me. "You there?"

"Huh?"

"I've been talking for ten minutes, and I don't think you've heard a word I've said."

The cake was gone; somehow we'd eaten it all.

"I'm sorry. What were you saying?"

"I was saying that if Dr. Royer can't locate his old partner, or find another surgeon he thinks can do the job, it won't matter what he learns today."

"So where is this ex-partner? What happened to him?"

"Pulled a Houdini. All Royer would say was that he suffered a personal tragedy and left medicine. Royer thinks that if Jonathan Mitchell can recover from whatever took him out of medicine, he'll make one of the finest heart surgeons the world has ever known."

The sound of my own name shook me like a cold shower.

"Annie's prayed for over a year that we'd just run into him in the street. That he'd walk up and buy a cup of lemonade from her. She's sure that he'd know what she needed just as soon as he saw her and would want to help her."

We stood up and pushed in our chairs.

"I keep telling her that sometimes adults have reasons for doing things or not doing things that most kids just don't understand. But you know Annie. She's hardheaded."

We crossed the cafeteria, and I held the door for her.

"So every night," Cindy continued, starting down the hall, "she prays for Jonathan Mitchell. And even though I haven't met the guy, I already love him, because he's given Annie something that no other doctor except Royer has ever given her."

I looked confused. "What's that?" I said.

Cindy looked at me and raised her eyebrows matter-of-factly. "He's given her hope."

"And what if he doesn't show up?" I asked.

She shrugged and looped her backpack purse over

her shoulder. "It's not up to me, but this much I know—if anybody's got a direct line to God, it's Annie. If I've seen it once, I've seen it a dozen times. But—" She put one finger in the air and gave a knowing shake of her head. "If He's going to answer this one, He'd better hurry up, because His hourglass is running low on sand."

Chapter 46

We didn't have to wait long before nurses wheeled Annie's bed back into the room. She was quiet, and when they reattached her to all the machines at the end of her bed, she continued sleeping beneath the whitish glow of the fluorescent lights.

Royer followed a few minutes later. He checked the face numbers on the machines over Annie's head, and the connection to and tape around her IV, and then placed his hand on her cheek and forehead. One of the things I admired most about Royer was the way he so seamlessly switched between father figure and doctor. Seldom since meeting him had I not sat beside a patient's bed and asked myself, either consciously or unconsciously, *How would Royer do this?*

Finally he turned to Cindy. "She's fine. Other than one small hiccup, the test went great." He brushed the hair out of Annie's face and tucked it behind her ear. "She'll wake up in a couple of hours. I'm not opposed to keeping her overnight just as a precaution, so—"

Cindy raised her hand, and I could tell that the economic side of her brain had just clued in to what he was saying. The term *overnight* translated into higher bills, and she was trying desperately to keep those within lifetime-reachable limits. "But, Doc—"

"Nope," Royer cut her off and shook his head. He sipped his coffee and continued, "Here's what I saw . . ."

I stood in the shadows, pressed against the wall, listening to the echoes of remembrance that reverberate off a hollow heart. I was stuck in that horrible place, one I knew all too well—that narrow and slippery ridge of hope that rises above the pits of despair that live on each side.

It's a fast track to circling the drain.

"First, ASD. Atrial septal defect. Long story short . . . because the heart has had to work so hard for so long, it's grown bigger. It's a muscle. It'll respond that way. Even since her last surgery. That causes a couple of things to happen. It puts more pressure on itself, causing it to work less efficiently." Royer began to talk with his hands.

"While the heart can grow bigger in response to the exercise, the chest cavity is only so large. So it's compounding its own problem. The right atrium enlarges and sends multiple signals to the ventricle. Normally, the sinoatrial node sends a one-for-one signal from the top of the heart to the bottom. It's what creates the beat, the lub-dub. It's like a drill sergeant that determines the cadence for the march.

"When the atrium gets this big, all those different cells can't hear the signal, and it becomes like a radio with static on every channel. So to compensate, the atrium sends multiple signals. The ventricle hears all of them, so it naturally beats with each signal." Royer held up his right index finger. "But when the heart gets this big and flabby, the entire muscle doesn't know what the rest of the muscle is doing. The heart can't hear itself." He smiled. "When we say Annie has a big heart, we're not kidding."

Cindy faked a responsive smile and wrapped her arms tighter about herself while she braced for the bad news.

Royer continued, "So just to make sure, various portions of the muscle send their own signals. The ventricle receives all of them, and we get a confused heart. For every pump of the atrium, we might get two or three pumps of the ventricle. It's like two people dancing, arm in arm, but one is listening to Dean Martin"—he looked at me—"while the other is listening to Elvis."

Royer loves Elvis.

"They're just not in tune. And to make matters more complicated, she's also got what's called VSD, or ventricular septal defect. The ventricle gets big and floppy, and then becomes an ineffective pump. Bottom line, it's just worn out and needs a break. Once the ventricle gets like this, the atrium dilates, sends out several signals per heartbeat rather than just one, and we get what Annie feels every second of every day, multifocal atrial tachycardia. Meaning, whereas your resting heart rate is 60 beats a minute, hers is more like 130."

Deep inside, I smiled. Royer was still the best. I missed his bedside explanations, the care with which he gave his delivery. I took a deep breath and relaxed.

"Now, there's one more thing."

Cindy perked up as if she already knew all that he'd just told her.

"That hole I was telling you about, that's open when we're in the womb and closes when we're born?"

Cindy nodded.

"Well, Annie's is still open, and while it's probably not going to get any larger, it's not going to get any smaller either. This causes greater pressure at the exit holes of the heart than at the entrance, and reverses the flow. It's rare, and it's called Eisenmenger's syndrome."

Cindy's face faded to a shade of white as pale as the sheet next to her. I knew Royer wasn't telling her everything. I could read his body language and knew he was deliberating as to whether or not to give her all the results or all but one. I think my presence there shifted the balance.

Royer placed his fingers to his lips, paused, and lowered his voice. "I also found one other thing." He punched the intercom button to the nurses' station and said, "Jan? Can you patch in the last fifteen seconds of Annie's TEE?"

A lady quickly responded, "It'll be on channel 3."

Royer changed the channel, and pretty soon something that looked like a baby ultrasound appeared on the screen. Royer took a pen from his pocket and tapped the screen, but I had already seen it.

He circled the screen with the end of his pen and said, "There, right there is an area along the stitch line of her previous surgery that has weakened. The tissue has thinned, become more brittle. If, and I do say 'if,' Annie undergoes any violent stress or impact to her body, it could rupture."

Cindy held her hands to her mouth, looked at Annie, and said, "What's that mean?"

Royer took a deep breath. "Annie's condition is worsening on an exponential scale. She's not growing worse daily, she's getting worse by the minute."

Cindy sat down in a chair next to the bed and hid her hands in her face, sobbing quietly.

Royer continued, "This means we've still got some time, but . . . not much. With the right medicine, right care, right everything, Annie might have . . ." Royer pressed his lips together and thought hard. "Three months on the outside. Two is more like it."

Cindy shook under the quiet sobs, and tears fell out from between her fingers and off the insides of her palms.

I took a step closer, then stopped and took two steps back. Royer watched me, considered, and then returned to Cindy.

"We need to list her, find a donor, and get her transplanted." He pointed toward Annie's chest. "If that tissue ruptures before Annie gets a new heart, she'll have about two minutes before the pericardium fills up with her own blood and . . . she'll never make it to the hospital. I'm not even sure my old partner could help her then." He didn't look at me, but kept his eyes trained on Cindy, who sat hunched quietly next to Annie. She was wiping her eyes with the sheet and smearing mascara across the word *Hospital* stamped along the hem.

"Cindy." Royer's tone changed from father figure to doctor. "I need you to listen to me. I told you two years ago, this is a marathon, not a sprint. Take a deep breath, because it's going to get worse before it gets better."

Cindy looked up.

"I know a doctor in Macon. Admittedly he's my second choice, but I've worked with him, he's a good man, and he's had great success with kids. I've already talked with him."

Cindy smeared what remained of her mascara across her face and said, "It's not me. It's Annie. She's had a dream and she's convinced—"

"I believe Annie's hope could move mountains, but I'm not sure it'll bring Jonny Mitchell out of retirement. Given our options and what I saw this morning, we better go with option B. We no longer have the luxury of time."

Cindy looked at Annie and nodded. "Dr. Royer, I, um . . . we got turned down from the last bank, and . . ."

Royer cut her off, and his fatherly tone returned. "It's no longer an issue."

Cindy looked up, smearing her running nose along her sleeve. "What do you mean?"

"I mean," Royer said with a smile, "an anonymous

313

donor . . . or donors"—Royer knew better, but he threw that in anyway—"created a benevolence fund in Annie's name. Accounting called me just before you arrived. I meant to tell you this morning, but I was thinking about the surgery. Currently, the balance is enough to pay for your hospital bills for the next several years. Including the transplant."

Cindy looked at the floor, at Annie, at me, then back at Royer. "Who?"

Royer shrugged. "Don't know. They didn't say." He smiled. "That's why it's called anonymous. Atlanta's a pretty good town. People hear about needs, and it's not uncommon to wake up one morning and find that . . ."

"Yeah, but . . . ." Cindy worked her fingers across the keys to the calculator in her mind. "All this? And an entire transplant? That's close to $150,000."

Royer smiled and patted Annie's toes. "Actually the account balance is closer to $200,000. Whoever did it knew that she'd have follow-up care for years to come. Chances are good that you won't see another bill for close to a decade."

Cindy rested her head on the bed and placed her hand beneath Annie's.

Royer walked around the bed and put his hand on her shoulder, his back to me. "Hey, right now, Annie needs you to sit here quietly, paint her toenails, treat her like a kid with her whole life ahead of her. Just spend the day with her. Hold her hand when she wakes up. I'll probably keep her here, just to be safe. Matter of fact, I think I will." He glanced over his shoulder at me.

"It's looking like I'll be here tonight, and there's really nothing quite like a hospital at night. While the rest of the world is sleeping, it's a rather busy place. Besides, the more rest we can give her here, the more energy we can put back in her muscle banks. I'll check back in a little while."

When the sound of Royer's heels had faded down the hall, I walked over next to Annie, dug the chain from my pocket, clasped it around her neck, and laid the sandal flat across her chest as it rose beneath one more breath.

Cindy spent much of the day sitting quietly next to Annie's bed, stroking her hair and whispering to her. At 3:47 p.m., Annie opened her eyes lazily and looked around the room. Before she ever said a word, her right hand came up from under the sheet and unconsciously felt for the sandal. Then her eyes found Cindy, who had fallen asleep on the edge of the bed. Annie searched the remainder of the room, and when her eyes found me, she closed them again and slept until 4:32, when she woke again and whispered, "I didn't wake up."

Cindy tried to smile and said, "I know, baby. I know."

Cindy held a water cup with a straw to Annie's mouth.

When Annie swallowed, which was painful and would be for a few days, she said with a half smile, "Hey, I was just wondering if, while I was asleep, you guys went ahead and found a heart and put it inside me without telling me. That way, we could just skip the whole waiting thing that comes next."

She and Cindy spent the evening watching movies, sending their personal chauffeur for non-hospital food and napping while I watched them.

About midnight, I stepped from the corner of the room and walked out into the hall. Cindy was asleep on the pullout sofa, and Annie had dozed off some time ago. The shift change had come and gone an hour ago, but that wasn't what brought me out of the room.

About eight minutes earlier, a helicopter had landed atop the hospital on the helipad. Given the chatter on the intercom and the excitement among the nurses, I knew Royer would be in the thick of things about now.

I climbed the service stairs—the "back way" that doctors used when they didn't want to be delayed—punched the numbers of Emma's birthday into the keypad, and waited to see if the light would turn green. When it did, I realized that Royer still had hope. I pushed on the door I had sworn I would never walk through again. The air was cold, the hallway clear, and at the far end stood the nurses' station and a half-sleeping security guard I didn't know.

OR2 sat at the other end of the hall, where the corridors crawled with nurses and ICU personnel. The cameras would catch my every move, but they'd go back to them only in the event that I slipped up. If no one knew I was here, they'd have no need to go back and look.

I slipped through a few side doors, crossed a hall,

grabbed a white doctor's coat from the back of a supply closet, and tied a surgeon's cap over my head. I slipped into the doctors' locker room and into a pair of blue scrubs and covers for my shoes, and grabbed a stainless clipboard. I walked through a back door, down a small hallway traveled only by doctors, and once again punched Emma's birth date into the keypad. The light turned green, I climbed the single flight of stairs, and walked into the observation post above OR2. The far wall was constructed of tinted one-way glass. I crept up to the glass, looked down upon the nine-member team, and started looking over Royer's shoulder.

He had just removed the old, diseased heart and placed it into a stainless bowl held by another doctor, who immediately left the room to go study that heart for several days, maybe even weeks, because dead hearts tell us much. Another doctor, whom I didn't know, stood next to the red-and-white Igloo. Upon Royer's silent command—an open palm and accompanying nod—the doctor reached in, grabbed the cold, lifeless heart, removed it from the plastic bag, and put it in Royer's hand.

Royer placed it in the patient's chest and began his work. Twenty-seven minutes later, he brought the patient "off pump" to test a series of stitches; then, satisfied with what he saw, requested that the patient be placed back "on pump" while he stitched another artery. After fifty-one minutes, Royer looked to the doctor across from him, who nodded, and the two requested the patient once again be taken off pump. Royer released one final clamp, blood filled the heart, turning it a bright, vibrant red, and then the true miracle occurred.

It beat on its own.

In all my years fixing hearts, it never ceased to amaze me how a lifeless, unbeating, and cold heart that had not been inside a human chest for almost four hours could be removed from ice water, placed inside another's chest, and, when filled with blood, beat as though it had never quit.

Life is where the blood flows.

A minute later, the heart pumping perfectly and the patient once again alive, Royer stepped back, broke scrub, and nodded to the other doctor, who began closing the patient. For the patient, a new life. For Royer, it was simply another day at the office.

I sat down in the chair behind me and took it all in. Another man will see his children grow up, get to know his grandchildren, make love with his wife, go fishing, watch a movie, or drive the outskirts of Burton in an old wooden boat.

The amazing thing about transplantation, aside from the fact that it worked, was that it allowed people to feel again. The thing I liked best about my previous life was the first smile when a patient woke up. Because with that smile, I knew that I hadn't simply given that person a new pump, I had given him or her a new pump that allowed that person to live, to express emotion. It was the smile, even more than the first beat of the heart, that told me it had worked.

The heart doesn't just pump blood, it is our source of emotion. Out of it and because of it, people laugh, cry, get angry, grow sad, know joy, empathize, live with a full range of emotions.

Yes, the road after transplantation is not without its challenges. They are multiple and complex. The patient will forever maintain a regimen of some dozen medications a day, designed to force the body to accept the alien organ. And the doctor has to specifically and proactively target and weaken the immune system so that it will not reject the new heart. But given the choice, the pain of surgery, the agony of recovery, the long road back to health, and the constant maintenance of it, we still meet people who would give anything for the chance to lie down on our table and let us cut their hearts out.

When I turned to leave, I saw the yellow sticky note taped to the glass. Just three words, in Royer's handwriting, characteristically visible due to the all-caps: *ABOVE ALL ELSE . . .*

I crept back to Annie's room to find Royer bent over the bed checking her vitals. Cindy lay sleeping quietly on the pullout against the wall. In stocking feet, I slipped into the shadows and watched him. Royer was meticulous. He recorded some notes in her chart slipped into the foot of her bed.

As he stood to go, Cindy jerked, sat upright, and said quickly, "She okay?"

"Fine," Royer whispered. "Just checking before I

head home. Go back to sleep."

She put her head down, tucked both her hands under the pillow, and drifted off.

Royer stood, his starched white jacket draped with stethoscope and the day's notes, his blue scrubs wrinkled and splattered. Married to his job, he had sacrificed his love life at the altar of this hospital. He still dated, but at fifty-four, he lived mostly at the hospital and seldom went home, which was nothing more than a condo a few blocks away stuffed with some never-used furniture.

His bedside manner, his professionalism, his huge hands, kind smile, and tender voice—he was everything good in a doctor. In all my time here, in all my time across the table from him, we'd never had a cross word, never even close. Royer and I worked the way Charlie and I rowed. In perfect unison. And for the first time since Emma's death, I missed that.

He walked out, and I slipped from behind the door, sat in a chair opposite Annie, and wished I had Emma's letter.

I dozed fitfully, because my dream wouldn't let me sleep. No matter how hard I tried to pour that water, I just couldn't hold it on my own. It just got too heavy.

When streaks of the morning broke through the glass and lit my face with a white glow, I finally realized the one thought that had kept me awake all night. Something I had known and yet forgotten, something so simple yet so profound, something I promised Emma I'd never forget.

While the heart is an amazing organ, transplantation doesn't allow you to choose the emotions you want. It's not a Mr. Potato Head. You elect to go ahead with transplantation, and you get the whole package. That means with great joy, you also get immense sadness. It's not like a rib eye, where you can trim the fat before you eat it.

Transplant patients are lucky in one regard. They are guaranteed they will never physically feel heart pain again. When you transplant a heart, you sever all the nerve endings leading to it. Given current medical techniques and knowledge, it is impossible to reattach those nerve endings. Arteries yes, nerves no. So, while the patient gets the benefit of emotions, they do not get the burden of pain associated with them.

If they have another heart attack, they don't feel it. They could have a complete and total blockage of the entire heart, the most massive attack to ever hit a human being, and they wouldn't know something had happened until they quit breathing and passed out. About like an engine running out of gas. No signal other than a last sputter, and then silence. That's why transplanting children is so delicate—because if they don't recognize the signs, and if their communication skills aren't fully developed enough, they'll never know anything is wrong, and you, as their doctor, probably won't either, because they can't tell you.

It struck me as I sat not sleeping, letting the sunlight warm my face, that I had taken the last five years and attempted to sever the nerve endings in my own heart.

I had taken a scalpel and carefully carved a swath around my own heart, cutting the nerves, while allowing the arteries to stay intact.

Self-diagnosis is painful at best. Or, to quote Dr. Trainer, "The doctor who treats himself has a fool for a patient, and a fool for a doctor."

And while medicine is helpless to regenerate the nerves, the heart can self-generate them, regrowing those tied to emotions in literally a matter of milliseconds. All they needed to take root, sprout, and begin the path back around my hardened and diseased heart was to talk with Royer at the bedside of a patient, watch Annie bravely undergo anesthesia and then simply breathe beneath a labored heart, and listen to Cindy care for everybody but herself.

And there, not far from the surface, floated the memories of Emma and Charlie. After more than thirty years of studying the heart, more than a hundred transplants and countless other surgeries, I could not cut out my own heart. I looked down, saw the tears that were now soaking my shirt, and realized that I hadn't even come close.

Chapter 47

Breakfast came early, and Annie ate as if she hadn't seen food in a week. Nurses from all around the hospital had heard she was in and awake, and began dropping in unannounced. That proved too risky for me, so I told Cindy I was going to get a paper, and stayed gone until she called me on my cell phone and asked me to bring the Suburban around.

Mike Ramirez accompanied the nurse who rolled Annie out. I clicked the door unlocked and rudely sat behind the wheel while Mike helped Annie out of the chair and into the car. Cindy grabbed Annie's new supply of stuffed animals and hugged Royer, who had walked out behind them. Mike pushed the chair back inside, a relief to me, and Royer leaned in the window. He looked back at Annie, then at Cindy, and his face switched once again from father to doctor.

The switch told Cindy that she needed to prepare herself. She sat upright and took a deep breath.

Royer said, "I'll list Annie tonight." He put his hand on her shoulder and said, "It's time."

Cindy nodded and said, "Will you try to reach Dr. Mitchell one more time?"

Royer nodded. "Already did. You might say . . . I left him a message. If I don't hear from him by tomorrow, I'll call Macon. Basically, once we list her, we could go any day. Could be tomorrow, could be next month, could be three months."

He handed Cindy a plastic bag containing two pagers and one cell phone. "Keep these close. Pagers on you both twenty-four hours a day. Keep the cell phone with you, and don't forget to charge it." He smiled. "The phone is equipped with a GPS, so if I need to find you with the helicopter, we'll be in good shape. Basically, if that pager goes off, and your cell phone is on, I'll already know where you are. Oh, and when that pager goes off? You'll need to be thinking about getting to the hospital."

Cindy held the bundle in her hands like a map that led to the lost treasure in the Sierra Madre.

He pointed at both of them. "Remember, never without your pager. Even in the shower, I want it close enough to touch."

Cindy patted Royer on his wrist and mouthed, *Thank you.*

"You bet. Now, get her home, get her some rest, but don't treat her like an invalid. Let her get out. Some sunshine will do her some good. She's still very much alive. Let's treat her that way."

We weren't even out of the parking lot before Annie said, "Reese? Did you hear that my test went well and that I didn't wake up?"

"Yeah," I said, looking in the rearview mirror. "I did."

Cindy handed Annie her pager, and they both clipped them to the waistlines of their clothes. Cindy spent a few minutes getting familiar with the cell phone. Finally she slipped it into her purse and smiled sheepishly. "I've never had a cell phone before. Hope I can figure out how to use it before I need to."

We stopped at the well for lunch. I fed them as much as they cared to eat and then drove them home.

When we turned into the drive, the sight was not pretty. Condensation was running down the insides of the windows, and a steady stream of water was bubbling up from under the door and spilling across the concrete front porch. Cindy covered her mouth, and I said, "Wait here."

I opened the door to find the entire house soaked from ceiling to carpet. I sloshed into the kitchen beneath a spray of water from the busted pipe in the ceiling and discovered that a crawl-space pipe had sprung a leak. From the multiple sag holes in the ceiling, it looked like a tiny leak had initially emitted a fine and quiet spray until it split the pipe, deluging the ceiling. The attic river then sought lower ground and found it. Three inches of water stood in the bedroom, and the living room was no better. Annie's stuffed animals looked like they'd been invited to a swimming party. I could turn the water off, but drying out the house would take the better part of a week, and by that time black, sporous mold would be growing off the walls like sprayed-in insulation.

I went back outside.

Cindy asked, "Do I even want to look?"

"It's pretty bad," I said. "Listen, let's worry about this tomorrow. Right now, let's get you two to my house."

I switched off the main water line and left the doors open. The rest would have to wait.

I got them settled at my house, then returned to theirs and collected a few things they had asked for. I opened the windows and spent three hours mopping out as much water as I could, then set three floor fans blowing across the house.

Looking at the mess, I phoned Cindy and asked, "Do you want to contact your insurance agent and have them send someone out while I'm still here?"

"No need."

"Why not?"

"You might say we're . . . self-insured." Cindy paused, and I thought I heard her chewing on a fingernail. "Well, anyway. We didn't have much, so losing what we had doesn't hurt as much as if we were running over with stuff and money."

Annie slept through the afternoon while Cindy spent it pacing back and forth atop the boathouse, thinking through her options. I tinkered with whatever I could get my hands on in the workshop, which wasn't much. I had finished their table and benches and didn't feel like tackling the Hacker. So I cleaned tools, waxed the hull of the shell, and watched Cindy through the crack of the sliding door.

When she descended the stairs along with the sun, I decided I'd try to cheer her up. "Hey, I wanted to show you something."

Cindy walked in, and I led her to the table and pulled off the canvas cover. I slid out the benches and pointed with an open palm. "It's for you and Annie."

Her mouth dropped and she sat gingerly, as if she were afraid it might break.

"Don't worry, it's pretty stout. It'd take a tornado to rip this apart."

She ran her hands across the top, following the grain,

and then said, "You made this?"

"Well . . . yeah. It's not—"

"It's incredible," she interrupted. "I've never seen anything like it. What's it made out of?"

"This is heart of pine. About two years ago Charlie and I salvaged it out of an old barn like yours, but a bit older. The wood itself comes from the 1840s."

Cindy's eyes grew large and round, and the corners filled with tears.

"I put it together with mortise and tenon. Meaning, there's not a nail in it. It's all sort of dovetailed together."

She ran her fingers along the edges, holding back the flood for as long as she could. Finally, she broke. After a minute or two, her shoulders were shaking, and a mixture of both fear and anger poured out of her.

I sat next to her, unsure whether I should just sit or put an arm around her. She fell against me and buried her face in my chest.

"Reese," she said through the sobs, "I don't care about my stuff, I really don't. I don't have anything anyway. But that little girl up there is barely clinging to life . . ." She sat upright. "Why? God knows what's going on down here. He's not unaware. But why all this? Huh? Why?"

I didn't attempt to answer.

Ten minutes later, my shirt soaked and her tear ducts empty, she sat upright and shook her head. "I have tried to be so strong for so long. First my sister, then

Annie. Now the house. I just don't know how much more I can take."

Cindy was starting to show the signs classic of all family members who endure alongside the patient waiting a transplant. I'd seen it before. Only difference was, Cindy was right. She had borne this burden alone and for a long time. She'd worked two jobs, sometimes three, sacrificed anything she'd wanted to provide for Annie and now, at the end of it, she felt as though she'd failed. Or was failing. She was also looking at the possibility of being left alone.

We walked out onto the dock, where Charlie sat soaking wet with Georgia lying just as wet, sprawled across his lap.

"Hey, buddy," I said.

He waved. "Sorry to barge in on you, but I heard some noise that I hadn't heard over here . . . at least in a long time . . . and I guess I got a little panicky."

I turned to Cindy. "How long's it been since you've been more than a hundred feet from Annie?"

Cindy looked at me, a little unsure, but said, "Long time. Why?"

"Would you be okay if Charlie babysat for an hour or so?"

Cindy looked up at the house, then down at Charlie, then over at me. "No offense, but what if—"

I broke in. "She'll be fine. Nothing's going to happen to her today, and I'd like to show you something. We won't be gone either long or far."

Cindy looked back up at the house and said, "Well . . ."

"Wait here," I said. I walked upstairs, pulled Annie off the couch where she was awake and reading, and brought her down to my hammock.

So, while Charlie and Georgia entertained Annie atop the boathouse, I slid the shell into the water and helped Cindy into her seat. We eased out of the creek and into the Tallulah. Cindy's shoulders tensed up as the boathouse fell out of sight. I tapped her on the back and said, "Okay, no free rides."

She grabbed the oars, sank them in rhythm with me, and the two of us rowed upriver against the smooth and slow-rolling current. Ten minutes in, and some of the tension had eased. Another five and Cindy was sweating. Five more and she was smiling and beginning to see the world around her.

We slid under the bridge, steered up the smaller creeks, and after half an hour she turned, looked around, and waved her hand across the landscape. "I had no idea."

"You ought to see it at sunup."

She looked behind the boat, at the perfect circles appearing and then disappearing behind the boat. "I'd like that."

After an hour she said, "Reese, this is great. Really, but . . ."

I nodded. "I know." I turned us around and said, "We'll get there a lot faster if you help."

She smiled and dug in her oars, and I watched her row. When we arrived at the boathouse, Charlie was doing his best blind-man routine and Annie was laughing so hard she was holding her stomach.

I fixed some soup and cold tuna salad and spread dinner across the porch for the four of us while Annie showered.

Cindy hollered down from upstairs. "Reese? You mind if I borrow your tub?"

The question stopped me. Charlie, standing next to me and slowly stirring the soup, turned toward me and nodded. And I guessed, as I thought about it, he was right. Emma would have wanted that.

"Sure!" I said. "Towels are in the cabinet behind."

An hour later, after Annie, Charlie, and I had finished supper, Cindy walked down the stairs, jelly-legged and pruny. Her hair was pulled up in a bun, sweat still beaded around her temples, and her cheeks were flushed. "That," she said, pointing upstairs, "is the best tub I've ever sat in."

Charlie smiled, and I brought Cindy a plate.

The four of us watched the sun go down, then Charlie and Georgia swam home. When Annie fell asleep on the couch around ten, I carried her upstairs, and Cindy pulled down the sheets in my guest bedroom. I walked to the door, and she followed.

She stood leaning against the half-closed door and stopped me just before I walked back downstairs. "Reese."

I looked up.

"Thanks for today. For listening. I'll be better tomorrow."

I nodded. "I know. Get some rest."

I sat on the porch, hovering above a cup of cold tea and listening to Cindy shuffle around and turn out the lights.

At midnight I unlocked the office, grabbed the letter from the top drawer of my desk, and walked out into the moonlight. It was getting cooler. A light breeze filtered off the lake and rattled the leaves, which were starting to turn varying shades of red and yellow. The stars were many, and the moon cast my shadow along the steps. I grabbed a candle from the woodshed, climbed into my hammock, and lit the wick.

I held the letter up to the stars, up to the moon, and then over the candle. Unable to make out anything, I slid my finger inside the tab and held it there. Caught once again.

Upstairs, coming from the window of the guest room, I heard Annie cough. She coughed once, then twice, then almost twenty times in a row. I saw a light turn on, heard the bathroom sink running. Annie quit coughing, the light clicked off, and it was quiet once again.

A moment later, Charlie and Georgia appeared on his dock across the way. He stood listening, then looked up to where he knew I was swinging.

He called softly, "You hear that?"

I looked up at the house, then down at Charlie. "Yes."

He waited a long moment, then spoke. "You doing what I think you're doing?"

I looked at the letter. Next to me the candle flickered

and wax spilled around me on the wood. "Yeah."

Charlie nodded and waited another long, pregnant moment. Just about the time I thought he was going to turn and walk into his house, he looked up again and said, "Stitch?"

I didn't answer. I knew what he wanted.

Charlie waited, then spoke again. "Jonny?"

It'd been a long time since Charlie had called me that. I stood and walked to the railing, the water shining black below me.

"Yeah, Charlie."

"Please . . . please read the letter." Charlie turned, patted Georgia, who ran ahead of him, and then climbed the stairs, holding the rope railing to guide him.

I sat in the hammock, placed my finger beneath the flap, and pushed against the glue that had held fast for so long. Finally I pushed, and the paper tore open. I pulled out the letter and held the candle close. A gentle breeze ushered itself up off the lake and blew out my candle. I didn't bother to relight it. The moon was all I needed.

Dear Reese . . .

After Emma's death, I had started going by my middle name because, one—it allowed me to hide, and two—it was the name she used for me when we were alone.

Remember, I am not the only one. There are others. And we all cry, "Be near me when my light

332

is low, when the blood creeps, and the nerves prick and tingle; and the heart is sick, and all the wheels of Being slow. Be near me when the sensuous frame is rack'd with pains that conquer trust; and Time, a maniac scattering dust, and Life, a Fury slinging flame."

Do this, Reese. Do this for me, but more importantly, do this for the others like me who cry like the cardinal on our windowsill. I love you. I will always love you.

Yours, Emma

I stood from the hammock, walked downstairs, and pulled what I needed from the woodshop. I constructed my small boat, slid the sail into place, doused it in lighter fluid, and pushed it off. It floated smoothly, aided by the breeze, and when it caught the outskirts of the Tallulah, it turned south and headed toward the moon. A few hundred yards later, the candle burned down, lit the fuel, and the sail rose in flames. In the distance, the flames climbed, sputtered, then disappeared into the black beneath.

I am ashes where once I was fire.

I stood on the beach, straddling that narrow ridge upon which I had built my home. I turned, not really knowing where to go or what to do, and saw Cindy highlighted by the moon, her faded, ankle-length flannel gown almost translucent in the light. She didn't say a word, but on her face, I saw shared pain.

"I need to show you something," I said.

She swallowed and nodded slowly.

"You're going to be angry, but I need to show you." I took her by the hand, led her upstairs, and unlocked the door to my office. I turned on the light and stepped aside so she could go in.

On the walls hung the diplomas and degrees and special medical recommendations of Jonathan Reese Mitchell. Hung about the room and sitting on the desktop and shelves were pictures of Dr. Jonny Mitchell with his patients—each one smiling and alive. On my desk sat a stethoscope, a key to a small city in south Georgia given me by the mayor whose bypass had gone flawlessly, various old retired pacemakers or mechanical hearts that I used for paperweights. Beneath the window sat a teaching model of the heart, about the size of a child's football. Filtered in and around all of this were pictures of Emma and me. Charlie was in many of them as well. And scattered around my desk were the medical files and records of Annie Stephens I had retrieved off-line.

Cindy walked the perimeter of the room, her mouth open, her fingers walking the edges of the frames and the lines of the windowsill. Finally she sat at my desk, saw the files, the work in progress, and all the pieces fell into place with a thunderclap.

Waves of emotion flashed across her face like the northern lights: confusion, anger, hurt, betrayal. Each appeared, disappeared, bled seamlessly into the next. "How could you?" she whispered.

"It's a long story."

Cindy rose from the chair, walked to the edge of the office, slid down against the wall, and tucked her knees up into her chest. She didn't say a word, but her rigid body language told me all I needed to hear.

I took a deep breath and started with the pictures of Emma and Charlie and me as kids. I told her about our childhood, Emma's medication, the faith healers, her parents' struggle, high school, our falling in love, college, getting married, medical school, Dr. Trainer, Nashville, my fascination with transplantation, the trip to Atlanta, Emma's worsening condition, and our dinner with Royer. I told her about my work, about putting together the team, and then about our last weekend at the lake. And when I got to that story, I told her almost all of it.

Four o'clock in the morning found us spent, aching, not knowing what to say.

After a silence that lasted a long time, Cindy spoke in a broken whisper. "Reese, I'll only ask you one time. If you say no, I'll kindly ask you to take us home. But if you say yes, I want you to say it completely. I don't want half of you, because Annie needs all of you. I want to know right now, will you save Annie?"

Sitting on the floor, beneath the shadow of all that I once was and everything I had once hoped to be, I said yes. The word formed slowly and came up from someplace deep, recessed behind my soul where the nerve endings to my heart tingled with feeling.

Cindy took a deep breath, looked around the room, and shook her head. And for a long time, we just sat there, letting the truth sink in, or drain out, depending on where you sat. We didn't speak for almost an hour.

I finally stood and said, "I've got one more thing to do. I need to tell Charlie."

She looked confused. "Doesn't he know everything already?"

"Not everything."

"Do I?"

"No, but I need to tell him first."

She nodded, and as I walked out onto the dock, I turned and saw that she had followed me out and was standing on the porch, arms crossed but shoulders relaxed. She called softly, "You mind if I call Royer?"

"No. I mean, I don't mind. Tell him I'll be in touch." I looked across the lake, then back at her. "Maybe later this afternoon."

I dived in, pulled myself up on Charlie's dock, and was met by Georgia's licking. She wagged her tail and then ran back over to Charlie, who sat on the bottom steps, harmonica in hand, playing quietly to himself. He heard me climb up on the dock, wring the water out, and then sit down beside him.

He spoke first. "You told her?"

"Yeah."

"How'd she take it?"

I looked through the trees and saw her rocking slowly on the porch, looking out over the lake. "I'm not sure . . . I mean, she's shocked and she's angry, but I guess she took it okay."

Charlie nodded and turned the harmonica in his fin-

336

gers. "So you finally came over here to say the thing that's been on the tip of your tongue for five years and yet you haven't had the guts to tell me?"

I was stunned.

Charlie leaned against the railing and turned to me. He ran his fingers along my face and then held my face in his hands. "Stitch . . . I'm blind, not stupid." He put his hands down and waited.

"Somewhere in medical school," I said, looking down at my hands, ashamed, "I began taking them. I'm not excusing it, but between the days on end with no sleep, the pressures and the responsibilities, I found what I needed in several different meds. They allowed me to stay awake long hours, work more focused, and then sleep short amounts of time." I paused. "They also allowed me to come home heavy with sleep, lie in bed with Emma, and listen to her heart beat." I closed my eyes and ran my fingers through my hair. "I wanted . . . I wanted to know that she was alive. The drugs let me live beyond what my body was capable of. They let me . . ." I shook my head.

Charlie took a deep breath and let it out slowly.

"That went on through my residency, through my specialty in transplantation. I told myself that once we got past the surgery, I'd cut back, cut them out altogether, go someplace to get clean if I had to, that I was only doing it for Emma, for us. But that never happened. The night Emma died, I had . . . I had taken several earlier in the day . . . more than I'd ever taken, to help me through the transplant of a lady named Shirley.

337

When I got home, I was coming down and . . . by that time, I hadn't slept in almost four days. Then we laid down, and I couldn't hold it off anymore. I crashed.

"When I woke and heard the crash in the kitchen, I was so . . . well, I hadn't been that tired in a long time. For the last week, I'd been trying to plan, put the team together, think ahead, make sure I had everything I needed . . ." I was quiet for a moment. "I think she tried to wake me for probably close to thirty minutes. Slowly at first, then more . . . more violently as her pain grew."

Charlie ran his fingers along my arm and felt the faint scars of Emma's claw marks.

"Charlie, if she'd been able to wake me . . . we wouldn't be having this conversation."

Charlie stood, walked to the edge of the dock, sank his hands in the water, and splashed his face. Then he sat down against a piling and pulled his knees up just as the first signs of the sun crept above the trees.

"Stitch," he said, "I never expected to see my sister graduate high school, let alone have a twenty-first birthday. And if you'd told me when we were kids that I'd get to stand as the best man in her wedding, I'd have said you were smoking something. Emma lived to be thirty because you gave her the hope that she might live past that." Charlie shook his head.

"That girl loved you, brother. You gave her twenty more years than anyone else on the planet could have ever given her. That had little to nothing to do with your ability as a doctor, but it had everything to do with you as a person. You put a new heart in Emma a long time ago, it just wasn't the kind you were thinking of."

He laughed to himself. "Hope is an amazing thing. I saw it in Emma, saw it with my own eyes." Charlie stood, walked over to me, and squatted.

I looked up and saw his chiseled face searching mine.

"I was thinking just today about Helen Keller and the day Annie Sullivan took her down to the pump house and thrust her hand beneath the flowing water and then wrote w-a-t-e-r in her hand. When Helen realized that cool, liquidy stuff flowing through her fingers was w-a-t-e-r, something inexplicable happened. She said that 'living word awakened her soul, gave it light, hope, joy, and set it free.'"

Charlie stood up and reached for my hand. I gave it to him, and he walked me to the edge of the dock, knelt down, thrust my hand into the water, and brought his face just inches from mine. I felt his breath on my face and saw the strain behind his eyes while the tears cascaded off his face. Charlie's words were pained. "Close your eyes."

I did.

He waved my hand through the water and said, "You were that water for Emma." Charlie leaned in closer. "I'd like my eyes back, Reese, but I'm not waiting around. I'm living. And that's the thing. You're not. I'm soaking it in, feeling every minute, and you're the walking dead." He gripped my face with a stern hand and turned my chin up toward my house.

"Emma died. Not you. But I swear, you might as well have. Now, there's a little girl up there who's God's spitting image of my sister. Some people never get their chance at redemption, but . . ." He let go and shook his head. "Yours is up there sleeping."

I walked to the edge and stood, staring back at Charlie. "Charlie . . . I'm . . ."

"You're one of the smartest people I've ever known, but you don't always catch on too fast."

"How's that?"

"I forgave you the night it happened. How else do you think I've been living here across the creek from you? If I was all torn up about it, you think I'd be living here, day in and day out, rowing up and down this lake? I don't even like to row."

"You don't?"

"No." Charlie laughed. "It's boring as all get out, and it's not like the scenery is any good."

"How come you never told me?"

Charlie shrugged. "You're my best friend. Besides, it gets me out of the house and keeps my heart in shape. And that's important," he said, laughing and patting his chest, " 'cause Lord knows I don't want you cutting on me."

He pointed to the house while Georgia leaned against his leg. "Go on. You got some explaining to do, and the little girl ain't gonna understand it in the same way the woman did."

"Yeah," I said, looking back at the house, "I know that."

Chapter 48

Annie lay on a reclining chair, surrounded by pillows and a blanket, a picture of Emma ten years ago.

I sat down and she sat up. "Annie, I want to tell you a story."

Cindy sat close by, elbows on her knees, hands tucked under her chin.

"When I was your age, I fell in love with a girl whose heart was very much like yours."

"What? You mean sick?"

"No." I shook my head and smiled. "Full of love."

Annie smiled too, enjoying the game we seemed to be playing.

"As we grew older, we did discover that her heart was like yours in another way. It too was sick. Very sick."

"As sick as mine?"

"In some ways, worse. In other ways, not so bad. On a scale of one to ten, you two are bringing up the bottom end."

Annie nodded like she already knew that.

I continued. "So, thinking I could make her better, I spent most of my life studying how to do just that. Eventually . . . I became a doctor . . . and got pretty good at fixing sick hearts."

Annie began to look confused and listened more intently.

I took her hand and placed it inside mine. "I even

took good hearts out of brain-dead people and—"

Annie's face turned white.

"—put them in people who needed them."

Her look of disbelief grew.

I nodded. "Dr. Royer was my partner and—"

Annie interrupted me. "You're the miracle maker?" She looked around the room as the conversation swirled about her mind.

"Let me show you something." I held out my hand and led her to the office. She turned in a slow circle, looking all around. I started to speak, but she stopped me.

"How come you didn't . . . why . . ."

I picked up a picture of Emma, taken just weeks before she died. "Because I made some mistakes and . . . I've never really stopped paying for them."

Annie looked at the picture, then at me. "Did your wife die because of something you did?"

I stood for a moment while the question settled in me. "Yes."

"Did you do something wrong?"

I nodded.

Annie sat down and looked around the room for several minutes. Finally she stood and walked into my arms and laid her head on my shoulder. She was pale, tired, breathing shallow breaths.

I carried her out to the porch and set her in a chair. Cindy wrapped her in a blanket. Annie finally opened her eyes and looked at me. The look was transparent and deep, and both scared and soothed me. Finally she said, "Will you be my doctor?"

For the first time in more than five years, I took in a breath deep enough to fill me. "Yes."

Chapter 49

A month passed. A month of long days, quiet nights, and every minute attuned to the possible rattling hum of a pager vibrating across the tabletop. To simplify all our lives, Cindy and Annie stayed at my house. With no mold in the air, Annie improved slightly, even regaining some strength. Cindy too. She relaxed, slept a little more, and some of the color returned to her face—a face that never failed to greet me with a smile. Charlie seemed to like his new neighbors, because most nights he'd entertain us with his humorous antics and harmonica.

I gave Termite a job planing the wood at my warehouse up in the hills and working with Charlie and me on the Hacker. He was good too. And when Annie, standing atop the boathouse, told him that I was going to be her doctor, he thumbed a cigarette and slammed the Zippo across his thigh. When he had drawn deeply, turning the tip bright red, he exhaled away from her and looked at me, his eyes misty. "That's good."

Sometimes I think that hell is two places: it's a place you end up, but it's also a place that you live before you get there. I don't know if the devil's got horns and a spear for a tail, but I don't think that's the point. The point is that hell is separate from love. If Lucifer knows anything, he knows that. And ever since Emma left, I'd known the same thing. It's a lonely, desolate place.

With Annie and Cindy roaming about my house, making things pretty, fussing over things that had never been a concern, something inside me stirred. It had a sweet smell. A sweet feeling. And every night, while they slept in the room next to mine, I walked to the dock and basked in the warmth of it.

Because Cindy had learned how to save money on just about everything, I sat on a chair atop the boathouse one afternoon and succumbed to a haircut. A real one. She cropped it close around my neck and ears. Emma would have loved it.

Charlie ran his fingers over my head and said with a smile, "I remember you. Seems like we've met somewhere before."

I also hung a mirror in the bathroom and shaved. And when I walked back downstairs where the girls were setting the table for dinner, I noticed Cindy watching me out of the corner of her eye.

Charlie returned to his old self and, despite his confession regarding rowing, met me every morning on the dock. Not a day went by that he didn't pop in unannounced and uninvited. He resumed his bingo nights and dancing lessons; one afternoon he waved his cane from his dock. He was dressed in the blue and white seersucker suit, top hat, penguin wingtips, hair slicked back.

"Your hair looks rather slick," I said. "You need

some help changing that oil?"

He smiled and turned around like a model on the runway. "Nope, I change it every three thousand miles whether I need to or not."

We ate several times a week at The Well, where Davis created a new menu item called the Annie Special: grilled chicken, mustard, French roll, with a side of coleslaw and one scoop of chocolate ice cream.

I walked in and out of my office without ever locking it and took to the pager and cell phone as though I'd never put them down.

Royer came up once a week to eat, check on Annie, and—probably more important—check on me. After about three weeks of that I finally walked him to his car, looked at him, and said, "Royer, it's me. I'm okay."

He said, "You sure?"

"Well . . ." I shrugged. "Given everything that's gone on, I'm not hooked on any drugs, don't want any, and . . . other than a recurring dream, I'm sleeping at night."

That was good enough for him.

Chapter 50

My patients used to ask me why most transplants occur at night. It's simple, really. During the day, the loved ones are waiting for test results conducted by medical personnel who work primarily during the day. When those results show that the patient's body is not responding to large amounts of carbon dioxide buildup in their system, and the brain is no longer responding to the most fundamental of tasks, only then is the "brain-dead" declaration made. This is often a difficult diagnosis to accept, but the sight of a loved one kept alive solely by a piece of cold, hard machinery is often the final straw.

That final straw tends to fall at night, after the hospital has quieted and the family is left alone with their thoughts and the possibilities of the future. That's when they make their painful peace and contact their doctor, saying they'd like to donate. Then the hospital performs its own battery of tests, determines whether or not the patient is a viable donor, and lists him or her. By the time that's all done, it's somewhere around the witching hour.

Rarely did I get a call to go pick up an organ at nine in the morning. It just never worked that way. So when my pager and cell phone rattled simultaneously at 2:00 a.m., I wasn't surprised.

"We may have a heart. In Texas. A twenty-six-year-old woman. Husband says they were in a car crash. She wasn't wearing a seat belt. EEG's been flat since this morning, team down there wants to declare her brain-dead as soon as they've prepared the family for the possibility. Coordinator talked to the husband. He'll donate."

"They know how we want the body managed?" I asked. "Nobody does anything until you or I get there?"

Royer chuckled; it was as if five years had not passed without a phone call between us and we had made a midnight run as recently as last night. "Yeah, but I think it better be me. Annie needs you with her. The last face she sees before the drip turns out the lights should be yours."

"Yeah, I'm with you."

"I told them which antibiotics to give and how we want the fluids handled. I'm waiting on urine output, and central pressure readings now. I'll call you back in five."

I hung up the phone and pulled an old pair of blue scrubs from the closet. They were a little baggier than the last time I wore them.

Cindy walked in and saw me staring at myself in the mirror. Her flannel men's pajamas looked warm and comfortable. She eyed the phone, then me.

"It was Royer," I said, but held out my hand in caution. "We don't know enough yet. Might be a false alarm. Anytime that phone goes off, chances are better that it's not a match than that it is. Remember that."

Cindy folded her arms and nodded at my scrubs. "That why you're wearing those?"

I shrugged and said, " 'Course, it might be too." I looked at the phone, almost willing it to ring, and five seconds later, it did.

Cindy jumped, and I answered it.

"What do you know?"

"Liver and kidney functions all normal. Serologies

on hepatitis and AIDS are negative. The girl's clean. We're a go."

"Dopamine?"

Dopamine was a great drug. In a donor, it made the heart pump harder, raised blood pressure, and increased blood flowing to the brain. But if used to excess, it could damage the heart.

"Currently, she's on a small dose, but as they rehydrate her over the next few hours, she'll be weaned off that."

"I've got . . ." I looked at my watch and unscrewed the pin to set it. "1:57 a.m . . . right now." I heard the clasp snap shut on Royer's Omega Seamaster. Knowing we'd be in touch at least every thirty minutes during the next six hours, we had to be precise.

"Me too," he said.

"You take care of everything at the door? I don't want any delays when we get there. Nothing to cause Annie any stress. I want a rolling seat and a fast track."

"Done," Royer said. "They'll meet you at the door."

"Blood bank?"

"They've got sixteen units of packed red blood cells."

"Sixteen? We've never needed more than six."

"Yeah." Royer laughed. "I wish all of them were this easy. Folks around here have taken a liking to Annie. They want to make sure she's got all the chances she needs. A week ago, there was a line out the door of nurses and doctors waiting to give blood."

"That little girl has touched a lot of hearts," I said.

"You might say," Royer agreed, letting it sink in. "You all get down here, but you better not cut skin there until I'm sure of what we have in Texas."

"Agreed." I thought through our trip south to Atlanta. "And Life Flight?"

"In the air. Took off seven minutes ago. Should touch down in about thirty-eight, give or take a couple for wind and whatnot."

"Same pad as before?"

"Yup. You guys get dressed, take a few minutes to get comfortable with the idea, and then get on down to the pad. We'll talk in thirty."

I held the phone and realized that I had just had the conversation I had waited my whole life to have. Mixed emotion—joy and sadness—fell on me in equal parts.

Royer heard it in my hesitation. "And Reese?"

"Yeah."

"I wish this was five years ago."

I looked out the window over the lake, which sat silent and unrippled beneath a quarter moon. My voice fell to a whisper. "Me too."

He took a deep breath, and I knew what was coming before he said it. "Hey, Doc?"

"Yeah," I said.

"It's time to put on your chinstrap, get off the bench, and get in the game."

The fatherly kick in the pants felt good, and brought me back. "Talk to you in thirty."

I hung up, and while Royer boarded a Learjet with a

red-and-white Igloo cooler, I walked into the room next door and shook the shoulder of a little girl who sold lemonade, raised crickets, and called most of a town by their first names.

Chapter 51

I grabbed my just-in-case bag, Cindy grabbed their small suitcase, and I carried Annie, wearing pink sweats and sock-slippers, to the Suburban. Then I took one look at the lake and at Charlie's dock, because I knew he'd heard the phone ring.

Sure enough, Charlie, wearing his pajama bottoms, was leaning on a canoe paddle and scratching Georgia's head, listening to us load up. I walked slowly through the trees, the branches brushing my face, and onto the bulkhead.

Charlie heard my footsteps and pointed his chin at me.

"Hey, buddy," I said.

"That time?"

"Maybe. Won't know for an hour or so."

"When you do, holler. I'll spread the word." He waited to hear my footsteps walking away. When he didn't, he nodded, and we stood in the silence separated by the water. Finally he whispered, "Reese?"

"Yeah?"

Charlie wiped his eyes and scratched one arm. "Can you see?"

His words echoed off the water and then drifted off,

following my sailboats onto the Tallulah, where they ignited, flamed, and then sank.

I knew what he was asking. "Working on it."

Charlie nodded, whistled Georgia up ahead of him, and climbed the steps to his house.

I got into the car, and we idled down the gravel drive to the hardtop that would take us the six miles to the hospital helipad. Annie and Cindy sat in back, huddled together, their eyes reflecting the dash lights through the rearview mirror. In my mind I began walking through the process, every stitch, snip, and reading. Every detail, no matter how small, held significance because there were no second chances.

I looked at my watch. Royer would be on the plane, talking to the coordinator, and he would be with the donor in an hour. In two hours, he would recover the heart, and be back at the hospital in four. Bottom line, we had time, but not much wiggle room. Once he placed the heart in that cooler, ischemic time started ticking. After four hours ischemic, too much damage had occurred to the heart to make it viable. We reached the outskirts of Clayton and pulled into the Rabun County Hospital. Life Flight was sitting at the pad, lit up like a huge white bird, the rotors slowly spinning. The pilot, Steve Ashdale, whom I had known well at one time, stood alongside, body erect and his clothes creased with starch. A product of several thousand hours' flying helicopters for the marines.

We parked, and I carried Annie to the helicopter. Steve shook my hand and smiled. "Good to see you.

Royer filled me in. Let's get airborne."

Ordinarily, Life Flight helicopters are only large enough to accommodate two medical personnel—one of whom also happens to be a pilot—and up to two patients, depending on the extent of their injuries. Due to the expansive sprawl of the Atlanta area and the need to fly greater distances, this bird had been designed a bit bigger. We had room to spare.

I placed Annie on the cot that lay down the middle of the helicopter, and Cindy and I took our seats on either side. Steve pointed to our seat belts and headphones, and we put both on. We lifted off, swayed backward, tilted forward, and sped through the night. He pulled higher, and within seconds Lake Burton stretched out beneath us.

Steve spoke. "Sure is pretty at night." He pointed at the trout hatchery and the green meadow next to it, now covered in darkness. "Set down there about three years ago. Good pad too."

Cindy gripped the handles, watched Annie, who was peeking out the window next to her head, and took purposeful and deep breaths.

"First helicopter ride?" I said.

She nodded. "And last, hopefully."

Annie grabbed my hand. "What's Dr. Royer doing right now?"

I wondered how to best answer her question. "He's flying to Texas, to go get your heart."

Annie pulled me closer and spoke quietly into the microphone that looped around her face from ear to lips. The sound of the motor and rotor blades made a dull roar above us.

"No," she said, "tell me what he's doing."

The heart was going inside her; I figured she had a right to know. "You sure?"

She thought for a moment, then nodded slowly.

"Right now, Dr. Royer is flying to a hospital in Texas. Once there, he'll open up the donor, inject a solution into the heart to make it stop, and the doctor across from him will declare a time of death."

Annie swallowed hard, and a tear puddled in the corner of her eye.

"Then he'll pour buckets of ice-cold saline onto the heart to try to get it as cold as possible. About five liters of real cold stuff. What they call either Ringer's lactate or normal saline."

The detail seemed to lessen the personal and emotional blow for Annie, and for Cindy, who couldn't help but listen.

"It won't take him but a couple of minutes to cut out the heart. The instant it's cut free, ischemic time starts—when no blood flows to the heart. From then on, every second counts. He'll put the heart in a sterile bowl, rinse it thoroughly to get rid of the old blood, stick it in double plastic bags, and then into a red-and-white plastic container—like the ones you see at the beach."

Annie attempted a smile.

"Then he'll hop back on that same plane and jet back to Atlanta, where you and I will be waiting for him."

Annie swallowed. "What's going to happen to me?"

"We'll get you to the hospital, whisk you up to your room, put you to sleep, and in a few hours, you'll wake up with a new ticker."

"That's not what I meant."

I thought for a moment. "Do you believe in the tooth fairy?"

Annie shook her head.

"Remember when you used to?"

She nodded.

"Well, let's just say that I still believe in the tooth fairy, and sometimes the best things happen while you're asleep."

Annie looked out the window into the darkness that was speeding beneath us at just over a hundred miles an hour. A few minutes later she asked, "Do you know anything about the person in Texas?"

I nodded.

Annie's eyes waited expectantly while her shoulders tensed.

"Somebody who was in a real bad car accident, who's not ever going to wake up, who's alive because there's a machine keeping her alive, and whose loved one wants you to have a new heart."

Annie coughed, and her eyes crowded in toward her nose, almost wrinkling the pale skin above her eyes. "It's a girl?" she asked. "How old is she?"

I made it a practice never to tell recipients information about their donors until after they had recovered, but something in Annie's eyes told me she wasn't asking for her benefit. She was asking for the donor's. "Mid-twenties."

Annie's eyes whirled around the inside of the helicopter, studying the lights, gauges, and odd mixture of medical supplies with aeronautical function and design. "Do you think she's already in heaven?"

I shrugged. "I don't know, Annie. I guess she's the only one who really knows that right now."

Annie thought for a minute, rubbed her sandal, and said, "God knows."

I nodded. "I guess He knows too."

Annie continued studying the instruments around her. Her pulse was elevated, but her color was good and her breathing, while forced, was deep and controlled. Her eyes steadied on mine. "Reese?"

"Yes."

Just then, Steve crackled from the pilot's seat, "Jonny?"

I looked up front and saw the lights of Atlanta growing closer through the glass.

"Royer's calling from Texas. I'm patching him through."

I nodded, understanding that Steve could selectively do so and would patch him through to only my set of headphones.

"Jonny?"

"Go ahead."

"We've landed and I've had a look at her. The donor's BP has not dropped, which is good, seeing as how they've weaned her from dopamine. The electrocardiogram looks good, heart rate normal, and from what I can tell, the heart muscle itself suffered no damage. 'Course I won't know for sure until I open her up. The chest X-ray is clear, neither lung is collapsed, and no pneumonia. We're at 90 percent go."

I made several mental notes and said, "Call me when you know."

"Will do."

Royer hung up and no doubt returned to the OR, where other doctors were performing their tests to determine if other tissues were also viable. The sequence of removal follows the best physiological progression, not the order of arrival. First the heart, then liver, kidneys, corneas, bone, and then other tissue, like skin. That meant nobody would touch the donor until after Royer was finished.

Annie squeezed my hand again and brought my thoughts eastward from Texas, up through the kitchen floor at the lake, and down into the helicopter. "Reese?"

"Yes?"

"Don't worry. Okay?"

I nodded and watched Atlanta growing closer over Steve's shoulder.

Annie tugged on my arm and pulled me closer. "Reese?"

My face hung just a few inches from hers. I didn't say a word.

"You don't need to worry," she said again.

I tried to smile and shrug her off and act as though

my attention were needed up front.

She tapped my hand and feigned a smile. "What would Shakespeare say about all this?"

I thought for a moment and attempted the same smile. My ability to remember the words that had brought me such comfort had disappeared. I had almost completely forgotten every passage I'd ever read. It was as if they knew they were no longer needed, so they had taken flight and found another soul in need. I pawed at the air, trying to remember. When nothing came, I felt lonely and cold. "No, not tonight."

She pulled my ear to her lips, tapped her chest, and whispered, "Whether or not I wake up . . . I'll have a new heart."

Cindy covered her mouth and looked out the window toward the east and the lights of Stone Mountain. The darkness hid her eyes, but the blue glow from the instrument panel lit up the shiny streaks cascading down her face. Before us spread the urban sprawl of Atlanta, which now covered Sherman's once-scorched earth.

Highway 400 stretched out below us, marked by the occasional junction lights or northbound headlights. We circled once, then landed amid a sea of lights and scurrying medical personnel, many of whom seemed as anxious to see me as Annie. Word had spread fast, and I knew my life of anonymity was over.

At first they were afraid to say hello, but when we placed Annie in the chair, and the two electric doors closed behind us, I turned to Mike Ramirez and said, "How's your family?"

He smiled a wide grin and said, "Fine." His chest swelled a bit, and his grin grew wider. "The boys are in school, and we have two little girls at home."

One by one, nurses and doctors came to wish Annie well and shake my hand or offer a quiet hug. We loaded onto the elevator, and while the doors closed, I reminded myself that while I needed those hugs and handshakes, this wasn't about me. And we weren't simply taking out a girl's tonsils. We were taking out her heart.

Chapter 52

We descended two floors in the elevator, and I thought about Royer. When he first inspected the heart, he had to be absolutely certain. I knew he would look for signs of damage. He would feel for flutters—like water running rapidly through a pipe—that meant the heart was not functioning properly. Next he would run his finger down each of the three major coronary arteries, the vessels that lie on the surface of the heart, that feed it with oxygen and nutrients. He'd look for plaque, any sign of hardening, the first signs of disease. Like Charlie, Royer would "read" the heart with his hands.

We rolled Annie into her room at the end of a long and quiet hall in the heart wing of the hospital. Immediately, the nurses began invisibly flurrying about, performing a battery of tests. After a few minutes, a nurse

I did not know whispered, "Doctor?" When I didn't move, she whispered again, this time louder, "Doctor."

Finally, Cindy got my attention and pointed discreetly at the nurse.

I turned and read *Jenny* on the shoulder of her scrubs. She held two things: a white jacket with *Jonny* stitched above the top-right pocket and two syringes, out of Annie's view.

I had been expecting the syringes, but not the jacket.

She held it forth and whispered, "Royer's had this hanging on the back of his door for I don't know how long. Said to give it to you when you arrived."

I nodded, and she helped me slip into it, like a tailor at a men's shop. In the pocket I found a stethoscope. I unfolded it, and she whispered again, "He's been keeping that for you too. Said he's been waiting till it fit you again." She hung it around my neck and smiled.

Then she held the syringes, eyed Annie, and said, "You or me?"

"Me," I whispered. It was a kind gesture, and I appreciated her offering. Those shots were the first step, and a very painful one, in what would become a lifetime routine of taking immuno-suppressants. The shots had to be given in the thigh, and Annie was not going to like it.

Jenny stood behind me, ready to help but not in my way, and I turned to Cindy. "You might ought to leave us alone a minute."

Cindy shook her head, grasped Annie's hand, and

gritted her teeth. I looked at Annie, and she eyed the needles in my hand.

"Dr. Royer told me about those." She lifted her gown, I swabbed the skin, and she grabbed my hand. She looked up with a forced smile and whispered, "I keep a close watch on this heart of mine. I keep my eyes wide open all the time. Because you're mine, I walk the line."

The rhyme puzzled me, and I knew I'd heard it someplace before.

Annie tilted her head. "My mom was a big fan of Johnny Cash."

She closed her eyes, gritted her teeth, and I quickly injected the drugs. She winced, and her eyelids squeezed the tears out from underneath. I straightened her gown, kissed her on the forehead, and she looked up at me, offering another whisper through still-gritted teeth. "I guess sometimes it's got to hurt before it can get better."

I nodded. "Hearts are like that."

Jenny returned with a small cup of water and a pill, which would put Annie on a more sedated field. It wouldn't quite put her to sleep, but it'd take away any anxiety.

Annie swallowed obediently, and someone paged me over the intercom. "Dr. Mitchell? Dr. Morgan's on line two."

I checked my watch. He was three seconds early.

I stepped out into the hall and picked up the phone. "Talk to me."

"I'm here. Other doctors are checking her out now; I'll have a look in ten minutes or so. I'd say, get Annie to sleep and get her prepped. This woman looks healthy. I'll call you in twenty when I know for sure."

I hung up, and Jenny ran the IV into Annie's arm. The drugs worked slowly, giving us about five minutes. I sat down next to the bed, and Annie slid her hand beneath mine. For the next three minutes I watched her fight a losing battle against her eyelids. During that time, her mouth said nothing, but her heart spoke volumes.

A minute later, she was asleep.

Cindy waited in the room while I walked down the hall to the OR and met, or got reacquainted with, the team. When I entered OR4, the phone lit up and the perfusionist, who stood closest, picked it up. She turned to me. "It's Royer." His calling meant bad news. I took the phone.

"Reese, the heart is showing signs of disease. Getting crunchy. Not a problem now. We can put it in her, but then we've got to tell her that she's got to go through this again in five years or so. How do you think she'll handle that?"

"Probably not too well."

"You've spent time with her. Day-in, day-out time. What's your call?"

I leaned against the wall, closed my eyes, and thought of Annie, trusting me with her life. I wondered whether she had the strength to wake up and hear that she didn't have a new heart. I also wondered whether we had time to find another one.

"Jonny," Royer said, "at best, this is a Band-Aid. Can she hold off?"

One of the most difficult aspects of transplantation was making decisions with people's lives that could kill them if you were wrong. It made it that much worse when you loved them.

"Yes."

"Let her sleep, and we'll break the news tomorrow. The rest will do her some good."

"See you in a few hours."

"And, Jonny?" I heard my friend talking, not my partner. "We'll find one."

"See you shortly."

On the surface, Cindy took the news pretty well. When I suggested we go to the Varsity and grab a chocolate shake, she nodded, and not until we got in the car and away from the hospital did she crack. The tears came all at once. Niagara Falls and she cried loudly.

I pulled off the interstate and wound through the buildings at Georgia Tech. When I found an open parking spot, I parked, and Cindy fell against my shoulder. She shook, clenched her fists, buried her face in my chest, and screamed at the top of her lungs. The years of worry and holding it all together had finally crumbled.

"I can't live like this! I can't! Please! What kind of a sick life is this?" Cindy pulled at her shirt. "Just cut me open. Take mine. I don't want it anymore, and if she can't live, I don't want to." She cried and shook her head as though bees were stinging her face.

I held her tight and said nothing. I felt the release, the warmth of tears on my chest, the rise and fall of anguish and despair.

How many times had I wanted to scream the same way? To purge myself and release the pain in my soul. But somehow, I never had. Maybe those who felt free to do so were only those who didn't possess the guilt of having put the pain there in the first place.

Minutes passed. Finally she wiped her eyes, sat back in the seat, and propped her feet on the dashboard. I put the stick in drive, and we wound slowly through the campus and into the drive-through at The Varsity. I ordered a shake and a PC: short for "pure chocolate." Nothing but some chocolate milk poured over crushed ice. When the drinks arrived, we sipped in silence.

A week passed. A long one. Annie had grown quiet since she woke, but she took the news as well as could be expected. While I tinkered with the surface coating on the Hacker and the surface coating on my heart, Cindy and Annie read some of the books in my house and ran their toes through the sand along the shore of the lake.

Without their knowledge, Royer and I had delivered a perfusion machine to Rabun County, along with half the sixteen pints of blood donated by her many friends. It was a just-in-case precaution. If Annie ran into trouble and we were lucky enough to get her to Rabun, that machine would give us options that we might not have otherwise. We also, with Annie's knowledge, gave her stepped-up doses of what might be considered ultrahigh amounts of antibiotics. Since we had given her the painful shots in her legs, we had kept Annie's blood swimming in the best and most aggressive antibiotics we could administer without killing her.

One morning, after I had made her swallow her horse pills, she gulped, wrinkled her lips, and then tugged on the leg of my jeans. I knelt on the kitchen floor and brought my face level to hers. Reaching behind her neck, she unclasped her sandal, gave it a long look, and motioned me closer. As I leaned in, she hung it around my neck. "It's yours now."

Cindy held up the doorframe and watched, her eyes on Annie.

I shook my head. "Annie, I can't . . ."

Annie shook her head, held out her hand like a stop sign, and took a deep breath. "Nope, we've talked about it." She looked at Cindy, Cindy looked at me, and Annie looked back. "Besides, I already told you . . . I won't need it."

I looked down and read the thumb-worn letters on the back.

Annie continued, "But! There's one condition."

I looked up. "What's that?"

She stood up on her chair and pulled me up with her—her eyes level with mine. "You must always remember . . ." She patted my heart gently with her hand.

My heart knew what was coming, and it took every ounce of strength within me to let her finish. The tears collected in the corners of my eyes, but she caught them before they fell.

"Whether I wake up or not . . . ," she whispered, "I'll have a new heart."

I picked her off the chair, wrapped my arms around her neck, and knew then that she was right.

It was now late September, what Charlie and I referred to as the wet and ugly month. When the late summer hurricanes made their annual migration across Florida, they would demolish whatever cities happened to be in their paths, spin out their madness across the rest of the state, and then turn northeast and drive the residue of their systems up through Georgia and beyond. There they would continue their terror, mostly through rainfall, before flinging themselves back out into the northern Atlantic and disappearing.

Most systems spun out their anger and dwindled by the time they reached Atlanta, but occasionally, one system would reach the residue of another system moving south out of Canada. When those two systems collided, cold air from Canada hitting the warm air from the Gulf, problems arose. The Palm Sunday Killer caught everyone by surprise because of the time of year and the fact that, according to the weatherman, no system was soon to collide with any other system. I guess that's why it was remembered as a "killer."

At least with hurricanes, we knew to be on the

lookout. Problem was, on Saturday evening, we were quietly listening for the ringing or pulsating of cell phones and pagers. Not the sound of a freight train pummeling straight up the lake.

There's not a train track within several miles of Lake Burton. Sometimes, at night, when the air is clear, you can hear a faraway whistle, but never during daylight hours. That's why the sound of a coming train brought me running out of the woodshop.

I saw the waterspout rising above the trees and felt the air charged with electricity. By the time I got to Annie, she had seen the spout and frozen in fear. I picked her up, and she and Cindy and I ran back toward the workshop. We reached the doors just as the trees started snapping around us. I turned, and the spout rose about a mile high out of the lake and toppled from side to side like a flag waving in the breeze.

I leaned against a rolling toolbox, inching it out of the way, and the roof started to shake. When the tin started peeling back and the glass windows shattered, I flipped their heart-of-pine kitchen table on end, covering half the door, rolled the toolbox in front of it to wedge it into place, and we slipped farther back into the L-shaped bunk room and turned the corner.

Inside the rock, it was quiet, damp, and very dark. We sat on my bunk, huddled together, unable to see our hands in front of our faces. Cindy cradled Annie in her lap while I blanketed the both of them. The noise and flashing light around the corner told me that the workshop was coming apart at the seams.

Behind it all, Annie was whispering. I could only hear bits and pieces.

". . . bind up the brokenhearted . . . beauty for ashes . . . oil of joy for mourning . . ."

For maybe thirty seconds, we braced for the blow that would bring the rock down around us, and then, just as quickly as it had appeared, it was gone. Blue light and silence crept around the corner. We sat in the dark rock hole, listening to the sound of our breathing. And that's when it hit me.

Annie had quit whispering.

I felt her wrist for a distal pulse and didn't find one. I touched her neck and felt the fibrillation.

In the dark, Cindy couldn't see what was going on, but she didn't need to. "Reese?" she said with the panic building.

I grabbed Annie and pushed against the table and toolbox that now lay on its side. I walked out into where the workshop had once been and looked around, but it was gone. Tools, power cords, and wood splinters covered the ground as though someone had taken a weed whacker to every tool I'd ever owned. The only thing still in its place was the concrete floor. The walls, roof, everything, had disappeared.

Before me lay the lake, scattered in debris that had once made up homes for miles down the lake. I looked for the boathouse, but the only thing that remained were the twenty-four pilings it had once stood on. No walls, no deck, no hammock. If I had to guess, I'd say the Hacker never even hit the water before the tornado gave it wings and sent it heavenward.

I looked at Annie. Her color was ashen, her lips blue, her eyes were falling back behind her lids, and her body was a twitching combination of limpness and lockjaw rigidity. She had maybe three minutes. If I could make it to the house, I might have time. I turned, but except for the chimney, the house too was gone. And along with it, everything I needed.

I laid Annie on the floor and flung open the drawer of the toolbox, slinging tools and parts of tools across the floor. Inside, I found Charlie's bag of barbecue basting utensils. Inside was the injecting needle. I pulled the needle, lit the lighter in my pocket, and fanned the needle through the flame.

While Cindy watched, I spoke slowly and didn't look at her. I nodded toward the bunk room. "The bag beneath the bed." I kept a small first-aid kit beneath our bunks in the event that either of us ever got cut or hurt in the workshop.

Cindy flung herself into the bunk room and just as quickly returned, dropping the bag on the ground and kneeling opposite me, awaiting orders.

I looked at her. "Do you trust me?"

She nodded and placed her hands along Annie's sides, as if to brace her for whatever I was about to do. I thought about Annie's body and how what I was about to do would ravage her body with infection. The only hope we had was that the stepped-up doses of antibiotics could hold off whatever would creep into her system until we could get her into a sterile field.

I pulled off the top of Annie's bathing suit, ran my fingers along her sternum, found the point I was looking for, and slammed the needle down and into her chest. When it pierced the pericardium, it showered me in Annie's blood, releasing the pressure. I pointed toward the toolbox and said as calmly as I could. "Second drawer, blue-handled pliers."

Cindy ripped open the drawer, fumbled through eight or ten different sets of pliers, until she found the angled wire cutters I was looking for. I turned Annie on her side and slit the skin along her rib. It was about that time Charlie climbed through the debris and out of the lake. He had a cut on his face, another cut somewhere on his head, and his left arm was hanging limp and lifeless.

He spoke softly, "Stitch, what do you need?"

I knew from the look of the trees around me that there was no way I could get the Suburban down the drive and out onto the hard road. "I need a ride out of here." In the distance, I heard the high-pitched whine of a Jet Ski screaming across the lake. "Get to the edge of the lake and wave your arms. If that's Termite, I need him."

Charlie disappeared, and the fear across Cindy's face told me all I needed to know. Annie had started breathing, but I had about one minute to patch the hole in her heart before I lost all ability to keep it pumping. I pointed at the bottle of Betadine and nodded at Cindy. "Cover my hands."

The sound of the Jet Ski approached, stopped, then

screamed away as quickly as it had appeared. In ten seconds it was gone, and in all probability, Termite was traveling somewhere around ninety miles an hour across a lake littered with nail-split debris. Cindy doused my hands, turning them an ugly yellowish brown. I washed in Betadine and looked at her. She held out the pliers and nodded.

I opened a suture pack and bit the thread like a seamstress. I grabbed the pliers, clipped the rib, spread open the cavity, cut the pericardium, and there before me lay Annie's disease-ridden, sick and dying heart. With blue skies above and no roof or tree limbs to obstruct it, light was not a problem.

I found the small hole, which was not difficult, made five quick stitches, and pulled the purse string tight. Unlike Emma's, Annie's tissue was not brittle. Her youth might just get her to the hospital.

Annie's heart fibrillated, twitched violently, and jolted, pumping weakly but pumping. It held. Looking at the mess around me, we had fifteen minutes on the outside. After which Annie would most likely bleed to death if her heart didn't quit first.

I motioned to the cell phone on my belt. Cindy picked it up and dialed Royer without having to be told. Three seconds later she had him on the line. She nodded and held the phone for me to speak. My tone of voice told him as much as anything.

"Royer, transmural rupture with pericardial tamponade." In the distance I heard a ski boat screaming toward us. "We've got no fluids, and ten minutes max.

Tell Life Flight I'll meet them on the meadow next to the trout hatchery."

"The what?!"

"Just tell them! They'll understand. And tell the folks at Rabun to get the pump up and running."

Annie's loss of fluids was about to become a problem, and I had no lactated Ringer's. I looked around. *Think, Reese! Think!*

Charlie reappeared, his left arm dangling. The picture of him, hurt and holding his arm, reminded me. I motioned again at the contents of the medical bag scattered around Cindy on the floor. "That plastic bag there."

She picked it up, bit off a corner, and pulled out the IV tubing from inside.

"Good," I said. "Now, insert those needles into each end."

Cindy plugged the needle-tipped ends of the IV into the ends of the tubing, then held it out to me. Dipping it in Betadine, I inserted one end into my right arm, and immediately the tube filled with blood. When it began running out the other end, I dipped the other end in Betadine and inserted it into the large vein in Annie's right groin. The advantage of using so large a vein was that it would carry large amounts of my blood directly into Annie's heart.

I pulled the watch off my wrist and handed it to Cindy. "Tell me when eight minutes are up." I lifted Annie off the ground, made sure the line wasn't crimped, and walked quickly to the beach. When I got there, Termite was docking what looked like a cigarette boat. It was probably twenty-eight feet long, had two engines on the back, and looked like it would travel a hundred miles an hour. By the looks of Termite's face and hair, it had.

I stepped into the boat, Cindy and Charlie did likewise, and Termite looked at me. Panic and disbelief riddled his face.

"Termite," I said, "I need you to get us to the ramp at the hatchery."

He looked at Annie and nodded. I laid Annie down in the boat, her head toward the engines, and knelt above her. I was counting on gravity and the angle of the boat in the water to pull the blood more quickly down into her chest cavity—and brain.

"Termite," I said, looking up from Annie, *"now."*

He threw the boat into reverse, backed us out of the finger, and then pushed the stick forward, never stopping. He slammed the stick as far forward as it would go. Cindy and Charlie braced in the seats next to me, I knelt over Annie, and the boat screamed across the glassy lake. When I saw the speedometer, we were moving at eighty-seven miles an hour.

Three minutes later, Termite turned the corner, slowed the boat to maybe thirty miles an hour, cut the engines, and trimmed them above the waterline. When they were clear, we hit the boat ramp square in the middle. The ramp launched us up along the carpeted runners and into the grassy meadow next to the playground along the hatchery. The boat slid along the grass and into the soft sand of the playground, where it dug in and slowed to a tilted stop.

I laid Annie on the grass and waited for the sound of the helicopter. Cindy tapped me on the shoulder, biting her lip. She held out my watch. It'd been eight and a half minutes. Charlie knelt nearby, running his hands along Annie's legs. When he got to the IV, he ran his other hand along my right arm. When his fingers hit the tape, he pointed his face toward mine.

He said, "How long you been doing that?"

I was growing light-headed. "About ten minutes."

Charlie ripped off his shirt and held out his arm. If Annie was to have any chance at all, I had to get that tube out of my arm. I pinched the tube, pulled it out of my vein, and immediately thrust it deep into the vine-like vein running down Charlie's arm. He never winced.

Annie's eyes searched the world as if the light around her were growing dim.

"Annie, honey. Hang on." I hovered over her, trying to force her eyes to focus on mine. "I need you to hang on a few more minutes. Do you understand me?"

She swallowed and tried to nod, but her eyes rolled back in her head, and she coughed. I pulled the pill container from around her neck, emptied the pills onto her chest, and nodded at Cindy. She held one to her teeth to bite it in half, and I shook my head.

"No, not this time. We need the whole thing."

She placed the nitroglycerin tablet beneath Annie's tongue, and within ten seconds some color returned to

Annie's face. In the distance, I heard the chopper. I looked at Termite, who stood wide-eyed and open-jawed above me. Then I nodded toward a Coke machine some hundred yards away.

"Think you can get a couple of Cokes out of that machine?"

Termite disappeared, only to return with two Mountain Dews about the time the helicopter landed in the grass next to us. Charlie had given Annie about eight minutes of his own blood when the chopper arrived. I lifted Annie up into the bird, pinched the IV tube, and immediately spliced into it the IV line running from a bag of lactated Ringer's that hung from the top of the helicopter. The medic immediately started squeezing that bag to increase the pressure and flow into Annie's heart.

The door shut behind us, and as the pilot pulled skyward, I looked back at the three of them, Charlie, Cindy, and Termite, standing together against a backdrop of green grass, a trail of Annie's blood, and somebody's one-hundred-thousand-dollar cigarette boat that now lay beached like a dying whale. Just before we cleared the treetops, Cindy covered her mouth and buried her head in Charlie's shoulder.

Chapter 53

We landed at Rabun amid a flurry of well-meaning medical personnel who had little to no idea how to handle a Level 1 trauma. The only one with any wits about her was the medic who had just picked us up.

I looked at her. "You got any trauma experience?"

"Grady Memorial, four years, weekend shift."

"Good enough. Follow me."

We rolled Annie inside, where people in white coats and multicolored scrubs were scurrying about like ants after someone had just poured gasoline on their hill. At the center of the room stood Sal Cohen, barking orders like a drill sergeant.

He pointed toward the hospital's only operating room. I nodded, rolled Annie inside, and saw the perfusionist readying the heart-lung machine. When I turned around, Sal was jamming his right hand into a rubber glove and looking at me for direction.

I looked at both him and the female medic from the copter. "I need a sternal saw."

The medic turned to the perfusionist, who held up a finger, disappeared around the corner, and then reappeared carrying an antiquated saw. Sal spread Annie across the operating table and began swabbing her chest with Betadine. Annie's radial pulse was nowhere to be found, and her carotid pulse was vague at best.

Time was out.

An anesthesiologist appeared out of nowhere. Annie was mostly unconscious already, but he quickly injected her and made sure she wouldn't wake up anytime soon. He pushed the free end of a long tube, the other end of which was attached to a ventilator, into Annie's mouth, down between her vocal cords and into her windpipe. The ventilator rhythmically blew air down her endotracheal tube, breathing for her.

With Annie's air supply operative, and drinking in oxygen-rich air, I slit her chest alongside the older scar, cut the sternum up to the base of her neck, and stepped aside as the medic inserted the chest spreader and cranked open Annie's chest. I pulled aside the pierced pericardium and immediately went to work freeing the scar tissue that surrounded it. With every pull, I feared my purse stitch would give. It did not.

Annie's previous open-heart had left a lot of scar tissue that slowed me down. I put one suture into the ascending aorta, then two sutures in the right atrium. I injected a drug called heparin directly into the heart to keep her blood from clotting as it passed through the oxygenator and bypass machine, then inserted tubes called cannulas through these three new purse-string sutures, in order to connect Annie to the heart-lung bypass machine. I stitched them in, and as I did, Annie's heart flatlined. I nodded to the perfusionist. "Your turn."

She nodded, opened the lines, and immediately the plasma filled Annie's deflated frame. Within seconds, her arteries and veins flowed, oxygen reached the far corners of her body and, at least for the time being, Annie was alive.

What I wouldn't know for some time was how long she'd been dead, or, when she woke up, if she woke up, how much damage had been done to her brain. I pushed the sweat-streaked hair out of her face, stepped back, and stumbled under my own lightheadedness. I'd worry about the damage in the days to come. Right now I had to find a heart.

Sal instructed a team of nurses and doctors to sterilize everything from Annie's chest outward. I watched the machines that monitored Annie's life and realized that, though sleeping, she was more alive at that moment than she had been in years. While I thought about how to get Annie and myself out of the mess I'd just got us into, a nurse tapped me on the shoulder.

"Doctor?" she whispered.

"Yes."

She pointed toward a phone along the wall just outside the room. "Line one."

I looked to Sal. "Think you can keep things in here under control 'til I get back?"

He nodded and continued directing the medics and nurses, who were looking at me as if I'd just lost my mind.

I stepped into the hall, scrubbed my hands in the sink, and picked up the phone. "Talk to me."

"How's our girl?" It was Royer.

"Alive."

"How long you think we've got?"

I considered. "We've got some time. I just put her on pump a few minutes ago."

I could see Royer looking at his watch, noting the time.

"Good, keep her that way. I'm headed to Nashville. Might have a heart."

The sound of "might have a heart" resonated through

me like the plasma now coursing through Annie's body. In my mind, I saw her standing on her toes, arching her back, yellow ribbon bouncing on the wind, and screaming "Lemonaaade!" for all the world to hear. "What do you know?"

"Not much, but I'll call you when we touch down and I get a look . . . say in about twenty-seven minutes."

I looked around at the near-uncontrolled chaos of scurrying doctors and nurses around me. "I'm not going anywhere until you get here with a heart, or"—I paused, thinking for the first time about the possibilities—"until you don't."

Royer was quiet for a minute. "Twenty-six minutes. Keep the lines open. And keep your eyes open for our team. They should be there shortly. They'll take care of everything. All you need to do is lead them to Annie."

"Will do."

I hung up the phone and looked at a tech, who was furiously scribbling on a chart nearby. "You busy?"

"No, sir, not really."

"Good. I want you to sit right here and make sure that nobody, and I mean nobody, not even the president himself, gets on this phone. Clear?"

He stood, stepped in front of the phone, crossed his arms like a bouncer, and said, "Yes, sir."

Just then I heard a woman screaming in the waiting area of the emergency room. I heard a scuffle, something slammed into the wall, and Cindy came running through the double doors and down the hall toward me.

She was headed for the operating room when I stepped in front of her. We collided, and she sent us both to the floor, hard.

She put her finger in my face. "Reese! You tell me right now! Tell me right now!"

I pulled her to me, tucked her arms inside mine, and wrapped my hand around the back of her wet head. "She's alive."

Cindy pounded my chest and then gripped my shirt, pulled me to her and her to me.

I could see the thought hadn't registered, so I pointed toward the OR and said it again. "She's alive."

"How?" she asked.

I shook my head. "Not now." I nodded toward the phone. "Royer just called. He's got a heart. He's en route and he's calling back in . . ." I looked for my watch, which wasn't on my wrist. "In twenty minutes or so."

Cindy placed her hands to her face, composed herself, and I saw my Omega flipping about on her wrist. I gently unclasped it and then fastened it about mine.

She looked at me. "What do you need?"

I thought about myself for a moment. I tried to smile. "I need some lemonade."

Cindy dropped her head and nodded. "Me too."

We sat on the floor, and I cradled her in my arms while medical personnel scurried around us. Once she caught her breath, I said, "I need to get an IV in me, to put back some of the fluid I lost, and then I need to eat something. We've got a long couple of hours coming up, and I'm going to need a bit more energy than I've got right now."

Cindy wiped her eyes and set out for the cafeteria.

I found Charlie and Termite in the waiting room and escorted them back to the lounge, where the medic from the helicopter ran two IVs, first Charlie's and then mine. I ate a Clif bar while she monitored us both. She washed and examined Charlie's cuts, which were deep and still bleeding, and then looked at me.

"You better take a look at this."

I studied Charlie's face and head and knew he had taken a pretty big blow. The medic returned with some #3 monofilament, and I put a total of twenty-seven stitches in two places on his cheekbone and scalp. He'd heal, but he might be sore awhile. Not to mention his dislocated left shoulder.

After Charlie was patched up and our fluid levels topped off, Cindy returned with some pasta covered in red sauce and cornered by four large meatballs. I ate slowly, watching the phone and begging God to make it ring.

Minutes later, it did. My phone guard stuck his head in the door and pointed to the phone on the counter. "Line two."

I picked it up, and Royer spoke before I said a word. "We're a go. I cut in ten, then back on the plane in twenty, and I touch down there in less than ninety. Have the chopper waiting."

"Will do."

"Think she can hold on until I bring the Pepsi?"

I looked across the hall toward the OR, where I knew Sal had sewn up the incision I'd made across Annie's rib cage. "Yeah, she'll hold." A few seconds passed. "Royer?"

"Yeah," Royer said in little more than a whisper.

I turned away from Cindy, making it difficult for her to hear. "It's now or nothing."

He took a deep breath. "Just have the chopper waiting and blades turning."

I hung up the phone, saw the first members of Royer's team run through the doors toward the OR, and felt Annie's golden sandal burning hot against my chest.

I took a long, hot shower, changed into some clean scrubs, and ate some more spaghetti. In my mind, I went through the operation. Every stitch, every possible problem, not the least of which was transplanting a patient in a hospital not designed to perform a transplant. I shook my head. The odds were not in our favor. Not in our favor at all.

In the OR, Royer's team had transformed the county hospital into a state-of-the-art operating theater. Calm-and-collected had replaced the chaos. Seasoned professionals now tended Annie's monitors. Sal sat in the hall, holding his unlit pipe and smiling as if he had been responsible for the transformation.

The room was stage-bright, totally sterile, and nondescript, not a picture anywhere, stainless steel tables, draped in pale blue-green, an assortment of odd-looking instruments laid out in some order across what looked like a sterile tablecloth. One whole wall was covered in gauges, machines, and sterile battleship gray. All the machines gave varying but equally important readings on anesthesia, the volumetric infusion pump, the ventilator, and different lines leading from tanks somewhere out of the room that piped in helium, oxygen, and nitrous oxide.

When the anesthesiologist had put Annie into a deep sleep with an intravenous medication, and while I put Annie on pump, the on-call surgeon poked a catheter into the artery in her left wrist—a small arterial line that allowed us to monitor blood pressure moment by moment. This finished, he stuck another catheter into a vein in her chest—to give her medicines and measure intravascular volume.

A scrub nurse ran a small tube catheter into her bladder so we could follow her urine output. Normally we would shave a patient's body hair, but Annie didn't have any, so they simply swabbed her down with soap and water.

In my past life, I would have sat back and watched, honoring the line drawn between doctors and nurses. But for the first time since my internship, I stepped up to the chief resident and honored my relationship with the patient above all else. I said, "You mind?"

A bit surprised, he shook his head and stepped aside, allowing me to set the pace and tone. As we sponged her with Betadine, I noticed how thin her arms had grown, how drawn and skinny her hips. Like Emma's those last few days at the lake, Annie's skin had become almost translucent.

People used to ask me, amid so much terror, pain, and hardship, how transplant surgeons could stay so hopeful. So positive. Whenever asked that, I remembered the look behind Emma's eyes and asked how could we not.

We covered Annie's chest with the surgical equivalent of Saran Wrap and then gently draped her with two sterile sheets, leaving a small strip of exposed chest and upper abdomen. In medical school, we learned to call that the surgical field, where we'd focus all our energies. Ordinarily, it helped distance us from the person attached to it.

Maybe that's why I stepped up and swabbed Annie. I didn't want that distance.

I stepped to the foot of the bed, felt Annie's cold toes, and turned to a nurse. "Think you could find some socks?"

She smiled and disappeared.

As a result of her previous open-heart surgery, Annie's chest cavity possessed a lot of dense scar tissue, or adhesions, between the back side of her breastbone and her heart. I knew when Royer arrived I'd have to further divide the scar carefully, making sure not to injure or rupture the cavity any more than I already had.

Most of the hearts I had removed were two or three times the size of normal ones, suffering from dilated cardiomyopathy. That meant they were big, flabby, swollen sacs that didn't beat too well. Annie's was no different. I hoped that the heart Royer found would fit in the space we had, because I didn't want to have to trim it. And hearts are fickle, they don't let you trim them much. I also hoped that he would hurry, because thousands and thousands of its cells were dying every minute it was out of the body. Every second it failed to pump, the farther we traveled from getting it going again.

The moment Annie went on bypass, the tubes shunted her blood away from her heart and ran it into what looked like a cross between the back of a pipe organ and something out of Frankenstein's laboratory. On one side of the cardiopulmonary bypass machine was a row of glass canisters that some have compared to high-tech versions of ice-cream makers. As Annie's blood fed into the canisters, the machine gave it oxygen and then pumped the enriched blood out again, back into Annie's ascending aorta.

On the other side of the bypass machine, the perfusionist closely watched a series of calibrated gauges; just a few feet away, the anesthesiologist tracked a series of gauges, looking at pressure and how much oxygen she took in and how much carbon dioxide she expelled. When we got her going again, there were two things I didn't want to hear from him: "Pressure's getting low" or "Flow's fallen off." In order not to hear that, I needed him on his toes. At the same time, I didn't need him mad at me. That wouldn't help Annie. I caught him in the hall and pulled him aside. "Can I ask you a favor?"

Expecting a barked order, the question caught him off guard. He looked at me through his glasses and shrugged. "Sure."

"In her last surgery, she woke up."

He gulped, shook his head in disgust, and then nodded. I didn't have to continue.

"Don't worry. I've got some sweet dreams planned for that girl."

Anticipating a long day and the fact that, normally, doctors hand off their patients sometime around mid-morning, I asked him, "When are you scheduled to sign out?"

He shook his head. "My partner arrived an hour ago. She's handling the other seven in my care." He looked at Annie. "But . . . not her. I'm here as long as you need me."

I put a hand on his shoulder. "Thanks."

I walked down the hall and past the one-way window that gave medical staff a view of the waiting room. Charlie, bloody but unharmed, sat listening to and smelling the world around him while Cindy stood at a nearby window, staring five thousand miles beyond the walls of the hospital and biting her nails to the quick. Termite leaned against a soda machine, looking at the choices but not really looking at the choices, unconsciously turning his Zippo over and over in his hand. And in the far corner, off by himself, eyes closed, forehead matted with sweat, lips moving, Davis knelt against a chair, his elbows leaning on a tattered Bible.

I closed the door of the doctors' lounge and looked

out through the window that viewed a pasture and a dozen or so milk cows all vying for a chance to stand in the center of the creek. Their udders looked like taut balloons and their jaws worked in rhythm with one another. A light, gentle rain had begun to fall.

I leaned against the window, closed my eyes, and thought of Emma. The way she had told me to take a nap, the tired look behind her eyes, the assuring smile she'd given me as I carried us off to bed. And I thought of the sleep I couldn't hold off. I looked at my arms and ran my fingertips along the fading reminders of her panic. Last, I thought of the pain she must have known and felt for the half hour that I didn't wake up.

All my life, I'd had an almost photographic memory. But while I looked out that window, with Annie breathing through a machine just over my shoulder and Cindy tied in knots in the waiting room just around the corner and Royer speeding toward us, I could not, for the life of me, remember anything Shakespeare had ever written. Nor, for that matter, anything by Tennyson, Milton, or Coleridge. My companions were gone and had taken their comfort with them.

I reached for Annie's sandal around my neck. Beneath it hung Emma's medallion. Draped in memory, I had none of my own. My mind felt as if someone had walked to the chalkboard and wiped the slate clean. I rubbed the sandal, felt the worn letters, closed my eyes, and searched again. All I could see was Emma's face just before the medic placed his hand over her face and closed her eyes.

The intercom crackled above me. "Dr. Jonathan Mitchell, line one. Dr. Jonathan Mitchell, line one."

Royer.

I reached up for the phone—one last time. I could hear the helicopter in the background.

"Jonny? Twelve minutes."

"We'll be waiting." I hung up and stood there. I knew that if my life had led to one moment, it was coming now.

I told the chief resident that Royer would be there in twelve minutes and then walked to the room where the others waited. Cindy saw my face, the puffy, tired look of passing pain, and she stood up, looking cold and reflecting me. Charlie heard her stand and did likewise.

"It's not long now," I said quietly. "I'll keep you posted as best I can." Cindy tried to say something, but I shook my head and put my hand on Charlie's shoulder. "Keep her company, will you?"

Charlie looped his arm inside Cindy's and nodded. I walked back down the hall and through the double doors and hit the button above the sink. Nine minutes later, I walked into the OR, hands held high, and a nurse held my gloves while I sank my hands in deep. Then she helped wrap me in a sterile gown, tied my mask behind my head, and turned on my headlamp. I peeked below the sheet to make sure Annie's eyes were closed. The anesthesiologist sat behind the sheet monitoring six machines and noting numbers on a clipboard.

The helicopter set down outside and an alarm

sounded, accompanied by a series of flashing red lights running up and down the halls. Royer walked in the door carrying a red-and-white cooler, with the calm and collectedness of a man delivering a pizza.

"Sorry to keep you waiting," he said. "Traffic on the perimeter was a bear, and . . ." He shrugged. "We lost the directions." He stepped to the sink and punched the button on the timer. Eight minutes later the timer sounded. He rinsed, sank his hands into 7-$\frac{1}{4}$ gloves, stepped into the waiting sterile green gown, and asked the nurse to adjust his mask and the angle of his lamp. Then he looked at me. "Your move, Doctor."

Around us, the team had assembled: a resident ready at my left, the perfusionist behind Royer, a scrub nurse at the table next to him, several more waiting at the foot of the bed, the anesthesiologist at Annie's head. All eyes were on me.

I had never sought the attention garnered by transplant surgeons. That wasn't why I took this job. But one thing about it, like a quarterback, you had it whether you wanted it or not. If you fumbled, everyone knew it, and if you scored, everyone knew that too.

I held out my hand and whispered, "Scalpel . . . please."

In a few moments I was reaching in and sinking my hand beneath Annie's still heart. I made six precise cuts, careful not to disturb the lines running into her, then pulled and lifted out the heart.

Royer held out a metal pan, looked at me above his

mask, and whispered, "There's a lot of love in that one."

Just before I dropped it into the pan, he noticed the purse stitch I had made amid the rubble on the floor of what used to be my workshop. He ran his fingers across the lines and looked at me. "That how you got her here?"

I nodded.

"And she made it to this table still pumping?"

I nodded again.

He turned to the nurse next to him. "Make sure we keep that." He looked at me. "A lot of folks in our profession have doubted that could ever be done. This might make a few believers. Cardiac pathologists for years to come will study that stitch and, who knows? It might just save a few lives."

Even dead, Annie's old heart was about to begin a new journey, which, when ended would open doors for other Annies.

I laid it gently in the pan while Royer reached into the cooler, dipped his hands below the ice level, and pulled out the grayish-pink donor heart, carefully passing it to me. Feeling for any sign of disease, I ran my fingers along the arteries. I felt the muscles, the valves, and dimensions of the heart in relation to one another. It was larger than normal, but its tone told me that it was large due to exercise, not disease. Somebody had worked this heart, and as a result, it would fit. In fact, it was near perfect.

Royer spoke up. "What your fingers won't tell you is

that she was a high-school kid. A cross-country runner. Parents say she was pretty good too."

He was suctioning excess blood from Annie's chest cavity and placing the first stitch while I lowered the new heart into Annie's chest. Hearts are slippery, so you never want to hold too tightly. But also not too loosely. It's sort of like holding a puppy. You need a good firm hold, but there's a limit.

I held the symbol of life in my hands and marveled just as much then as I had the first time in my anatomy class. *This is it. The wellspring.*

Royer placed a hand on mine, and eyes smiled at me above his mask. "Remember, right side up."

A heart transplant is a rather straightforward operation, comprising four anastomoses—a derivation of a Greek word meaning "to join mouth to mouth." First we connected the donor heart's left atrial chamber to what remained of Annie's left atrium, creating an entirely new chamber. Next we sewed the two right atrial chambers together. Then we took the donor's aorta and attached it to Annie's, end to end. Finally, we attached the pulmonary arteries.

I sewed while Royer positioned the heart and kept tension on the suture material to assure good apposition of the tissues. Despite the way he bragged about my abilities as a surgeon, transplantation was very much a team act.

Royer poured a bucket of ice-cold saline on the heart as I continued sewing, in order to keep it as cold as possible during its exposure to the hot operating room lights. He looked at the clock on the wall. "We're in good shape. Lots of time. It's 10:07."

"Ischemic?" I asked.

"Still have almost an hour."

Stitching in the heart took about an hour minus a few minutes. All the while, the circulating nurse made trips to pick up more blood products or drop off a blood gas sample for the lab. When she returned, her arms full of clear plastic bags of plasma, she was met by the anesthesiologist, who checked the receipt of each one.

When we needed blood, the anesthesiologist would hook up a packet to one of the tubes running into Annie's body and suspend it high in the air on a pole. While Annie was on bypass, the accordion-like pump of the ventilator would remain still and deflated because the heart-lung machine did the breathing for her.

Royer checked the lines and said without looking at me, "Heard you gave blood today."

It was a leading statement. I nodded without looking up.

The sutures required in transplantation are large and take big bites into the tissue, taking into account the full thickness of the heart's wall and its surrounding fat. In contrast to the almost minute stitches needed in a routine bypass operation, where magnifying glasses were helpful, these seemed gigantic.

Royer poured another bucket of cold saline, and I took more large bites to prevent further bleeding. He pulled on the lines to make sure the sutures were tight enough to withstand the changing pressures of a beating heart over one hundred thousand times a day for the next four or five decades. Ever the teacher, he turned to the resident to my left. "Big bites like these guarantee a secure anastomosis and allow us to achieve hemostasis."

The resident nodded.

I finished the left atrium, then made an incision in the right. I reminded myself that it's important to make the incision away from the sinus node, the region of the heart that produced all its electrical activity. If every heart has its own beat, and it does, then it's the sinus node that is the drum.

I finished the anastomosis of the right atrium, leaving only the final connections of the two aortas and pulmonary arteries. That meant we were about an hour away from coming off bypass. I turned to a nurse.

"Would you please tell Cindy everything's going fine?" I checked the numbers on the machines all about me. "Annie's doing well. I'll be out in a bit."

She nodded and disappeared.

I trimmed the aorta of the donor heart. Of Annie's new heart. If God had given me a gift, part of it occurred here. In these incisions. It was vital, both now and in the decades to come, that this fit be perfect. Textbooks couldn't teach it. It was like sculpting; the doctor either could or could not fit the two together.

When I placed the arteries against Annie's own, Royer smiled and shook his head. I sewed the two aortas together and turned to the perfusionist.

"Let's warm her up."

I did this not to restart the heart, but to check my stitching and determine if I had any leaks—a trial run.

During the operation we had cooled the blood in the heart-lung machine by about twenty degrees, to slow Annie's metabolism. This would decrease the body's demand for oxygen, and preserve the vitality of the heart-muscle cells. Once I stitched together the aortas, we reheated the oxygenated blood, and as it flowed through the machine and into the coronary arteries that fed the heart, the heart slowly warmed up. As it did, its color changed—from dead gray to alive red. I wrapped my fingers gently around its growing volume, felt the chambers grow taut, and felt life fill the emptiness.

I placed the final sutures in the pulmonary artery, and the rich, warm blood began pouring into the new heart, feeding its millions of cells that had been starving for three hours and forty-eight minutes. I tugged gently on the heart and noticed one anastomosis that did not hold the way I thought it should. I turned to the perfusionist and said, "Hold her off and give me about five minutes."

I made the adjustments, turned once again to the perfusionist, and nodded. Again the heart filled and began to quiver like a steaming kettle just before it boiled. I held my breath.

I reached for the defibrillator paddles behind me, often used to start up a transplanted heart or shock it into a sinus rhythm—a regular pattern. I massaged the heart once, using my hand to remind it that it once had a rhythm. Hearts forget, but up to a point, they can be reminded.

It beat once, a hard jolting, pounding beat. It torqued, pumped itself empty, and refilled. The screaming flat-line above me beeped once. Around the table, we waited for the second and the third and the . . .

It didn't come.

Royer's face wrinkled with concern. I reached for the paddles and said calmly, "Charge to 100."

The nurse waited for the light to turn green and nodded at me. I slid the paddles alongside Annie's heart and said, "Clear." The heart jerked, almost shaking itself free of the current that swam through it, and then lay still.

I said it again. "Charge to 200."

Royer's face studied mine while I studied Annie's heart. It jumped again, and fell quiet, limp, and unresponsive. I paused, thought back through the process. *Everything had been perfect. Why won't it start?*

I shook my head and whispered, knowing it would be the last time. "Charge to 300."

The light turned green, and I shocked Annie's heart to where it rocked and spasmed, tugging violently against the sutures that held it. I pulled out the paddles and waited, but Annie's heart didn't even twitch. I reached in with my hand, wrapped it around the heart and massaged, pumping for her. Trying to pass life from my hand to her heart. I felt it fill and empty with each successive squeeze. And each time, it fell limp and melted into my aching palm. I squeezed for several minutes until my hand began to cramp. After ten minutes, it locked up.

Royer put his hand on my arm and shook his head. Around us, the nurses began crying. The chief resident turned from the table, the perfusionist buried her face in her hands. Royer eyed the clock. His voice cracked. "Time of death, 11:11 p.m."

The tears came slowly. First a trickle, then the Tallulah. For the first time since Emma died, I set sail into the current. The years of muffled pain, unvented anguish, and stifled sorrow caught me and swept me toward the dam. When I got there, the water flowed over, cracked the concrete, and flooded the valley below.

I fell backward, sending my instruments flying across the room. I bounced off the sterile stainless-steel table, hit the floor, pulled my knees in under my chest, and could not breathe. I opened the eyes of my mind, pulled hard, but could not reach the surface. Below me, the old town of Burton reached up, caught my ankles, and pulled me downward toward the darkness and remnant. Struggling, flailing for the surface, I screamed at Charlie, at the medics to "charge to 300!" and then at Emma to "wake up!" "Hold on!" and "Don't go!" Then I thought of a yellow dress, of a yellow bow floating in the wind, of a little girl yelling "Lemonaaaade!" at the top of her lungs and how something had awakened in me the moment I saw her.

My body shook. I cried hard, out beyond the pain. With every wail, I paid penance for the guilt of my soul, for the sorrow that knows no end, and the shame that was me. It was there I realized there were some sins for which I would never quit paying.

Down in the green, murky coldness near the bottom, I saw Emma. She swam to me, and on her chest I saw no scar. She touched my chin, kissed my cheek, and pulled me up to Annie, lying still, cold, and dead on the table. As quickly as she appeared, she was gone.

Annie lay still, her chest a cold, open wound holding a lifeless heart. On the table next to me sat the pitcher of water. Out of several cracks, holes and crevices, it was leaking water across the table, which was spilling all about me on the floor. I tried to lift it with one hand, but it was too heavy. I leaned in, lifted it off the table, poured it over Annie. As I poured, the blood washed away. The more and longer I poured, the cleaner she became, but the heavier the pitcher felt. With every passing second, Annie's heart filled with blood, her chest began to close itself—no scar.

The pitcher pulled against me, growing too heavy. I slipped, regained my balance, and held the stream over Annie. Losing my grip, I screamed against the weight of it. The weight of everything. Unable to hold it any longer, I lifted it high and poured the water over us both. Standing in the waterfall, I bathed. And for one brief second, came clean. Then my fingers gave way and the pitcher came crashing down, shattering on the stone floor beneath us.

The sound shocked me. I opened my eyes, ripped off my mask, and the wet air filled my lungs. I gasped, coughed, and found the room awash in light. From the distance, Emma whispered. The echo reached out of the void that had been us and spoke and it was then, there, that the words returned. I stood over Annie, my tears falling onto her cold, gray heart, and whispered— the one thing I had not done.

If life is where the blood flows, then death is where it does not.

Chapter 54

Six weeks passed. The summer swell of peace-seekers had long since returned home, and the engineers cracked open the dam, dropping the level of the lake several inches. The quiet residue left in their wake spread across the water and brought with it the cold promise of a long winter. As winter progressed and water needs increased from Burton to Atlanta, the level would drop farther until next spring, when the rains would refill it.

With my home destroyed and the life I had come to lead changed forever, I returned, stood amid the wreckage, and sifted my hands through the rubble. Not much remained. Certainly, not much of worth. I found a few pictures and a couple of kitchen utensils, but little else. As best I could figure, the storm had picked up what was once mine and sent it scattering over the surrounding counties or dropped it in the lake north of us. The disheveled sight of every physical thing I had once held dear left me dumbstruck.

In hopes of finding anything that had been mine, I circled out from the house and spent three days searching the woods. Most of the trees were snapped in two about ten feet up, and all the tops were laid like pickup sticks across the landscape, making it difficult to get around. A couple hundred yards from the house, I found Emma's tub lying on its side with three of the four feet broken off. I ran my fingers along the edge, remembered Emma leaning her head against the rim and smiling at me as the steam rose off her face. I let it be. Another day and I called off the search. I never found the transit case.

After a week, I looked out over the lake—now clear of debris—and took it in. Maybe it was telling me something. I looked down in the water, saw my reflection, and decided it was.

I drove around the lake to my warehouse, pulled back the canvas, sneezed under a cloud of dust, and loaded up the trailer. By the end of the afternoon, I had made several trips and forced the return of my blisters.

Termite offered to help, so every afternoon when he got off work at the marina, he'd scream across the lake, beach his Jet Ski, and pitch in. The first day he showed up, he handed me several magazines. He shook his head and looked away. "I won't be needing these no more. I seen enough."

Most nights he'd work until midnight. He was tireless, and Charlie taught him, much as he'd taught me, how to turn and craft wood into something that, when finished, exceeded the sum of its parts.

While Charlie and Termite worked to rebuild the workshop and frame a new boathouse, I worked at cleaning up the mess. It took me the better part of a month. Finally, I hired a bulldozer and pushed what remained into a large pile. I got a burn permit, alerted the fire department (who sent a truck just in case), and then Termite lit the pile with a flick from his Zippo.

The fire burned for three days. The only particle of my past that remained was the shirt on my back and what hung around my neck.

We never found the Hacker. We found the engine and part of the steering column at the bottom of the lake beneath where the dock once stood, but the hull, cut-water, and most everything else disappeared into the whirlwind. The same went for most of our tools. We found power cords, a few screwdrivers, and whatever had been stored in the red toolbox, but on the whole, $15,000 worth of machinery had disappeared into the wind.

Oddly enough, the two-man shell that I had restored for Emma and in which she and then Charlie and I had spent many an hour, came to rest in the arms of a dogwood up the hill. Termite helped me pull her down. I patched up a hole in her hull, sanded her, applied several coats of spar varnish, and set her up to dry.

Charlie's house fared pretty well. It had been built into the side of the hill, and the tornado bounced over his house and landed squarely on mine. He got hurt when he ran out the door to scream for us, only to be thrown back inside by the wind.

Since the day that Annie's heart died, I'd slept in a sleeping bag in the "cave" at the back of the wood-shop. Most nights, when I turned out the lantern that lit my small world, Georgia appeared out of the night air, checked my nose, and then disappeared back to Charlie's side. I've heard that submarines deep in the ocean will send sound beacons to search each other out. Between Charlie and me, Georgia is that *ping*.

The purse stitch I had sewn into Annie's heart created quite a buzz in the medical world. Royer's phone had been ringing off the hook, but I asked him not to give out my number. He said, "It's time you get back on the horse that threw you."

It was Friday. I rolled out of my sleeping bag and walked out of my hole. The morning sun broke the skyline and sent the sunkist screaming across the atmosphere. Standing on the bulkhead, watching the bream and bass dart below me, I watched my shadow stretch out across the water in front of me.

I jumped into the cold lake, washed off, and was standing in my birthday suit toweling dry when Sal walked down the steps and emptied his pipe. I pulled on my clothes and met him at the bulkhead.

He didn't look at me, but studied the lake, methodically packing his pipe. He lit it and puffed thoughtfully. Exhaling, he spoke. "Now that your secret's out, I've got something I want to say to you."

I raised my eyebrows and waited.

"I've been the only doctor around here for . . . well,

a long time. Probably too long." He looked at me. "It's time to pass the baton. But—" He nodded sternly and pointed the tip of his pipe at me. "I'm passing it to somebody who can run with it. Someone who understands new medicine, and who can offer it to these folks."

He painted the perimeter of the lake with his wafting pipe. "I'm talking about the high-tech stuff that only exists in places like Atlanta, Nashville, and New York." He paused. "I'll pay you the same thing I'm making. Sixty thousand. Royer says that's about a tenth of what you were making in Atlanta, but that's tough. I've never made more than sixty and besides, people around here don't have too much money. And as best I can figure, you ain't in it for the money."

He turned and began walking up the steps, scanning the lake again. Then he looked at me. "Folks around here need a good doctor, and you, boy, are a doctor. One of the best I ever seen.

"I'll wait to hear from you. Offer's open until you close it." He pulled his handkerchief from his back pocket and wiped his eyes. "I saw what you did with Annie. I was standing in the corner of the room." He shook his head. "Don't let the doubt get you." He poked me in the chest. "It almost got me, but . . . well, if you're going to be a doctor, and I mean *be* a doctor, you've got to deal with that now. 'Cause it's not going to get any easier." He paused long enough to catch his breath. "But that's the thing about doctoring. It's not about you. It's about them."

He took a long look across the lake, then eyed my neighbor's empty house next door and Charlie's cabin across the lake. "And them," he whispered, "is worth it."

Sal walked away, climbed into his Cadillac, and drove off.

I dangled my legs over the bulkhead and looked across the finger of the lake where Georgia lay sunning herself just outside Charlie's front door. Her sprawling across the doormat was akin to a DO NOT DISTURB sign on a hotel door. Charlie had found Georgia useful, but not in all the ways I had anticipated. His new sleep schedule had been difficult to get used to, and made training for next week's Burton Rally all the more difficult. Some days we were lucky if we got on the lake by noon. Occasionally I went alone. Although, I'm not sure I've ever been truly alone on the lake.

Around ten, Cindy tiptoed down to the lake and dangled her legs beside mine. She was staying in a house up the road a couple hundred yards. My neighbor, a broker from New York, had rented it to me for the next couple of months. At least until we could find Cindy someone who would grant her a mortgage to buy someplace else. The process had been working more smoothly since I called the bank and told them I'd cosign.

Ever since the surgery, she had come down here daily about this time to check on me. In a sense, she was taking my pulse—checking to make sure I still had one. She seldom said much, but neither did I. She'd

402

dangle a few minutes, soak in the sun, breathe deeply, and then disappear. We shared something now that few others did or could. I'd often spot her down here at night as well, walking along the bulkhead. I guess the quiet soothed her. We both needed some of that.

After a few minutes, she turned to me and said, "Your turn or mine?"

"Mine," I said, smiling, knowing full well that she knew whose turn it was.

She nodded, hid her smile, and leaned her head back, closing her eyes behind the sunglasses that had been propped on top of her head. I walked up the stone walk and out the gravel road that led from where my house used to stand, and would one day stand again.

At the neighbor's doorstep I took off my shoes and crept silently to the door of the master bedroom on the first floor. The windows all around the house were open, and a gentle breeze brought fresh air into the house. I pushed open the door, and there, propped in bed, eyes closed, and face flush under the warmth of too many blankets, lay Annie.

I knelt next to the bed, and her eyes opened. "Is it time?" she asked.

I nodded.

She opened her mouth, I placed the two pills on her tongue and held the glass of water for her to swallow. She blinked lazily and whispered, "I had a dream."

I leaned closer.

"I met your wife. She was walking along the lake."

I nodded. "It was one of her favorite places."

"Then she did the strangest thing."

"What's that?" I said, taking her temperature and counting her pulse.

"She knelt down next to the water, lifted out a little boat, and gave it to me."

"That's not so strange."

"No, that wasn't the strange part. It was the sail. It was made from a letter. One she'd written to you."

I had never told Annie about Emma's letters. Other than Charlie, no one knew about them.

I checked Annie's bandages, pulled the covers up around her neck, and tucked her in. I kissed her on the forehead, crept out, and pulled the door behind me. Walking down the back steps, I bumped into Charlie coming to read to Annie. He had *Eloise* in one hand and was feeling his way up the steps.

When he heard me, he stepped out of the way and said, "Been looking for you."

"Yeah?" I said doubtfully, knowing by the look of his hair that he'd just woken up.

"Yeah," he said. He reached up, ran his fingers across my face, held them there for a moment, and then squeezed my cheeks in an attempt to point my face and eyes toward his. When he was sure he had my attention, he cracked the book he was carrying and slipped an envelope from inside. "She said I'd know when to give this to you. Best I can figure, it's time."

Emma's handwriting was unmistakable. I snatched it out of his hand. "She gave this to you?" I said in disbelief.

Charlie nodded.

"When?"

" 'Bout the time she and I drove to town and opened that safe-deposit box."

"You knew about that all along?"

"Yup."

"When were you going to tell me?"

Charlie shrugged. "I wasn't."

I stared at the envelope. "You got any more secrets I need to know about?"

Charlie smiled. "Not at this time, but I'll keep you posted."

I ripped open the envelope and unfolded the letter.

Dear Reese, If Charlie's given you this letter, then you've met someone.

I looked at Charlie in disbelief.

I asked him to hold it until he saw you wanting to offer that tender heart of yours to someone else. Don't worry. There's enough love in your heart for two women, and when you get here, we'll let God sort it out. Whoever she is, she is blessed and better for it. Reese, never forget that you were born, and sent . . . to bind up broken hearts. I know. I've always known.

I looked out across the lake and heard Emma's whisper.

Reese, don't hold it in. Please don't live any

longer in pain and loss. Remember, I'm better now. I'm me. When you get here, you'll see. But between now and then, offer the gift that is you.

I was thinking yesterday of how the water looks whenever we go rowing. The wake disappears, the ripples from the oars fade into the shore and are erased forever. Life on the water, there's never any past. And up front, the view is all future.

I love you. Always will. Death can't take that away. Now, go. And live where the life flows.

Ever yours, Emma

Charlie looked at me. "Well?" He raised his eyebrows and searched the sky for flashes of light. Waving his head back and forth, he asked, "What's it say?"

I smiled, tucked the letter inside my shirt, and held his hand up to my face, where his fingers traced the lines of my smile and felt the slippery tracks of tears cascading down the cracks. I whispered, "Charlie . . . I can see."

I jumped off the porch, landing on a pad of evergreen needles, and ran flat out. I flew through the woods, the tree branches pulling at me, and jumped over the downed trees like hurdles. I slid down a small hill and felt the earth give beneath me. Somewhere above me, I flushed a mourning dove that rocketed through the treetops like a jet. I reached what used to be the dock and would be again and dropped the shell into the water. I zipped up my shirt, the letter pressing against me, strapped in my feet, and pulled hard on the oars.

The shell jumped forward. I pulled again. Three more long, deep pulls and the Tallulah caught me. I dug in, arching my back against the water. The water pulled back, but I dug in deeper and pressed hard in with my legs. Lighter without a second person, I glided atop the water like the breeze. Within minutes, sweat stuck the letter to my chest.

Crouching into a spring, my knees tucked into my chest with arms extended, having sucked in as much air as my lungs would allow—I dug in. Pushing with my legs and starting the long pull with my arms, I exhaled. Fully extended, body bloated on lactic acid, I gorged on air as deeply as my lungs would allow. At the top of my pull, I lifted the blades and pulled my knees into my chest, once again sucking in air the entire way back down the boat. With each pull, I emptied myself, again and again and again.

On the water with Emma, one last time.

In our wake, circles appeared. They grew outward, overlapped, then disappeared completely. The sun warmed our backs, sweat stung my eyes, and the breeze pressed against us. Over my shoulder, the water spread out like polished ebony. I saw all future and a fading, and forgiving, past. And on the air, I heard the echoing whisper of Emma's laughter and felt the gentle touch of her fingers on my face.

I turned around at the dam, my head caked with sweat that trickled down my face, stung my eyes, and sat salty on my lips. The sun sat low and painfully bright. *No man is an island.* I pulled against the current and pushed my back into the breeze that would slow me. Three hours later, I returned, spent and clean.

With Charlie's help, Annie—wearing a hat, the yellow ribbon trailing behind her—had walked down the hill. They stood on the bank, focused on her cricket box. After the surgery, Charlie and Termite had transported it and placed it on the porch just outside her window. Given the pain of her surgery and the strangeness of a new house and bed, we thought maybe it'd help her sleep better.

Now, at Annie's request, Cindy and Charlie had moved the box down to the bank. Annie stood next to the box while Charlie leaned it on its side. Slowly at first, then all at once, the crickets started hopping and crawling out. Pretty soon the box was empty, and around us the earth moved like drops of water on a sizzling stove as fifty thousand crickets headed for the safety of the trees.

I listened closely, as did Annie. She looked at me, smiled, and whispered, "Shhhh."

In seconds, the crickets had ascended the trees and were singing. Annie closed her eyes, smiled, then danced like a ballerina, being careful where she stepped. When I looked down on the beach, I saw the imprint of her small foot alongside mine.

Charlie stood and headed for the Suburban. "Last one to the truck buys dinner!"

Annie looped her arm around Cindy's as the three of them made their way to the Suburban. That meant I was buying dinner—five Transplants. I said five because I was pretty sure Termite would show about the time we put in our orders.

Charlie shouted out the driver's-side window, "Come on, Stitch! Hurry up, or I'm driving!"

I stood looking out over the lake, not wanting to say good-bye. A moment later, I felt a tug on my arm. It was Annie. "Reese? You coming?"

I nodded. For a minute, we stood watching the water ripple beneath the wind.

Then she arched her back, stood on her tiptoes, and whispered in my ear, "You said you'd tell me today. You promised."

I nodded again, and hollered to Charlie and Cindy that we'd be there in a minute.

Annie pulled on my hand, and we sat down on the bulkhead and dangled our legs.

"The trick to transplanting hearts," I said, "is getting them going again." I paused, trying to figure out how to say what I needed to say.

Annie tapped me on the thigh. "It's okay, you can tell me. I'm a big girl now. I turn eight next week."

Tiger's heart in a china-doll body.

"No matter how much I studied, how much I prepared, or how good a doctor folks say I am, the difficult part is knowing that, in truth, I am powerless to get it going again. It is . . . a miracle . . . that I do not understand."

Annie leaned against me and listened. The sunlight reflected off the water, lit the blonde fuzz on her legs and the smile on her face.

I pointed over my shoulder, toward Rabun County Hospital. "That night . . . I couldn't get your heart going. We had done everything, medically speaking, that we knew to do. Royer, that big crying teddy bear, shook his head and recorded the time as 11:11 p.m."

Annie nodded, remembering her mother's dream.

"He was waiting for me to agree with him. It's something doctors do when somebody dies. But I couldn't. Or wouldn't. I just knew you weren't supposed to die on that table. I'd die first." I tapped Annie gently on the chest. "I leaned over and whispered to your heart, speaking aloud the one thing I had not said in a long, long time. And, when I did, your heart heard me."

Annie smiled and pressed her hands to her heart.

"It was as if it'd been waiting for me to simply speak the words, and remind it. Because when I did, for reasons I cannot and never will explain, it filled like a balloon, swelled a bright, healthy red, and then, as if it had never stopped, it beat. Hard, powerful, and rhythmic."

Annie looked out across the lake, her whole life before her. "Do you think it'll stop again?"

I nodded. "Yes . . . but not until you're finished here. All hearts stop, Annie. What matters is what you do with it while it's still pumping."

Annie wrapped her arms around my waist and pressed her cheek to my chest. Her arms had strengthened, giving greater expression to the bubbling inside her.

"How long do I have?"

I looked at her, her big round eyes, her melting smile,

410

the tender shoots of hope showing beneath the surface. I brushed the now-growing and healthy hair out of her face and said, "Long enough to turn gray."

Annie looked over her shoulder at the Suburban, then tugged gently on my arm. "Reese? What did you whisper?"

It was time. I lifted Emma's medallion over my head, watched it spin, dangle, and mirror the sun's reflection off the water. I held it in my palm and ran my fingers along the worn engraving. When the tear finally broke from the corner of my eye and sped down my face, I spread the chain, hung it around Annie's neck, and watched it come to rest just above the scar on her chest.

Acknowledgments

Thank you to all of you who have read my books, passed them to your friends or stopped to talk with me. Your stories have touched me and, on the days when the words won't come—which do occur—I carry them with me. I'm grateful.

Many thanks to:

Allen Arnold—my publisher with a vision. Jenny Baumgartner—my editor with patience. L.B. Norton—my copy editor with a gift. Heather Adams, Caroline Craddock, Amanda Bostic and all the folks at Westbow—my hat's off to you. Thank you for helping me tell the stories rattling about inside me.

Carol Fitzgerald—thank you for your wit, enthusiasm and excitement for my stories. You're a great encouragement.

Chris—agent, counselor and friend. You're the best.

Steve and Elaine—some of my richest memories include you. If you were hoping to make a difference, you have.

John Trainer, MD—friend and doctor. I could not have written this without you. Thank you for your care of this story, my family and me. You're the real deal— a true healer. Thanks for dropping out of law school.

Dave—you had more of a hand in this than you'll ever give yourself credit. Thanks for the phone calls. And your life.

Charlie, Todd, Jon, and Terry—Thanks for holding

up the mirror, looking into it with me and then doing something about it.

My Family—you bless me. I'd never have gotten here without you.

Charlie, John T., and Rives—*Above all else . . .*

Christy— *. . . you surpass them all.*

Lord—thank you for this—again, for the people above and for replacing my heart of stone.

A message from the author about the
When Crickets Cry Heart-Care Fund

Heart disease is far-and-away the greatest killer of all Americans, taking the lives of over 300,000 of our family members, friends, and neighbors each year. Sadly, children are also affected with life-threatening heart conditions. There are many children in our nation who, like Annie in *When Crickets Cry*, struggle with heart defects and diseases.

The *When Crickets Cry* Heart-Care Fund was formed to raise the standard of heart-safety for our nation's youth. Through this fund, Thomas Nelson, in partnership with Saint Thomas Health Services and Life-Guard Medical Solutions, has made it their goal to raise money for the cause of heart health in our children.

To initiate this program, a portion of the sale of each copy of *When Crickets Cry* will be placed within the fund. We are also seeking individual or corporate donations. All donations are tax-deductible and 100% of the proceeds will be used to place safe and reliable Automatic External Defibrillators (AED's) within public schools that would otherwise be unable to afford these life-saving devices.

If you are interested in joining us in this important project, please go to www.sths.com/whencricketscry to make a gift to the *When Crickets Cry* Heart Care Fund.

Thank you for your support,
Charles Martin

Center Point Publishing
600 Brooks Road ● PO Box 1
Thorndike ME 04986-0001 USA

(207) 568-3717

US & Canada:
1 800 929-9108

Opal C